ALL THAT WE BURN

MARISA BILLIONS

For Cat Benson. Thank you for not only being an amazing beta reader but also for becoming a friend and giving me the push for this story.

For all of those couples that have come together against the odds, from opposite backgrounds, lives, and experiences, and found each other because you were meant to be.

For the black sheep girls who have been written off and cast aside. You are the ones who make this world a better and more interesting place.

As always, for my wife, Stephanie. Thank you for your patience and your support in dealing with this little hobby of mine. And I still love you, MOST.

FOREWORD

This book was definitely an adventure to write. I think it's the messiest, most toxic, and most complicated story I've written thus far. And I couldn't have done it without Cat Benson's suggestion, and her Alpha Read.

I also couldn't have done it without my wife Stephanie and her support. She inspires me daily. And of course, my friends and family who constantly listen to me talking about my characters like they are real people, boost my ego, and buy my books and read them.

Last but not least, the inspiration I get from music. Whether it be a whole song, a single line, or just the vibe, below is the playlist that shaped this book and its three hot mess main characters. I've included the chapters that the songs pair with. You can also find the playlist on Apple Music.

"Hymn to Virgil" – Hozier ––(This is like the theme song to the whole book—so start here.)

"A Little Bit" – Ella Boh – Chapter 1

"Kool Thing" – Sonic Youth – Chapter 1

"her name" – Beneld, Cheyanne & Omido – Chapter 6

"How Bad Do U Want Me" – Lady Gaga – Chapter 6

"Messy" – Lola Young – Chapter 8

"Contemplations" – Elijah Lee – Chapter 9

"Sin" – Ash to Eden – Chapter 9

"Mile High (feat. Travis Scott and Metro Boomin)" – James Blake – Chapter 10

"7" – Prince & the New Power Generation – Chapter 11

"Find Me Here (Extended Mix) – Helsloot – Chapter 13

"Fire on Fire" – Sam Smith – Chapter 16

"Broken Man" – St. Vincent – Chapter 17

"Feel" – Beneld & Bury – Chapter 18

"Fire for You" – Cannons – Chapter 20

"Think of Me" – Hidden Voices – Chapter 21

"Obsessed" – Sophie Powers & Ashley Sienna – Chapter 25

"Cocoa Hooves Part II" – Glass Animals – Chapter 28

"affection" – BETWEEN FRIENDS – Chapter 32

"Heat" – breathe. & L.A. Rose – Chapter 33

"Disposable" – Blaise Moore – Chapter 34

"Dark Side" – Bishop Briggs – Chapter 35

"temptation" – Ashley Sienna – Chapter 35

"Cut You Off" – CHINCHILLA – Chapter 36

"Unknown / Nth" – Hozier – Chapter 36

"Would That I" – Hozier – Chapter 38

"Silk" – Wolf Alice – Chapter 39

"The Last Beat of My Heart" – Siouxsie & the Banshees – Chapter 41

"Faithless" – The Airborne Toxic Event – Chapter 44

"Barbwire Kiss" – Night Club – Chapter 47

"My Kink is Karma" – Chappell Roan – Chapter 48

"Everybody Supports Women" – SOFIA ISELLA – Chapter 49

"bellyache"– Billie Eilish – Chapter 50
"Wicked Little Monster" – Veda – Chapter 52
"Burn It Down"– Siobhan Sainte – Epilogue

Scan to link to the Apple Music Playlist

PART I
THE FOUNDATION

1 THE STAND

EIGHT YEARS AGO JUNE 12

MACY

This was going to be a cakewalk. No sweat off her back. Macy had been sworn in on the witness stand, and she was confident in herself and her testimony. The case being heard marked her first truly high-profile case and her last arrest as a beat cop. The arrest had taken place in an alley behind a crowded shopping center, where she chased the perp down, cuffed him, and hauled him in. The defendant, a known drug kingpin, eluded arrest for years for the distribution of oxycodone, Fentanyl, and other pharmaceuticals. This arrest earned her a promotion to detective and a coveted spot on the Organized Crime Task Force.

The defense team mostly sat with their heads down, scribbling notes while she testified. Now she sat waiting to be cross-examined. The female attorney, in a bespoke black three-piece suit and tie, her black hair in a short pompadour, gazed up at her with bright green eyes. The suspect's defense team owned a proud reputation for being the best in the business. The prosecutor had prepped Macy relentlessly for this trial. Not to mention, she had sat in the witness stand countless times and gone through trial prep a million times, albeit never for a case of this magnitude. The prosecutor issued her a sharp warning that this would be a tough cross-examination. Harrington and Harrington, the defendant's defense team, was a very well-known firm with a reputation for fighting slightly dirty while still playing within the rules, and they did their homework. He told her to pray that the father questioned her, not the daughter. The father was for the most part partially retired, but the daughter, Parker, now only took on the most high-profile cases, and the word most often used to describe her in the courtroom was *vicious*. And when Parker Harrington's green eyes met hers for the first time and a cocky smile played on Parker's lips as she took Macy in, Macy's heart stopped, and a ball of need grew within her.

This trial had seemed to take forever to come. Harrington and Harrington filed motion after motion, causing this trial to be delayed. She waited eagerly to prove to everyone that her work on this case was flawless. Nothing less than clean and perfect. This defendant should be going to jail for a long ass time. With her prep solid, her notes clear, and the evidence she meticulously collected, this dirtbag would rot in prison.

And now she sat looking in the eyes of the attorney who wanted to invalidate it all. And she fell in love—or at least lust.

She exhaled, trying to center herself. She didn't want to prove anyone right about Parker Harrington's reputation or her record. But no one warned her that Parker Harrington was the sexiest butch in a bespoke suit she would ever lay eyes on.

Parker Harrington rarely ever lost in a trial. But neither did Macy. Her arrests *always* held up in court. Earning that reputation of clean police work, in combination with *this* case, won her that coveted detective shield. The lead prosecutor, Jared Cline, who prepped her, warned her that being a defense attorney ran in Parker's blood, literally. Her father and his father before him, and probably the father before that, worked as defense attorneys. Their firm, Harrington and Harrington, now existed as the most sought-after firm if you found yourself charged with any crime in Southern California. Considered a brilliant attorney in her own right, *nepo baby* would never be used to describe Parker. Macy wished the prosecutor told her that Parker could be best described as hot as fuck.

Pushing her red hair back and opening her eyes, she attempted to steady herself with a deep inhale. Only to find herself shaken to the core of her razor-sharp brain—

all because of this woman standing in front of her, looking in her eyes.

She would swear all the way to her last day that Parker winked at her as they made eye contact. Did Parker Harrington take the time to research hard enough to uncover the fact that she ticked every box for Macy's type? She most definitely appeared to be *flirting* with Macy. No. No. That wasn't not possible. How would she even obtain that information?

"Detective Quinn, is it?" Parker's smooth and velvety voice resonated in Macy's chest.

"Ye—" She cleared her throat. "Yes." Heat crept up from her center and flushed her cheeks. In Macy's opinion, the worst thing about being a natural redhead was how obvious it could be for anyone and everyone to see when she blushed, which hadn't happened often until this moment.

"You note the time of day of the arrest as eight-thirty p.m. in your police report, correct?" Parker didn't even glance at her notes. Her emerald-green eyes bored into Macy with utter intensity.

"Yes. That's what's in the report." Macy tried so hard but failed to stay confident and match Parker's cocky assuredness.

"This alleged transaction took place outdoors, correct?"

"Um. Yes."

"That time of year, it's dark outside at that time, correct?"

"Yes."

"So, it's possible that you may not have clearly seen what transpired between my client and the other gentleman?" By *gentleman*, she must have meant *junkie*, but okay.

"No. I clearly saw it."

"So, they stood under a streetlamp?"

"No. They—"

Before she uttered another word, "according to your report, you spotted them in an alley, correct?"

"Yes. But—" Her pulse ramped up, and she couldn't finish a sentence before Parker cut her off with more of her aggressive, rapid-fire questioning.

"You also noted that you observed this while sitting in your patrol car, which was at least twenty yards away, correct?"

"I'm not sure the exact distance—" Macy eyed Jared as he closed his eyes and shook his head subtly.

"Can you take a look at this photo?" Parker pointed to a large photo displayed on an easel within her line of sight as well as the jury's.

"Objection," Jared stood. "Lack of foundation."

"Miss Harrington?" The judge's gruff voice came exasperated.

Parker's eyes drilled directly at Macy with an eyebrow cocked. "Your Honor, I'm not using this photo for foundation, I'm using it to impeach this witness's testimony regarding visibility at the scene."

Macy's heart stopped, and her mouth went dry.

Parker continued, "But if opposing counsel would like me to lay foundation—"

"Miss Harrington, you're dancing on a thin line. Overruled." The crotchety old man seated as judge in this case turned to face Macy, "Answer the question, Detective."

Macy examined it. The scene in the photo appeared dark, and the images were blurry due to the low lighting.

"What do you see in this photo?"

"Um, it looks like two people in a dark alley." Macy's voice came weak and soft.

"Do you recognize the location in the photo?"

"Yes."

"Can you tell me what that location is?"

"The alleyway where the arrest took place. Behind the Santa Rosa strip mall on the exterior of the Bradly Housing Project."

"Are you certain?" A single lift of an eyebrow as she smirked at Macy.

"No. Yes. I mean, yes."

"Yes or no will do. So would you say that is a definitive yes?"

Macy nodded. "Yes, it is."

"What if I told you that it is not?"

"I— It is."

"Actually, no, it isn't. That's a different alley in another city. The photo is, however, shot from the same distance as your patrol car would have been."

"Objection—" Jared called as he stood. "Counsel is testifying, not cross-examining." He was trying to do his best to salvage Macy's testimony. But it turned out to be a hopeless cause. She remained unraveled and unnerved.

Parker grinned at the judge before looking at the jury. "Withdrawn, Your Honor." She wore a Cheshire cat–like grin on her face.

She removed the photo from the easel and held up another one. "Can you recognize this location?"

With tears in her eyes that she fought hard not to release, Macy struggled to maintain her composure. "No." Her voice came out weak, and she shook her head, because now reasonable doubt and uncertainty overtook her, as it probably had within the jury. This case had died in the water.

"Can you make out what the two people in the photograph are doing?"

"No."

"Is it possible that this is the alleyway you witnessed my client and his friend in?"

"It could be?" Her answer came as a question, and she cringed.

"Would this be the distance from which you would have witnessed them?"

"Approximately, yes."

"So you couldn't with one hundred percent certainty say that you witnessed a drug deal, correct?"

"I had all—"

"A simple yes or no will do, Detective Quinn."

She hesitated. "No?" Jared mouthed the word *fuck* as he set his pen down and leaned back in his chair, and she wanted to die right then and there.

"They may have merely been exchanging a 'dap' handshake as they parted ways for the night, as the defendant claims?"

"But we—"

"Yes or no."

"We seize—"

"Objection, Your Honor." Both Parker and Jared called at the same time. Melting into the chair and disappearing would have been preferable to this.

The judge gave an exasperated sigh. "Let's hear from you, Miss Harrington, first."

"This witness is unresponsive," Parker said matter-of-factly.

"Mr. Cline?" The judge asked.

"She's badgering my witness." Cline offered.

"I'm merely asking her to answer a simple yes or no question. She's refusing to answer." Parker's lip curled at the judge, cool, calm, and smooth.

"Miss Harrington, your objection is sustained. Detective Quinn, you will answer the question as directed." The judge directed her. "Mr. Cline, sit down. Overruled."

Macy, for the first time ever, was impeached, appearing as a complete idiot. Cline spent the rest of the time shrinking in his chair. All the effort he put into prepping Macy went for naught.

Macy hadn't felt that humiliated, that low, since she left New Orleans with her tail between her legs over a decade ago. Her love life had been in shambles, and it was impacting her job. Fleeing to California seemed to be a good idea—the only option if she was being honest—at the time.

A dimple in Parker's left cheek appeared as Parker grinned at her as she unbuttoned her suit jacket and sat back behind the defense table. Her client smiled, satisfied with his counsel's performance.

* * *

JUNE 22

Her embarrassing disaster on the witness stand didn't stop Macy from fantasizing about Parker that night. And the next one, too. Or looking up all of Parker's social media accounts and going through her Instagram posts regularly (albeit carefully so as not to "like" any of them, because that would be weird and stalkerish).

Needless to say, two days later, the defense rested, and one day after that, the defendant ended up released after being found not guilty. It resulted in a massive blow to her ego. But she still caught herself looking at Parker Harrington's Instagram and fantasizing about her that night, too.

A little over a week later, when she went to Mo's, a local bar near the court where all the cops and lawyers hung out, she spotted Parker sitting at the bar alone.

Her jacket off, sleeves rolled up, collar unbuttoned, and tie loosened. She sat looking at her phone, a cocktail in front of her.

Macy pulled her shoulders back and approached Parker.

When Parker didn't look up from her phone, Macy held her breath and tapped her shoulder, which got Parker to turn and face her. Those sharp green eyes focused on her, registering her presence. Grateful she wore her favorite jeans and a tight t-shirt to show off her toned and athletic physique, she felt a boost of confidence. Something Parker wouldn't have been able to see as she sat in the witness box. Her silky red hair swept up and back into a perfect ponytail. She showed a confident side that was achingly absent when Parker cross-examined her. She looked good. If there ever existed an excellent time to run into Parker, it would be now.

"Hi?" Parker said, more in question than anything else.

"Hi. Macy Quinn. Do you remember me?"

Parker smiled, that dimple popping in her left cheek.

Macy wanted to kiss that dimple. "I do. The flustered detective."

Macy found herself glad for the darkness of the bar, aware that her cheeks resumed flushing bright pink as they were when Parker cross-examined her. "Yeah . . . I don't . . . That's never been something that happened to me in court before."

Parker's expression let her know she didn't believe her. "Hmmm."

Damn. She's cocky. Macy became flustered all over again. "So, um. I just wanted to say hi."

"Have a seat, Detective." Parker acknowledged the empty seat next to her.

"You can call me Macy."

"Okay, Macy. Have a seat."

Macy followed Parker's order with utter obedience. She sat on the barstool, and the way Parker turned to face her, their knees wound up touching. Macy inhaled the scent of the cologne Parker wore, and her mouth watered. She wanted to pull Parker in by her necktie and taste her lips. Instead, she licked her lips and forced herself to try to act normal.

"So you don't have some big case to be working on right now?" Parker chided.

"Just working some cold cases right now. No new clients to send your way, Counselor." Macy jabbed back, getting her bearings.

Parker gave a small laugh. "That's fair. You can call me Parker."

"It's an interesting name. Where did that come from?" Macy did a mental facepalm. That sounded lame as hell.

"My mom's maiden name. What are you drinking?"

"Nothing, yet." Macy indicated her empty hands and the bar in front of her.

Parker gave a slight nod to the bartender, and he hopped to, coming to her. "What's up, Parker?" He asked.

"She needs a drink. Add it to my tab."

"No—Parker—"

"I owe you one for what I did to you when I cross-examined you." That slight dimple popped in her left cheek. She came across so fucking cocky. If anyone else acted this way, Macy would be turned off. But with Parker, it only made her more appealing. And she plainly saw it—Parker flaunted her attitude, a badge of honor she wore proudly.

"You're never going to let me live that down, are you?"

"Probably not."

Three drinks later, Macy got her wish, pulled Parker in by the necktie, and landed her lips on Parker's. Her body became electrified and heat pooled in her as Parker's tongue met hers. The lingering of Parker's breath on her skin as she pinned Macy to the brick wall in front of Mo's caused Macy to let out a whimper. The cool coarseness of the bricks at her back, in contrast to the soft warmth of Parker in front, made her want the world to stop. She wanted to surrender herself to this feeling. This woman.

Fifteen minutes later, Parker landed in Macy's bed in her condo a few blocks outside of the downtown area. Macy had hoped it would have been Parker's hillside home with a stunning view of downtown from high above—a space that Macy thought to be too much for one person. (Not that she took the liberty to research Parker's address and search it on Google Earth, and then search the listings in Zillow.) Defending criminals must have been exceedingly lucrative for Parker, apparently. It didn't matter. Macy was in bed with her.

With Macy's body under her complete control, it was as if Parker read all of her thoughts, ventured inside Macy's mind, and caught on to how she had spent the last week fantasizing about her. Parker's fingers gripped Macy's hips as her tongue worked against her. Parker's fingers dug into her hips and held her in place as her back arched and her fingers gripped the bed sheets, certain that she saw stars, as her heart hammered and her body completely rocked.

She pulled Parker up to her and let her hands glide down the smooth and firm curves of Parker's body. Finding Parker slick and hot as her fingers worked on her. Her lips against Parker's, tasting herself on them, finding it more than she expected. Better. Hotter. She loved the sound of Parker's breath and cries as her body responded. Though Parker's typical demeanor could be best described as cool, calm, and in control, she easily let herself go in bed. And nothing was more beautiful than Parker letting go of control, and not calculating.

Macy lay next to Parker as the sky began to lighten. All the way on the other side of the bed, Parker apparently didn't snuggle. Macy wormed her way closer to Parker under the blankets with an overwhelming need to feel Parker's skin against hers again.

Parker read the need in Macy's eyes. She gave an awkward *ahem* and sat up. "I probably should have mentioned this before we ended up here," sending Macy a concerned look as she sat up. "I don't do relationships. I don't have time. I don't need the drama. I don't want it."

Macy flinched a bit. "I understand." The lie spilled from her lips as the disappointment hit her heart hard. She *didn't* understand.

Parker exited the bed and turned to Macy as she began to get dressed. "I mean, I had fun with you. I did. To be frank, I wouldn't mind hanging out with you again. But I don't want to lead you on and let you think you will get any more than this from me."

Nodding in agreement so she wouldn't come across as

desperate, she chewed on her lower lip. She wouldn't mind getting *this* again. But *that* would make it harder for her not to have Parker be exclusively hers.

Parker pulled on her pants and eyed Macy as she made her way into the bathroom. "I also don't do overnights. It gives the wrong impression, so I'm gonna head out."

Macy swallowed the lump in her throat as she fixed on Parker slipping out of sight through to the stairs, her coat and tie in hand.

She got the message loud and clear. She picked up her clothes from the floor, and tossed them in the hamper in the corner. She was hurt and she was embarrassed. But all that she ever wanted since she was a child was to be picked. To be someone's number one. Their person. She tried to not take it personally. But how could she not?

2 UNLIKELY FRIENDSHIP

PARKER

*P*arker regretted sleeping with the detective almost immediately. Not that she didn't find her cute. She possessed a unique charm that Parker appreciated. And Parker found her to be surprisingly great in bed. Definitely the furthest thing from being a pillow princess. Not that Parker always minded that either. But she preferred active participation much more.

As Parker was about to head down the stairs, she turned and made her way back to Macy's bedroom. She saw that Macy had removed herself from the bed and thrown on a pair of shorts and a tank top. Parker felt bad as Macy tied her silky red hair up into a messy bun. The disappointment still showing on Macy's face kind of pulled at Parker's heartstrings a bit. Typically, the no-relationships disclaimer occurred before she hooked up with women. But Macy came on to her so hard and so fast, Parker didn't have a chance to say anything more. Macy's tongue found its way into her mouth and her hands gripped Parker's tie. Parker got the hint loud and clear and took Macy home. The way Macy came on to her, Parker assumed it would be a hookup, but she glimpsed the hurt in Macy's blue eyes when she broke it to her. She felt responsible to be up front, though.

Parker meant every word she told Macy. She worked hard, and she didn't want to be responsible for someone else's feelings. It's why she owned a cat and not a dog. The cat, same as its owner, was fiercely independent. It didn't even have a name. Parker referred to it as The Cat, or Kitty. The Cat had no qualms about being left alone for an entire day, as long as his bowl stayed full and the cleaning lady cleared the litter box—an ideal relationship for Parker.

Parker exhaled. "Before I leave, I need you to understand, first of all, I'm sorry that I didn't tell you up front. And second, I do want to hang out again. Not to use you or abuse you. But I find you intriguing, even if we play on opposite teams." Parker hoped that would smooth it all over.

Parker sensed a bit of hope in Macy as they exchanged numbers before she left.

She would have to shut that shit down. Fast. Maybe forming a friendship wouldn't be the best idea. Stalking frequently occurred after Parker cut off clingy bedmates. Women she brought home who wanted to claim her and tie her down (literally and figuratively) resulted in a few restraining orders, too. She felt hopeful this wouldn't be the case with Macy.

The night after their hookup, she received a text from Macy. Parker braced herself for the give-me-a-chance texts that sometimes came after a casual tryst. In its place, she found a pleasant surprise. "Regardless of what it is that comes of this, I'm glad we got to hang out. And I'm cool with only being friends."

An sigh of relief escaped Parker's lips.

It evolved into a regular meetup, with lots of calls and chats in between. But Macy never dared to cross the boundary. After a few drinks, Macy, it turned out, happened to be a lot of fun to hang out with. She laughed easily and carried herself in a super-chill manner.

Parker enjoyed hanging out with Macy. She didn't come across as clingy or jealous. Parker did not hide the string of one-night stands that occurred since their friendship began. Macy remained cool and unenvious.

After six months or so of regular meetups, Parker began referring to Macy as her bestie. Macy wore that title with absolute pride.

And she turned out to be a useful bestie at that. If Parker needed information on a case, Macy provided it, despite the risk to her career. Usually, after a few drinks, she would casually spill intel on cases. Parker never questioned it, and Macy never said no. There wasn't much Macy would say no to when it came to Parker. If Parker wanted to meet up, Macy would be there, come hell or high water. If Parker needed information, as long as it wasn't one of her own cases, Macy risked it all to make sure Parker had it. Macy was totally breaking protocol, but as long as Macy was willing, Parker was going to ask.

Seven Years Ago, September 12

About two months into their friendship, Macy ended up in a relationship with another woman, Nikki, a corrections officer at the county jail. They met when Macy brought in a suspect. Parker congratulated Macy on her newfound happiness and took her for a drink.

However, when Parker met Macy and Nikki out for dinner one night, it didn't take Parker long to decide how much she detested her. *Jealous*, *controlling*, and *demanding* were the first words that came to Parker's mind when asked about Nikki. The epitome of the type of person Parker didn't care much for and could never be friends with. Her actions showed her to be mentally unstable at the very least and volatile at the most. She possessively threw her arm over Macy's shoulder when Parker showed up, and then spent most of the night mad dogging Parker. Not that Parker cared. She considered herself well versed in how some women can be, especially with someone who had previously slept with their girlfriend. She didn't have time for that kind of insecurity. So Parker excused herself from the dinner early and went home.

Parker didn't hesitate to tell Macy her impression of Nikki on their next hangout, though. Macy shrugged it off. Parker understood that Macy was one of those women who *needed* to be in a relationship, though it saddened her that she was choosing to settle for such a bitch.

A little over a year into their friendship and a year into Macy's relationship with Nikki, Parker invited Macy to her house. She was opting for a meetup at her home because she knew if they went out, none of the work waiting to be completed that night would get done. So Parker offered wine, and DoorDash delivered tacos. She also wanted to talk to Macy alone.

Sitting on the patio, overlooking the twinkling lights of downtown in the distance, Parker asked Macy about how her relationship was going, and with a smile that never reached her sad blue eyes, Macy gave the typical, "It's fine."

Parker poured Macy a glass of wine, but Macy wouldn't make eye contact with her.

"I can tell something isn't right." Parker gently prodded as she turned the outdoor fireplace on.

"What do you mean?"

"I mean, I can see a change in your behavior. You aren't *you*. Word on the street is that you are getting aggressive with your questioning. Physical, not just verbal. Macy, you're laying hands on suspects in the interrogation room. That's not you. That's not solid detective work. That's abuse. Some folks are worried that your behavior will lead to suspects being found not guilty—especially if they land a good attorney. Or a lawsuit. You know I would have a field day with that if it were one of my clients. You are going to set your career on fire. And I know how much you love your job. How hard you worked to get where you are, and it's going to go up in smoke. That's not even considering your personal life. Something's up." Parker may not have been romantically involved with Macy, but anyone who considered her a friend knew Macy to be loyal—someone who went above and beyond for those she cared about—and Parker shared that trait. She wanted the best for her friends, Macy included.

"What do you mean?" Macy asked. "Sometimes it gets rough. You. know that. Suspects see that I'm a woman and they think they can bully me. It's my way of maintaining control. How is that not me? How is that something being up?"

"I mean, you aren't making stupid jokes. You barely call. And when we hang out, you barely talk." Parker couldn't hide her concern.

Setting her unfinished glass of wine (from an expensive bottle Parker hated to see wasted) on the table between them, Macy nodded. "I think I am going to go home." She stood up.

"Dinner isn't even here yet. And since when do you turn

down tacos and leave a drink unfinished?" Parker teased her. Macy put Parker to shame easily drink for drink when they went out, and Parker was no teetotaler.

"I just think I need to go home. I have a lot on my mind, and you said you have a lot of work to do. It's best if I just leave."

Parker worried about her as she walked to her car. Parker had come to realize over the past year that Macy desperately needed to be loved. She validated herself through having a relationship. She knew Macy had had a rough upbringing, being raised by her mom's parents after her mom died. Parker didn't know the specifics behind any of it, and she didn't want to pry.

Parker assumed that the talk would have led nowhere, and they would be sitting here having this same conversation again and again.

"Text me when you arrive home so I know you made it safely." Parker hugged her friend and hoped she would be okay.

Macy nodded and drove off. Parker lowered her head and went back inside.

After two days of not hearing a word from Macy, Parker finally got a call from her with good news. She finally ended her relationship with Nikki. She did it that night after leaving Parker's and made a point to call Parker as soon as Nikki left after picking up the last of her personal items. "I ended it with Nikki. I kicked her out. It's done." The calm was evident in Macy's voice.

"Excellent news." Relief washed over Parker. "I think we need to go celebrate tomorrow night."

"Abso-fucking-lutely."

While Parker was waiting in Macy's living room for her to change before they hit the local gay bar to celebrate Macy's newfound freedom, Nikki showed up, letting herself in through the front door as if she still belonged at this address. "What the absolute fuck are you doing here?" Parker asked from the couch, glaring in Nikki's direction, but not giving her the satisfaction of rising.

Macy came out of the bathroom at the sound of Parker's question and stared at Nikki. The color in her face drained. That reaction alone told Parker that Macy held back on telling her all that happened between them. Parker had witnessed that face on other women who suffered violence at the hands of their partners.

"What in the fuck are *you* doing here?" Nikki tossed the question back at Parker.

"Actually, we are on our way out to celebrate Macy kicking your ass out. I think it's best you leave. Now." Parker's voice came out cold and calm, finally taking it upon herself to rise from her seat.

"Babe?" Nikki's eyes softened as she fixed her gaze on Macy. "I'm so sorry. Can't we just work on things?" Nikki ran her hand through her short brown pixie-cut hair. Her rich brown eyes grew glassy with tears. Parker sensed the bullshit from where she stood.

Macy turned to face Parker before looking back at Nikki. "No. I think I'm done. I think Parker's right. You need to leave." Parker fought the compulsion to applaud Macy's strength.

It was reflexive and instant. As Nikki launched herself at Macy, Parker lunged toward Nikki, putting herself in Nikki's way. "I think it's best if you get the fuck out," Parker growled at Nikki, nose to nose with her.

Nikki sneered at Parker. "And what are you going to do to stop me?"

The sour breath from too much whiskey poured out of Nikki's mouth. "I think you need to fuck off and sober up. This is not going to end well for you." Parker challenged her, walking forward, which forced Nikki to walk backwards until her back was against the door.

"Oooohhhh. Parker the bad bitch." Nikki laughed. Nikki glanced over at Macy, "You think you are going to get rid of me and jump into Parker's bed? The same bitch who left you right after fucking you? The same bitch you obviously still have a thing for?"

"Okay. That's enough." Parker's hand was behind Nikki, opening the door. Macy stood back, watching the whole thing. Being a cop, most people didn't think she needed protecting, and in truth, she didn't. Parker realized full well how capable Macy came across, but she would be damned if this crazy bitch would be allowed to come into her friend's home and throw her weight around, especially after all that she had already put Macy through.

"It's time for you to go now." Another step forward succeeded in pushing Nikki back out to the porch, sending her stumbling back, almost falling down the steps of the porch. Parker slammed the door and locked the deadbolt before anyone could bat an eyelash.

"Wow. No one's ever stood up for me before." Macy cast her eyes on Parker with utter awe. "People assume because I'm a cop that I'm impenetrable or something."

"We all need a little protection. Someone to stand up for us once in a while." Parker put her arm around Macy's shoulder for a gentle hug.

Nikki pounded on the door on the other side. "Macy! Get out here!"

Macy backed away from Parker's embrace as she quietly typed on her phone.

"What are you doing?" Parker asked.

"Texting my former partner. He's going to come and take her. We might be late for dinner. Fuck. I'm gonna need to change my locks."

"How long have you been living like this?" Parker asked, not subtly and not at all delicately.

"I mean . . . I . . ." Macy's eyes glazed over with tears.

Parker couldn't help it; she pulled Macy into a big, warm hug, and she let Macy cry it out, even if she melted a bit too much into that embrace.

3 SOME OF THAT VOODOO

CALYPSO

Calypso stood in the empty retail space in the heart of downtown, looking around. The space was in the bottom floor of an office building, sandwiched between an upscale clothing boutique and an Irish pub.

This was a huge gamble, starting her tattoo studio here. There was a lot of competition, even considering that she wouldn't have to work hard to build up the clientele, as she had a long line of loyal clients who would follow her. Three artists had already jumped at the chance to work with her, including her bestie, Xander (whom she had worked for at one point, until his shop closed due to mismanagement and a poor location). Xander also came with a long and very loyal client list. The risk still lingered. There's always a risk. But what's life without risk, right?

The space was ample. A former jewelry store, it came

with a vast open floor and large glass-paneled windows that lined the entire front of the space. There would be workstations built in, along with adjustable chairs, cabinets, rolling carts, and tables set up at the stations. The delivery men and the contractor would be arriving soon. This was absolutely happening. Calypso let the pride and anticipation course through her. She wished for the ability to go back in time and tell sixteen-year-old homeless Calypso, living on the streets and couch surfing at her friends' homes in New Orleans, that one day she would be a business owner and live in a swanky downtown loft in California, no less.

The space fell within walking distance of her loft. Everything was falling into place as it should. Calypso let out a squeal. She turned and caught her reflection staring back from the mirror, standing in her own business. Her space. Her golden eyes appeared happy. A small smile played on her dark burgundy lips. Her neo-gothic filigree blackwork tattoos were on full display from her hands up to her neck and down her cleavage. She adjusted her cut and torn black t-shirt and smoothed a stray lock that fell from her inky black ponytail.

The signage person arrived to create the window sign that Calypso had designed for her business, which she aptly named Voodoo Ink—an image of a voodoo doll covered in old-school sailor tattoos, with the name underneath. The name paid homage to her New Orleans roots. A past and a town that flowed through every bit of her being, making her who she was today. Even though she could never go back to New Orleans. But that didn't mean she didn't miss it or that she didn't leave steeped in the blood of the former love of her life.

It had been a long journey for her. She moved to SoCal in the wake of a hurricane evacuation, creating an opportune time to start her life over and put the past behind her—a past that she didn't want to think about and never mentioned or discussed since arriving in California.

Being one of the few who evacuated before the storm hit, Calypso never understood those folks who refused to leave, especially after Katrina. She took herself and her scant possessions in her car up to Baton Rouge and planned her cross-country journey from there.

After watching the coverage of her hometown struggling with the threat of drowning in another flood again—her beautiful, haunted, and old city—she— knew she should go now or never. She flew from Baton Rouge to LAX with nothing more than a tattoo machine and the clothes she fit into an old, beat-up suitcase, leaving behind her car and almost everything she owned in the airport parking lot— enough living in fear and hiding from the ghosts of her past. The time to put her pain in her past and move on so she could heal started now. The only rational thing left to do was leave.

Nightmares of what she saw and what she experienced still occasionally plagued her. Blood on her hands. Watching life drain from their eyes as they stared unseeing into hers. The nightmares slowly came less frequently now, but they were no less disturbing. As she established herself, she found that she moved past seeing the bodies every time her eyelids slid shut. When they did revisit her, she would wake to the smell of blood in the air so thick it lingered metallic on her tongue and in her nostrils—the heat of blood on her hands.

Before the death and the violence, after being cast out by her very Catholic family, after living on the streets and couch-surfing with friends, after the abuse and the first death, Calypso learned her trade, fell in love. But that ended in violence and bloodshed. It was time to leave that all behind and begin again.

Her parents kicked her out when she came out of the

closet after being caught making out with a girl in the school bathroom. They called her a sinner. Only a junior in high school, sixteen, and on her own, it was no wonder she fell prey to such horrors.

After six months, Gilian, one of her school friends, convinced her parents to let Calypso stay with them. Grateful and not wanting to wear out her welcome, she dropped out, got her GED, and worked at a sno-ball stand. She saved up and got her own place a month after she turned eighteen.

That's when the horrors started. And they didn't end. It was a domino effect of lies and violence that turned her bitter. Twice. Two times too many. And the threat of life in prison or worse, the death penalty, was too much.

Hurricanes, though they usually end in tragedy, became an opportunity for Calypso to begin again. When the evacuation warnings hit, Calypso seized the opportunity and left. She would start over from scratch and build herself a completely new life.

Calypso would rebuild. She would live her perfect life. Far away from her past and her trauma. She would never have to deal with the ghosts of her past in California. Or the threat of a murder charge hanging over her head. Because, for as big a city as New Orleans is, it's not that big. You can't escape the people you know. And everyone knows everybody. And they all talk. And the lesbian community is small and tight-knit. Everyone was always up in everyone else's business.

Every time she walked into the bar, she heard people talking about her. They didn't know—but they suspected. And the dirty looks and the whispers and the gossip were also a life sentence of a different sort.

Her dreams and her independence called her, leading her

west. Instead of staying and dealing with speculations and the accusations, she would go as far away as possible.

She came to California, and she found a tattoo shop that jumped at the chance to hire her. She found friends within the art community. She built up a client list and established her niche and notable style. Several magazines, both local and national, featured her, which helped build a buzz around her. She grew a long waiting list of clients.

She occasionally dated. But she feared that if she ever got too close, she would have to talk about her past. Or they would eventually figure it out. She firmly believed she would be better off alone. Maybe the trauma of her past made her aromantic. Satisfied with her life as it stood, she didn't need a girlfriend to distract her. With her pin-up body and pretty face, she easily and effortlessly landed hookups when she found herself a little lonely.

Many tried, though, to make her theirs. They would attempt to wine and dine her. Sometimes she would go, if only to see if the ability to fall in love still lived within her. Or if she could go deep enough to find that place in her heart and feel something for someone. But it never happened. She would go back to their places—she never let anyone into hers. Letting someone into her home, her private space, seemed too close to letting them into her heart. It over-whelmed her. It struck her as getting too close. A total no for her.

Her friends would try to set her up. None of it worked. They would ask her, "aren't you lonely?"

She would shrug. "Not really. I kind of like my life as it is. If it's not broke, why fix it? I don't need someone in my life or in my bed to make me whole or complete."

She attended the weddings and baby showers for her friends and found family she made in California. She stood as the bridesmaid for many of them. Almost all of her friends tried to set her up with every lesbian they met. As much as she loved them, she finally sat them down and told them, "enough."

With her single mom friends, she held the role of the person in the delivery room. She held their hands as they were in labor, and, on a few occasions, cut the cord. She served as godmother to a few of those babies.

She hugged her friends and members of her found family, holding them through both their celebrations and their hurt. But she didn't need anyone.

Instead of pouring energy into a love life, she worked hard and saved. She got her loft in a foreclosure deal. She loved the space. In its previous life, it served as an old slaughterhouse that became part of a gentrification effort (not that she ever agreed with the gentrification concept, but this deal ended up being too good to pass up) and was converted into eight two-story loft units, four on each floor. She loved the natural light in the afternoons that filled her west-facing windows, the exposed brick walls, and the wrought iron spiral stairs that led up to her bedroom. The space occupied just over thirteen hundred square feet, with the only walls and doors enclosing the upstairs bathroom and downstairs powder room, and one utility closet that housed her washer and dryer. Perfect for one person. Herself.

Being friends with a bunch of creatives paid off. When she closed on it, many of them gifted her with their art pieces to hang on her walls—and many were gifting more to hang in the shop. The ample space and golden natural light in her home provided her with a place to create her own art. She painted the scenes that haunted her. She painted the streets of New Orleans that she missed. She painted as her way of communicating her pain and her past.

She continued to work and save, qualifying for a small business loan in conjunction with her savings, which allowed her to open her own business. It took her thirteen years to finally find herself in the place in her life where she wanted to be.

But she made it. And she only owed it to herself. She did it on her own. Proving she didn't need anyone in her life. She persisted fine all by herself.

The sign maker carefully placed her business name and logo on the window as she allowed herself to reminisce about how far she had come. If all those who cast her aside as a young girl could see her now.

4 HE'S MALNACIDO

SEVEN YEARS AGO JUNE 7

CALYPSO

ith only one appointment scheduled for tonight (it should have been to*day*, but whatever), and with a client Calypso considered a bit sketchy, Javier, she sat and glared at the clock as she waited for him to arrive. She worked on him regularly and was well aware he manifested as bad news. But she got paid to tattoo him, not judge him. He came in a lot. Sometimes he would bring a girlfriend to get his initials tattooed on their hip. She thought he got off on it. Those girlfriends always seemed to be very young, even though Javi, same as her, was in his mid-thirties, and it struck her as gross, but again, he paid her. And he always paid in cash. And he always gave her more than the price she charged. Sometimes double. He also brought all of his brothers, cousins, and friends to her. So no judgment. Sit in the chair, don't fidget. Don't complain. Don't whine. Take care of the ink when you leave. Wear sunscreen. Thank you. Goodbye.

It turned out to be a sweltering hot June day. Javier called her three times throughout the day to push his appointment later in the evening. At this point, Calypso would never get home. He scheduled her to work on a giant back piece of a naked woman with a sugar skull instead of a face. It would take his entire back from shoulder to waist, to the spot above the crack of his hairy ass. At this point, she made up her mind that she didn't care how long he believed he was able to sit under the needle. She decided that tonight, only the outline and shading would be completed. He would have to reschedule to have the color added.

Three other artists and two piercers rented space from her. Every one of them booked out in advance. Walk-ins were hardly accommodated. She considered passing him on to another artist, but he would never accept that. She knew better. Knowing his pain tolerance and the size of this piece, she cleared her schedule for him. So, his repeatedly rescheduling the appointment wound up costing her a day of clients she could have brought in from the waiting list.

Her level of irritation with Javier reached record levels, and Calypso couldn't deny it. She recognized that his piece — the outline and shading alone — would take at least five hours to complete. She would end up alone with him in the studio for most of it, based on when he would finally come sauntering in. He always ended up hitting on her, no matter how many times she told him she preferred women. Only women. Not interested. A proud gold star lesbian, she never let a man touch her. And she maintained zero plans of ever going there, especially not with Javi.

But that didn't deter him. He would touch the neo-gothic filigree patterns tattooed onto her neck, down, down to her chest, both arms, and onto her hands. He would trail his finger down the pattern on her neck. She would bat his hand away and threaten to kick him out.

He would laugh her off. "Don't be so serious, chula. Smile."

She would narrow her golden eyes at him and cuss him out under her breath; the words drowned out by the sound of the machine humming in her hand, the music overhead, and the chatter of the other artists and clients.

Calypso sat at her drafting table and began to sketch a custom piece for another client. Her phone pinged with an alert. Javier: "I'm parking right now. Be in soon."

"Xander, can you stay late tonight?" Calypso called over to him. He peered up from the client he labored over and stopped his machine.

"Javi is coming in?" he asked.

"Mmmhmmm."

"Yeah, I gotchu girl. No worries. I can think of a million things I need to do to stay. I'll walk you home tonight, too." Xander's six-foot-three, tatted head to toe—literally—frame was considered to be imposing by most who came across him. A complete facade, though. Xander was the biggest teddy bear Calypso ever met. Calypso considered him her adopted older brother from the second they met.

Xander could be relied on to have her back at any given time, even after he met his now wife, Xochitl. (When Xander met his wife, he went by Alexander, but dropped the *ale*—first as a joke, and then it stuck.) After Xander and Xochitl got together, Calypso often ended up a third wheel. Once Xochitl (a blank canvas that quickly became brightly colored as she ended up covered in tattoos herself) came into the picture, she promptly became her best friend. Often, Xochitl would end up inviting her to come out with them. So when Xander found out Calypso planned to open her studio, he asked to work with her again (as if she would say no). Calypso loved it when Xochitl cooked and brought food in for Xander, and she always made sure to bring a plate for Calypso as well. Xochitl managed to cook beautiful and tasty meals even though she worked full-time as a social worker. The two of them became the closest thing to family for Calypso, and for them, she would be forever grateful.

"Is Xochitl coming by tonight?" Calypso asked as Xander's machine started its buzzing, and Xander carefully outlined a string of butterflies wrapping up the leg of a woman who finally got an appointment after she patiently sat on the waiting list, trying to get booked for over a month.

"Yeah. She made enchiladas. She's got a plate set aside for you. Extra hot sauce for yours." He didn't peer up from his work while he talked to her.

Calypso's mouth watered. Xochitl's cooking beat takeout any day.

Before Calypso said another word, Javi swaggered in through the door. "Calypso, beautiful . . . I'm so sorry. I got caught up with some business."

Some business most likely pertained to activities she wanted nothing to do with.

He wasted no time taking his shirt off and lowering his boxer shorts, exposing the top of his crack (so gross), to avoid the smear of ink and blood when Calypso got started. "How do you want me, beautiful?"

Calypso caught sight of Xander rolling his eyes.

"Face down on the table." Calypso snapped her black latex gloves in place. Calypso inspected some of his healed pieces before taking the razor to his back. The inside of his forearm was one of her favorites she had done for him. A custom piece she made for Javier and his three brothers, Santa Muerta. A few of his friends even came in for the piece. Since each tattoo was an original—she never worked from flash at this point—she asked Javi first. He said he wanted them to have it.

Calypso put the stencil on his back after shaving it. "Get up and go look in the mirror. Tell me if that works."

Javi got up from the table and checked his reflection. "Yeah. That works, baby girl." She wished he would use her given name. "I know I caused you a lot of shit today, being late. Don't you worry. I'm gonna take care of you. You'll be paid for the hours I made you wait." *Good. Thank you. It's the least he can do. Time is money after all.*

He lay face down on the table. Calypso snapped on a new pair of gloves and started in on Javi's back.

When she stopped after finishing a section of the outline, he ran his finger down the length of her neck. She swatted him away. "What are you doing after you leave, baby girl?"

"I'm busy. Lay down, keep your arms by your side, please."

Xander's client had left, and he raised an eyebrow, fixing his gaze on her. His eyes expressed his concern for her.

"What are you doing that you are too busy for me?" Javi asked her.

Xander pulled up an extra chair and sat next to Calypso and Javi, crossing his arms over his chest.

"Bless your little heart, Javi. You just don't understand," Calypso murmured.

"I heard that." Javi picked his head up and glared at her with an image that could only be considered slightly menacing.

"I meant you to." Calypso arched an eyebrow at him, amused. "Do you want this piece to come out like you want it?"

"What's that supposed to mean?"

"It means don't fuck with me. I have the power to make you look really good, or really fucking stupid. You decide."

Xander snickered silently.

"Man. Lighten up." Javi stuck his face back down, and Calypso continued to work.

As Calypso worked, Javi put in his earbuds and took a call. Calypso did her best to ignore his conversation. She realized he involved himself in shady shit, but she didn't want to even think about the various possibilities. Not on any level whatsoever. "Where is she?. . . Why did you let her go without you? . . . ¿Qué pinche chingados? What the actual fuck is wrong with you? . . . Are you stupid? . . . Do you know how much that's going to cost me? . . . No. . . . No. . . . Stay—don't you dare leave." He pulled one of the AirPods from his ear for a second and looked back at Calypso. "How much longer do you think we will be?"

"Three hours. At least." Calypso answered.

"I'll be there in a few hours. I'm at Calypso's. Stay put. Don't let anyone else go either."

When he hung up his call, he peered over at Calypso. "Mami, why won't you let me take you out, just once? I would treat you so right."

Xander cleared his throat.

"What?" Javi turned his head to glare at Xander.

Xander cracked his tatted knuckles and leaned his elbows on his knees to be eye level with Javi. "You will treat her with respect. She said no. If you keep hounding her, I will make sure you leave with or without your finished work, and that you have a tough time walking from this point on."

Calypso smiled to herself. Xander was a blessing in her life.

* * *

THREE AND A HALF HOURS LATER, with a finished outline and shading, Javi finally left. Xander and Xochitl helped Calypso clean up and made sure she got home safe and without incident.

"I'll just say this," Xander said as they stood in front of Calypso's building, "I really think you need to stop letting Javi come in. He's bad news, and I'm not fully convinced he's not going to try something, regardless, no matter if I'm here with you. I'm only one person. He's got a goon squad in unknown numbers. You don't need his business."

Calypso glanced at him and Xochitl. "I appreciate everything you do. Both of you. You're right. Absolutely right."

"It's only because we love you," Xochitl said as she wrapped Calypso in a big hug. "You are like family to us. You know I went to high school with Javi, right?"

Calypso nodded.

"He was malnacido even then. Bad news. Steer clear, Calypso."

"I know. I'll see what I can do to keep him from coming back." Calypso hugged both of them, and as always, they waited on the step until she made it up the stairwell and into her loft and waved at them from the window.

5 TRIAL AND ERROR

SIX YEARS AGO MAY 25

MACY

Despite not being able to sleep the night before, Macy drank in the sight of the woman in the bed with her, Sam. They began their relationship a little over a year ago. Macy met Sam, one of the district attorneys in the county, when she was assigned to prosecute one of Macy's cases.

Once they solidified their relationship, Sam passed on the case that had kept Macy up all night, dreading her cross-examination. This being a case that could make or break either of their careers, Macy took it as the ultimate sign of love.

Macy and her team busted the perp almost a year earlier for human trafficking, homicide, and sale of narcotics, and now, twelve months later, the case had finally made it on the docket. He was the head of an international cartel that ran prostitutes and various substances from Mexico into California, New Mexico, and Nevada. Ironically, the defendant retained Harrington and Harrington for their representation (leading directly to Macy's anxiety over her pending cross-examination).

Up until now, Macy had been kept on the lower profile cases, and she was hoping this would elevate her status and allow her better cases. She felt her career had been stunted ever since her promotion. Her partner, Brent Caldwell, constantly had to remind her that they were still part of the Organized Crime Task Force and that they would get better cases as they came. She appreciated his low-key attitude; it was a great counter to her high-strung overachiever attitude. A former Marine who served two tours in Afghanistan, he had learned to let a lot of shit not get to him. He knew life was valuable and too short to sweat what he couldn't control. He was also the only person who didn't get frustrated or angry with her on the occasions she blundered her court appearances when she had to go up against Parker. He also never questioned her friendship with Parker.

Sam, on the other hand, never understood how Macy and Parker were such close friends. Sam faced off against Parker several times, and those encounters led Sam to form a deeply negative opinion of her. Macy always ended up playing interference between the two of them, and she would mostly go out with Parker alone to avoid any conflicts. If the two of them spent any time together, it would dissolve into insults and petty barbs thrown back and forth, and Macy would be caught in the middle.

Macy and Caldwell fell into this case by dumb luck as they were investigating one of the lower-level members of the organization, and their investigation led straight to the top. They built this case with strong, straightforward, and clean evidence, including solid witness testimony; it should have been an open-and-shut case.

Macy discovered that out of all the attorneys on staff at Harrington and Harrington, Parker would be cross-examining her. Over the course of their friendship, Parker had only defended a small handful of the suspects in Macy's cases since they met, (and each time it ended badly for Macy). Most of Macy's cases would be considered minor to Parker. Sometimes, other attorneys at her firm took those cases, as Parker essentially only handled the most significant and high-profile cases. Parker obviously took the lead on this one.

Because of the recent case at hand, and Macy's relationship with Sam, Macy and Parker didn't spend a lot of time together or talk often. She missed Parker. She missed her best friend. As expected, Macy also expressed concern about being cross-examined by Parker today. She chalked it up to PTSD from the three other times she had faced Parker in court. It strained their friendship a bit when Macy found out Parker signed on to defend this shitbag. But she hoped that, given their years of close friendship, Parker would not be so aggressive with her cross-examination.

She took in Sam's features with her bed-ruffled pixie cut and her pale blue eyes closed, sleeping peacefully. Macy loved her. She did. She loved that they both worked on the same side. Their relationship got serious relatively fast. Macy rarely thought about Parker. At least not consciously. She couldn't control her dreams.

Sam worked her ass off to prepare Macy thoroughly for trial, even though it wasn't even her case anymore. She ran Macy through a battery of questions, acting as she perceived Parker would—even imitating Parker's way of walking, inflection, and facial expressions. Sam impressed Macy with her spot-on (albeit exaggerated) impression of Parker. And it kind of turned her on a bit if she was going to be honest.

That didn't mean shit, though. She fully realized Parker would chew her up and spit her out. She suspected, based on history, that Parker would fight dirty. Sam's perception only touched the surface of the depths Parker would go to defend a client. The anxiety of what Macy understood to be coming her way kept her from getting a good night's sleep.

"Hey, babe . . . wake up." Macy nudged Sam gently.

Sam's eyes fluttered open and she sat up. "Are you going to be okay today?"

Not even a good morning? Damn. "What do you mean?" Macy was automatically thrown into being defensive.

"I'm extremely aware of the soft spot you have for Parker." Sam stretched and got out of bed.

"I do *not.*" And there went the cheeks flaming red in a mixture of anger and embarrassment.

"You have crumbled almost every single time she's crossed you. You have a history of falling apart during your testimony when she cross-examines you. People are starting to talk. The only time you ever crumble and fall apart on the witness stand is when you are face to face with Parker fucking Harrington."

"What do you mean by *talk?*"

"It's a long-standing rumor amongst my office that you have been paid off to throw cases for Parker. I've come to your defense more than a few times."

"You actually believe that?" Macy flinched.

"No. It's just what people say. I realize you don't *intentionally* throw cases for Parker. But there's a weakness you have for her. I'm not sure if it's because of your friendship or something deeper. But something happens to you when you are around her, most specifically on the witness stand. She's won every single case she's defended against one of your cases. Every single one. It usually falls back on your inability to handle her questioning you."

"I'm not going to entertain that." Macy got out of bed and left the room on that note.

As Sam made her way into the shower upstairs, Macy made her coffee, despising the fact that Sam bore the need to throw that in her face. Especially this morning. Her nerves were already raw and on edge. This was definitely not helping. The extra pressure was making her extra self-conscious.

ONCE CALLED TO TESTIFY, Macy gave a brilliant performance on direct examination. Her answers came across as clear and concise, and she didn't falter once. However, when Parker stood and began her cross-examination of Macy, Sam's words echoed in the back of her mind. She told herself she wouldn't crumble. She wouldn't show weakness. She wouldn't prove "everyone" right.

But as "everyone" predicted, she caved. Not intentionally. But it happened. Parker somehow got under her skin and hit the right buttons. It all happened with her first question— "You have a history of getting physical with your suspects, don't you?" Forcing Macy to stumble, and once she stumbled, she couldn't regain her footing.

Parker immediately following with, "The lead that led you to my client was given through coercion, correct?" Followed by the introduction of a photo into evidence, a picture of the informant with a black eye.

"Your department has consistently turned a blind eye to your behavior, has it not?" was the question that followed.

By the time Parker finished with her, she even began questioning herself and her whole investigation. She was rattled. She was confused. She was angry.

When she got off the stand, she marched herself out of the courtroom and to the bathroom, locked herself in a stall, and cried quietly, banging her head against the metal divider. She'd barely held herself together as she left the courtroom. As she had walked out, the heat flushed in her cheeks, and the tears began prickling under her eyelids. She found sweet relief when she closed the stall door and let the tears flow.

"Macy?" She heard Parker's voice asking for her.

The court must be in recess. Fuck. Why is she even here? Is it to gloat?

Macy opened the door, and glared at Parker through her red, watery eyes. "Why?"

"Why what?" Parker leaned against the counter and crossed her arms over her chest. She had to be kidding. *Why? She knows full well the fuckery she played at in that courtroom.* Parker wore a royal blue bespoke suit, crisp white button-up with Tiffany cufflinks, her coral-colored tie in a double Windsor knot, and not a hair out of place. Macy hated that Parker was in here looking so smug and so good. She hated that she even considered Parker to be so alluring to her. She should *hate* Parker Harrington. She *wanted* to hate Parker Harrington.

"Why do you do that to me when you question me? Why would you bring up the accusations of me getting physical? Why would you have everyone doubt me like that?" Macy tried her best to sound angry and indignant, but she only sounded weak and pathetic.

"I'm doing my job, Macy. What do you want me to do? Softball you?" Parker's eyebrow raised as she smirked.

"You don't have to go so hard, Parker. You don't. It's like you figured out exactly how to question me to make me look like a bumbling idiot on the stand, and you exploit it every chance you can."

"It's my job. It's not personal." Parker came across so

straightforward and snarky, the need to scream took over. She wanted to throw something. She wanted to hit Parker. She wanted Parker to hold her and tell her she was sorry. Macy's emotions fell all over the spectrum.

"Sam thinks you're a lowlife for how dirty you fight and how you work so hard to get these guilty pieces of shit off the hook."

"I really don't give a single flying fuck what Sam thinks of me. I'm not doing anything other than my job. My job is to make sure the defendants in your cases are not having their constitutional rights trampled on. I'm merely ensuring that the law is being followed and they are receiving a fair trial. If the judge or jury can't see their guilt beyond a reasonable doubt, it's their right to be let go. It's. My. Job."

A woman walked into the bathroom, caught sight of Parker and Macy in their showdown, and turned around and walked back out. Parker went over and locked the door so no one else would come in. She came back and resumed her spot at the counter.

Macy leaned against the stall door, looking at her disheveled reflection in the mirror standing next to a perfectly polished Parker. She hastily wiped the tears off her cheeks. "Sam told me about the rumors that I throw cases for you."

"Sam is also jealous. She lacks credibility on that. She would say anything for you to cut me out of your life." The mind-blowing level of Parker's hubris infuriated Macy, despite the dead-on accurate assumption.

Macy snickered wryly. "Well . . . maybe it's best if I do step away."

Parker flinched and gave a snort. "Really?"

Before Macy answered, Parker's phone dinged with an alert.

Parker glanced at the screen and back at Macy. "I have to

go back. You might want to think about that before you make a hasty decision you will end up regretting."

Macy waited for Parker to walk out. She locked the door behind Parker and sat on the floor of the bathroom, her nicest pantsuit be damned, until she composed herself. She was truly losing her shit. And she knew the root of this insanity was Parker. Parker was the reason she had a bad reputation. Parker throwing her off in court is what kept her from rising further faster. All of the problems in her life came back to her feelings for Parker. The feelings she couldn't seem to control or manage. She had to do it. She had to let her go once and for all.

Once she deemed herself capable enough to get through the courthouse and to her car without a complete public meltdown, she stood in front of the mirror and splashed cold water on her face to try to shrink the puffiness of her eyes. It didn't help.

Someone tried to open the door and then knocked. She stayed quiet. She didn't want to see anyone or deal with anyone.

Macy waited until the knocking subsided and the hallway went quiet before she left.

* * *

SHE DIDN'T WANT to go to the station and she didn't want to go home, so she took herself to the bar. She went to a dark booth in the back with dim lighting so she wouldn't be spotted.

She had texted Caldwell and asked him to meet her there.

She slouched in the booth and glared at her phone. Sam sent a text asking her to check in. She scrolled past it. Caldwell, responding to her text, asked how it went at court, trying to gauge the climate before he testified later that day.

She put her phone back down on the table and put her head down without even responding.

Jill, her favorite waitress at this bar, came up and set a glass of red wine in front of her. "How did you know?" Macy asked her. A strand of Jill's long, wildly curly black hair, which she had piled up atop her head, had fallen loose and trailed down her cheek, and her tight shorts and crop top accentuated her ample curves. She and Macy made out once after she got off work, and they got drunk together. But Jill couldn't help being straight, and wrote the incident off as a drunken oops. She didn't let it interfere with their somewhat friendship.

"It's kinda obvious when you sulk to the back and put your head down. What's going on?"

"Fuck Parker Harrington. That's what's going on."

"I thought she was your best friend?"

"I thought so, too."

Jill sat down in the booth across from Macy. "Wanna talk about it?"

"No. I just want to drink and feel sorry for myself."

"Is Sam meeting you here?"

"No. Sam has no idea I'm here. Caldwell is on his way after he gets done in court." Macy took a drink and set the glass back down. Jill's eyes sparked at the news that Caldwell was coming. She had a huge crush on him. Macy ignored her reaction to Caldwell's impending arrival and gave a huff, putting her head back down on the table.

Jill caught her lip between her teeth and crossed her arms. "Why are you friends with Parker when she makes you feel this way?"

"What do you mean?"

"This isn't the first time you've come in here pouting about something she did or said to you."

"It's complicated."

"You have Sam in your life. She's good for you. Maybe you should focus less on Parker and more on Sam?" Jill offered.

Macy took another deep drink of the wine and rested her eyes on Jill. "Yeah. That's probably good advice."

Caldwell arrived and slipped into the booth across from Macy. "That bad, huh?" He asked as Jill gave him her most dazzling smile. He gave Jill a wink. "Can I get a Stone IPA?" He asked her.

"Of course. I'll be right back." She spun and walked off.

Macy sat back up and cocked her head at him. He was the epitome of the Southern California surfer boy, all grown up. He was sun-kissed, blond with blue eyes, and well-toned, he still spent his off days surfing. Macy nodded at him. It was all she could muster.

Jill brought Caldwell's IPA back and sat it in front of him, sliding into the booth next to him. "She needs to get Parker out of her life," Jill informed him.

"I couldn't agree more." Caldwell sighed and took a sip of his beer. He had been her shoulder to cry on regarding Parker since day one. He knew. He knew far too well.

Macy pouted in their general direction. "I'm trying. I have tried. I can only continue to try."

6 WITNESS THIS

PARKER

*P*arker went back into the courtroom after her bathroom run-in with Macy in time for the prosecution to call its last witness, Macy's partner, and then rest its case after she crossed him. He did much better than Macy, but even he couldn't repair the damage of Macy's disastrous performance. Memorial Day weekend approached, and the court would be recessed for four days. When they resumed on Tuesday, Parker would take her turn to argue the case.

That didn't mean *she* would be allowed to be in recess for four days. Witness prep for a reluctant witness awaited her. The witness in question didn't want the attention of testifying in a high-profile case. The witness was a tattoo artist whom Javier insisted she call as a character witness—not that she needed this witness. Parker planned this one to be the icing on the cake.

Parker's client frequented this artist and brought several of the alleged victims through her shop. It took Parker several days of attempting to reach her and then even more days on the phone with her, trying to persuade her to agree to testify. But in the end, Parker's powers of persuasion won out. Parker wanted every last witness and piece of evidence in place to create reasonable doubt.

As she drove back to her office, she thought about her encounter with Macy in the bathroom.

Parker considered Macy to be her closest friend in a long time. She didn't want Macy to have to make a choice between a possible future with someone she loved and their friendship. Make no mistake about it, Parker didn't have a high opinion of Sam. She considered her to be a stick-up-the-ass, stuck-up Goody Two-shoes. But to have to choose between your friend and your lover—that's a shitty position for anyone to be in. But she didn't want to lose a good friend either. Case in point as to why Parker stayed single. She didn't want to be put in the position of having to choose between her friends, her career, or her girlfriend. Life is so much easier when you stay single and have an occasional fling or friend with benefits.

Parker pulled into the garage that her office building used, and shook the drama from her head. She didn't want, nor could she afford, to be bothered by Macy's melodrama. This decision fell on Macy's shoulders and not hers.

She put herself back into work mode to focus on meeting with the tattoo artist and preparing her to testify. Gun-shy witnesses who are already ambivalent about testifying tended to be the hardest to deal with. She wanted to skip the whole meeting, turn around, and head home to have a cocktail and something to eat, and then pass out in her bed.

As she walked into the office, she took note that only one person sat in the lobby waiting.

Parker approached the receptionist, who didn't even turn away from her screen to make eye contact as she typed away, responding to an email. "Stacy? Is that my witness?" Parker asked, looking at the woman sitting in the lobby. Parker took in her long, inky black hair, shaved on the sides and flowing freely in waves that reached her mid-back. Her eyes appeared to be literally the color of honey, not brown or even hazel-gold, and a silver septum piercing sat above her full, deep burgundy upper lip. Blackwork neo-gothic filigree pattern tattoos sleeved both of her arms, extending to her hands and fingers, tattoos climbing up her neck and across her chest and solar plexus. Clad in a black tube top, an unbuttoned blazer with sleeves rolled up, distressed jeans barely held together at the seams, and black patent leather Doc Martens, she sat scrolling on her phone, looking bored as she waited.

"Yes, Miss Harrington." Stacy continued to work.

"Is everyone else gone for the night?" Parker asked, stalling. Parker's eyes were glued to the woman in the lobby. She couldn't help but be drawn to her, a completely foreign feeling to her. She was intrigued not only by her unusual features, but the desire to explore where all those patterns inked into her skin went.

"Yes, Miss Harrington," Stacy repeated. "Except Juliana. She stayed in case you needed anything." She still didn't look up from her work.

"Thank you. If you want to head out, you can." Parker stole another glimpse of the woman in the lobby and licked her lips as she took her in.

Stacy only nodded without any other reaction. Parker couldn't stand Stacy, but her father adored her. Parker would have selected someone with more personality for that role.

But her father valued Stacy's precision and therefore, she stayed.

"Calypso Boudreaux?" Parker made her way back into the lobby.

She turned her golden gaze on Parker and smiled. "Hi. Yes. That's me." Absolutely. Stunning.

Parker paused, frozen in that eye contact. She wished this encounter had happened under any other circumstances than those where she felt forced to remain professional. "Parker Harrington. So sorry I made you wait. Come this way." Parker, for the first time in a long time, found herself utterly distracted by a woman. She fixated on watching Calypso move as she stood and walked toward her. She fought the craving to take Calypso and lay her out on the conference room table and—Nope. Can't go there right now. She tried to erase the thought as she led Calypso down the hall toward her office. She was shorter than Parker, with a figure that was soft and curvy, reminiscent of the old Hollywood starlets or pinup girls. Calypso was eyeing her subtly, assessing her. A static pull of energy flowed between them as they walked. It was terrifying.

"No problem." Calypso's voice carried a soft lilt as she followed Parker from the waiting room down the hall to the end.

Parker took Calypso to her impressive office suite (regrettably bypassing the conference room). As managing partners, she and her father occupied corner offices on opposing sides of the building, with large windows and grand views. Her view looked out over downtown, and she considered it beautiful no matter what time of day (her father's office had a view of the San Gabriel mountains). Their offices featured dark mahogany and black leather furniture, complemented by plush dark carpeting on the floors. Parker's degrees and awards lined the cream-colored wall behind where she sat at the desk. Parker studied Calypso as she decided where to sit. Parker found herself mesmerized by the intricate black pattern that adorned Calypso's skin. Imagining how it would feel to trace that pattern with her fingertips, Parker flexed and released her hands subtly to shake herself from the thought.

Calypso sat in the chair across from Parker's desk, resting her elbows on the arms of the chair, and folded her hands in front of her on her lap. Parker unbuttoned her jacket and slipped it off, loosening her tie. It seemed hot in the office as she draped her suit jacket over the back of her chair.

"Can I fetch you anything before we start? Coffee? Water? Soda?" Parker asked as she got herself settled into her chair. The heat of Calypso's eyes on her told her a lot. She suspected that the attraction was obviously mutual. She intuitively sensed it, which made it that much harder for Parker to focus on the business at hand.

"Water would be great," Calypso replied as she fidgeted with a silver spoon ring with the figure of a goddess molded into it.

Parker pressed a button, and her assistant came in. "Juliana, can you grab us two bottles of water, please?" Even as Parker talked to Juliana, she couldn't help but look at Calypso.

"Thank you," Calypso said to Juliana. Parker found herself looking at the lines of Calypso's neck as she tilted her head up and over to speak to Juliana. Focusing on this meeting was already showing itself to be a considerable challenge. She wanted to trace each of those patterns with her—Stop. Not now.

Parker gave a small ahem as she pulled out her yellow pad and her favorite Montblanc pen. Calypso seemed calm sitting across from her. Parker took her in, studying her perfectly arched eyebrows, perfect cat eyeliner, and burgundy lips before she finally said, "you have an accent. Where are you from?" Not at all relevant to the case, but whatever.

"New Orleans." Calypso's honey-gold eyes bore directly into Parker's. For as hardcore as she appeared, her voice carried a soft sweetness and matched the honey color of her eyes.

Parker shifted in her seat and turned her attention to her notes. "Calypso . . . that's an unusual name. Is that your real name?" Again, not related. But that voice.

"Yes. It's Greek. It's the name of a character in *The Odyssey*. It also means mystery, or secrets. It also means strong feminine energy. Calypso tried to seduce Odysseus to leave his wife for her."

Parker recalled having read *The Odyssey* in high school. But she never considered it once after she aced the essay on it. Now she wanted to re-read it and deep dive into the section on Odysseus and the seductress this captivating woman was named after.

Parker struggled hard to keep her composure and professionalism; before now, she couldn't say another time when she encountered a name that matched the person so well. She took her cufflinks off and rolled up her sleeves before asking, "California is a long way away. Why here?" These questions had zero to do with the case or Calypso's testimony. But Parker wanted to learn everything about this woman. And she could easily pawn it off as small talk to make this witness more at ease.

"My family didn't want anything to do with me, and I fell in with a bad crowd, so I came here to start over about ten years ago."

Parker nodded. "Do you want to tell me what kind of trouble you got into? Is it something the prosecutor would use against you? Something that can invalidate your testimony?" The latter part of the question she added in an attempt to steer the questions to Calypso's impending testimony.

"Let's just say there is a reason I was hesitant to testify. And add to that, I don't care for police presence. But I don't think they would know. And if they did, I don't think it would get in the way of my testimony."

"But you can't tell me?" Parker leaned back in her chair, crossing her ankle over her knee, raising her eyebrow as she tapped her pen against the yellow pad that she had not taken a single note on.

Calypso's eye contact didn't waver as she sighed. Parker sensed Calypso staring directly into her soul with those hypnotic, black cat eye-lined, golden eyes. She again reminded herself to focus. "I saw some things. But if I were to report any of it, or testify to it, I would be in trouble— well, danger actually." That eye contact that stirred too many emotions in her broke momentarily through Calypso's confession. Parker wanted to be in that gaze again. She wanted to study everything about the woman sitting before her and listen to all of her stories and confessions with that subtle, soft accent.

Parker inhaled. "Let's get to it, then? Calypso." Parker relished the feel of her name on her tongue. "Tell me how you know Javier Ortiz Sanchez."

"He's a regular client of mine."

"And what is it you do, exactly?"

"I'm a tattoo artist. I own a studio downtown. Voodoo Ink."

"Good, Calypso. At that point, I'm going to have you point him out and say something he is wearing."

She nodded.

"Can you tell me about your interactions with Javier on June seventh of last year?"

"Javi had come in for work on his back piece. He came in around four and didn't leave until well after ten."

Juliana returned to the office with two bottles of water. She handed one to Calypso and one to Parker. "Anything else, Parker?"

"Calypso? Is there anything else we can bring you before we continue?" Parker asked.

Calypso took a drink of the water and set the bottle on a coaster on the table between the two chairs. "If you don't mind, I would like to use the bathroom before we continue."

"Juliana will show you where it is." Parker planted both feet on the floor and brought herself in closer to the desk as Juliana opened the door for Calypso.

"I'm going to head out after I show her where the restroom is, if that's okay?" Juliana asked.

"Yeah. That's fine." Parker took a deep breath in as Calypso exited with Juliana, and she caught the faint scent of Calypso's perfume. A tantalizing blend of vanilla, orange, and lavender.

Goddamn. Get a fucking grip. Parker closed her eyes and worked so very hard to remind herself to maintain professionalism. She kind of hated herself for having ethics. It was one thing to fight a little dirty in the courtroom. It's another to throw all professionalism out the window and jeopardize her whole case.

Parker exhaled and glanced at her phone. Javier texted her seven times, asking if Calypso had ever made it to her office.

"Don't worry about any of that. It's my job to worry. You just relax. I got you." she texted back.

Calypso came back in, sat down across from Parker, and reached over to grab her bottle of water. "Sorry." She smiled. "Ok. I'm ready to continue."

Parker set her phone down and took a breath. "Okay. Let's do this."

7 QUESTIONS AND ANSWERS

MAY 25

CALYPSO

*C*alypso found herself intrigued by Parker. It was obvious the attraction went both ways; Parker's eyes kept roaming over her body as she talked. The atmosphere definitely carried an electric charge around them. Calypso wondered what the odds were that she could get Parker's number or her Instagram and maybe ask her to have a drink after this meeting. The charged air in the office drove Calypso crazy. She couldn't remember the last time she experienced this much chemistry with someone.

Calypso never thought she would be into the professional types. She always did her best to stay cognizant about sticking with her kind. But this woman, in her obviously expensive suit, with the fresh haircut and those green eyes and the slight dimple in the left cheek . . . This was new. This was different. This was exciting—a new kind of challenge.

"How long have you known Javier?" Parker's question broke her from her thoughts.

"I've known him for about five years."

"Calypso, can you tell me how many times you've tattooed Javier?" Hearing her name tumbling from Parker's lips made goosebumps crop up on her body.

"Countless times. A lot of times."

Parker fished around on her desk and held up a picture. "Do you recognize this tattoo?" She showed Calypso a photograph of the tattoo of Santa Muerta on the inside of Javi's forearm.

"Yes. Javier and all of his brothers got it . . . I don't know . . . about a year and a half ago."

"What is this a portrait of?"

"It's a portrait of Santa Muerta."

"Can you tell me about Santa Muerta?"

"I'm not entirely familiar with it. Only that she's a patron saint of something or other in their culture. I don't typically question my clients on the significance of the work they commission. It's my job to draw the picture, and then if they approve, I ink it into their flesh."

Parker smirked at Calypso's snark. A warmth flushed through Calypso under Parker's seeming approval, and she returned Parker's grin. "Do you do a lot of those portraits?" Parker continued with her questions. Calypso registered that, though there was a pad and a pen for notes in front of Parker, she didn't write down a single note. She kept her intent gaze on Calypso.

"It's fairly common. I do variations of them quite often."

"So it's fair to say that there are a lot of people with this tattoo?"

"Yes. You can say that."

"Other than his siblings, did Javier bring in anyone else to get tattooed?"

"A few of his girlfriends."

"Girlfriends? As in plural?"

"Again, that's not for me to judge. But as it seemed, yes. Plural."

"All at the same time?"

"No. Just one or sometimes two at a time."

"What did they get?"

"All of them got his initials. Near their bikini line."

"And these girlfriends, what can you tell me about their demeanor while they were in your shop?"

Calypso paused. These questions came at her rapid fire, which she appreciated as it kept her mind on the situation at hand, and not the more base thoughts that she couldn't stop from running in an undercurrent in her mind. "Demeanor?"

"Yes. How were they acting?"

"Normal."

"What does that mean? Normal—in the context of being tattooed."

"They came in. He paid, they lay on the table, they made conversation while I worked on them."

"Conversation with you or just Javi?"

"Both of us. It's always kind of a lively environment when they come in."

"Would you say that they appeared distressed in any way?"

"No."

"Did they seem as if they had been forced to be there?"

"If by forced you mean laughing, joking, talking about their plans when they leave the shop, sure."

Parker gave another smirk. "I like that answer here, but in the courtroom, don't say that. You will confuse the jury. Just answer the question. Next question—did they seem drugged or under the influence in any way?"

That curl in Parker's lip gave her a thrill, leading her to

wonder what else would make Parker smile, and it had nothing to do with answering questions about Javi. "No. There are strict laws about working on people who are under the influence. They have to sign the consent forms with a clear head."

"That's all of the questions I'm going to ask you. When I'm done, you will be cross-examined by the other side. They are going to try to trip you up. They are going to try to make you angry. They will try to discredit you. You need to remain calm."

"I can do that." Calypso internally kicked herself for saying that. She discerned that, by speaking those words, Parker would let her leave. She thought quickly. "But just to be sure, maybe you should ask me what you think they will ask me."

Parker smiled and sat back in her chair. She suspected Parker wanted her to stay.

After Parker ran her through the assumed cross-examination questions and gave her feedback on her responses, Calypso paused and flicked her gaze over at Parker. She wanted to ask Parker to have a drink with her, but she didn't seem to know how to do so. Calypso didn't have a history of being the nervous or self-conscious type, but she was so very out of her league with Parker.

Parker paused and fixed her eyes back on Calypso, obviously sensing a question waiting to be asked. Parker narrowed her eyes. "Is there something wrong?"

"Um." Calypso worried her lip and fidgeted with her ring.

"What's up?" Parker asked, putting the cap on her pen.

"I was just . . . What are you doing when you leave here?"

Parker lowered her lids and exhaled.

"I was just . . . I am going to go grab a bite to eat and a drink. And . . . If . . . If you aren't busy, maybe you want to come with?"

"Fuck." Parker let it out in a low exhale.

Calypso's heart dropped. Maybe she misread this whole situation, and it was all one sided in her head. "I'm sorry. I didn't mean to—"

"No." Parker cut her off quickly, opened her eyes, and glanced at Calypso. "It's not that I *don't* want to. I can't, *ethically,* go. Not until this case wraps up. It's not good form, and it can damage the credibility of this case and you as a trustworthy witness."

Calypso smiled. She got it loud and clear. She didn't misread it at all. Parker appeared to be, in fact, every bit as interested as her. "So . . . after this case wraps?"

Parker caught her lower lip and smiled, that dimple in her left cheek showing, causing Calypso's heart to melt a little further. "After. Certainly." She couldn't be entirely sure, but she thought she saw Parker blush a little bit.

Calypso stood and made her way to the door, lingering. She hoped to at least walk out with Parker. She wanted even just a few more minutes with her if possible. What on earth was going on? This was totally out of character. She would normally leave the room and the woman left behind in it to chase her.

Calypso waited, lingering at the doorway, as Parker packed up to leave. When Parker made her way with her attaché case and stood next to Calypso at the door, Calypso breathed in the earthy scent of Parker's cologne. It made her mouth water slightly. She wanted to say something else to Parker. She wanted to talk to her, but she found herself suddenly shy and unsure. Instead, she walked quietly with Parker to the elevator.

"If you need reassurance this weekend, before you testify,

you *can* call me." Parker pulled a silver business card case from her jacket pocket and extracted a card.

Calypso took the thick cream-colored card from Parker and peered at it.

"My cell is on there," Parker instructed as they got onto the elevator and took it to the bottom floor.

Calypso shot her gaze up at Parker. "I might." She played it cool as her heart beat hard and fast.

Parker smiled and shook her head. That damn dimple.

Yeah. Parker felt it, too. And that made Calypso smile as she walked outside the building. She gazed at Parker's back as she walked in the opposite direction to the garage before heading down the street.

She called Xander to check in on how things had been going at the shop as she walked down the street—Voodoo Ink being only a few blocks away, and true to Southern California, the weather was perfect. She could walk there and check in, but she kept walking even though she had to talk to someone now. She needed help processing this situation with Parker—the sensation of being this off-balance over a woman. She opted to call Xander.

"Hey, kid," Xander answered.

"How's everything?" Calypso asked him.

"Good. You coming back in or going home?"

"Home, if you don't need me."

"How did it go with the lawyer?"

Calypso paused and peeked back over her shoulder to make sure Parker didn't magically appear behind her. "Why didn't anyone tell me the lawyer is hot as fuck?"

"Really?" Xander laughed.

"On god." Calypso laughed. "And then I made an ass of myself and asked her out."

"She said no? Do I need to kick her ass?"

"No. She said not until the case wraps up. But she's probably only saying that to make sure I testify on Tuesday. So yeah. I'm positive I looked extremely stupid."

"She said after the case wraps. So I wouldn't feel too stupid."

Calypso made it around the corner and eyed her building, but stopped moving toward it. "It's weird. I've never been so self-conscious asking someone out. Maybe it's because she's just like . . . so different? Does that make sense?"

"Different because she's the professional type?"

"Yeah. And not like . . . us?"

"That can be good, too."

"Yeah. It can be, I guess. But it's just . . . I actually care about what she thinks. I don't normally ask people out, and I don't normally care what they think."

"Think about Xochitl and me. She's not—well she wasn't—'like us.' Maybe you, for whatever reason, sense something deeper with her?"

"I don't think I'm the 'deeper' kind."

"From what I've heard about her, she isn't either."

"Then it's perfect, right?"

Calypso sighed as she let herself into the building. "Sure. Yeah. I guess."

"I said I wasn't looking for a commitment, and then I ended up married to Xochitl."

"But you would have been stupid not to marry Xochitl. She's a goddess."

Xander laughed. "And so are you, so this Parker Harrington will be stupid if she turns you down." God, she loved him. He was the person she always needed in her corner.

8 HEARTACHE AND PAIN

MACY

Macy returned home, still heavily buzzed from the bar, and found Sam sitting on the sofa waiting for her. Sam, still clad in her work suit, gave an air of officiality. Whereas Parker wore masculine suits that she paid way too much money to have custom-made, Sam wore more feminine suits she bought from the high-end shops and occasionally had tailored to fit better.

By the brooding look on her face and the energy boiling off her, Sam gave a clear impression of being in a mood. Macy kicked her shoes off at the door and ran her hand through her hair. This was about to be brutal.

"I heard about today." Sam didn't even say hello, and her voice dripped with acid.

Macy collapsed on the couch next to her. "It wasn't my best day."

"Are you drunk?" Sam's voice came out incredulous.

"I had a few drinks after court. It was definitely not a good day for me. There's nothing wrong with that."

"It never is when Parker is concerned." Sam's icy cold eyes glared at her. "Did you drive like this?"

Macy didn't have it in her to fight. "I don't think I'm friends with her any longer. After today, I can't." Macy folded her arms over her belly as she lay back against the cushions of the couch. "And Caldwell drove me home."

"Macy, I don't think I can do this with you." Sam leaned forward, with her elbows on her knees.

Macy sat back up. "What do you mean?"

"It's obvious. You're in love with Parker. I thought maybe that might be the case. But I thought as time went on, you and I could really be something. But I can't be her. I'm not her. I wouldn't want to be her. And you *want her.*"

"Just because I struggle on the stand, you think I'm in love with her?"

"It's only ever with her. You are fine with every other case, under every other cross. But with Parker, something happens to you. And I see it clearly now."

"I can't lie. At one point, yes. That was the case. But Sam . . . I love you. I do love you. I want it to work with us."

"I think it's still the case that you love her. I think if she gave you a chance to be with her . . . A real chance . . . you wouldn't hesitate."

Macy thought she had finished with the crying, but the tears began running freely down her cheeks again. Annoyed at the show of weakness, she swiped the tears away. "Why does everyone say that? Everything always points back to her when I fuck up. Why is that always everyone's answer to my problems?"

"Because it's true. And it's obvious. And because of that, I have no choice. I'm done."

"Sam, I can't convince you, obviously. You have your opinion, and no amount of talking to you is going to convince you. I can already see that."

"Maybe I need that. Maybe I want you to show me I'm worth fighting for?"

"What's the point? You will always doubt me."

Sam nodded and stood. She dropped her house key on the coffee table. "I'm going to head out now. I will grab the rest of my stuff this weekend." She made her way to the door and grabbed her keys from the table next to the door. She made her way out without another word, only the sound of the door slamming behind her.

Macy took the remaining days of that week off. She spent them in a drunken stupor. She woke up and started her day with vodka. By lunch, she managed to be sufficiently drunk. She passed out, nestled into the sofa, by dinner time.

When Sam came to get her things, Macy locked herself in the bathroom and sat in the tub with her bottle of vodka, the door closed and locked. She put her AirPods in and listened to the playlist of songs she put together using the ones that Sam sent to her over the year they spent supposedly in love. Yes, she was still drawn to Parker, but she had it in check. She did love Sam. If she didn't, it wouldn't hurt so bad.

Throughout her entire life, Macy had only ever wanted to be loved. Her father skipped out on her and her mom before Macy had even been born. Her mom never seemed interested in raising her, and by the time she turned ten, her mother dumped her off with her grandparents and disappeared with some guy. Her grandparents had no interest in raising another child. They provided food and shelter for her, but beyond that, they gave nothing. They spent their years with her completely checked out when it came to any other facet of Macy's life or feelings. She began to wonder, as she sat in the empty bathtub torturing herself with the playlist of songs sent by Sam, if she was completely unlovable. Maybe she was broken, and everyone but her noticed it.

Sam knocked on the door lightly, at one point. Macy didn't answer. She drank and laid her head on the cool ceramic of the tub while the music blared in her ears. There was nothing more to say to Sam at this point that would change her mind. Locked in, nothing would get her to change course and convince her to stay.

MAY 31

By the following Monday when she went back to work, she sensed the eyes on her. Her colleagues were whispering. She sat behind her desk, and Caldwell glanced up at her from his stack of papers. "So, you're aware Javier Ortiz Sanchez was found not guilty."

"I can tell. I can tell also, everyone thinks it's my fault." Macy straightened a pile of papers on her desk.

"Some people, yeah. But most people can plainly see that it's just Parker Harrington. I swear that bitch has the judicial system on her payroll."

"Are we keeping eyes on him?"

"He fucked up once; he will fuck up again. Where were you last week? I tried calling you like a million times. I was starting to take it personally that you weren't answering me."

"I needed some time. Personal stuff." Macy didn't make eye contact with him; she sorted through papers to avoid any further conversation.

"Oh, yeah. We all heard about that, too. Sam and you split."

If Macy didn't love Brent so much, she would have punched him in the throat. Instead, she balled a piece of paper and threw it at him.

He ducked and flipped her off. "Meanwhile, let me catch

you up on everything you missed . . ." Caldwell started going through all of the updates for their current case, and Macy, glad to have something to focus on instead of herself, listened intently.

She loved Caldwell—he'd become closer to her than her own blood. She often caught herself wishing either that he were a woman or that she could be attracted to men. She was hard-pressed to find anyone else as loyal, sweet, and fun to be around. He would make an excellent life partner—not merely a work partner. And they did kiss once after a night of celebrating the close of a case. But both of them ended up so not into it, they came apart laughing. They were only meant to be close friends and partners.

June 16

Two weeks later, after being warned by the higher ups that she had to work on her anger management and stop taking it out on her suspects or she would be put on administrative leave without pay, she found herself working nearly ten days straight without a day off—she and Caldwell spent three days on surveillance , followed by a conference on digital forensics in San Francisco, Macy finally got a day off. She was tired of feeling lonely, and aside from Caldwell she didn't have anyone else in her life since Sam left. Sam wouldn't even respond to any of her texts or answer her calls. It was whatever. Nothing new or unexpected. This seemed to happen with all of her relationships.

So, her loneliness led Macy to decide that three, almost four, weeks of the silent treatment would have to be enough. That and the forced anger management group she was going to—she was being challenged to forgive her perceived wrongs. She decided to finally call Parker.

Macy sat on the balcony of her condo overlooking a

courtyard with a pool. The sun shone bright and hot, and the kids on summer vacation were beginning to stir on the grounds below her. Moms and bored children took over the pool. The sounds of kids shrieking and splashing carried the thirty yards from the pool to where she sat. The summertime fragrance of cocoa butter sunscreen floated toward her on the breeze.

Macy took a small pull of her iced coffee, sat back in her chair, put her feet up on the table, and selected the call option under Parker's contact information. She almost gave up when the phone rang several times and Parker still didn't answer.

She almost hung up when Parker's voice came across the line.

"Hey," Parker answered the phone tentatively.

"Hi." Macy pushed her sunglasses up to the crown of her head. Parker's voice caused heat and hope to build inside of her chest.

"Are you still mad at me?"

"I wasn't mad."

"Okay." Sarcasm dripped from Parker's tone. She should have expected that Parker would be far more perceptive and able to see right through her.

"I wasn't."

"Mmmmm. Okay."

"I was hurt." Macy folded with a pout.

"I would love to say I am sorry. I really would. But I can't apologize for doing my job. That's not fair."

"I'm not expecting you to."

"So what's up?"

"Are you busy?"

"I'm always busy."

"Too busy for lunch?"

The sound of Parker moving papers around came across

the line as she waited for a reply. "I can meet you around one."

"Mo's?"

"No, that's too far for me to go. I'm gonna have to make it a quick lunch."

"Lemon Lark, then?" Macy suggested, knowing that Parker could walk there from her office building.

"Yeah. That's better for me. See you soon." Parker hung up.

Macy sat back in her chair, relieved to know Parker's friendship didn't die with her petty fit. Having her in her life as a friend was better than nothing at all. Maybe it was a good thing that Sam dumped her. It was hard to be friends with someone that your girlfriend didn't care for. And she didn't have to guess that feelings must be mutual for Parker.

Macy went to the mirror and fixed her hair and touched up her makeup. Even though she's been friend-zoned by Parker, an ember of hope still burned. That hope would probably never die. This thought was absolute insanity. Parker would never be the one to settle. Parker would never be the type of person for a relationship.

9 BUT YOU DON'T DATE

JUNE 16

PARKER

*P*arker beat Macy to the restaurant. She had no business taking time out for lunch. But she considered her friendship with Macy important; Macy was a good friend that she enjoyed spending time with. Given the fact that Sam had driven a bit of a wedge into that friendship over the last year, Parker deemed it only right to take some time for Macy.

Macy came in, obviously on a day off. On the days she worked, she wore a blazer with her holster under it. Today, Macy sashayed into the restaurant in a maxi skirt and a tank top, with her silky red hair tied up in a messy bun. Even if she was a bit odd and a bit crazy, Parker considered Macy to definitely be cute. Pity flooded Parker for Macy's horrible luck in finding a person to love. She wished that Macy would find someone to truly love her for who she was.

Parker stood and hugged her. She drew back slightly as Macy melted against her a little bit, holding on a bit too long, a bit too closely.

"Hey, stranger. It's been like forever." Parker pulled away and sat back in her seat.

Macy's gaze fell heavily on Parker in the brightly lit restaurant. The trendy pop music seemed almost too loud for Parker. She sat back in her seat, annoyed, and kind of regretted the restaurant choice.

Macy exhaled before looking away. "It has. I'm sorry. I was out of town getting my digital forensics certification." *Yeah. Sure. That's the only reason.*

"That can't be all."

On a sigh, Macy confessed, , "I've been kind of a mess recently." She sat in the chair across from Parker.

"What's going on?"

"Sam split."

Parker forced herself to frown, even though she despised Sam. "What happened?" She should be sad about this turn of events, but she couldn't. Sam was a bitch, and Macy deserved better.

"She accused me of being in love with you."

Because you are, Parker wanted to say. *You shouldn't be. But here we still are.* Parker took a swallow of her coffee. She felt an acute awareness of Macy's feelings; it lingered in the background over the years of their friendship. She also recognized that Macy valued their friendship more than trying to sabotage it with a failed relationship. She bit her tongue and nodded sympathetically. "I'm sorry. That sucks." She ran through a list of friends in her head that she might be able to set Macy up with. It would achieve a double goal: Macy could be happy, and she would hopefully stop crushing on her. Immediately, her friend A.D., who happened to be a hopeless romantic, came to mind. Parker pondered a way to put them in front of each other.

Macy shrugged and darted a glance at Parker with sad eyes and a defeated sigh. "What's new with you?"

Parker hesitated. "You worked for New Orleans PD for a while, didn't you? Before you came here?"

"Briefly. Yeah. Why?"

"Did you know a Calypso Boudreaux?"

Macy's eyebrows knitted together. "It's been a lifetime. Was she a cop? A suspect? The name is kind of familiar."

"Possibly a witness of some sort? She told me she 'saw some things.'"

"I don't think I can place her. I wish I could. Why?" Her answer came quickly.

Parker sat back in her chair. "I have a date with her tonight."

"You don't date." Her voice carried an edge. Fuck. Here's the jealousy.

"Yeah, yeah. You're funny. But she's . . . I don't . . . I'm curious about her. About who she is. What makes her . . . her."

"You want to *fuck* her." Macy opened the menu and put it in front of her. Color crept into Macy's cheeks. Her tone was straight up acid.

"That too. But I want to *know* her. Like, figure out who she is and why."

"How did you meet her? How did she manage to get you to be so invested in her?" Macy set the menu back down.

"She was a witness in Javier's trial. I'm surprised you didn't know that. It's not like her name is common. But after the trial, she called me to ask a random question. She was using it as an excuse to call. And we ended up on the phone for over an hour."

"You don't talk on the phone, either. Are you okay?" Macy

let one brow raise as she picked her menu back up and perused the selections, not bothering to make eye contact with Parker.

"It's weird, right? She has me all off my game. And she's not even my typical type."

"You have a type?"

"Fuck off. You know what I mean."

"What did you even talk to for over an hour?"

Parker was beginning to pick up on some obvious irritation. She was tempted to let it go, but if they were going to be friends, she needed to be able to talk about these things. "Everything. Families. Music. Football. Religion. Spirituality. Life. And we've been basically texting each other all day, calling each other every night, every day since. It's been like two weeks."

Macy snorted. No doubt about it—Parker picked up on Macy's annoyance (and jealousy). "And how is she not your type?" The question came out exceedingly forced as she set the menu down with more gusto than necessary.

"She's . . . Raw and edged. Tattoos and piercings and combat boots. But she's *beautiful*. And she's *intelligent* and . . . I just want to see where this can go."

Dark clouds took form in Macy's eyes. "Just be careful."

"What's that supposed to mean?"

"Only that, if she's that unpolished, be careful. That's all."

Parker shrugged off Macy's jealousy. She suspected that if she asked Macy for an actual date, Macy would jump at the chance. This is where being friends sometimes became difficult to navigate with her. Instead, she changed the subject and asked Macy about her digital forensics certification trip.

* * *

Parker showed up at Calypso's building right on time. She'd shed the tie and vest of her dark slate-gray suit and unbuttoned the top button of her crisp black shirt in the car, keeping the slacks and blazer. Parker grew up in the city, going to the law office. She was familiar with this building, though it had been abandoned for much of her childhood, at one time operated as a slaughterhouse before being converted into six different loft condos. It totally fit Calypso's image. She rang the buzzer on the security door, and Calypso's silken voice came over the intercom, "Parker?"

"Are you expecting anyone else?" Parker smirked.

A throaty laugh followed. "No. But you can never be too safe." The harsh buzz sounded, and Parker opened the door. Calypso's loft took the third and fourth floors of the building on the west-facing side. The wrought iron stairs leading up, lit with industrial lights, gave the building a more trendy and edgy vibe. A stark contrast to Parker's hillside house in a remote subdivision with acre lots, and where people pretended to be ranchers and vintners.

She got to Calypso's door and found it cracked open, so she let herself in. The walls, all exposed brick with large art pieces in various styles hung in random places, spoke to Calypso's artistic nature. On the wall between the large floor-to-ceiling windows, was a large black-and-white canvas of Jackson Square, before another of Calypso's nude form from the burgundy lips to a few inches below her belly button, one tattooed arm around her porcelain pale torso, and the other covering her ample breasts, holding a blade to her own throat. As Parker considered the piece with her head cocked, she didn't see Calypso anywhere until a poke on her shoulder broke her reverie. "Hi."

Parker had mentioned to her where she planned to take her to dinner—an upscale seafood place on the water that had a dress code. She'd called in a favor to obtain reservations for a sunset dinner. This was not Parker's style at all. On a typical day, she wouldn't go through such a hassle to have dinner with someone, much less make reservations. But Calypso did not fall under the *typical* category.

Parker turned around to be met with Calypso's golden eyes. Calypso's hair was pulled up into a faux-hawk by several small ponytail holders and teased up in wild curls, paired with a black form-fitting, short-sleeved turtleneck; a pencil skirt that hit below the knee; and black patent leather heels, which caused Parker's heart to flutter hard. She found herself slightly disoriented, a sensation so unfamiliar to her as she took Calypso in. "Hi." She paused and cleared her throat. "This is some place."

"Thank you. I like it. It's home." Calypso smiled.

"The art on the walls—is it all yours?" Parker needed to learn everything about her.

"Some of it. That one—"she pointed to the nude Parker had been studying when she came in, "was done by a friend for his portfolio. But I liked it, so he gifted me with an over-sized print." She laughed lightly. "I realize it's an extreme level of hubris to hang a picture like that of yourself."

Parker smiled at her. "I mean, it's art, so I think there's a clause around that rule or something. Are you ready?"

"Whenever you are."

Parker studied Calypso as she walked ahead and took in the sight of the back-seamed stockings that completed her aesthetic. She fought hard to keep her thoughts from derailing into the gutter.

* * *

THE RESTAURANT WAS PERCHED on a cliff overlooking the beach. Parker's connection did not disappoint. Their table was positioned right in front of an open window, allowing the warm summer sea breeze and the salt air in. Parker didn't look out once. Transfixed watching Calypso as she drank in the sunset, the way the pink and orange came through the window as it reflected off the water and onto Calypso's face, Parker realized this was deeper than simple curiosity. The sun cast a golden and amber hue on her face, highlighting the effect of her honey-colored eyes. She was focused only on the woman sitting across the table, lit by the golden glow of the sunset. Parker was captivated. Looking at Calypso across the table from her, the thoughts of work, friends, family, all of the background noise in her brain had gone quiet. She was focused on only one thing: Calypso.

Parker's gaze must have weighed on her. She turned her eyes back to Parker. "It's so beautiful out here. I've lived here for years, and it just never gets old. This is an excellent choice. Thank you."

Parker smiled. It was beautiful indeed, more so because of the woman who sat across from her and the palpable chemistry between them. Parker caught Calypso gazing at her across the table as well. She sensed it. This was different. There was more here, and Parker didn't want this to be the only time.

Throughout dinner, Parker caught herself amazed by the easy flow of their conversation and Calypso's wit. She was not only beautiful; Parker found her to be smart and cultured, despite her rough-around-the-edges appearance. Even though they'd spent the last three weeks texting and talking, there was no shortage of topics to discuss. Parker ate up the way Calypso fixed her eyes on her across the table. The way she leaned in as Parker spoke and hung on every word.

Dinner extended into dessert, and then one more drink.

After dinner, when Parker walked Calypso to the door, Calypso invited her up. Parker sat on the burgundy chenille couch as Calypso poured two glasses of wine. Not being distracted by the large canvas of naked Calypso, Parker actually got a good look at the space she occupied. The bottom floor consisted of one big open space, with a wrought iron spiral staircase leading up to the bedroom, the furniture a mix of dark wood and antiques painted black. Several bookshelves filled of an array of books lined the wall between the two floor-to-ceiling windows. Parker couldn't read the titles from where she sat, but she loved that they were organized by the colors of their spines.

Calypso came around the kitchen island and brought the glasses, handing one to Parker, and set her own on the end table as she sat facing Parker. She sat close, and Parker was absolutely positive that she didn't need the wine; she was already drunk on Calypso's intoxicating perfume—that scent that had distracted her in the office when they first met.

Pausing for a beat before setting her glass down without taking a sip, Parker locked her eyes on Calypso, and the need to touch her skin took over. Primal, strong and aching. Nothing had ever felt so natural as this pull. Natural and terrifying.

Almost of its own accord, Parker's hand drifted up the exposed tattooed skin on Calypso's forearm and up to her neck. Calypso's gaze followed the motion of Parker's fingertips. A current of heat passed from Calypso's skin through Parker's fingers. Catlike, Calypso leaned into Parker's touch. Parker's thumb brushed against the smoothness of Calypso's cheek as she pulled her in closer. The whisper of Calypso's breath, so close, danced off of her lips, as she hesitated, breathing her in. Absolutely positive that this kiss carried life-altering consequences, Parker knew there was no way she could have only a one-night fling with this woman. The gap was bridged by Calypso, her lips velvet and lush, her tongue tasting of wine. The kiss started tentatively with the knowledge that she was going to be an absolute goner for this woman when all was said and done. She ultimately relented to the urgency in Calypso's kiss.

Calypso's hands grasped Parker's jacket lapels and pulled her closer. If anyone else dared to do so, Parker would have slapped her hands down—no one messed with her suits. Parker already realized she would be putty in Calypso's hands. Whatever Calypso wanted, she would be willing to give.

A gentle bite on Parker's lower lip broke the kiss, and Calypso stood up from the couch, pulling Parker to stand with her. Looking into Calypso's golden eyes, her pupils blown wide, Parker took a few steps forward, causing Calypso to take a step back, so she was now against the island that separated the kitchen from the living area, with three barstools lined up underneath.

Calypso took Parker's hand to the top of her skirt, where Parker was met with the velvet heat of Calypso's skin under her fingertips as Calypso's skin pebbled and her pulse quickened. Parker's hands skimmed over Calypso's waist, grabbed the bottom hem of Calypso's shirt, and pulled it over her head. Calypso didn't break eye contact with her. Parker found herself almost obsessed with Calypso's bold and fearless attitude, and she found herself helpless. Her hands traveled down, grazing over the scant fabric of her bra, letting her lips follow the pattern of her hands. Calypso's heart beat fast and her breath was shallow. Parker lingered at her pierced navel and casting her eyes up to meet that mesmerizing golden gaze.

Before Parker could think, Calypso pushed Parker's jacket off her shoulders, and Parker shrugged it off the rest of the way, letting it drop to the floor. With a need to see and feel all of her, Parker's hand slipped up behind Calypso and unhooked her bra, pulling the fabric away, letting her lips graze over Calypso's pierced nipples, followed by her thumbs, causing a quiet whimper to slip from Calypso's mouth. Parker's own heart matched that escalated rhythm of Calypso's.

She had done a little digging on Calypso before this night. Calypso shared an identical reputation as a player. Parker, given how she was feeling, realized going this far with this woman would be putting herself at risk. Looking at Calypso, light glinting off the rings in her nipples, eyeing her, waiting for her to make the next move, Parker decided this would definitely be a risk worth taking. She took a step back and spun Calypso around. Calypso gasped and braced herself against the granite counter. Whether this was going to be one night or not, she decided to make it worth it for both of them.

Obsessed and compelled to explore Calypso, Parker let her hands trace down her back—where the intricate patterns that adorned her neck continued, ending in a V shape below her shoulder blades—to the zipper of Calypso's skirt, pulling it down and letting it fall from Calypso's hips, revealing the luscious perfection of her curves.

No amount of words or grattitude could match the appreciation of the sight in front of her. Calypso turned her head to look over her shoulder at Parker, still braced against the island. Taking in the sight of Calypso's back-seamed thigh highs, black heels, and black panties, Parker wanted nothing more than to make sure Calypso was hers. For as long as she lived, this was the one image she wanted burned into her memory.

She stepped forward and let her hands explore Calypso's body. Measuring how Calypso's breath changed with each variation of her touch. Pulling her back so that her body was against Parker's—Calypso's back against her with one arm, Parker buried in that intoxicating perfume with her lips against Calypso's neck. Her other hand travel down and slipped into Calypso's black panties. Calypso's breath hitched, and her hands gripped the edge of the counter as Parker's fingers stroked and worked. Calypso's hand let go of the counter and slipped up and around Parker's neck, gripping the back of Parker's hair as her excitement mounted.

When Calypso cried out, legs shaking, Parker turned her around and sat her up on the granite island, slipping the panties down her legs and to the floor, as she sat on the bar stool in front of Calypso, parting Calypso's still trembling knees.

Consumed by the need for her, Parker lost herself in the way Calypso tasted, the way her body moved, the way she unabashedly surrendered to her. She could not get enough.

When Calypso came undone a second time, she pulled Parker up by the collar of her shirt. There was a scramble to undo the buttons and shrug it off as Calypso pulled her in closer.

Goosebumps cropped up on Parker's skin as a shiver ran through her while Calypso's hands began to skim over her skin. Parker moved to step back away from the island and held out her hand to help Calypso down, but Calypso wrapped her legs around Parker's hips and held her in place as she pulled Parker in and let her lips meet Parker's.

Parker was no stranger to women wanting her—and she definitely got around—but something in the absolute abandon and fire of Calypso's kiss had her reeling. Calypso's whole energy was a tidal wave crashing over her. And it was so good to be pulled in and drowned in it.

Calypso broke the kiss. "Shall I have my way with you here or upstairs?" She smiled against Parker's lips.

Taking a step back, she up helped Calypso down. "Upstairs." Parker was also not used to women being forward or taking charge in such a manner. Most of the women

Parker hooked up with expected her to be in charge constantly. To have someone who wanted to take the lead was a welcome change.

Calypso's warm hand slipped into hers, and with a gentle tug she led her up to the loft to her bed. In stark contrast to all of the dark furniture and coloring, Calypso's bed had crisp white pillowcases and a fluffy white duvet on top. Green plants sat by the window. Not that Parker paid attention to any of that at the time.

Parker found herself pushed back onto the bed as Calypso's hands deftly undid Parker's slacks and slid them off. Breathless and in awe, Parker propped herself up on her elbows and arched an eyebrow at Calypso, trying to play it cool. Calypso straddled Parker's hips and pushed her back down with a firm hand on Parker's chest. "Uh-uh." She shook her head. "I'm still hungry after dinner. You need to let me have my way." She gave Parker an impish smile. Parker lay back, letting her take control, a luxury she rarely enjoyed. She watched while Calypso paused and let her gaze slowly drift over Parker's body as it glowed in the silvery light of the moon filtering in from the large windows. Surrendering, Parker lay back, allowing herself to enjoy the vulnerability of being under Calypso's command.

Anticipation built in Parker as Calypso took her time exploring every inch of her, smiling deviously as Parker whimpered and writhed beneath her. Calypso kept her on the edge and refused to let Parker come.

"Is there something you want?" Calypso teased, centimeters from Parker's center.

Definitely different from anyone else. Parker pulled Calypso into where she needed her. Calypso may be different, but she would be damned if she was going to beg. Calypso took the hint and didn't back off. This time.

Spent and exhausted, Parker did something else she never

did. She pulled Calypso close to her under the covers and let her hands trail over Calypso's curves lazily. Calypso nuzzled into Parker. The warmth and softness of her, and the overwhelming sense of how right it felt to be with this woman, led Parker to drift off to sleep with a certain peace. There was no rushing. There was no getting up or explaining why she didn't do relationships. She was perfectly content for the first time in her life, with this fascinating woman, who in so many ways was her match. There was no way this would only be a one-time deal. It couldn't. Overtaken by the peace, Parker fell asleep in Calypso's bed, with Calypso in her arms. A life-changing emotional high that was both beautiful and foreign.

10 GOOD MORNING

CALYPSO

Calypso rolled over and peered at the woman lying in the bed next to her, and the rumpled suit pants that she had tossed onto the chair in the corner at some point last night. Calypso didn't normally bring women home, much less spend the night with them. But she had no intention of kicking Parker Harrington out of her bed. She also didn't call them out of the blue to ask them out. Attachment scared her. But not with Parker. Something about Parker made her feel protected.

Unable to sleep, Calypso slipped out of the bed and threw on a faded old Siouxsie and the Banshees T-shirt and a pair of sweats and tiptoed down the stairs. The light in the kitchen area still being on did not help her fall asleep.

She contemplated this desire for Parker while standing at the sink, pouring a glass of water. Parker was different. And

Parker treated her differently, too. Throughout dinner, Parker didn't talk down to her or assume she couldn't keep up.

Parker made eye contact with her when they talked. She also didn't stop to explain every little bit of minutia with the assumption that Calypso didn't understand. She listened when Calypso talked. She didn't stare at Calypso's tits or glaze over bored. Parker asked questions and wanted to learn more details, showing interest in Calypso's opinions, thoughts, and stories.

She picked up Parker's jacket and shirt from where they had been discarded near the island and smoothed them out before draping them over her arm, cutting the kitchen light, and making her way back to the loft bedroom, climbing the staircase by the silvery moonlight that filtered in from the large windows.

She didn't want a fling with Parker. She wanted to see where this might go. She had never experienced emotions anywhere near this level of intensity since Shae. And for good reason. Shae's death nearly killed her. She didn't want to risk dealing with that devastation ever again.

Calypso grabbed the slacks off the chair, took the pieces of Parker's suit, pulled a hanger off the silver clothing rack that was pushed against the brick wall on the other side of the bedroom, and hung them from the bathroom door. She loved the way the simple gesture of hanging Parker's clothes, and the way they smelled, lit her senses on fire. Whatever expensive cologne it was, it made Calypso's heart flutter.

All the reasons why this wouldn't work also played through her mind. They had completely different backgrounds. Different classes. Different educations. Would Parker even *want* to see where it went? Judging by how peacefully Parker slept in her bed, Calypso suspected there was a good chance.

Calypso made her way back to the bed, curled up against Parker, and fell asleep watching Parker as she slept. Studying her sleep-softened features. Listening to the steady sound of Parker's heartbeat and breathing.

In the morning, Calypso woke before Parker. She tiptoed back down the stairs and did her best to make coffee quietly. With no real doors except for the bathroom upstairs and the powder room downstairs, sound carried in this loft space. For one person who stayed more or less to herself, it was perfect. Not so perfect when someone stayed the night. Which was never, until last night.

While she waited for the coffee to brew, she picked up her rumpled clothes from the floor and threw them in the laundry basket she kept in the downstairs closet. Since the windows faced west, it was still somewhat dark in the space.

As she poured herself a cup of coffee and sat on the stool at the island, she could hear Parker rustling around upstairs. Calypso's heart did a thing. Something she wasn't used to. And she found herself excited to see Parker.

When Parker came down the stairs, her button-down untucked, jacket in hand, and bed-rumpled hair, Calypso smiled. She wanted to play it cool, but she couldn't help herself.

"Good morning." Wrapping her hands around her warm coffee mug, Calypso greeted Parker. She worked hard to restrain herself from getting up and wrapping her arms around Parker. She didn't know how it would be received. She had done some asking around before this date and knew Parker's reputation for being a love-them-and-leave-them kind of woman, as she herself was.

Parker made her way over to the island. "I'm sorry I fell asleep last night. I don't typically do that."

"Sleep or stay the night? Do you want coffee?"

"Absolutely, I'd love some coffee. As for the other question, stay the night." Parker nibbled at her lower lip; Calypso recognized that expression from the office—Parker's tendency to bite her lip when she was about to ask a personal question or show some sort of vulnerability. She studied Parker's features and how she cast her eyes down at her hands as Calypso set a mug of coffee in front of Parker.

"Do you want cream or sugar?" She made herself appear calm and steady on the outside, but inside she was anxious. If Parker didn't usually stay the night, that led Calypso to believe that this might be a one-off with Parker. It typically would have been for her, so she had no reason to be so judgmental. She still tried to prepare herself for the letdown.

"I take it black." Parker glanced up and took the mug into her own hands. "Thank you. On the rare occasions I stayed the night, I don't think I ever stayed for coffee. There are a lot of firsts happening right now." Parker said, her brow raised as she drank in the sight of Calypso, raking a hand through her bed head hair, and Calypso fought yet another urge, to rake her fingers through Parker's hair and smooth the wild, random locks for her.

Calypso sat back down beside Parker. She remained silent as she took her seat, for two reasons: first and foremost, she wasn't a morning person, and second, she wanted to see what Parker was going to say or do next. She wanted to keep the ball in Parker's court and preserve her own dignity. There was a long list of women who wanted exactly what she wanted from Parker Harrington. She would not lower herself to their standards and make herself appear desperate.

Parker took a deep drink of the coffee. Her eyes fluttered closed, and she smiled as it went down. Calypso may have left New Orleans, but some things she refused to give up, the biggest one being chicory coffee. Apparently, Parker approved.

"That being said," Parker continued as Calypso hoped she

would. "I have a rule about not getting involved in relationships."

"I kind of figured when you said you don't typically stay the night." Calypso forced a smile that she hoped came off as genuine.

"I'm not done yet." Parker took another sip of her coffee and set the mug down, biting her lip again. It was actually very cute. Calypso wanted to reach out and caress Parker's cheek where the dimple popped. "How did you feel about last night?"

"Am I under oath?" Calypso said, playfully.

Parker smiled at Calypso's joke. "Let's pretend you are."

"Well, counselor, I would say this—I, too, am known to not get serious with anyone. But I did have a really excellent time with you."

"What was excellent about it?" Parker let a slight smile play on her lips (that Calypso desperately wanted on hers this instant), as if she already detected the answer.

"Aside from the mind-blowing sex?"

"Aside from the mind-blowing sex," Parker affirmed with a laugh.

"The way you treated me. The way you *saw me* when I spoke. The way you listened when I answered questions. The way you paid attention. You didn't treat me like I'm dumb, or an object, or just rush to get me home and in bed."

Parker still had that slight smile playing on her lips. Her green eyes were laser focused on Calypso.

Calypso cocked her head to the side. "What about you?" Her voice sounded tentative. She was almost afraid to ask.

"I can't lie . . ." Parker paused. "I had a great time."

"What was great about it?" Calypso asked, turning the tables. "Besides the mind-blowing sex, that is." She couldn't help but smile herself.

"I don't normally talk on the phone or text this much

with anyone. But I've enjoyed getting to know you. I also really enjoyed talking to you over dinner. You aren't just beautiful and creative, you're deep and thoughtful. I've been able to talk to you about things that are important to me, and you've added to the conversation, giving me other angles to consider. I liked that you offered to pay for your own dinner —which I will never, ever let you do, by the way —but that tells me you are independent. I could go on and on." Parker kept her gaze intent as she held Calypso's eyes.

Calypso couldn't help the flutter in her chest. Her heart suddenly became a bird beating its wings in a cage.

Parker paused thoughtfully before she said, "I would like to maybe shelve the 'I don't do relationships' thing and see where this," Parker pointed at Calypso and back at herself, "can go."

"I think I can manage that. If it keeps going the way it is now, I think it can be beautiful." She was suddenly a relation-ship person after all. For Parker, she would be anything at all if she were asked.

11 SAVOIR FAIRE

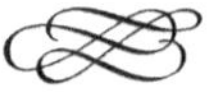

Macy

Macy sat on the patio at Parker's house, surrounded by about a dozen attorneys from Harrington and Harrington and their significant others, including the formidable Mr. Harrington (Parker was indeed a Daddy's girl, taking right after him. Macy totally got it), and the buttoned-up Mrs. Harrington. If you looked up *wealthy white privilege with generational wealth* Parker and her parents would be pictured under the definition. Oftentimes, she questioned her attraction to Parker. This was one of those times.

In addition to the swarm of lawyers, a motley crew of tattooed, pierced people with brightly colored hair and an array of distressed pants, cut shirts, and fishnets—obviously Calypso's friends—gathered around. Though the two worlds were colliding in their clashing styles, everyone was mingling with everyone. Lawyers were talking to the "artists," and everyone seemed to be having a good time. A few of Parker's other friends from college and high school also milled around. Macy found herself standing next to the pool with a cocktail in her hand, talking to a cute butch who met Parker in undergrad at UCLA. She had short-cropped hair with tight edges, in black dress slacks and a crisp white button-down that was unbuttoned to the middle of her chest.

Macy wasn't sure whether she should flirt with her or keep it friendly. She couldn't remember if she got her name or not, being a bit tipsy after three very strong cocktails. She also wasn't very sure she should be here at all. Since Parker had introduced her to Calypso, she had seen very little of Parker at all. That night, Calypso had left the restaurant before dinner even came. She said she didn't feel good, but it was utter bullshit. For the brief amount of time Calypso sat at the table, she scowled and gave Macy death glares. Since then, they'd had lunch together a few times, sans Calypso. It couldn't be more evident that Calypso didn't want to be around Macy. And since Parker had been whipped from the beginning by Calypso, that meant she rarely spent any time with Parker. Their bar nights at Mo's were seemingly over and done with—or DoorDash and wine in the yard. It was all seemingly over.

Add this to the number of things going wrong in her world right now. She had been written up at work for "misplacing" crucial evidence in a case, which led to the discovery of a few other "errors" in the chain of custody, including her reports leaving out essential details or recording the wrong times, and she may or may not have doctored a few reports. As if she was the only cop to do that—it moved the cases along faster. And regardless, it was a means to an end, and those arrests were solid. Again. Whatever. Another drink would be great. But not advised.

From the corner of her eye, she studied Parker in cream-colored linen pants and a pink button-down shirt. She spotted Calypso smiling and talking to Mr. Harrington, who seemed to genuinely enjoy her presence. He was laughing at whatever Calypso said, patting her lovingly on the back. She wore a black strapless, fitted-to-the-waist maxi dress with a flowing skirt that brushed the floor, and bare feet. Macy wondered if she was wrong for hoping that Calypso would trip on the hem of it and fall into the pool and drown. She wouldn't even mind holding Calypso's head under the water. Sigh. Whatever.

The double bifold glass doors from Parker's living room opened to the patio, creating an extended living space. Some of the art on the far wall of the living space indoors was visible from her vantage point, including a large portrait of Calypso, from a few inches below her belly button to right below her nose, her arm covering her bare breasts, holding a knife to her throat. *Classy* (meant with all the sarcasm in the world). Admittedly—to herself only—she had come to Parker's house in the middle of the night to feel near to her. From where she sat in her car, she wasn't able to spot that tacky art. But she could spot Calypso coming and going, which made her sick. She couldn't figure out what it was about Calypso that had Parker so invested in her.

She felt sick now as she took in the tables with white linen draped over them that were set up around the yard, and the caterer and bartender stationed toward the back of the patio, accompanied by a playlist of downtempo music played on Bluetooth speakers placed throughout the yard. Parker knew how to throw a party.

Everyone began to move to their tables, and the cute butch put her hand on the small of Macy's back and led her to a table, pulling out her chair. She smelled so good. Macy smoothed the skirt of her floral-print lavender halter dress as she sat.

Setting her drink down, she resolved not to get another and to order water when the waiter came by. Making a fool of herself at Parker's party was not on her agenda for the night.

"I'm sorry," she said, looking at the cute butch. "Typically, I can muster a lot more savoir faire . But I'm awful with names, and I'm," she laughed nervously, "a bit tipsy. Can you remind me?" She hoped she came off flirty instead of bitchy.

The cute butch smiled broadly. She had a great smile. "Damn, it's like that, huh?"

A warm flush over her cheeks as she moved her beach-waved hair over her shoulder. "I'm sorry!" She forced a smile.

"They call me A. D., but my name is Antoinette, which is my grandmother's name, but our middle names are different. Mine is Dyanne. So, A.D. has always been what I answer to."

Nodding as a waiter placed salads around the table. "Can I get a water?" Macy asked him, not taking her eyes off of A.D.

"Of course. Flat or sparkling?" He was dead-ass serious.

"Leave it to Parker to have such a bougie party." A.D. laughed. "Flat or sparkling. Damn. Just serve some water."

"Sparkling?" Macy requested more as a question.

The waiter nodded, unamused, and made his way back to the bar area.

"How do you know Parker?" A.D. asked.

"What makes you think I'm Parker's friend and not Calypso's?" Macy questioned with an eyebrow raised.

"Um . . ." A.D. grinned and shifted her eyes amongst the partygoers. "I think there's a clear distinction in whose friends are whose." So it wasn't only Macy who thought it was weird.

"Parker cross-examined me a few years ago, and then we ran into each other at a bar a week later, and we've been friends ever since. How about you?" Leaving out the super-hot one-night stand seemed appropriate.

"We dated the same girl at the same time. Correction. My girlfriend cheated on me with Parker. But I just couldn't be mad at Parker for it. I wanted to be. I really wanted to be. But logically, it wasn't Parker's fault. She didn't know. I dumped the girl, and Parker and I went out to the bar. This was in undergrad at UCLA. We've been friends since."

"Parker definitely gets around." Macy's sparkling water had been placed in front of her. She took a big sip.

"Parker *used to* get around. I think she's found her person, though." A.D. put her napkin in her lap and picked up her silverware to start on her salad.

Macy picked at a cherry tomato with her fork. "You don't think it's a bit odd? Those two?"

A.D. shrugged. "Opposites attract." She took a bite.

Macy sobered up some as she ate and talked with A.D. She found A.D. charming. A.D. was an ad executive at a firm in LA. She was extremely smart and politically astute. Macy got the vibe A.D. might feel some kind of way for her, too. This might be the one that will help get her over the Parker thing. So she hoped. A.D. couldn't seem to take her eyes off her. It eased the sting of slowly losing Parker.

When dessert came out, the sky turned a dark purple as the sun set, and the market lights strung up over the yard glowed. Parker stood up, and a friend of hers cut the music. Parker tapped her glass with a fork, and everyone turned their attention to her.

"I'm so honored that all of you made it here tonight. A year ago, I was focused on nothing but work. I thought I had it good. I thought I had it all figured out. I had Kitty, my friends, and my family, an excellent career that I love. What more could I possibly want or need? And then, out of nowhere, I was able to schedule an unexpected reluctant witness in a case. She stunned me as she sat across from me. Not just because she's beautiful. She's smart and witty. She lit something inside of me on fire. I wanted to get to know her—and those of you who know me well know that is something outside of my norm. A week after the trial ended, she called me. And that was it. I was toast. I was addicted to the sound of her voice. I looked forward to talking to her every day. After a few weeks of trying to manage our schedules, she let me take her to dinner, and that was the night I fell in love. And every day I spend with her reminds me how rare it is to find a love like this." Macy shot a glance over at Calypso at the same time Parker did. She was blushing as she peered at Parker from under her dark lashes. "Calypso Boudreaux, can you come here, please?"

Calypso stood and made her way to stand beside Parker. Macy's stomach lurched. She picked up on exactly what was going to happen. Everyone seemed to. People were murmuring excitedly as Calypso picked up the hem of her dress as she walked.

Parker got on her knee, ring in hand—and Calypso's hands went over her face in shock. As if she hadn't seen it coming. Whatever. Macy fought the urge to roll her eyes. "Calypso, every day I spend with you, I love you more. I want you to be my forever. Will you marry me?"

Calypso nodded as she put a trembling hand down in front of Parker. Parker tilted her head up at Calypso as she slid a large diamond onto her finger and stood, landing her lips on Calypso's. Everyone cheered and whistled, champagne corks popped, and flutes were being passed around. Macy's heart sank. But she forced a smile and clapped. A.D. popped two fingers in her mouth and whistled. Everyone around her was happy. Macy started to find keeping up the facade to be tiring, but she pushed through it.

Calypso was holding her hand out as her friends inspected her ring, and Macy turned back to her cupcake. A flute of champagne had been placed next to it. She took a deep sip. Water wasn't going to cut it any longer. From where she sat, she took note that the rock Parker put on Calypso couldn't be less than two and a half carats. It flashed and sparkled under the market lights. Ostentatious. Overboard. *It's whatever.*

Someone turned the music back on. It changed from downtempo music to a pop playlist. And couples started dancing. Mr. and Mrs. Harrington had now moved to examine the ring and hug Calypso. They were smiling and hugging Calypso. Weird that they would be so fond of Calypso. Again, whatever.

None of this was right. This shouldn't be happening. Macy couldn't allow Parker to make a mistake as grave as this. She had to protect her friend from ruining her life.

Making her way over to Mr. Harrington after Calypso had moved on, Macy tapped him on the shoulder. "Hello."

He turned quite abruptly. "Yes?"

Fuck. He's scary. "I'm Detective Macy Quinn. It's really nice to meet you."

"Can I help you with something, Detective?" His eyebrows furrowed, and his voice carried an edge of irritation.

Macy guided him away from the fray. "I'm a close friend of Parker's. I just want you to know, Calypso . . . she's not who or what Parker thinks she is. But I can't tell her that. She doesn't listen to me. Maybe . . . maybe she would listen to you. She needs to be careful. Protect herself. Calypso's past is dangerous, to say the least." She didn't give him a chance to respond. She spun on her heel and walked back to her table.

A slow song came on, and A.D. cast her eyes over to Macy. "Wanna dance?"

Macy nodded. A.D. held out her hand, and Macy took it. A.D.'s hands were soft and warm–a convenient distraction amidst her heartache–as she let A.D. lead her to the area where everyone danced slowly.

She tried not to stare at Calypso looking up into Parker's eyes, and Parker looking so happy. Macy had never seen her that happy. But honestly, what *did* she know about this woman?

If you love something, you're supposed to let it go. *Blah blah whatever*. It hurt. It hurt that Parker chose Calypso over her. It hurt more than any other loss she could remember. And she had lost so much in her life. It seemed she lost everything all the time. Her heart clenched and her throat constricted as she fought back the tears that were brewing from that empty space. All she ever wanted was for someone to choose her first. She wanted to be loved. She'd spent her whole lifetime chasing it to no avail.

A.D.'s hands snaked around Macy's waist. Macy turned her head to look at A.D. This may work. This might be her person if she would let it happen. A.D. appeared cute in the daylight when she was drunk. Slightly more sober, Macy thought she was definitely cute under the market lights. And she smelled good. She wasn't Parker. No one else possessed the capability to match Parker. But she was being forced to move on.

"What are you thinking about in there?" A.D. asked her.

"Just how sweet it is that they found each other." There was absolutely no way she would tell A.D. what she was thinking about.

"It's crazy how when you least expect it, you find it."

Macy let her fingertips glide up the back of A.D.'s neck to

where her hair was shaved close in a tight fade. *She is so fucking cute.*

A.D. inhaled sharply. The slow song transitioned into a second one. A.D. pulled her a little closer. "Do I have the privilege of seeing you again?"

"Do you want to see me again?" Macy turned her charm on, blocking Parker and Calypso from her peripheral vision by slightly turning them as they danced.

A.D. rested her eyes on Macy. "Maybe it's the atmosphere, or the whole *being here to celebrate love,* but I think there's something worth exploring here. That is if you're down?"

Macy smiled and nodded. She was down because there was no other choice but to be. Desperately.

12 GOLD DIGGER?

Parker

Parker stared at Calypso, her *fiancée* (holy shit!), in the glowing market lights as she hugged Parker's parents. Calypso's parents, Parker, learned, did not have any part in her life. Nor did anyone from her past in New Orleans, except for her friend Gilian. For as much as the city lived in Calypso's heart and soul, the people in it were not. And she never spoke about it. Her past was a ghost she was not willing to face. Parker's own family quickly welcomed her into their fold—not that they weren't skeptical of her at first. Calypso certainly did not belong to the country club set that her parents had raised her with and continued to run with.

Parker noted Macy in the distance, slow dancing with A.D. It would be a good fit if those two were to work out. They both fell in love quickly, and Macy was the type of woman who needed a steady partner in life. Parker set her eyes back on Calypso, glowing under the lights. *Unbelievable. This isn't a dream.* She bought the ring only six months into their relationship, three days after Calypso moved in with her. She sat on it for nearly another six months, trying to decide if she could actually be ready. Each day with Calypso proved this was right.

Parker swept in and took Calypso's hand without a word of apology to her friends, who were mid-conversation with Calypso, and spun her out onto the dance floor. Calypso laughed as she pulled Parker closer. "That was kind of rude."

"I mean, you're mine," Parker teased her with a sly wink.

Parker was literally on cloud nine. She turned her head and stole a glance at Macy. She hadn't spent much time with Macy recently. Respecting Calypso's wishes, Parker didn't bring Macy around. Calypso never quite told Parker why she didn't want Macy around. Calypso didn't trust the police, and she chalked it up to that, never bothering to press the issue.

But she still cared about Macy and considered her a friend. She tried her best to squeeze in lunches with Macy, knowing how Macy struggled with loneliness, and Parker felt slightly guilty for, in effect, abandoning her friend.

A.D. spun Macy around, and Macy made eye contact with Parker. Parker winked at her and smiled. She was happy to see Macy there and having a good time.

She turned around to see her father and Xander standing behind her.

"May I cut in?" Xander asked.

Parker smiled and handed Calypso's hand over to Xander. "Of course, sir." Calypso spun off with her adopted big brother, and Parker stepped closer to her father.

"Parker, we should have a talk." Her father, tall with silver hair and dark, brooding eyes, was still handsome even in his later years. A lot of it, though, came from the way he carried himself as if he owned every room he walked into. He walked past Parker and into the house, forcing Parker to follow. It didn't matter how old she was, how many accomplishments she had under her belt, or how independent she was; she consistently deferred to her father.

He walked across the yard and through the opened bifold doors, through the living room, to Parker's home office, and shut the door behind her. It didn't matter that it was *Parker's* office; he took over the space as if it belonged to him as he sat behind *her* desk.

"What's up, Dad?" Parker sat in the chair across from the desk. If it were anyone other than her father, she would have ejected them from the chair. Forcefully. Instead, she sat across from him, subconsciously mirroring his exact body language, leaning back, elbows on the arm of the chair, fingers steepled under the chin. After a lifetime of mimicking him as a child and growing up as his shadow. She idolized him.

"You're aware that we love Calypso, right?"

"Of course. Who wouldn't?" While he kept his hands steepled and calm, a defensiveness fell over her and she dropped her hands, gripping the arms of the chair.

"What do you know of her past? *Really* know?" He leaned forward slightly. A tactic that was definitely intended to put the other person in check and remind them that he was in command.

"She's from New Orleans. Her family cut her off for being gay. She was on her own for a while, and then she witnessed something terrible and left. To be honest, I'm not at all concerned with her past. It's her *now*, and *us* going forward."

Her father gave a sigh and leaned back in Parker's chair. It never went well when the two of them matched wits. "You're a grown woman and you're going to make your own choices.

But I'm begging you, Parker, write a prenup or have one written up for you. I will even draft it for you. But you've got to remember how you have built yourself up. You have equity in this home, a stake in the firm, and savings and investments. Protect yourself. This is moving fast. You barely knew her when you moved her in. Now, scarcely a year in it with her, and you are proposing to her.

"It is all very understandable. You never allowed yourself to have a long-term relationship. You're excited. You're in love. This is all virgin territory for you. But Parker, don't lose your head to your heart. I wanted to wait to have this talk, but your friend Macy brought up a good point earlier—in that none of us really know much about her before she landed in your lap."

Parker leaned back in the chair across the desk from him. "For someone who claims to love her, you are certainly not talking like someone who thinks very highly of her. And to top it off, no offense to Macy, but she's been in love with me since we met. And she and Calypso hate each other. So take whatever she says with a grain of salt." It was disconcerting to be on the opposite side of the desk. Almost tempted to ask him to move out of her chair, she bit her tongue.

"It has nothing to do with liking her. It's a safety net just in case. Parker, your mother and I are very happy for you. We wondered if you would ever settle down with someone. And we *do* love Calypso. She's charming, and she's witty, and she's a good match for you. But Parker, you never can tell what the future holds. Your mother even signed one before we got married. It's simply smart thinking."

Parker nodded. "Okay. I understand. I'll talk to her about it."

"That's the prudent thing to do."

"I want to be the one to write it, though. I want to parse it out with Calypso."

"If you don't ensure it's handled, *I* will write it up in a way that I think it should be." So typical of her father to be controlling. And as far as this situation went, he was justified. His father was the one who founded the firm, he grew it, and Parker took it to the next level—the epitome of a family legacy.

* * *

JULY 14

Parker woke earlier than Calypso *most* mornings. Today being no exception. Calypso was sleeping soundly, curled up on her side. After the first night together, Parker knew full well that she was in love, a scary and very foreign emotion for her. But Calypso fit perfectly into her life. She made very few demands of Parker's time. She accepted Parker for her demanding and often bratty ways. Parker honored Calypso's drive to be independent and her black-cat nature.

Her father questioning Calypso's intentions set her teeth on edge. She did understand the importance of having a prenup. But she wanted to have the talk with Calypso and discuss what she would think is fair. She wanted to have it on her terms when she deemed the timing to be appropriate. Doing it the day after their engagement was not in her plans. But she didn't want her father in charge of it, so she recognized would have to take the initiative sooner rather than later.

Parker sat at the kitchen table with her coffee as Calypso came shuffling in. Furry pink bunny slippers and a black fluffy robe, her hair piled up in a messy bun fastened up on her head. No makeup and sleepy-eyed. Parker loved groggy morning Calypso.

Parker reached out and gently grabbed her, pulling her

down onto her lap. Calypso giggled as she wrapped her arms around Parker and nuzzled into her. Parker lifted Calypso's chin with a finger and kissed her. "Good morning."

"We should go back to bed," Calypso purred. Parker wanted nothing more than to not have this conversation and fall back into bed with Calypso. That was her favorite place to be.

"I agree, but first, make your coffee. We need to have a little talk." Parker released her, and Calypso went to the counter and popped a pod into the machine. A convenience Calypso came to enjoy when she didn't want to get up and wait for what she called "real coffee."

When her coffee finished brewing, she took her mug and sat across from Parker.

"I need to preface this conversation with the fact that there is no doubt in my mind that you love me. There is no doubt in my mind that when we get married, you are in it for the long run. For life."

Calypso nodded and sipped her coffee. "I did give up my amazing loft space downtown to live in the country with you." She smiled.

"It's not the country." Parker kicked Calypso playfully.

"We are not within walking distance of *anything*. But, please, continue."

"And you didn't really give it up. You still own it. You can kick your tenants out and take it back if you feel so inclined."

"Okay. You win." Calypso smiled into her coffee.

"I was going to talk to you about this later, but a conversation with my dad prompted me to speed up my timeline." Parker paused and let it out on the exhale. "Are you going to be okay with signing a prenup?"

"Do I have any say in what's in it?" She handled it better than anticipated.

"Of course you will."

"Because I don't want it to just be about me. You came with a certain reputation, so I need to protect myself, too."

"Absolutely. I would expect nothing less." It was only fair. And she was right. Parker did have a reputation.

"Are you drafting it?"

"If I don't, my father will. I would rather the two of us sort it out without him involved. That's why I'm bringing it up now. You might want to obtain independent counsel before signing it. It's only fair for you to have someone not involved with me or my firm look it over so you fully understand what's in it."

"I don't need that. What are you going to put in it?"

"Calypso, if we are going to do this, it needs to be done the right way. I'm certain you trust me. As you should trust me, if we are getting married. But for something like this, it's best. Just so if anything that we don't see coming happens, you fully understand what you are or are not entitled to."

Calypso rolled her eyes. "I will check into it if it makes you happy. But really, Parker, this is a nonissue."

"Thank you. It would make me feel much better. And they may decide that there is something you *should* include that's not already in there. So, with that being said, what would you like included?"

"You tell me your terms first. It will determine what I think is fair," she tapped her black lacquered nails against her mug.

"Okay. If we divorce due to your own actions, i.e., cheating, or just wanting to walk, you will receive five grand a month for one year to supplement your lifestyle, allowing you time to adjust. Nothing more. You will hold no claim to this house, or stake in the firm, or anything that you didn't bring into this relationship. Of course, if something happens to me and I die, obviously, it's null and void, and you get everything. What terms would you like added?"

"If *you* cheat on me, or *you* decide to walk, *ten* grand a month for *five* years."

Parker raised her eyebrow. "That's it?"

Calypso smiled. "It's not going to be necessary, though. You're mine. You're not going anywhere." She nudged Parker with her foot beneath the table and winked. She paused after drinking a quick sip of her coffee. "Can I talk to you about something else?"

13 UNFRIENDLY DEMANDS

JULY 14

CALYPSO

"*Y*ou can talk to me about anything." Parker regarded Calypso.

Calypso paused. "I don't want Macy Quinn in our house again. Ever."

"What's your beef with Macy? She's harmless."

Calypso hated Parker questioning her. Or the way she pooh-poohed her very simple request. She gave a sarcastic laugh. "Ha! What's my beef with her? One, I don't trust her. Not one bit. And two, I'm very aware that you slept with her—"

Parker cut her off. And her annoyance was evident. "One time, *four* years ago, which was two years before you and I ever met."

Calypso sensed that Parker wasn't thrilled with where this conversation was going. "Let me finish. Let's just say, I don't like the way she looks at you. I don't even understand how you are friends with her. You are on two different sides. And she's just . . . weird. Something about her is *off*."

"Calypso, I can't just cut off a friendship off because you don't like her. That's not okay."

Calypso realized that much of what made the two of them work was that neither of them was jealous or possessive. But Calypso couldn't stress her distaste and distrust for Macy any other way. "I'm not asking you to cut her out. I just don't want her in our house. I *would* love for you to cut her off completely, but I *know* it's not right of me to ask that of you. But to be frank, I feel like this is a compromise on my part."

Parker sighed. "It's not like she spends time here."

"She was here last night."

"Because I wanted *all* of our friends and family to be present when I proposed to you. She *is* my friend."

"Okay. But no more?"

"Okay. Fine. No more Macy at our house."

"Thank you."

* * *

CALYPSO DROVE to work a few hours after their conversation. Her car, a black Mercedes-AMG Coupé with tinted windows, was a birthday gift from Parker a few months ago. Parker claimed she gifted it for two reasons: Calypso had recently moved in with her and the commute was long, so she wanted her to have something safe and new. The other reason being that she said she couldn't tolerate Calypso's beat-up old Toyota in her driveway any longer. She feared it would leak oil on her otherwise pristine concrete driveway in front of her garage. Calypso had never driven a car this nice. She never thought about it. But it was beautiful and sleek, and she couldn't say no. The car was a big deal. That's when Calypso first suspected that Parker would probably be proposing.

Parker spoiled her from the start. Not that the gifts were what kept Calypso there. They were merely an added bonus. She would have been with Parker if Parker lived in a cardboard box on the beach. And to be honest, she never had someone in her life spoil her. It was a welcome surprise. Parker understood her. Parker intuitively selected what she would pick for herself. Understood her style. Every one of the gifts Parker hand-selected were well thought out and spoke to who Calypso was a person. She loved that Parker didn't try to change her or change her style. Parker *saw* her.

Parker would come home with all kinds of gifts randomly for no reason, from the HardWear collection from Tiffany one night, to flowers, to her favorite perfume—Libre Intense by YSL (because Parker noticed the almost-empty bottle on the bathroom counter)—spa retreats, Chanel bag (in black leather of course, and it was a tote so she could carry everything she needed), designer clothes (that came in her style— Parker didn't want to change her, she only wanted to spoil her). It wasn't every day. It wasn't even once a week. Randomly, Parker came home with a bag or a box. Sometimes she randomly showed up at Calypso's shop with a little surprise.

At first, Calypso sat Parker down and told her that she didn't need to buy her love. Parker smiled and said she knew. She explained that she enjoyed giving her gifts. It was her love language. Parker also explained to her that she deserved the finer things in life, and if she had the ability to provide them, she was going to.

With no other choice, Calypso relented.

As she drove, she glimpsed the sun glinting off her engagement ring. Something she never thought she would see on her hand. Her whole lifestyle since she met Parker had ultimately evolved into something she never thought she would see, much less want. At times, Calypso found it to be a little overwhelming. Living a life she never imagined, as if she lived in some sort of Cinderella story of sorts. The house. The car. The clothes. The ring. And most of all, Parker herself. She was scared she would wake up one day, and it would have all been a dream, or something from her past would come barreling into her present and destroy it all.

And it wasn't one-sided. Calypso was totally smitten with Parker. She didn't make the money that Parker did, obviously. So instead of gifts, she took over cooking on the days she got home early enough to send the housekeeper home (certainly never thought she would live in a house that came with a housekeeper). Calypso would leave love notes around the house for Parker to find, or slip them into Parker's bag for her to discover later. On her off days, if Parker was working, she would prepare a lunch for herself and Parker and bring it to the office so they could have a few minutes together. She would check on how Parker's day was going. She would do whatever it took to ensure Parker knew she was loved and appreciated.

Calypso found herself living a life she never imagined would be in the cards for her.

When she arrived at Voodoo Ink, she did the obligatory showing off of the ring, to the sounds of whistles and congratulations, though almost everyone at the shop had been present last night.

"That's not a rock, that's a boulder!" Xander exclaimed. "Seriously, Calypso . . . Congratulations!" He gave her a big hug and went back to setting up for his next client.

Calypso went to her own corner of the shop and opened her Instagram. She posted a picture taken of her and Parker as Parker proposed earlier that morning, before she left for work. The caption underneath read, 'Fairytales do come true.' With hundreds of comments and likes, Calypso did her best to read through them and respond to the ones from people she'd met personally. Her account, @Caly-VoodooArt, mainly focused on her art and her tattoos. It was public, which is how she got a lot of her business. She only occasionally posted something personal—weekend getaways with Parker, her kitchen bloopers when her attempts to cook for Parker failed, Kitty hiding in her closet.

As she scrolled, she found a private account. The profile picture was of a dog, and it had the the generic and unfamiliar name @JaneDoe69. The comment read "you white trash whore. you don't deserve parker Harrington. go crawl back to the gutter you crawled out of. gutter slut." Redundant. Rude. And poor grammar.

Calypso considered responding, but kept scrolling. Another private account, this one with the profile picture of a silhouetted couple kissing in front of a sunset, the name @SamFink11, "Be careful. The past always comes back around. Hope you are sleeping well. For soon you will sleep the permanent sleep," from another account. And yet another one, "Wait until Parker finds out who you really are. She will throw you away like the trash you are." Another one, "The past always comes back to bite. And it will bite you hard."

Calypso's hands began to shake. She took a deep breath, put the phone down, and started setting up for her next client. She sensed, deep down in her gut, who was behind those accounts and making those comments. She only hoped that her bubble wouldn't be burst by Parker believing them. Parker wouldn't buy into that, would she?

Javier being her next client didn't do much to help her nerves. After his back piece had been finished, he began working on sleeving out both of his arms. Xochitl had encouraged her to cut him off, but money was money and he always paid well and above what she charged.

"Hey, beautiful," he drawled as he came through the door. "I see congratulations are in order. I should get, like, a free piece or something, since I'm the reason you even met. Or are we counting that as my returning the favor for you testifying at my trial?"

Her teeth were set on edge. "I told you I'm not asking for any return favors, Javi."

"If we don't count you and Parker getting a happily ever after together as the payback, I know one day you will need me for something. And you know, whatever you want," he winked suggestively and licked his lips, "I'll give."

She wasn't in the mood to even justify his lewd suggestion. She motioned for him to sit in the chair and began shaving his arm.

"What? You got nothing to say to me?" He slipped his finger under her chin.

Slapping his hand away, giving him her meanest *don't fuck with me* glare, she continued prepping his arm.

"Alright. Alright. I'll leave you alone to bask in your newly engaged glory. Just know the offer stands."

She stayed silent.

As she worked on Javi, she let herself get lost in the music playing overhead. It was Xander's turn to control the music —a heavy bass, deep house techno playlist with very few lyrics. This song was about finding someone at night, or something. Between the music and the hum and vibration of the machines throughout the shop, she didn't even notice Parker standing near the counter watching her.

Parker would come in occasionally, but it was rare. Usually, she gave Calypso advance notice.

Xander calling out, "Hey, Parker! Congratulations!" from

his station in the opposite corner alerted Calypso to Parker's presence.

Calypso finished the lines of the crucifix she was working on as Javi called out over her to Parker, "How's my high-powered lawyer doing?" he was grinning as Calypso sprayed the paper towel with green soap spray and wiped the section she just finished.

"I'll be right back." She snapped off her gloves, went over to the counter and leaned across it so she could kiss Parker.

Parker looped her finger through Calypso's engagement ring, hanging from a chain around her neck. "I can't wear it when I'm working, this is my work-around for that." Calypso let her finger trace the platinum band of the ring Parker's finger had slipped through. "What are you doing here?"

Parker shrugged. "I don't have anything going on today. I figured I would come see if you wanted to go grab lunch." Parker smiled and stepped aside as Xander's client left. "Plus, I like watching you work." Xander made his way to the front and dapped Parker, giving her a half-hug.

"Let me finish up here, I've got maybe another forty-five minutes left," Calypso informed her. "You don't mind if Parker has a seat over here while we finish up?" She asked Javi.

"You don't even need to ask. She was my girl before she was yours." Parker took the seat across from Calypso, next to the chair Javi sat in with his arm, a work in progress, on a padded armrest. Calypso noted how his behavior changed from predatory and lewd to deferential now that Parker was sitting next to him.

As Calypso put on fresh gloves and gave another green soap spray wipe down of Javi's arm, she shot a quick look over at Parker. "I think there are some people who are not so happy we are engaged."

"Who?"

"I'm not sure. But like five people posted some very odd, veiled threats on my picture of you and me."

"You don't know who it is?"

"No. They're screen names I don't know, with generic profile pictures and private accounts." Calypso picked up her machine and resumed her work on Javi.

"You've never had comments like that before?" Calypso watched as Parker pulled up Instagram to search for them.

"I mean, occasionally. But never to this level."

"Did you report them?"

"No. Instagram never does anything about them."

"I can look into it and make it stop," Javi offered.

"No." Parker and Calypso said in unison.

Parker continued to scroll, and based on her expression, she found the comments. "Calypso, there are like twenty of these. Not just five." Parker began typing on her phone.

"You aren't responding to them, are you?"

"No. I'm going to send screenshots of them to Macy. She's in the loop with people who can track down cyber stuff like this. She has some sort of certification in cybercrime."

"Nope. Abso-fucking-lutely no. Do *not* involve her." Calypso popped her gaze up from her work. "I'd rather *not* know and take my chances than involve *her*." Calypso could see her client arch an eyebrow at the drama unfolding around her.

"The ginger cop bitch that tried to get me locked up?" Javi was appalled.

"The same one. Believe it or not, she's Parker's bestie." Calypso didn't even stop or look up.

"That doesn't make any sense," Javi grumbled.

"I know, right?" Calypso mumbled.

Parker ignored both of them. "She can help us figure out who this is. Why wouldn't we take it to her?" Parker, obviously irritated, glowered up from her phone.

"Just don't. I'm sure it's nothing. It's only some trolls trying to get a reaction."

Parker put her phone back in her pocket and crossed her arms over her chest.

As Calypso kept working, Parker pulled her phone back out of her pocket to continue reading through the comments. Apparently, a lot more hate comments were posted based on Parker's expression. Parker was tapping on them.

"You better not be responding to those." Calypso chided.

"No. I'm reporting them to Instagram. If we aren't taking them to the police, the least we can do is this."

Calypso loved that Parker respected her wish not to involve Macy, but she didn't love Parker's annoyance with her over it.

When Javi left, she cleaned her station as Parker moved to the chair where the clients typically sat.

Calypso grinned. "Are you next?"

"As much as I love yours on you, that would be a negative. My canvas stays blank."

"I can put my name right on—"

"Nope." Parker's smile faded. "Calypso, this could be something serious. Those comments are flooding your post. And some of them are straight-up threats."

"Well, I can tell you, Macy Quinn would not do anything to help the situation."

"Just because you don't like her doesn't mean she's not good at her job."

"It's a fact she's lost every case when you defend the client."

"That's because I'm better at my job than she is at hers," Parker smirked.

"Your ego knows no limits." Calypso grinned as she finished cleaning up her area.

"And if I didn't have this ego, you probably wouldn't have fallen in love with me."

"I fell in love with you *despite* your ego." Calypso finished cleaning her area.

"Enough, you two!" Xander called out as Parker got out of the chair.

Parker pulled Calypso up and into her arms. "You're lucky you're cute." She teased.

"No. *You're* lucky I'm cute." Calypso loved the teasing banter they would have back and forth. It only reaffirmed for her that she had found her person. Someone she was unabashedly herself around. And no anonymous comment was going to change that.

14 LIKE RAIN ON
YOUR WEDDING DAY

Macy

It sucks being at the wedding of the woman you are truly, madly, deeply in love with, and you are not the other bride. It wasn't a big grand affair. It was just a small affair inside a conservatory at an estate of some old, dead, rich white dude that he donated to the state or city or whatever and turned into a museum (it was supposed to be in the garden, but by some fluke, it was raining in Southern California). Macy found herself sitting in the second row behind Parker's family.

Normally, the rain in Southern California came as a mist —hardly worth calling rain, at least not the same as the rain in New Orleans. But today, thunder rolled and lightning burst overhead as the rain pelted the glass roof of the conservatory, and all of the glass windowpanes began to fog with the heat and the breath of the guests. Macy found it all a bit oppressive—taking her back to her grandparents' living room during a summer rain, no air conditioning running because her Papa didn't want to run up the electric bill, the smoke from their cigarettes hanging in the air and choking her out. The overwhelming feeling of being stuck and the hopelessness of it all. It was hard to breathe. She was suffocating.

Macy wore a lavender dress that flattered her red hair. She wore it up with curling loose strands framing her face. A.D. sat beside her in a nice suit. Not as nice as any of Parker's, but it still worked for her. Her tie matched Macy's dress, and they did, in a very real sense, look good together.

Calypso chose black for her wedding dress—because of course she did—with a pink sash ribbon around her waist. Her jet-black hair, which had previously been shaved on the sides, was grown out and even, and hung in loose beach-wave curls down a little bit past her shoulders, with a rhinestone and pink feather clip holding her hair up on the right side. A fat diamond solitaire sat at her throat, gaudy against her blackwork tattooed patterns underneath. For sure, that was real. Most certainly a gift from Parker. Her honey-colored eyes were dramatically shaded in smoky black. Macy couldn't bring herself to admit that Calypso, though not in any conventional sense, was a total smoke show. She hated A.D. a little bit for even commenting on it. She shot A.D. a fake smile and a quiet "mm-hmm." She would look better with a knife in her chest or back or whatever as long as she was no longer breathing. *But it's whatever. Focus. Pay attention. Pretend to be happy.*

Calypso's best friend was a riot of color standing next to her—covered in brightly colored tattoos, with dyed pink hair, in a pink dress that matched Calypso's sash as maid of honor. Macy met her briefly at the engagement party. Xochitl or something or other. She wondered if Calypso had any friends who could be considered normal. Her side of the seating contained a motley crew of freaks.

Parker's cousin stood at her side. An attractive guy who definitely hailed from her father's side, as he carried the Harrington bloodline look. Parker had mentioned him before—Teddy Harrington. Unlike Parker, he *was* a true nepo baby hire at the firm. Macy heard all about it when Parker was annoyed with one of his screwups. Mr. Harrington's brother, Parker's uncle, died of a massive heart attack. He had earned the same reputation as a fierce litigator, in the same vein as Mr. Harrington and Parker herself. His son, Theodore Harrington III, not so much. He was a hand-picked brother to Parker, even though he also frustrated her to no end. She stuck him in the trusts and estates branch of the firm and let him handle those cases. Not because he wasn't smart, but because he was a pushover, according to Parker.

The officiant began, and Macy eyed Calypso as she turned her head to smile at Parker. She felt a small stab of pain in her chest. Macy didn't *hate* Calypso—okay, she hated her a little bit. That's not true either. She loathed her. She was jealous, and she fully admitted that (to herself only). She also didn't fully trust Calypso or particularly think very highly of her friends. And honestly, you couldn't find two people any more different than Calypso and Parker. Parker being the epitome of refinement and class. Calypso was all edges and bite. Granted, she had smoothed out a lot of those edges since she got with Parker. Or so she heard. She barely hung out with Parker any longer. And that was what hurt most. She barely got scraps of Parker's time. She cherished those brief lunches or quick drinks after work. Those precious moments meant the world to her.

She had come to terms (kind of) with not being in a romantic anything with Parker, as long as she had a spot in

Parker's life at all. And that had slowly been pulled away from her, too. This had to be what a drug addict felt when they were forced into rehab. But there was no rehab for this. No twelve-step program. No support group.

Parker stood with her trademark pompadour, fresh fade (because it always was), in her bespoke tux and spectator shoes, a pink ascot in lieu of a tie, and Macy had to admit, Parker appeared to be happy.

If you love something—set it free. Right? Right. And besides, she'd been serious with A.D. for over a year. It was time for her to let it all go. How long could she possibly hold onto this hope that she and Parker would end up together in the long run? It had been five years. And the last two, she only saw Parker a handful of times. Each time, though, Macy always hoped that Parker would tell her she and Calypso had broken it off. Hope can be so dangerous to hold on to. When you are let down, it's a knife wound directly to the heart.

But she was able to tell A.D. genuinely loved her. And A.D. was a good woman. And she considered A.D. sexy as hell. Macy loved her. Unfortunately, she loved Parker more.

But this was it. It was past time for her to put it all behind her. Let Parker go once and for all. She keeps telling herself this but never found the ability to do so.

Macy almost didn't even want to come to the wedding. But with A.D. being Parker's good friend, she was obligated to attend. And she was technically Parker's friend, too. Or at least she had been.

She got herself out of her own head long enough to listen to Parker saying her vows to Calypso. She forced herself to pay attention and (pretend to) be happy for the couple.

Rain pelting the glass made it hard for her to focus; the rain produced an irregular drumbeat, and the lighting was mottled and bluish through the panes. Macy would usually have thought this was a good thing, but she was familiar with the old wives' tale that rain on your wedding day is supposedly good luck. She wanted Calypso gone. Her chest hurt as Parker gazed into Calypso's eyes, as she recited, "I vow to love you with a fire that no storm can extinguish. In your arms, I find my home, my beginning, and my end. Should the world turn against us, I would stand beside you still. Should the world try to take you from me, I would burn the world to bring you back. My heart is yours, now and always, in this life and whatever waits beyond."

Did they have to be so dramatic? Macy forced herself not to roll her eyes. She also knew damn well that if Parker said those words to her, she would melt then and there. So, good for Calypso.

A.D. turned her head and stole a glance at Macy, giving her a subtle wink. She was onto the fact that A.D. was thinking about asking her to marry her. She overheard her talking to a friend. Not intentionally eavesdropping, but she happened to be walking down the hall and heard the conversation.

She would probably say yes. She should say yes. She was definitely going to say yes.

The minister, or judge, or whatever the officiant was, pronounced them married, and Parker and Calypso kissed. Macy's stomach lurched. She had seen pictures of them kissing on Parker's Instagram. But this was the first time it hit her for real—they were married. And it was weird. She busied herself with her purse instead.

As they went walking down the aisle, heading out of the conservatory to the waiting photographers, Macy caught Calypso glowering over at her, shooting daggers at her with her eyes. Macy would have been dead right there if looks actually killed. Macy regretted putting the hundred dollars in a card from her and A.D. She had conveniently forgotten to order the fancy whatever from their registry that A.D. had wanted to buy them, so they each threw a hundred-dollar bill into a card. It couldn't be that hard to fish the envelope out of the card drop box.

A.D. put her hand on Macy's shoulder and whispered in her ear. "I'll meet you in the library for cocktail hour. I'm going to go find the bathroom."

Macy nodded.

As the guests all filed out, she could see Parker and Calypso on a covered porch, kissing as the cameras snapped photos behind them, the rain adding to the atmosphere. Parker dipped Calypso back as she kissed her, and the photographer caught it as lightning struck in the distance behind them. Okay, that would make a badass picture, because of course it would work perfectly for them.

Employees of the museum escorted guests under umbrellas (because who in Southern California really owns or remembers to bring them?) to the main house, where another employee guided the guests to the library for cocktail hour before escorting them into the dining room for dinner.

A.D. was nowhere to be seen as the clusters of people began milling around and watching the photos being taken as they waited for their escort to the main house.

Macy didn't care if she got slightly wet. She worked her way through the crowd and ran to the house, holding her purse over her head.

She entered the foyer where a large mirror hung, and appraised herself. Aside from a stray hair she smoothed down, and brushing the water drops off her purse, she got across the walk unscathed. Macy found a tray of cocktails and selected one from the tray, along with a canapé from another one.

After spotting a window seat that remained unoccupied, with the lead-paned windows and the raindrops giving everything outside an ethereal, wavy, blue-tinted quality, Macy made her way over and sat. Now she had a distorted view of the brides and the bridal party, making them look alien as they took pictures. Parker's parents were also out there with them.

"Detective Quinn! How are you?" One of the public defenders Macy knew sat down next to her. He had been kissing the Harrington asses for the last two years, hoping to land a job working with the Great Parker Harrington. His tone came across as friendly and chipper. She tried to hate him, but his puppy dog nature made it somewhat challenging.

"Lovely, Lloyd. Have you scored an interview yet?" The question came out in an overly pandering tone.

"Ouch. You know I do genuinely like Parker. She's become more than a mentor for me. How's your new assignment? Working in computer and tech crimes?"

"I'm still on Organized Crime. But yeah. I'm focusing on that aspect of it. You know, it's a big thing. New challenge and all."

"It sounds pretty boring compared to being out on the streets."

"Not really. And I still get out there. But they keep sending me for these certifications in digital forensics and crime. So it's paying off."

Before Macy said anything more, A.D. found her way back inside, pulling her up out of the seat, placing a light kiss on her lips. "Having fun?"

Macy forced a smile, hoping A.D. found it convincing. "Yeah. Of course. A.D., this is Lloyd Whittaker. He's one of the public defenders; he's being mentored by Parker. Lloyd, this is my girlfriend, A.D."

A.D. stuck her hand out to shake Lloyd's hand. "Nice to meet you. I've heard Parker mention your name."

At the sound of being mentioned by his absolute idol, Lloyd's eyes lit up. Apparently, Macy wasn't the only one enamored with her. She wondered if he had a crush on her, too. "Nice to meet you." Lloyd shook A.D.'s hand.

The heat of angry eyes bored straight through her. Turning to glance over shoulder, Macy beheld Calypso glaring at her as she tapped her black tipped, French-manicured finger against her glass. Macy turned and glanced back at A.D. "Babe, if you want to grab a drink before dinner, we are running out of time." Macy wanted to escape to another room, if possible.

A.D. pulled a flute of champagne off a passing tray as she and Lloyd talked.

"I mean, do you want to go to the bar?" Macy tried to sound casual.

"No. Champagne is fine by me. I don't want to overdo it."

Thankfully, a tuxedo-clad waiter announced that dinner would be served shortly, recommending that the guests find their way to the dining room, allowing Macy to not have to say anything further. A.D., Lloyd, and Macy made their way as they were directed and took their seats at a table.

A lack of a formal seating chart and Lloyd not having a date put him on the other side of Macy for dinner.

"Don't you have a girlfriend or something?" Macy chided.

"I have plenty of them. But none that I would want to bring here. Weddings give women the wrong idea."

Macy gazed at A.D. quickly and back at Lloyd. "Not all women."

"Most women. Admit it. The romance. The idea of having that perfect love for a lifetime." He would fucking argue with a wall. Typical lawyer.

"It has no effect on me," Macy said as she brought her glass to her lips.

"Babe, you don't think this is romantic?" A.D. asked.

"I honestly don't understand big weddings. Or moderate-sized ones or whatever. It takes the focus off the couple and puts it on all of the guests."

"What do you mean?" A.D. asked. Shit. She must want a big wedding.

"Think about what Parker threw down for this venue. The catering. The DJ and photographers. She must have dropped at *least* forty grand." Macy defended her stance. "Think about what she could have done with that money. Buy a car. Pay for a hell of a vacation. That could go to *charity* if she didn't need it. There's just a better use of that kind of money."

"That's pocket change for the Harringtons." Lloyd offered. "She can pull that out of her couch cushions."

"Yes. But think about it. After tonight, what will people be talking about? The venue. The food. The drinks. The dress. And whatever gossip they parsed out while here. No one will talk about their marriage, or their love, or whatever."

A.D. shrugged. "I think it's romantic to celebrate love in a grand way like this. Hopefully, you only get to do it once. And for Parker, *no one* ever thought she would get married. She never had the interest or drive. So this is a pretty big deal. The devil is gonna have to ice skate home."

"If you're lucky. Fifty percent of all marriages end in divorce." Macy countered.

It was Lloyd's turn to shrug. "It's fun. I'm having a good time."

"*You* will do anything to make Parker happy." Macy directed it to Lloyd.

A.D. leaned over and whispered in Macy's ear. "Are you in a bad mood or something?"

Macy whispered back, "I'm just not a wedding person."

A hint of disappointment flashed in A.D.'s deep brown eyes.

Parker and Calypso were seated at a sweetheart table at the front of the room. They laughed and talked quietly. Parker's arm was protectively draped over the back of Calypso's chair, and the fingers of her free hand were laced through Calypso's on the table.

A.D. took Macy's hand in hers and gave it a light kiss. "Are you okay?" She asked.

Macy nodded. "I think it's the pressure change with the weather. I have a bit of a headache. That's all."

15 HAPPILY EVER AFTER

PARKER

*P*arker set her eyes on her wife and took in the crowd of friends and family who had gathered to witness what almost everyone (okay, not almost—literally everyone) thought would never happen.

As dinner was being served, Teddy stood up and tapped his glass for everyone's attention. His wife, Cassie, sat next to him.

Everyone turned their attention to Teddy. "I'm five years older than Parker. We grew up together, like brother and sister, being the only two children who hung out at a law firm. It's not often someone gets to say this about a younger family member, but I always looked up to Parker. I still look up to Parker. She has always known what she's wanted in life. She would play lawyer in the offices of our fathers from the time she was seven. She is the most self-assured and ambitious person I've ever met. She was also the biggest player I had ever met." The guests laughed, and Parker threw a faux glare at her cousin. "At one point, she even stole one of my girlfriends."

Everyone paused to laugh again. Parker mouthed, "It's true."

"Glad I wasn't the only one." A.D. laughed.

Teddy tipped his glass to A.D. with a wink before he continued. "So when Parker told me Calypso was moving in with her, I almost fell over. When she invited Cassie and me over for a party a year ago and she filled us in on why she was having a party—that she was planning to propose to Calypso, I think I fainted." Again, everyone laughed. "But honestly, seeing Parker this happy, this contented, and this loved is all anyone can ask for their family. To Parker and Calypso! And Calypso, welcome to the family!"

Everyone cheered and drank.

Xochitl stood next. "When Xander introduced me to Calypso and told me she was like a sister to him, I didn't really think much of it. But Calypso quickly became a valuable person in my life, too. She's the little sister we've both always wanted in our lives. We've watched her grow and establish herself. When Xander's shop closed, she followed Xander to the next shop, saving and stocking away, and eventually opened her own business. A testament to her business acumen and drive to be independent. When we first met Parker, Calypso brought her to dinner at our house, and we were blown away to see her this happy. To see the light in her eyes. And watching the two of them grow together has been nothing short of beautiful. Parker, Calypso, may you have many more years of growing together in happiness and love!" Xochitl lifted her glass in a toast, brushing a stray pink curl out of her eyes.

Overwhelmed by the sheer amount of love and support

she and Calypso were surrounded by on this day, Parker couldn't help but to feel the joy.

As the waiters began clearing the dinner plates, the guests started mingling, and the music changed from quiet classical music to pop hits.

Calypso went to greet some of her friends while Parker went to talk to Lloyd. A.D. and Macy had dispersed into the crowd.

As she made her way to Lloyd, she witnessed Macy and Calypso having a heated conversation in the corner of the room. Macy's face turned beet red and Calypso was staring daggers into her with her arms crossed over her chest as they went back and forth.

Over the last few years Parker learned Calypso's body language and personality extremely well. Calypso was typically extremely laid back about everything. She rarely got angry, and she almost never raised her voice. She wasn't yelling now, but if Calypso's death glare could physically destroy someone, Macy Quinn would be nothing but a pile of ash on the floor.

Lloyd eyed Parker expectantly as she moved around him, trying to find out what was going on between Macy and Calypso. She gave him a signal that she would be there in a minute and kept moving past him on her way through the crowd to where Macy and Calypso were. Before she could make it there, they split up. Macy made her way one way, Calypso made her way to the bathroom, and Parker followed.

It was a one-person powder room, and Parker made it right before Calypso closed the door, sliding in. "What was that?" Parker asked.

"What was what?" Calypso asked. The energy emanating from her was not good; her golden eyes flared with anger.

"Between you and Macy? What's going on?"

Calypso shifted her eyes away. "Nothing. I just . . . You know I don't like her. I don't trust her. I just don't want her coming around after today, okay?"

Parker drew Calypso in close to her. "Can you tell me the real reason?"

Calypso glared at Parker. "I just did. I don't like or trust her. Isn't that enough?"

"I have a feeling it's something deeper. Now, can you please tell me the real reason?" Parker tilted Calypso's face up to face hers.

"It's really nothing." Calypso dug in, refusing to go any further. It was obvious. She wouldn't say any more.

"Did she say something to you?" Parker was still going to try, though.

Calypso put her hands on Parker's chest. "Can we drop it for now? I want to enjoy the rest of today, and then the rest of my life with you." She adjusted Parker's ascot and used it to pull Parker closer to her.

Parker nodded and gave Calypso a light kiss. "You got it." She didn't want to ruin this day or have the memory of it be clouded by whatever beef Macy and Calypso had with each other. The gay community wasn't that big. Maybe they had mutual friends or dated the same girl in the past. Either way, it wasn't the time to push Calypso to talk about it. Calypso never talked about her past, and Parker never pushed.

Parker opened the door, and A.D. was standing there. "Y'all can't wait until you get home tonight?" She chided.

Parker grinned at her and shrugged. Calypso slipped out and back into the crowd as Parker held the door open for A.D.

"Nah, I don't need to go in there. I was just looking for you. Macy isn't feeling well. She's had a headache since before dinner. I'm gonna take her home."

"Hold up." Parker dragged A.D. into the powder room and locked the door.

"You know people are going to talk, you and me being in here." A.D. joked with her.

"I give zero fucks about what anyone thinks. Besides, everyone is very aware you aren't my type. What's going on between Macy and my wife?"

"Macy and Calypso?" A.D.'s expression was genuinely confused.

"Has Macy said anything about Calypso to you?"

"No. Not that I can recall. I understand she's not Calypso's biggest fan or anything. But she's never said anything specifically about her. Why?"

"I caught them arguing a few minutes ago, and Calypso is adamant that I stay away from Macy forever."

A.D. raised a concerned eyebrow. "I recognize Macy can be a little temperamental. But yeah, no. I don't know what's up."

Parker narrowed her eyes and nodded. "If you knew something you would tell me, right?"

A.D. approached her with a sense of caution as she moved to the door. "Yeah. And if you find the answer, let me know, too."

A.D. unlocked the door and walked out with Parker behind her.

Calypso wasted no time in sidling up to Parker and taking her hand to lead her to the dance floor. She'd obviously put aside whatever the fuck it was brewing between her and Macy as she peered up at Parker, and her energy finally settled.

"Are you okay?" Parker asked.

"Why wouldn't I be? I just married the love of my life." Calypso squeezed Parker's hand.

"I'm only doing a temperature check after all of that."

"As I said, I'm not letting her ruin our day. I'm chill."

"As you always are," Parker said. "I don't know how you do it."

"If I can't control it, why should I be upset about it?"

"Good point, my love. Good point." Parker kissed the top of Calypso's head.

16 FIRE ON FIRE

MAY 15

CALYPSO

The music changed to a slow song. Calypso took in Parker (her wife!) as she snaked her arms around Parker's neck and pulled her closer. Pictures were being snapped, and guests moved out of their way.

Calypso had begged Parker to let go of the "first dance" and song. She'd relented on a lot of the wedding traditions. Including having a wedding at all versus eloping. Having guests and a bridal party (she managed to get Parker to compromise on only one bridal attendant each). Calypso's rationale on the first dance was that she believed it was limiting to choose one song when she found so many that reminded her of their love. Parker let it go with that logic. Calypso had given the DJ a list of the songs she and Parker had sent to each other over the last three years, and the DJ did a good job of peppering those songs in. This particular song was Calypso's favorite for her and Parker, Sam Smith's "Fire on Fire."

As Parker spun Calypso around before bringing her back in, Calypso spotted Macy and A.D. talking in the corner. It appeared serious, as if they were arguing. Macy's body language spoke volumes as she hung her head and crossed her arms over her chest.

Calypso wasn't sad as she witnessed Macy huff and head to her table to grab her purse. A.D. put her jacket back on, and the two of them left. *Bye, Felicia.*

"What time is our flight tomorrow?" Calypso asked.

"A little after twelve noon," Parker answered. They were nose to nose, and Calypso wanted so badly to be skin-to-skin with her.

"How long are we required to stay?" Calypso murmured against Parker's lips.

"I think at least another hour."

The song changed to an upbeat dance song, and Parker escorted Calypso off the dance floor. Mrs. Harrington pulled Calypso away to meet and greet guests.

One of Mrs. Harrington's sisters came up to her and took her hand. "I'm Parker's Aunt Rebecca. Welcome to the family." Her snow-white hair swept up into a tight chignon, and her blue satin dress was obviously a designer piece.

Calypso smiled. "Thank you. The Harringtons have been wonderful. I'm very honored to be part of the family now." Mrs. Harrington beamed at Calypso's answer.

"Are you going to keep all of those tattoos?" Aunt Rebecca asked. Mrs. Harrington gave the impression she was uncomfortable and mumbled a reason to leave. Calypso thought it was to powder her nose.

Calypso flinched but kept her smile on her face. "Yes. I have no plans on removing them."

"What happens when you get old, dear?"

"My wrinkles will be pretty." Calypso forced herself to smile so hard it hurt. She couldn't remember the last time someone said anything so rude to her in her life.

Aunt Rebecca laughed. Thankfully, Parker swept in and put her hand on Calypso's back. "Aunt Rebecca! Thank you for making it."

"Parker, your new bride was just explaining her tattoos to me. They are very pretty and unique."

Calypso's brow crept up in skepticism. She didn't think that's what had happened.

She met cousins and family friends. It had never been made more clear to her the two different worlds in which she and Parker lived in. Many of Parker's family members spoke to her with what she perceived to be fake smiles and patronizing tones. She was used to that when she met these types. But Parker never made her feel that way. And neither did Teddy and his wife or Parker's parents. And for that, she was always grateful. But this group of aunts and uncles and cousins and friends of Parker's parents—it wasn't only Aunt Rebecca—it was almost all of them. "You are from New Orleans? That's a wild place. That explains your interesting style." "Your life certainly has changed since you got involved with Parker!" "What do those tattoos mean?" "Why did you choose black for your wedding day?" "How on Earth did you and Parker end up together?" "We never thought Parker was going to get married, much less to someone so . . . different."

The few other family functions Parker brought her to, she had Parker there to shield her from the comments and the judgment. Based on Mr. and Mrs. Harrington (does she still call them that now?), she perceived she was welcomed and didn't think their differences would be such a topic of conversation. Or as it seemed to be, by so many of these blue-blood snobs, such a scandal.

She took Parker to a group of her friends, various

creatives she had met in the art circles she spent her time in. They appeared to be far more accepting of Parker than Parker's friends and family seemed to be of her. They hugged Parker, complimenting her sense of style and noting that they understood why Calypso had all but disappeared.

After Parker disappeared from her side she spotted her talking to Lloyd Whitaker. Having met him a few times in passing she knew he was Parker's new pet project. She also suspected they were probably talking business because . . . well . . . Parker. Her only real complaint about Parker was the amount of time she focused on work. Parker commented that it wouldn't always be this way. She would slowly scale back eventually. Calypso brushed off her annoyance and let out a breath.

Calypso took advantage of the temporary downtime between talking to guests to grab a piece of cake and take it back to her seat, and kicked her heels off below the table.

"How's it going?" Xander pulled up a chair next to her, and Xochitl pulled up a chair on the other side.

"I'm ready to bust on out of here." Calypso took a bite of the cake. It was her favorite part of the whole wedding planning process—going to all the different bakeries until they found the *one.*

"Are you okay?" Xochitl expressed her concern.

"I'm tired. It's been a long day, and other than Teddy and Parker's parents, her family kind of sucks." She took another bite of the cake. "They're judgy and rude. And they have this perception of me that I'm some sort of gold-digging freak."

"Remember, this will probably be one of the only times you have to deal with most of them. And you didn't marry them. You married Parker." Xochitl put her arm around Calypso's shoulders.

"Most of the time I don't see the differences as being a big deal, but these people . . . I mean, they couldn't make it any more obvious what they think of me."

"Like Xochitl said—and she's an expert—don't pay them any mind. Parker's opinion is the only one that matters. And anyone can see, she loves you."

"I wonder, though, if she knew the truth about my past—"

"She would love you." Xochitl cut her off.

"It's just such a huge risk. And there are so many factors in play. It could ruin—"

"Now is not the time for that kind of thinking, though. Enjoy this day. Enjoy your wife." Xochitl stood up.

"Are you guys leaving?" Xochitl had her wrap, and Xander, who had given Calypso away during the ceremony, had quickly shed his tie and jacket once they entered the main house for the reception, only to have his jacket back on and his untied tie around his neck.

"Yeah. With you being gone on your swanky honeymoon, someone has to be at the shop early to handle business."

Calypso slipped her heels back on and stood up to hug them. "Thank you for being here, and thank you for being a part of this day. Such a huge part of it."

"We wouldn't have it any other way." Xander wrapped her up in a big bear hug, and Xochitl kissed each of her cheeks.

"See you when you get back. Go enjoy it." Xochitl whispered to her.

Calypso nodded and waited for them to walk out. Once they made it through the door, Calypso went down to where Lloyd and Parker sat chatting.

As predicted, they were talking about work. "I will have Juliana schedule you an interview for two weeks from Monday."

"You are *not* talking about work at our *wedding!*" Calypso teased Parker, leaning with her elbows on Parker's shoulders, kissing her on the tip of her nose.

"Not anymore. Just setting Lloyd up with an interview." Parker put her hands on Calypso's forearms.

"I'm sorry to have taken her away from you." Lloyd smiled at Calypso.

"It's to be expected with this one!" Calypso smiled at him. He was cute in a puppy dog kind of way, always sweet and always deferential when he dealt with Parker. Regardless of whether he was doing it to kiss Parker's ass for a shot to work at the firm.

Parker removed Calypso's arms from her shoulders and stood up. Lloyd followed suit, standing. Parker shook his hand. "See you in two weeks." She told him.

He nodded. "Thank you again, Parker. And congratulations! Go enjoy your honeymoon."

Parker nodded at him and turned to Calypso, intertwining their fingers. Calypso loved Parker's hands. The sensation of them on her, the shape of them, the fact that they were always warm and soft. "Are you ready to go?" Parker asked her.

"I've never been more ready to leave in my life." Calypso brushed her lips over Parker's lightly.

After making their rounds to say goodnight and goodbye, she held on tight to Parker's hand as they made their way to a waiting car to take them to their suite. She desperately wanted to be alone with Parker in the quiet of each other.

PART II

REVELATIONS

17 LIFE IS COMPLICATED

Macy

$\mathcal{M}$acy sat staring at her computer screen on her desk at the precinct. The cacophony of the space swirled around her. She'd been riding the desk for over four months now, and she hated life. At least she was getting to use all of the digital forensics training they sent her to. She spent her days looking at digital evidence to feed to the other detectives who got to go out and actually do the work. Honestly, she hadn't felt this demoralized since she left New Orleans.

She clicked the image and zoomed in on it. She zoomed back out, put her head in her hands, and stared at Brent's empty desk across from hers. After seven years of partnership, it was disconcerting to see that desk empty, knowing he was no longer her ride or die. He served two tours in Afghanistan only to die in a warehouse.

Looking at his desk took Macy back to that day only five short months ago to when he was killed. They were on a sting operation, and it all went south fast. The smell of the gunfire, the feeling of the bullet as it whizzed past her and hit Brent in the neck, were permanently ingrained within her senses. The blood as she tried to put pressure on it, and it continued to pump hard and fast, a hot and thick fountain pouring between her fingers, Macy had been in shootouts before. She was no stranger to this risk. She had even been present when other officers were killed in the line of duty. But this hit differently. It had been nearly two decades since she had lost someone she cared about so deeply.

As a matter of fact, nothing in her life had been going as she hoped.

She forced herself to return her attention back to the file in front of her. A plethora of documentation and police reports and a warrant. The buzzing of the lights overhead seemed way too loud. *When did they become so loud? Have they always been this way?* She sat back in her chair and closed the file. Uncertain about what to do with the information in front of her, she set it aside for now and clicked off her screen.

But Macy did miss Parker. They would wave hi whenever they ran across each other in the courthouse or ran into each other at various places. But that was it. No texts. No calls. No lunches. No face-to-face or one-on-one contact whatsoever.

A.D., who still hung out with Parker, mentioned that Calypso quit work as a tattoo artist and was spending her time volunteering with a queer youth shelter. Parker bought out the shop, so Calypso made residual income from the artists who rented space there—because, of course, Parker would do some grand gesture to show off. But the story went that the commute was a lot, and now that she had married Parker, she didn't have to work and could spend her time doing something more worthwhile. Shortly after the wedding, A.D. told her Parker seemed happy. To use A.D.'s words, "There's a calmness and peace I've never seen in Parker before. Not ever." A punch in the gut for Macy that led her to wind up divorced. She shouldn't feel that way about Parker when she had a whole wife. A whole awesome wife. A whole awesome wife who she wasn't in love with. Not the way she should be.

But anyway, good for Parker.

A.D. would try to bring the four of them together, but Parker explained to her that Calypso carried some weird hatred for Macy, and she didn't want to push it. She wanted to honor her wife's wishes. Whatever. Macy hated Calypso just as much. She had to stop lying to herself. She fucking hated her even more for taking her friend away. She was also hurt by Parker being so willing (so whipped, really) to cut her off.

A.D. asked Macy what Calypso's problem was with her, and Macy shrugged and said she didn't give a rat's ass. Calypso was known to run with a bad crowd. For fuck's sake, she met Parker by testifying in defense of Javier Ortiz Sanchez. She helped that dirtbag get away with human trafficking. Of *course* she would hate Macy.

When A.D. and Macy got married, Parker and Calypso were noticeably absent. It bothered A.D., but she didn't push the issue. After their wedding, A.D. kind of pulled away from Parker, though. In her opinion, Parker should have enough respect for their history and friendship to show up. A.D. said, "Some people are in your life for a reason, a season, or a lifetime. I thought Parker was a lifetime friend, but maybe she's merely a season after all." Macy kind of loved A.D. a little more after that sentiment, but still not enough. A.D.'s sentimental side got the best of her and she did try to have a few more get-togethers with Parker, and she did say that Parker didn't seem to be as happy. She was stressed. And apparently, Calypso was wearing on Parker's nerves. But there was no elaboration. And Macy didn't care. It was news to her ears.

It all came apart as she came in late one night after going and sitting in front of Parker's house. It was a day after Brent had been killed and she needed a friend. She missed Parker so much. She desperately wanted to feel close to her. She needed to see her, and not limited to a screen on her social media. She needed proximity. She had done it from time to time since she had been systematically cut out of Parker's life. But this time, A.D. had been looking at her location. She knew where she was. Macy let it out. Confessed her feelings for Parker and apologized to A.D. for being less than she deserved. A.D. was crushed, and it was over.

Macy left work early to meet with her divorce attorney. Her marriage to A.D. lasted all of a year and a half. It was the right thing to do. Cut A.D. loose and work on herself and get her life in order. A.D. deserved better. A.D. deserved to be loved in a way Macy couldn't seem to do.

She almost called Parker for a recommendation for a divorce attorney. But she hadn't spoken to Parker nor seen her since her wedding. After her confrontation with Calypso, she literally avoided Parker at all costs. Or rather, Parker avoided her.

She texted Lloyd instead. He ended up getting hired as a junior associate at Harrington and Harrington. She saw him and Parker walking into the courthouse together. He gave her a few numbers of some of the friends he met in law school. It wasn't going to be an ugly divorce. She and A.D. were on friendly terms. A.D. moved out. They still texted regularly, but it simply came down to the fact that they were better off as friends.

It was bittersweet that today she would be signing the final divorce agreement with her attorney. From there, it was all said and done. They didn't merge many assets when they married, so the process would be straightforward. She would no longer have A.D., and she no longer had Parker. And Brent was dead, too. So now she had no one. She was losing her grip on her life. She had zero control and it was frightening.

A.D. was letting Macy keep the condo (it was Macy's before they got married, but A.D. put a large chunk of her money into the interior renovations, not to mention the sweat equity she put in). Macy would pay her off for her share of the equity when she refinanced. A.D. got to keep the dog they adopted before they got married. Macy didn't have time for it.

A.D. took a job in New York. She said she wanted to start over somewhere else. Macy needed to start over, too. Her life was a mess. She was a mess. But she didn't have the slightest inclination as to where to begin to put the pieces back together.

From the attorney's office, Macy needed to meet with her department-assigned therapist. She was going to be riding the desk until the therapist cleared her. At this rate, she didn't think she would ever be cleared. She couldn't gather herself together to save her life. She couldn't see a way out of the hole she was in. It was too deep and too dark.

She landed in therapy, an escalation from the anger management group. She witnessed the life drain out of Brent's eyes. And the motherfucker who was responsible for it, when he was brought in for questioning, Macy cut the recorder and let herself into the interrogation room and beat him within an inch of his life for taking the one person she had left in her life away from her. The hole was increasingly deep. Increasingly dark. She couldn't fathom when it was she lost herself to this darkness. When it was she lost control.

Since then, Dr. Bennet, the therapist she had been

assigned to, wanted to keep her involved in therapy before letting her get back off the desk. In her professional opinion Macy held a lot of underlying trauma and needed a lot more than the standard minimal sessions and rubber stamp to go back out there. To be frank, the Dr. Bennet said that she believed Macy to be a danger to herself and the public and shouldn't have a firearm. She said it in therapist terms, which came across as much softer, but that's what she meant.

After scrawling her signature on the divorce papers, she drove across town and sat in the cozy (if bland) office of Dr. Bennet.

She sat on a soft loveseat, held a throw pillow, and darted her eyes over to the woman seated across from her. Dr. Brenda Bennet. A PhD in psychology, and old enough to be Macy's mother. Dr. Bennet was easy to talk to. Her grey hair was dyed dark brown, but the grey showed through at the roots. She wore cardigans, dress slacks, and flats to every appointment Macy had with her. Maybe the colors occasionally differed (how many cardigans in varying colors does one person actually need?). She wore little to no makeup, and her dark brown eyes always seemed to be tired. She was warm and easy for Macy to talk to. If Macy could have picked someone to be her mom, instead of the junkie that birthed her and then OD'd when Macy was barely three, she would pick Dr. Bennet.

"I signed my final divorce papers today." Macy opened with.

"And how do you feel about that?"

Macy shrugged. "I feel like it's the right thing. A.D. deserves better than what I can give."

"Why do you say that?"

"I love her. She's wonderful. But I'm not *in love* with her. She deserves to be with someone who loves her."

"When did you realize that?"

"I think I always realized. I just didn't want to admit it."

"Who would you say would be your support system?"

"What do you mean?"

"Like friends, family, colleagues that you could turn to?"

Macy paused. She opened her mouth to answer, but nothing came out.

"How's your relationship with your family?"

"My dad is . . . I don't know. I never met him, and he's not on my birth certificate. My mom . . . she's dead. I spent two years in and out of various foster homes before my grandparents finally took me. I haven't even spoken to them in I don't even know how long. They might even be dead by now, too. I don't really have any friends. I have acquaintances. But not friends. No one that I am particularly close to, anyway. Except Brent. We were partners for seven years. He was like the only person I trusted. I used to have a friend. Parker. But her wife didn't like me hanging around with her, so she kinda cut me out. I guess A.D. and I are still friends. I guess I can still rely on her if I really need someone."

"Would you say you have trust issues or a hard time letting people in?"

A tear slid down her cheek. She wiped it with the back of her hand. "Maybe?"

"What about abandonment issues?"

"Probably."

Dr. Bennet paused. "Let's do an activity, Macy. Can you play along with what we are going to do?"

"Yeah. Sure."

"Close your eyes. Picture yourself as a child again." Dr. Bennet paused to allow Macy to catch up. "Picture yourself outside. You are blowing bubbles." She paused again. "Take a deep breath in. Slow and deliberate."

Macy saw herself in the yard of her grandparents' home in Metairie. She breathed in the humid heat and the bright blue sky and hot sun. She was sitting alone on the swing that hung from the branch of a large magnolia tree. Her grandmother was looking out the window at her. Her grandfather was smoking in the chair in the garden. Neither of them was particularly interested in what she was doing. She took a deep breath as instructed.

"Now, exhale—but as you exhale, you are blowing the biggest bubble ever."

The bubble floated in front of Macy, rainbow colors iridescent in the relentless glare of the sun.

"Now, picture yourself in that bubble. You are floating. Up and over everything. You're safe here. Protected. But you are high above, looking back down. You can see things from here that you've never noticed or seen. Other perspectives. Other ideas. But most importantly, you see yourself. You can see things as you've never seen them before. Another side."

Macy looked down and saw her failures. She saw her first love. She saw herself leaving New Orleans. She saw Parker. She saw Calypso. She saw A.D. walking out their door for the last time. She felt the heat of her tears as they coursed down her cheeks.

"You see the paths others have chosen to take. You see that their choices are not yours to control, change, or intercede in. You only need to see your own path and decisions. You can see from above, that you can't change the past. But you can love yourself through this time and accept your decisions and yourself with love and compassion because you are safe up here. You are safe in your bubble. Macy, what do you see from your bubble?"

"I see all of my mistakes. I see all of the wrongs done to me. All. of the wrongs I've done to others."

"Do you see anything good?"

Macy choked out a sob. "I don't." Her eyes fluttered open.

"I want you to think about that. Journal about it. Also,

write down how you feel when you start to find yourself close to someone."

Macy nodded, grabbed a tissue, and dabbed her eyes. She wished she could climb into that bubble and float away for real. She was so tired of hurting. Of making mistakes. Of being left behind.

* * *

WHEN SHE LEFT, she went home to her empty home Quiet, lifeless, and bare without A.D. and the things she took with her. No dog. No wife. Even the wedding pictures had been taken down and placed in a box somewhere.

Her whole adult life, she had kept a clean space. But since A.D. left, cleaning was not a priority. Take-out cartons littered the coffee table, and the sink was full of dishes. It matched her insides right now. Messy. Complicated. Over-whelming. It could wait.

Macy curled up in the recliner and opened her social media. She saw posts of Parker and Calypso going to a benefit dinner for a non-profit that helped inmates get their convictions overturned. She knew Parker occasion-ally picked up pro bono cases for them. And Harrington and Harrington donated heavily to such causes. Parker was still hot as fuck. Calypso's appearance resembled an ex-con with all those gaudy tattoos. Someone who bene-fited from that organization. It didn't matter how expen-sive her dress was, or how many Tiffany diamonds Parker gifted her with. On the plus side, there had been rumors that Parker and Calypso were not so solid. It's amazing what information you can get from certain people with the right amount of pressure. Calypso apparently lamented it in her shop one day. It was overheard and reported back to Macy by a CI. It wasn't just Parker who was expressing unhappiness. Macy relished the information, though.

Macy closed the app and texted A.D. "Hey. I just wanted to inform you that I signed off. Everything is pretty much official."

A.D. messaged back immediately. "Be that as it may, I don't regret it. I still love you, and I'm always going to be there for you. No matter what."

Macy smiled and fought the tears that welled up. "I'm sorry I couldn't have been a better wife. You deserve so much more than I could ever offer. But I will always be there for you, too."

A.D. hearted the message.

Macy closed the messaging app and tossed her phone on the end table next to the recliner.

She couldn't sit in the silence any longer. She turned on the news for background noise. She couldn't care less about anything being covered. She turned it back off. The silence was deafening, though. And her thoughts were too loud. Her loneliness palpable. She wanted—no, she *needed* the presence of another person. She yearned to love someone and be loved in return. She still wanted Parker. And she hated that she still wanted her so badly.

She couldn't understand what Parker saw in Calypso. Why would she go from not wanting to be in a committed relationship to being with Calypso? It was absolute insanity to her. She'd spent the last five-plus years trying to make sense of it, to no avail.

Macy turned the television back on and made her way to the table with her work bag.

She sat at the table and pulled out the file she had been working on before she left for the day, studied the image on the printout, and decided it was time to call Parker. Without

Brent, she needed Parker. And this was going to be her in back into Parker's life.

18 MAYBE IT'S TIME TO LET IT GO

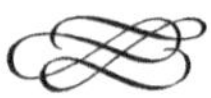

AUGUST 2

PARKER

*P*arker sat in the conference room she and Lloyd had taken over as a "war room" for the high profile defense case they were handling for a B-list celebrity who a decade ago starred in his own popular sitcom, Will Williamson, who was the person of interest in the mysterious disappearance of his on-again, off-again girlfriend who he met at a strip club.

"Do you have exhibit thirty-two?" she asked Lloyd. He had become her favorite person, aside from Calypso and her father. He was smart, capable, and dedicated to his career. She couldn't ask for anything more. He also hung on every single word Parker said, and did whatever she asked of him. Best decision ever, in her opinion, was to push him through the interview process.

"Yeah. Hold on." He went to the box next to him and began sifting through its contents.

Parker pulled her tie off and laid it on the table, stretched her neck, and called her assistant, Juliana, into the room. "Can you order me a spicy miso ramen, no meat, extra egg? Lloyd, do you want anything?"

"Spicy miso ramen *with* meat." Lloyd didn't even take a break from his task; he still sorted through the banker's box where the evidence was stored.

"Got it. Anything else?" Juliana asked.

"Two black coffees."

Lloyd popped up with the exhibit in his hand. "This is going to be a long night."

A small smile from Juliana in Lloyd's direction had him frozen in place before she turned and walked out.

Parker eyed Lloyd as he stared at Juliana's ass as she walked out. "Quit it. You're going to land this firm in a lawsuit. If you like her, ask her out like a normal human."

"I don't have time for a relationship, seeing as I'm *your* bitch." Lloyd joked. "And I'm not going to hit it and quit it with someone in the office. And I recall in my onboarding here, you told me no interoffice relationships. So, meanwhile, I do nothing but look."

"Good. I'm glad you paid attention. She's the best assistant I've ever had. I would die if she quit or I had to fire her."

"How many assistants *have* you had?"

"Just one other."

"What happened to her?"

"I fired her. She lied about a few things and tried to cover it up. I have zero tolerance for lying. And then lying on top of lying to cover your tracks."

"Damn. Was she stupid or something?"

Parker gave a humph as she raised an eyebrow. She pulled out her phone and texted Calypso. "I am going to be late. Don't wait for me for dinner. Don't wait up. I'm sorry. xoxo The xoxo was sent out of habit. Calypso and Parker were not seeing eye to eye. They hadn't seen eye to eye in a while. Ending it might be the only option at this point. Though Parker refused to quit anything, and didn't handle mistakes well either. For months, the atmosphere had been marked by constant silent treatments, arguments, snapping, and a lot of pretending in public. Including last night's fundraiser dinner, where the entire drive there was silent, as was the drive back. At the fundraiser, though, she held Calypso's hand as they walked and made conversation with everyone at the table. No one looking from the outside in would have the slightest clue that Parker and Calypso were anything but living their happily ever after.

Calypso's reply was "K." Parker rolled her eyes and shoved the phone away from her.

Thirty minutes later, Juliana placed to-go ramen in front of Parker and Lloyd. "Anything else?" She asked.

Lloyd smiled at her. "Parker?" He asked, not taking his eyes off of Juliana.

"I fucking hate this case." Parker leaned back in her chair. "No, Juliana. Unless you can fix my personal life," she grumbled.

"You and Calypso are perfect for one another. You will sort it out." Juliana leaned against the door frame.

"No, you don't hate this case. You love this shit. If you weren't married to Calypso, you would be married to this job." Lloyd tossed out.

"Calypso tells everyone I *am* married to my job and she's merely my mistress."

"That's why I'm single." He was still looking at Juliana, not at Parker.

"That's why I was single for so long. And I'm probably on

the road to being single again." Parker rubbed her hands down her face and opened the chopsticks.

"Married life isn't what you thought?" File forgotten, Lloyd moved to sit across from Parker, opening his container, before grabbing a pair of chopsticks from the bag.

"Parker, go home. All of this will be here tomorrow." Juliana gestured to the files and boxes. "Prioritize Calypso. She deserves it."

Parker paused. "I mean . . . it's been tough these last two months. How are you going to take her side? I pay you."

"What do you mean, tough time?" Lloyd asked.

Juliana rolled her eyes. "Well, I'm going to go home, then." She was teasing in her exasperation, but what she said struck a chord with Parker.

"Calypso is getting frustrated with the time I spend at work. She assumed once we got married, I would scale back a little. To be fair, I did promise her that I would once we got married. Especially since I hired you. And she's starting to feel very isolated and alone. Moreso since I paid off the loan for her business and she stopped working regularly. Now she just manages, and most of the time, she does it from home, because Xander takes care of everything. She goes in when a regular client requests her, or she goes and volunteers at the shelter. But really, she just sits at home alone. And her biggest complaint is the lack of sex. I work eighteen hours a day, sometimes. I'm not always in the mood for that. That last part is probably TMI."

With a shrug, Lloyd gave her a generic answer, "All couples seem to go through growing pains."

"This is a whole ordeal. And it seems like I can't do anything right. The only thing she wants is more time. And I should be honored. But she literally just said that she feels so alone, she would rather end up divorced and be single. She's tired of me coming home only long enough to sleep. Or when I am home, I'm in the office working."

"She threw out the D word?"

"She did. She used to wait up for me. Now she's asleep before I get home. All we seem to do is argue, for months now. And it's been awful. I'm not sure how much more I can take. I suggested we go to counseling. She said no. The only thing that's going to fix this is if I step back. Oh, and she thinks I may have something going on with Juliana. Oh, and periodically, I keep getting mail asking me to ask Calypso who she really is. Or something saying that she's not who she says she is. If I question her on it, she gets all weird and pissed off. It *is* a legitimate question, as she *never* talks about her past. But for me, it's the assumption that I would be having an affair with my secretary. How cliche."

Lloyd nearly choked on his ramen. "Do you have a thing for her—with her?" He asked around a mouthful of noodles.

With narrowed eyes in Lloyd's direction, Parker said, "It would be more believable that I had something going on with you, given I seem to spend every waking minute with you lately. If I were going to have an affair, it wouldn't be with someone who works for me. Calypso seems to think there is a correlation between Juliana's promotion and my time at work increasing. She feels there is a disparity in emotional effort. She's giving her all, and I'm giving a frac-tion, which is where the Juliana conspiracy comes in. So, between my not giving her enough time, the jealousy, and the perceived lack of effort, my inability to even ask her a question about her life in New Orleans, and she says I'm controlling and erasing her identity because I won't go to some stupid gallery openings for her friends or allow her to buy their awful art, and the D word being thrown around, yeah. I'm not sure we are going to make it. To be honest, it might be the right thing to do at this point. I mean, it was good when it was good, but maybe the experiment is over. I'm not cut out for this domestic life."

Cocking his head, Lloyd set his container down, wiped his mouth on a napkin. "I would think this could be easily cleared up with a discussion. Maybe take some time off and spend it somewhere quiet. I can field anything that comes up. You two can talk it out. Take a long weekend or something."

Parker crossed her arms over her chest, shaking her head in disbelief. "Oh. And she said I treat her like hired help, since she's quit going to work."

"Well, do you?"

"Fuck off. I don't. But for fuck's sake she lives in a nice house. She has anything and everything she could ask for. She wants for nothing. We do have a housekeeper, but I've reduced her hours to two days a week. Calypso is home *all the time*. I'm not asking too much for her to cook a dinner once in a while or run the vacuum between Karen's days. She says I don't love her, I control her. She hides behind her past traumas but won't talk to me about them. She doesn't trust me."

"What do you think the issue is with her past that she won't talk about?"

"That's the thing. I have no idea. She won't be honest with me about it. I tell her that if she can't trust me as her wife, she can't trust anyone. She tells me it's too painful to talk about and it's no longer relevant. And honestly, it's wearing on me. She thinks I'm fucking Juliana; she won't talk to me. She obviously has no trust or faith in me. That hurts. Why the fuck are we even married? Honestly, I should do right by her and let her go. As much as I love her, I'm not able to give her what she actually wants."

"You aren't able to, or you don't *want* to?"

Parker's eyes went wide. She was speechless; because

when you put it that way, she morphed into the world's worst wife.

Lloyed went to ask another question, but Parker's phone rang, and she glared down at the screen, annoyed—it was Macy's name on the screen. "What the hell?" She mumbled.

"What?" Lloyd asked.

"Macy Quinn is calling me." Lloyd mouthed a *what the fuck?* as Parker answered it. "Hey. What's up?"

There was a pause on the other end of the line. Parker waited as Macy took a breath. "Hey. Um. I know we haven't talked or . . . any real contact in a long-ass time. But, can you meet for lunch tomorrow?"

Parker remained silent.

"Please. I need to talk to you. In person."

"I'm in court tomorrow. But the day after?" Parker's voice was wary. "Is everything ok?"

"Yeah. Kind of. I mean, a lot has happened. Brent died. He was killed in front of me during a raid. And A.D. and I are divorced. But no, yeah. I just . . . I need to talk to you about something. And I would rather do it in person."

Parker exhaled. Humiliation painting her to be a total ass. She was failing everyone at this point, and for what? "Okay. Can you meet me at Charlie's?" The lunch place they used to meet up at before Parker cut her out.

"Yeah. I will see you there around noon."

Parker felt bad for Macy. They were good friends until Calypso demanded that Macy be cut off. And she couldn't even tell Parker why. Now her friend, actually two of her friends, were iced out, and she didn't even have a clue they had split up and gotten divorced, or that the only other person in Macy's life had been killed in front of her. "Mace, you gonna be good until then?"

"Yeah. I will be. I'll see you in a couple of days."

* * *

PARKER DRAGGED herself home around midnight. She made her way to the bedroom, where it was pitch dark, and Calypso was curled up sleeping peacefully as she had been for a while. She missed how Calypso used to wait up for her. Parker slipped past her and into the bathroom to get ready for bed, trying to be quiet so she wouldn't wake her.

Parker could never deny how much Calypso loved her until recently. Calypso would do little things all the time—from bringing Parker home-cooked meals to the office when she worked late, to leaving her little notes and drawings, or buying little trinkets for her. Or surprising Parker with romantic little day trips or activities on Parker's rare days off. Or waiting up for Parker to spend some time with her. This last week, well, fuck. The last several weeks, it had been anything but. Parker would come home bone tired, and Calypso would be sound asleep.

Thoughts tumbled around her head. The most concerning one being, that maybe she was pulling the strings and controlling Calypso. She wore the clothes that Parker picked out and bought for her. She went to the formal functions with her. She hosted dinner parties for Parker. She did those things out of love for Parker. But Parker was slowly erasing everything that made Calypso her unique and beautiful self.

After getting out of her suit and into pajamas, and brushing her teeth, Parker stared at herself in the glare of the mirror, running her hand over her face. All Calypso wanted was some time. And for Parker to do some of the things *she* loved with her. Was it such a horrible request? Calypso wanted time with her because she *loved* her. Parker stayed put in the bathroom, bracing herself on the counter, trying to think of how she *could* scale back to give Calypso this one simple wish. If she couldn't accommodate this, she had no business being married. She would have to do right by Calypso and end this.

When she came out, Calypso was sitting up in the center of the bed on her knees, looking at Parker. "Come here," Calypso demanded, her voice soft and low. Calypso had shed the tank top and panties that she often slept in. She knew she would be tired tomorrow (today, technically), but she didn't care. Calypso was worth it. She would give Calypso this time. She would figure out how to give her more time. Be more present.

Parker crawled onto the bed in front of Calypso.

On her knees in front of Calypso, she let her hands travel from Calypso's hips, up her waist, and to Calypso's breasts, letting her thumbs travel over her nipples as her lips met Calypso's. She couldn't think of a time that they had even kissed in the last week. It had been arguments, silent treatments, and hurt. The kiss began soft, but built with the urgency and want to bury the past few months.

Calypso tugged Parker closer to her so she could pull the shirt over Parker's head, her lips travelling down Parker's neck and chest before taking one of Parker's nipples into her mouth and giving it a slight bite. A low moan escaped Parker's lips. She had been dog tired when she got home, but was fully awake now.

Pajama pants shed, Calypso pushed Parker back down the bed. "You work so very hard," Calypso murmured as she nudged Parker's knees apart and positioned herself between them, lowering herself to kiss Parker again. "I think tonight, someone needs to take care of you."

Calypso's hand traveled down lightly, stroking Parker. With Calypso's very skilled fingers moving against her, Parker let herself relax in the hands of the woman she loved.

Calypso had long ago discovered Parker's body and her

responses. She stopped right as Parker was at the edge. Parker's breath was shallow. "Calypso . . ." Parker refused to beg for the longest time, but since Calypso's favorite game was to take her to the edge and leave her there, she relented and learned Calypso wanted to listen to her pleas.

"Yes, Parker." Calypso purred, a very wicked smile on her face in the moonlight that filtered into the room. Her fingertips glided whisper-light over Parker's body.

A whimper escaped Parker.

"I know what you want." Calypso taunted. "Patience, my love."

Lips trailed lightly over Parker's body, the whisper and heat of her breath teasing, as she dipped lower, and skipped over where Parker wanted her to be most. Calypso traveled down Parker's inner thigh before coming back up and finally giving Parker what she had been begging for. Parker's hands gripped Calypso's hair as her silky black locks spilled over Parker's thigh and belly. She needed this. She had to see that Calypso was still in this. In that very second, it was decided that as soon as this case ended, she would give Calypso what she was asking for: time.

When Calypso finally let her come, Parker pulled Calypso up to her and kissed her, holding her to her body as close as she could. "I love you," Parker whispered against Calypso's lips.

"I know you do. And I'm sorry. I want this to work. I love you. I don't want to lose you." Calypso's eyes glistened in the dim moonlight that spilled in through the windows.

"You won't lose me. We will work through this together." Parker kissed Calypso on her forehead and wiped a tear that escaped Calypso's eye with her thumb. "I will scale back. I promise. I have to be in court tomorrow, but it shouldn't be for long. I will come home right after, and we can spend the whole afternoon and evening together."

Calypso's eyes lit up. "Really?"

"Yeah. We can go spend the afternoon on the beach, or wine tasting, or at that animal sanctuary you always talk about, so you can hug cows or whatever." Parker smiled as Calypso lay her head back down on the pillow beside her.

"I really don't care if we just stay home. We don't *have* to do anything at all. I only want some time with you."

"We will spend more time together. I promise. I will work on this. I will make more of an effort. It's not like you ask a lot of me. I will do better."

* * *

AUGUST 3

Famous last words: I will do better.

The next day, while Parker sat in court wrapping up another case, she got a text from Lloyd. The Williamson case hit crisis mode. The body of Will's girlfriend had been found inside Joshua Tree National Forest, and it was an apparent homicide, with over thirty stab wounds.

Parker responded with one word, "Fuck."

Lloyd continued. "Will's been brought in for questioning. He's, of course, asked for you."

"Let them know I will be there soon." Parker closed her eyes and sat back in her chair. She promised Calypso she would be home early, but now it wasn't going to happen. She held her breath as she texted Calypso: "I'm so sorry. I know I promised you I would come home early, but there's been an emergency."

"Isn't there always?" The response came fast. Too fast. Calypso had been prepared for Parker to let her down. Again.

She didn't have to be a mind reader to be clear on the fact

that Calypso was beyond incensed. She fixed on those stupid three dots as they appeared and disappeared several times, but nothing more came over. It was as if the night before didn't happen. They regressed right back to where they sat for the last few months. "Fuck my life," Parker whispered under her breath.

And when she got home late that evening after meeting with Will, talking to the prosecutor, and getting the arraignment scheduled, Calypso wasn't home.

Parker rummaged in the refrigerator for leftovers, warmed up a plate of pasta, and texted Calypso: "Where are you?"

"Out with friends. Don't wait up." she texted in response.

They weren't going to make it.

19 A MATTER OF PERSPECTIVE

August 3

CALYPSO

*P*arker didn't even bother to respond to her text. She didn't even ask her to come home so they could talk about it. That's what hurt most. Calypso sat looking at her phone. Drama dots indicating a response or attempted response didn't even appear.

Well. Fuck.

"What's going on?" Xochitl asked her as the bartender set two espresso martinis before them.

"I love Parker. She's my world. My life. I never thought I would feel like this for anyone. But she . . . I don't think she feels the same. My life revolves around her. But I think she only wants me around to save money on the housekeeper."

"Don't you think you're being a bit overdramatic?" Xochitl's eyebrow raised as she took a sip of her cocktail.

The chilled glass sat in Calypso's hand, ready to drink, but she just stared at Xochitl, mouth agape. "Whose side are you on?"

"The side of your marriage. You know, marriages have ups and downs. You will get along, and then you won't. You won't feel seen or heard, and then she won't either. It happens. You need to be at home with your wife right now, talking this out. Running away from discussing this isn't helping."

"I'm not running away. I'm getting out of the house so I can process this. Xochitl, I'm alone all fucking day. I didn't get married to sit alone in Parker's house all day while she works. I volunteer. I go into the shop once in a while. But honestly, I might as well just be another painting on her wall. An object that she owns and gets out when she's bored and has a few minutes of downtime."

"Have you expressed this to Parker?"

"Yes. Maybe not effectively. I think it came across as more whining and begging than anything else. I don't know how to talk about these things without sounding ungrateful. I mean, we've only had sex once in the last several months. We barely kiss. She barely touches me. She used to struggle to keep her hands off me. I just want to feel like I matter to her. It's all promises, and then there's always—literally *always*—some sort of crisis that *only she* can handle at work. It's emotionally exhausting." There was no controlling the tears that streamed down her cheeks.

Xochitl's arm went over Calypso's shoulder, and she drew her in, handing her a napkin to wipe her tears. "You're going to hate me for this next question."

"Just let it fly. I can't feel any worse." Calypso sat back up, using her phone as a mirror to fix any smudges her tears may have caused.

"What have you done to show her that she matters to you?"

"I stayed up late last night so I could . . . uh . . . help her relieve some tension." Calypso had never been one to talk openly about her sex life, no matter how close her friends were.

"That's it? Just once in . . . what did you tell me? Months?"

Calypso shrugged. "She wasn't trying at all. I got tired of being the only one making an effort. I think accusing her of sleeping with her assistant didn't help either."

Xochitl shook her head. "I would presume not. Calypso, *why* would you think that, much less accuse her of that?"

"The stupid thing is, I know Parker would never cheat on me. Especially not with someone who works for her. She would be terrified of a lawsuit."

"So why did you say it?"

"I was mad. I was feeling alone. She wasn't fucking me. Or even trying to. So in the heat of it . . . I just threw it out there." Calypso finally brought her drink to her lips, downing almost all of it in one large gulp. The heat of the alcohol soothed her as it went down.

"Did you ever apologize for any of that? Try to talk it out?"

"She's never apologized for how she's made me feel. Why do I have to be the one to say it?"

"It sets the ball in motion. It will open the door to dialogue. Tell her you're sorry. Be the better person. Set the tone. Ask her what she feels she needs from you. You tell her what you need from her."

With her head heavy in her hands, her heart a ton of bricks in her chest, she let out a giant sigh. "I don't want to go home tonight. Can I crash at your place, if I do what you recommend tomorrow? I need to be away for a night."

"You know I'm never gonna tell you no, and neither is Xander. Even though the right thing is for you to go home to your wife and have a conversation."

Yeah. Yeah. Easier said than done.

* * *

IT HAD BEEN three hours since Calypso collapsed on the bed in Xochitl and Xander's guest room. For three straight hours, she stared at the ceiling, memorizing the crack above her, replaying her conversation with Xochitl over and over. Her heartbeat was hard and fast and loud in her ears. She regretted choosing espresso martinis as she lay there wide awake. She was forced to dwell on feeling stupid and immature for not going home.

With a groan, exasperated, exhausted, she rolled out of bed and scribbled a thank you note for Xochitl. It was time to go home to her wife. Sleeping without Parker next to her wasn't right. And of course those damn espresso martinis didn't help either.

When she finally got home and tiptoed up the stairs, she kicked off her shoes and crawled into bed next to her wife. This was where she belonged. Kitty jumped in the bed and curled up at Calypso's feet.

Wanting more than anything to snuggle up to Parker, but she nevertheless held back. If she woke Parker, it would make matters worse. She got as close as she could without disturbing her and watched her even breathing. Her face softened in sleep. Calypso knew she had to make things right. She couldn't live without Parker.

Calypso made her plan to right the ship. She would cook Parker's favorite dinner tomorrow. She would pour a bottle of wine. And she would apologize. She would get the ball rolling and set the tone like Xochitl suggested. She hoped Parker wanted to make this work, too.

20 THE TRUTH COMES OUT

PARKER

The next afternoon, Parker walked into Charlie's. Macy sat alone in a booth by herself toward the back.

Parker slid into the seat across from Macy and undid her plaid suit jacket. Macy hadn't changed: her red hair in a neat ponytail, fitted jeans, a tight plain white t-shirt, and a black blazer, with very little makeup. The only difference was that there was no holstered gun under her jacket. Parker heard along the way that Macy was riding a desk, but never thought to even ask about why.

The waitress dropped off a glass of water in front of Parker. "Can I get you anything to drink?"

"Black coffee, please." Parker stared at Macy, expectant. Between Calypso not coming home last night until the wee hours of the morning and being dragged away from her desk, her patience dipped below very little.

Macy smiled. "You don't change."

A half smile was all she could muster. She'd already fucked up with her wife. She needed to try a little harder with her friend. "So what happened with Brent?" Parker asked. "If you want to talk about it. You don't have to."

"We were raiding a warehouse outside of downtown, where we were tipped off that illegals were being stored for trafficking purposes. They were tipped off that we were coming. They opened fire. They got Brent in the neck. I dragged him behind a barrier and held him while he bled out. I tried to put pressure but..." Parker watched as Macy's eyes went glassy.

"I'm sorry." Parker patted the top of Macy's hand.

Macy dabbed at her eyes with the napkin and shook her head. "I'm working through it. The department put me on desk duty until I complete therapy. And this was all while A.D. and I were ending things. It just . . . Yeah. It's been tough. But I'm okay. I'm gonna be fine." Macy shook her head and put a smile on her face. "I'm just happy you came."

Parker eyed her warily as she perused the menu. "So what's up?"

"How are you?" Macy asked.

Her phone lit up with several notifications from the prosecutor on Will's case, and then from Will's manager, and they kept coming. She didn't have time to waste. "Look. You're aware my wife isn't a fan of me spending time with you. You asked me to meet you. I'm here. Why?" Parker closed her menu and set it on the table. She wasn't angry with Macy so much as impatient. She had no choice but to return to the office, leaving her no time for theatrics or drama. Will's arraignment didn't go well, and he was being held without bail. She had a lot of work to do.

Exhaling, she reached into her bag and pulled out a file. "I have been torn about this for days now, questioning whether or not to give this to you." She pushed it across the table to Parker.

Parker took it. "What is this?"

"Just open it." Macy clasped her hands together, elbows on the table, and locked her eyes directly on Parker's.

Parker opened it. The first thing she took note of was a mugshot of a younger Calypso. She wasn't tattooed. Her hair was bleached platinum, making her honey-gold eyes stand out more. "I'm already familiar with the fact that Calypso has a past." Parker went to close the file.

"There's more. Keep reading." Macy slapped her hand down on the open file to keep it open.

As Parker skimmed, her stomach dropped. Calypso Boudreaux wasn't her real name. Her real name was listed as Calliope Nikanidis. Calypso previously told Parker she "saw some things" when they first met. She didn't say she had committed murder. She stabbed and killed her girlfriend at the time. She was able to plead self-defense and got off completely.

Parker kept reading. She was also a person of interest in another murder. She allegedly killed someone else, a woman who was also linked to her romantically. A month before the hurricane that forced her to evacuate the city hit. She disappeared in the aftermath of the storm. She was still wanted. A long outstanding warrant sat in the file. This woman was reportedly stabbed, exactly like her previous ex, in the same pattern of injuries. Exact same number of stab wounds. Parker had defended enough murder cases that she recognized exactly what she was looking at. And it wasn't good.

Acid swirled in Parker's stomach, and breathing suddenly became difficult. The waitress approached and put Parker's coffee in front of her. She opened her mouth, ready to ask

Parker if she had selected what she wanted to order. A wave of Parker's hand dismissed her. No wonder Calypso never wanted to talk about it. She was a fucking felon. On the lam. For murder.

So much fell into place. This confirmed it all. The exhaustion of all the demands, professionally and personally, were caving in on her. Calypso's consistent refusal to even discuss a sliver of her life in New Orleans, writing it off as too painful, struck her as a form of rejection. And here, in this stack of papers in a folder in front of her, was all she needed to know. It was a key in a lock. It confirmed everything. This was her closure to this mistake of a marriage. An out. She was done. So fucking done.

"Parker, I'm sorry." Macy's voice was quiet.

"How long have you had this?" Hands shaking, she set the file down. She opened it and scanned the information again. It clicked. It really did. All of these facts. All of the lies came to light.

"Just this week. Riding the desk means I also cover the phones. So, I answered a call and it happened to be from New Orleans. When I started taking the information, I realized who he was talking about. I broke protocol in a big way and had him send me the file. He told me that he got some sort of a tip about this case and the suspect was here. It just so happened that I was the one who took the call since . . . you know . . . riding the desk and all. I'm taking a huge risk giving you this information."

"Who has knowledge of this?"

"No one. But I have a duty to report it. I wanted to tell you first, though."

21 SORRY NOT SORRY

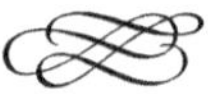

AUGUST 4

MACY

acy studied Parker's face. Parker always carried herself as unflappable. She had never seen Parker thrown. Parker's face grew pale, and tears made her eyes glassy. Macy's hand traveled across the table and rested on Parker's. Parker didn't move. Her head tilted to look Macy in the eye.

"Is this a joke?" Parker choked out. "Because if it is, it's not funny. Not at all."

"Parker, I wish it was. I do. I would never fuck with you like that. I care about you too much to do that to you. I just . . . I was as surprised as you are. Believe me. When the file came over, I looked at it three times. I couldn't believe what I was seeing. It was crazy."

"I can't. There's no way. There's *no* way. Are you sure this is accurate? There's not some mix-up?"

"When I got the file, I was as shocked as you are. It makes sense, the name Calypso. She who hides secrets."

"Answer me, Macy. I don't have time for suppositions."

"There's always room for error. You know that. Your whole career is based on it. But no. In this case, they are absolutely certain. Just look through it. Her fingerprints were on the murder weapon. Her hair was at the scene. Her DNA under the vic's fingernails. Her history. I highly doubt there's an error or fault in this."

Parker was stiff and coiled with her anger. "I need to go. I can't . . . I'll talk to you later." She set the file back on the table and got up.

"Wait. Parker. Where are you going?"

"I need to go talk to my wife. Well, I guess she's not technically my wife now, seeing as it's all a false pretense. A facade. She's not even who she said she is." Parker's voice was unsteady and a pitch above her normal, even-keeled, almost sultry voice.

"Sit back down. You are not in any position to talk to her right now." Macy tapped the table lightly. "And with as angry as you are, I highly doubt it's even safe for you to drive."

Parker sat back in the booth, resigned. "What are you going to do with this information?"

"I have to do the right thing. I wanted to give you a heads-up first, though."

"When?"

"I can sit on this for a few days. But I eventually have to let them take her in."

"Let me . . ." Parker trailed off. She seemed so lost and fragile. Cocky Parker was all she ever let anyone see. This version of Parker coming unglued was utterly fascinating to Macy.

"Parker, you can't hide her. You can be disbarred for harboring a fugitive."

"No shit, Macy. I'm not fucking stupid." Parker's sorrow turned back to anger.

"I know you aren't stupid. But you're *married* to her. I don't know if you have intentions to hide her. I don't have a clue as to what your intentions are."

"I can't stay with her. Not after this. I thought it was weird that I've been getting anonymous letters in the mail, implying that she is not who she says she is. When I question her, she gets angry and shuts me down." Parker gave a subtle shake of her head and ran a hand through her hair, messing up her smooth pompadour. A lock of hair fell over her forehead. It was a struggle for Macy to resist the impulse to smooth it away. She hated to see Parker distressed, but she had to give her this information. Parker needed this information—she was saving Parker by giving her this file.

"Are you going to tell her? Or are you going to let us just surprise her?"

"I can't not tell her. I can't just tell her to get the fuck out without explaining why. I just can't . . ." Parker opened the file again and examined the picture of a younger Calypso. Macy studied Parker as she traced the picture with her finger. She closed the file and slammed it on the table. "Motherfucker. Of all the women I could have fallen in love with . . ." Parker's voice trailed off as she shook her head.

Pausing for a beat, Macy pondered if she should ask the question that had been brewing in her mind for days now. She decided now was as good a time as any. "What was it about her? She's so . . . not—"

"Not what?" Arms crossed, Parker sat back, her evil eye piercing through Macy's soul. Macy wanted to die being in that glare. Parker may be angry with Calypso, but she still possessed some drive to protect her.

"I mean . . . Just to be frank, when you met her, she was kind of rough . . ."

"Macy, what in the absolute fuck? Why are you asking me this?" Parker snapped, exasperated.

"Because I never understood it. I always suspected there was more to her. I just had a sense. And normally, you're the kind of person who can sense bullshit a mile away. Something about her blinded you. I'm trying to put it all together. It's what I do. I figure things out. I solve puzzles. Just like you search for loopholes."

Macy beheld Parker while she glared up at the ceiling, and gazed at the tears that formed in Parker's eyes, threatening to spill over. She considered Parker hot as fuck when she was in control, but her the vulnerability, the softness she was showing, had Macy's heart melting. Macy got up, slid into the booth, and put her arms around Parker.

Parker stiffened in her embrace. She shrugged Macy off. "What the *fuck?* Just stop."

With her hands up, Macy slid back out to her side of the booth. Her cheeks were hot with embarrassment. The rejection stung hard.

"What was it about Calypso? That was your question, right?" Macy nodded. "She's different. Not just how she looks, but her whole being. Her whole persona. She's not only gorgeous, she's smart, she understands me, or at least she used to. There's this sense of coolness about her; a confidence to her that's really alluring. She knows what she wants and isn't afraid to go for it. She doesn't get jealous really . . . of . . . anyone . . . but Juliana because of the amount of time I'm with her when I'm working, and . . . *you.*" Parker's eyes got big. She took a deep inhale. "It all makes sense now." Those last words came out as a whisper on her exhale.

"What makes sense?" Transfixed by this revelation, Macy leaned in across the table.

"Why she hated you. Why she never wanted to be around you. Why she didn't want me around you. Ha!" A mirthless, sarcastic laugh came out as she slapped the table and slid out of the booth. "Okay, it's been real, Macy. Let's stay in touch." Parker buttoned her double-breasted jacket and straightened her tie.

"Parker, call me. I'm worried."

"You should be. I've never been this angry."

"Should I come with you?"

"For fuck's sake. No." On that note, she turned and made her way to the door.

Macy couldn't deny that she was butthurt by how Parker shrugged her off and told her not to come with her. She kind of wanted to see Calypso's face when Parker confronted her. She envisioned Parker strangling Calypso and dumping her in a shallow grave and grinned. She would totally help Parker bury Calypso's body.

She sat still and waited as Parker left the restaurant, letting the door slam behind her.

The waitress came back by. "Are you going to order lunch or are you fine with only coffee today?"

"I'll have the BLT, toasted on wheat, add avocado." Macy didn't even look at the waitress. She stared at the door Parker exited through.

22 IT ALL COMES APART

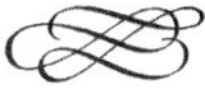

PARKER

*P*arker let herself into the house. It was past time for her to go back to work, but this couldn't wait. She called Lloyd and briefed him on what needed to be done, alerting him that she was currently dealing with a personal crisis.

"Calypso?" There was a hard edge in her voice as she called out. It had been breaking dawn when Calypso returned home. She stayed out with her friends and turned off her location sharing. Calypso was pissed.

"Kitchen!" A chipper response, oblivious to the sharpness of Parker's voice.

As she made her way into the kitchen, her heart cracked as she eyed Calypso moving around the kitchen. She was torn between the woman she knew and had fallen in love with and the woman she had been exposed to.

Barefoot in distressed jeans and a black tank top, her hair fixed atop her head in a loose, messy bun, Calypso placed a tray of stuffed peppers into the oven, and her trip-hop music played on the speaker on the counter as she moved across the floor to the island where Parker was standing. Parker studied her for a minute. She couldn't believe this was happening. The sharpness and the sorrow proved to be unbearable.

Smiling and wide-eyed, Calypso turned around and peered up at Parker. "You're home really early!" She wiped her hands on a dish towel and made her way across the floor to Parker. "I need to ap—"

Putting her hand up to stop Calypso from coming any closer, Parker growled, "I know."

Calypso's brow furrowed, confused, shaking her head. "You know what?"

"I *know* about New Orleans. I *know* what you did. I *know* you are in hiding. I *know* you lied to me. I *know* why you never wanted to talk about your past. I *know* it all now. I *know* your real name isn't Calypso Boudreaux, Calliope Nikanidis."

Calypso shook her head; her eyes were wide and innocent. Fuck, she's a good actress. "No—"

"Those anonymous letters I was getting and your refusal to even talk to me about your past. Your hatred for Macy. It all makes sense now. It's all been made clear. I know you stabbed your ex. I know you were wanted for another murder, an identical stabbing. You got lucky and disappeared when the storm hit. You were able to reinvent yourself. Clever. Very fucking clever—"

"Parker. Babe—"

"No. I don't want to hear it. I saw the file. Do you not understand what kind of danger you put me in? Harboring a fugitive? I could be disbarred! I could end up charged!"

"Pa—"

"I *saw* the file. I read it *all*. What I want is for you to go upstairs. Pack a bag. Get the fuck out. I don't care where you go. I just can't have you here." Even saying the words out loud caused Parker's heart to crack.

"You aren't even going to try to listen to my side? This is from Macy, isn't it?" Tears streamed down Calypso's cheeks. "What—"

"It doesn't matter if it's from Macy or someone else. There's nothing to say, Calypso. Calliope. Whatever the fuck your name really is. If we don't have trust, we have nothing." Trembling, Calypso swiped tears away. Parker did her best to turn off every bit of her feelings and put herself into her cold courtroom mode. "If you had been honest with me and told me all of this from the beginning, I could have helped you. I could have gotten this cleared. But you couldn't even trust me.

"Since this whole farce of a marriage was entered into under false pretenses, this marriage is void. It never happened. I'm going to have the trust changed over as well. I don't know what your intentions were. If it was money. If it was a lifestyle. Or if you thought I was stupid and would never have found out. But it's fucking over. And what's worse is until the point when I saw your file, I would have burned the fucking world down for you." Her facade was beginning to crumble, and her voice cracked at the end. "Goddammit." She whispered as she wiped tears.

"You've been looking for a reason to end this. This is just a convenient excuse. The last four months have been tough, and neither of us had any idea how to fix it. So now you have your reason to bail. That's why you won't hear me out." Tears flowed freely from Calypso's eyes.

"Caly—" Parker began to counter before she was cut off.

"No. No. Parker. You wouldn't hear me out. I'm not going to hear you out. You said all you needed to say. You're done.

You made it clear. I'll grant you your wish. I'm going to go pack. You need to grant me one wish, though—I know where you got this information. Take it with a grain of salt."

Parker wanted to tell her that she wasn't done. She didn't want it to be done. Over the last few days, she had committed to doing whatever it took to salvage this marriage. But she couldn't help the crisis that came up yesterday. She couldn't say anything. They were both done.

Calypso turned and walked out. She didn't try to say anything more. Parker didn't want to listen to it even if she did. She couldn't. This was clearly over. The sound of Calypso's footsteps as she charged up the steps and slammed the bedroom door was all too much for Parker. She couldn't be here either. It was all too overwhelming. Every room held a memory. And every memory was now tainted by betrayal. She didn't even know who Calypso was. Grabbing the hot pads Calypso had set on the counter minutes ago, she opened the oven and pulled the lentil and couscous stuffed peppers out. It was one of Parker's favorites, and Calypso took the time to learn it from Karen. Parker dumped them in the trash and turned the oven off. What a fucking waste. All of it, not only the dinner. The time. The effort. The love. And it hurt so much more than Parker ever imagined.

Calypso's footfalls tapped above her as she moved around upstairs. She walked into the living room and glowered at the large portrait of Calypso on the wall. When Calypso moved in, Parker insisted that the piece be hung. She loved it. She loved it because it displayed the epitome of Calypso's personality. Razor sharp, beautiful, and sensual. But she didn't know that woman. She thought she did. But what hurt even more was that she caught herself wishing she didn't know. That Macy would have never said anything to her. Which was ridiculous.

She waited in the kitchen leaning against the island until

Calypso, looking back at Parker once over her shoulder, was at the door. Her perfect cat eye makeup was smudged as she quietly left with a suitcase.

The house became eerily quiet and empty without Calypso. Lifeless. Before Calypso, her home was a sanctuary of solitude and peace. After five years of living with Calypso, the energy had shifted. It was no longer a sanctuary. It was hollow. She couldn't stay here. Making her way upstairs, she walked into the bedroom, and her eyes fell upon Calypso's wedding band and engagement ring on the surface of the dresser sitting in front of her favorite picture of them from their wedding day—when Parker had dipped her back as they kissed on the porch, the rain coming down behind them, and a strike of lightning in the distance. She turned it over face down. She took her own off and set it next to Calypso's. The totality of all of it hit her all at once. Her heart constricted in a vice. She desperately needed to get the fuck out of here.

A change of scenery for the next few days would be good. Some distance. She decided to stay at one of the hotels downtown. Tomorrow, she could start the paperwork to void the marriage. Calypso or Calliope or whoever the fuck she is was entitled to nothing. She entered into the marriage under false pretenses.

* * *

PARKER STOOD in the hotel lobby, with its crystal chandeliers and black-and-white marble floors wishing she had picked another location. She and Calypso stayed here after a fundraiser right before everything went wrong. Everything came with memories now. She should have stayed single and left Calypso alone, let her be a fantasy. But no. She had to have her. She had to throw caution to the wind and commit herself to a stranger. A stranger who refused to reveal her truth to her own wife. Her father was right to question her at the engagement party. What did she know about Calypso or her motives? Abso-fucking-lutely nothing.

Parker checked into her suite, hung up her clothes, and eyed her new surroundings. It was quiet and lonely there, too. She sat in the living room area of the suite and appraised the room service menu. She picked up the phone to order, but decided she wasn't hungry. She needed a drink or seven to numb the pain. The bar downstairs would be suitable.

23 LET'S GET LIT

AUGUST 4

MACY

$\mathscr{M}$acy gripped the top of Parker's headboard, on her knees, Parker's face between her thighs, as Macy writhed above her. Parker's tongue expertly moved in all the right places. Heat was building, and she wanted that sweet release.

She was close. So close. When her phone rang with a tone she hadn't heard in years—Parker's ringtone.

Her eyes flew open—the memory of that one night with Parker was forever burned into her mind, and the fantasy she most often recalled when getting herself off.

Rolling over, she rushed to answer the phone. "Hey, are you okay?"

"Not really. I can't believe how stupid I've been. How foolish I was. And I just let her cut you out of my life. I've been a shitty friend." Macy could hear a slight slurring in

Parker's voice, as well as the music and chatter in the background.

"Are you drunk?"

"Not yet. Heading in that direction, though. I've got a nice buzz right now."

"Where are you?"

Parker named the hotel she'd decided to call home for the next few days. "I'm at the bar."

"You in need of company?"

"Yeah. I think so."

"Be there in twenty." Macy hung up with a grin on her face. Maybe she would receive the opportunity of another shot at Parker after all. Perhaps a few drinks would lead to going back up to the room, and she wouldn't have to rely on her fantasies any longer.

Thirty minutes later (she only needed to change her outfit three times and freshen up her makeup—so she was ten minutes off from her promised twenty minutes), Macy was alongside Parker at the bar. Parker had a head start on her with two martini glasses already drained in front of her and a fresh one next to it. Parker had changed out of the suit she had been wearing earlier into jeans and a cream-colored cashmere sweater—and Macy found it equally appealing.

With raw red eyes from too many tears shed, Parker pulled the toothpick with the three olives on it out of the drink and slid one off with her teeth. Macy placed her hand on Parker's thigh. She sensed Parker tensing under her touch, so she pulled her hand away before Parker snapped at her again.

"Parker, I'm so sorry."

"No. I'm sorry. We were friends. Good friends. I let her cut you out of my life. I allowed it. And that's not fair." She leaned her head against Macy's shoulder, and Macy was able to catch the scent of Parker's cologne, which sent her mind spiraling back to what she had been doing when Parker called. Macy caught her breath as her body reacted to Parker's nearness. Parker, meanwhile, was obviously past the tense and stiff reactions to Macy's affection. Her perfect pompadour had fallen, and a lock of it tickled against Macy's neck.

"No matter what, I'm always going to be here for you, Parker." Macy purred as she rubbed Parker's back.

"I don't deserve it." Parker slurred, her breath hot against Macy's neck, the breath of her words causing goose bumps to spring up over Macy's body.

The bartender approached, and Macy ordered a martini as well. Extra dirty. Extra olives. She hadn't eaten dinner, so she hoped the olives would provide some sustenance. "Parker, you're a good woman. You are. And you were doing what you thought was right by your wife. It's understandable."

Parker picked her head up and nursed her drink. "I'm sorry about you and A.D. I figured you two would be in it all the way through to the end. A.D. is a sweetheart."

"She is. That's why she deserved better." Her heart ached as she said it.

"What do you mean by that?"

"I loved her. I still love her. But I'm not in love with her. She deserves someone who is totally crazy for her. And I just . . . there's someone else I can't get out of my head. I thought A.D. would help me move past it. It didn't work, and she ended up hurt in the end."

Parker gave her a knowing glance, and her cheeks flamed red. Parker nodded. "We all deserve that in the very least. And that's why, Macy, I'm not it for you. I'm not. I can never give you what you want. I thought I had it with Calypso. But now I'm questioning everything."

Macy shook her head. "I understand, Parker. I don't

expect anything from you. That's been clear since the beginning." There was a mix of disappointment and embarrassment swirling around in her. She chugged her martini to numb the stinging pain inside her. She dragged one of the olives off the pick to keep from saying anything else.

"Just like you have to be fair with A.D., I have to be fair with you." Parker plunged her olives into the drink before pulling them out and taking one into her mouth.

Grateful for the darkness of the bar, Macy could feel her cheeks were flaming red. "Like I said, Parker. I understand. I got it. I've had it for years. It's not even that."

"What is it then?"

Macy shrugged. "A conversation for a sober time, I think."

Parker shrugged and ordered them both another drink.

* * *

AUGUST 5

Macy found herself waking up in Parker's suite, in the bed, fully clothed. She didn't have a clue what time they made it back to the room, or if Parker even slept in the bed with her last night. Parker was noticeably absent. But hey, she woke up where she wanted to be—Parker's bed. Macy's head throbbed as she stood up, and her stomach lurched. The door to the bedroom was closed, and there was quiet shuffling around outside the bedroom door.

She padded her way across the plush carpeting and opened the door to see Parker sitting on the sofa with a room service tray on the table in front of her and a cup of coffee in her hand. Parker's hair was wet from the shower, and she was in sweats. And no matter how her head ached or stomach threatened to spill its contents, she wanted Parker in the worst way.

"Thank you for staying last night," Parker said, her voice husky with sleep.

"Any time." *No. Really. Any time. Please. All the time would be even better.* Sitting in the armchair next to the sofa, she caught sight of an extra cup on the tray. She reached over, grabbed the carafe, and poured herself a cup. "Where did you sleep last night?"

"The couch." Parker pointed to the folded blankets and extra pillow on the armchair next to the sofa before she picked up a croissant off the tray and tore off a piece.

Macy took the other one off the tray, hoping the carbs would soak up the alcohol in her system, and also soak up the disappointment that Parker didn't even try to sleep next to her as drunk as she was.

"What are you going to do now?" Macy asked her.

"Like today or going forward?"

"Both."

"I need to get dressed and finish preparing for the trial that's coming way too soon with Lloyd."

"Saving the world one criminal at a time." A common jab between the two of them, being on opposite sides of the law.

"Innocent until proven guilty." Parker grinned, putting another piece of croissant into her mouth. "As for Calypso ... I need to void the marriage and then get the trust taken out of her name and put in the name of my cousin's kid. I just don't know when I'm going to have time for all of it, though. This trial is going to be a nightmare, and my head for the first time isn't in it."

"You were dealt a huge blow." Macy popped a piece of the croissant in her mouth.

"If you didn't tell me, I would have never had a clue. Part of me wishes I'd never known."

It was a hard fight not to respond in anger. Instead, she took a breath before responding. "And when we showed up to take her, you would have found out. It was coming, and I didn't want to blindside you."

Parker ran her hand through her damp hair and collapsed against the back of the couch. She glanced at the clock on the end table. "I have to get going. Lloyd is waiting for me. Take your time. You don't need to rush out. But I have to make my way to the office."

Macy warmed her coffee by adding more and sat back in the cozy armchair. There was no way she was ready to face sunlight yet. Instead, she curled her feet underneath her, snuggled into the chair, and let her eyes fall closed. Her head throbbed with each beat of her heart, and her eyes burned, dry and heavy.

She sensed she should also leave so as not to wear out her welcome with Parker. That was not going to happen. Not right now. Not with how she was feeling.

She could hear Parker shuffling around behind the closed bedroom door. Knowing Parker was going to work, she would be donning one of her suits. Fully aware it was hope-less—*she* was hopeless—she let out a defeated sigh.

Based on the sounds of her movements, Parker moved on to the bathroom. The tap was running, and Macy kept her eyes closed as she listened to Parker getting ready. The spray of Parker's cologne came next. She was acutely familiar with that scent—Dior's Sauvage—peppery with earthy and amber undertones. Eight years later and she still remembered the scent of it on Parker's neck. She couldn't forget it. Macy inhaled deeply. She could almost taste Parker's skin under the essence. If Parker could get past this Calypso thing and see things clearly.

Before she sank too deep in her reverie, Macy heard the door to the bedroom open. Parker stood in the doorway looking at Macy. To her surprise, Parker wore jeans and a Stanford Law hoodie instead of her suit. Macy knew that

Stanford was also a legacy piece for Parker. Her grandfather and her father also went to law school there. Parker and her family were the traditional American example of generational wealth and privilege. Sometimes, Macy wondered what she saw in Parker. She couldn't explain it. She'd learned to face that it was something she couldn't fight.

Macy's heart simultaneously broke and accelerated. She would sell her soul for Parker to be hers.

"Are you okay?" Parker asked her.

"Yeah. Sorry. I'm just feeling like a truck hit me."

Parker laughed a little. "Yeah. Me too. Like I said, take your time. Shower. Eat. Whatever you need to do before you head out."

"Thanks. Don't work too hard." Macy forced a smile.

Parker slipped out the door.

After Parker's footfalls couldn't be heard in the hallway, Macy waited a bit longer to make sure she wasn't coming back in. When she was convinced Parker was gone for the day, she finally made her way into the bathroom, stood in front of the shower, and stripped. The smell of vodka and olive brine clung to the fabric and her skin.

Macy turned the knob for the shower and stepped under the rainfall spray. Parker's ginger awapuhi shampoo and conditioner sat on the tile shelf next to her body wash. A brand unfamiliar to Macy, Le Labo Hinoki. She let the water wash over her as she turned the temperature to scalding.

Lathering herself in Parker's products, she let the soap and her hands glide over her body.

Her pulse beat fast, and her body was in need.

After turning the water off, she stepped out onto the cool, fine marble floor as the steam billowed around her and fogged the mirrors. This suite would have broken her bank. A bottle of Parker's cologne sat on the counter in front of her. It was an impulse to spray some of it onto herself before wandering back into the bedroom.

Wrapped in Parker's scent, she lay back onto the bed and let her hands run down her body, imagining it to be Parker.

The cool air licked over the heat of her damp skin as she moved under her own touch. She understood she shouldn't be in Parker's suite alone, bathed in Parker's fragrance, touching herself, but she couldn't help it. She didn't get to finish last night, and being this close to Parker in an intimate kind of way was pushing her too far. Knowing it was something she shouldn't be doing made it all the more exciting. It didn't take her long to bring herself to climax.

24 IN THE DARK

PARKER

*A*ir conditioning cranked to subzero on high, Parker sat in her car and gripped the leather of the steering wheel. Her parked car still sat in the parking garage of the hotel. The only way to describe how she felt was *dog shit*, not because she was hungover. It was because she couldn't get Calypso's face out of her mind: her trembling lip and glassy eyes.

Calypso only wanted to be heard. She should have let her explain. Shouldn't she? *No. Fuck that.* Her inner war continued to rage. Calypso made a fool of her. Used her. Violated her trust.

She listened to the roar of the engine. She loved that sound under normal conditions. But right now, her head weighed a ton and throbbed.

When she finally emerged from the garage, she rolled her

window down, hoping the fresh air would help clear her head. She had a text from Lloyd wondering where she was and several other unread texts waiting for her. Those would have to wait. She was angry. She had to fucking get a hold on her emotions before she responded to or met with anyone.

After pulling into the office garage, she checked her messages and found a text from Calypso waiting for her: "I'm going to swing by and pick up some of my things today. I know you have trial prep, but maybe your anger has cooled, and we can make time to talk?"

"I have nothing to say." That response was a complete lie. She had plenty to say.

She glared at the three little dots dancing and disappearing, anticipating Calypso's response. They appeared again and then disappeared again. Parker was unsure what would have been worse, a response or this lack of one.

Parker sucked in a breath and exhaled. The sting of tears behind her eyes threatened to spill over. Another text notification popped up. This one from Macy. "If you need to talk or need company again, I'm here for you."

Parker groaned as she replayed her conversation with Macy from the night before. Choosing to not to respond, she instead made her way to the office.

"You look like shit," Lloyd greeted her. A cup of coffee was placed in her hand by Juliana as she passed her desk and went into the war room. She didn't think Lloyd ever saw her dressed in "normal" person fashion. She always put her best effort into presenting herself dressed to the nines.

"I look like shit because I feel like shit. My life is falling apart around me."

"What do you mean? You have a hot wife, a nice house, a managing stake in a huge law firm, and an inheritance that assures you never have to think about money ever again in your life."

"I don't have a 'hot wife' any longer." Parker gave him a rundown of her last twenty-four hours.

His eyes wide, he whispered, "Calypso?"

Parker nodded.

"Do you want to take the day and just kind of cope?"

"No. I need to keep my mind busy. If I think about it too much, I will go crazy."

"Where did she go?"

"I don't know. And right now, I don't give two fucks. Hopefully, far away from me. But probably Xander and Xochitl's." She pulled up a banker's box, set it on the table, and opened it. Across the table from her, Lloyd sat with the whiteboard behind him. Notes and timelines in black Expo marker adorned the board. With an open marker in his hand, he turned his chair to study the board. "Something with this timeline isn't fitting . . ."

Parker pushed the thoughts of Calypso out of her head and went into work mode.

Parker returned to the hotel suite after several hours with Lloyd, during which they reviewed Will's case, discussed a motion to be filed in the morning, and analyzed the timeline. She decided she would let Lloyd take the lead on this case. He started laying out the points for the opening statement. She ran him through tactics and words to use and how to stand, and which words to inflect. What is law other than the ability to tell a good story? Whoever tells it better wins. Lloyd had promise when she hired him. Since then, he had grown to be capable and skilled as she worked with him. She would eventually cut him loose to handle his own cases without her. But not this one.

Sitting on the end of the bed, neatly made by the hotel staff some hours earlier, she collapsed onto her back, toeing her shoes off. Not working allowed all of the thoughts and feelings to creep back in and invade her brain.

She still had a ton of text messages to sort through. After pulling her phone from her pocket, the first message waiting for her was from Calypso: "What do you want me to do with the picture over the couch?" That was three hours ago. There was a sharp pain in her chest and her eyes stung. She remembered standing back after she hung that portrait of Calypso, the one that captivated her so much on their first date. She walked past that portrait every single day, and it never ceased to take her breath away and bring her back to that feeling that hit on day one. She couldn't even think about what she would hang in its place. Another sharp pain in her chest. She bit her lip and tilted her head back to collect herself before reading the next message from Calypso below it in the thread.

Sent an hour later than the first one: "I'm going to leave the picture. I have no room for it." Parker was torn between a sense of relief that the picture was still hanging on the wall, and sadness, as she didn't think she could look at it without feeling hurt and betrayed.

A notification from Macy came through: "How are you?" She let out a groan and ran her hand over her face. She couldn't deal with talking to Macy about all of this right now.

Parker didn't respond to either of them. Instead she called her cell carrier and canceled Calypso's phone line. She didn't want to be able to reach Calypso, and she didn't want to know where she went. Or how she was. It hurt too much.

As a high-powered, highly-sought-after attorney, she was left to wonder how she allowed herself to be so blinded by her desire to have Calypso that she ignored all of the red flags. Every single one. She wrote them off. She rationalized them away. So fucking stupid. So. Absolutely. Stupid.

Foolishly, she opened her pictures. She was greeted with a series of selfies of her and Calypso. Pictures Calypso would send to entice her to come home from work, showing enough to make Parker blush and put her phone away. She thought to delete them, but couldn't bring herself to. She wasn't ready. She also wasn't ready to look at them any further.

A hot shower to wash it all away would solve everything. Grabbing her pajamas as she walked to the shower, stripping off her shirt, she passed the mirror. The lid to her cologne bottle was off and left on the counter. She was always meticulous about her products and how she kept the countertops, up to the distance between the bottles or items on them. She clearly remembered that she didn't leave the cap off it—she was always precise with her routine, no matter how hungover she happened to be. The products were also not organized the way she left them.

Macy must have gone through them after she left. She rolled her eyes and put them back the way they were supposed to go. She told Macy to make herself at home and take her time getting ready to go. But she hadn't expected Macy to go through her things. She put her annoyance aside. Macy didn't have her own items there. It's not as if she planned to get drunk and stay overnight. The least she could have done was put them back, though.

The hot shower did nothing to help clear her head.

Once she stepped out, she thought about calling Xander and asking if Calypso was there, but decided against it. What more was there to say? *I miss you. I wish you had been honest with me. I hate you for ruining what we built together.*

Bone tired and mind numb, she stared at the television, even though it wasn't on. As she stared at it, she listlessly picked at the room service she had ordered. After hardly eating any of it, she passed out.

* * *

AUGUST 7

After two full days of strategizing, meeting with clients, and meeting with junior associates, Parker decided to swing by the house to grab a few things. She still wasn't ready to stay there. She found herself seriously considering selling the place. When it had been only her and the Cat, it was the perfect sanctuary. Now there were five years of memories of a life she made with someone tainting every single room.

When she pulled in, the front door was cracked open. Calypso's car sat in the driveway. The keys to the car had been tossed in the cup holder on the center console with Calypso's fluffy black cat keychain still attached. Fuck, she didn't want to come face-to-face with Calypso. She didn't think she was ready for that. If Calypso left the keys in the car, she probably didn't plan to stay that long. She was probably grabbing a few extra things and leaving.

After a few seconds of hesitation, she considered turning around, walking back to her car, and leaving and waiting for Calypso to leave. But she also realized that at some point she would have to face Calypso.

Fuck it. She's a big girl. She would go in. Another long pause before heaving herself out of the car on an exhalation and marching up the walkway. As she walked through the already open front door she called out, "Calypso?" Dread that she would have another confrontation and hope that she would see her—just one more time—swirled through her as she waited for a response.

She was met with no response—utter silence. The house was dark. All of the blinds and curtains were drawn closed. Karen usually did that when she left for the day. Parker had given up on asking Karen to stop doing that. Annoyed that she had to open the shade, and even more annoyed that

Calypso wasn't here, she turned to the window and moved to open the living room shade.

As her hand reached for the shade, there was a click behind her, and she turned, expecting to see Calypso. She was unable to say for sure what was first, the burning sensation searing her back—once, twice—or the two loud bangs.

The pain burned through her. The world went black.

25 HER HERO

MACY

*M*acy sat in her car in Parker's driveway. Parker didn't invite her, but she was compelled to come to the house—but this time she planned to actually knock on the door and not watch from afar.

Although Macy was familiar with where the spare key was, she noticed the front door had been left propped open. The house was dark, but Parker's car sat in the driveway.

The house being dark was not typical for Parker; a dark house was one of Parker's pet peeves. Macy flipped the light switch next to the front door, illuminating Parker's vast living room. As her eyes adjusted to the light, her gaze froze on the sight of Parker lying on the floor, bleeding out. Falling to her knees next to Parker's body on the floor, she grabbed her phone and called 911.

"911. What's your emergency?"

"I came over to my friend's house and saw the front door propped open. I came in and found her lying on the floor. She's bleeding. There's a lot of blood. She's unconscious but breathing." Macy's voice came out shaking and high-pitched. She checked Parker's front for bleeding and wounds and didn't see anything, so she rolled her onto her side and saw two entrance wounds. She sat cross-legged with Parker on her side over Macy's lap. Setting the phone on the floor and putting it on speaker, she reached behind herself so she could grab the alpaca wool throw blanket lying over the arm of the couch, using it to apply pressure to the two wounds.

"What's the address?"

Macy gave the address. Parker's blood felt warm and slick on her hands, as it soaked through the blanket.

Parker's breath was shallow. Her skin was an ashy pale. She reported as much to the dispatcher, and her own pulse was fast and thready. Her heart beat loudly in her ears, and tears streamed down her face. She put her fingers to Parker's wrist. Her pulse felt weak. Trying to better apply pressure, she adjusted Parker in her lap, hoping to minimize Parker's bleeding.

"Parker, keep fighting. Stay with me. Don't leave me." Macy kept repeating it as she held Parker in her lap. Parker's crisp white shirt and light gray suit were darkening with her blood. Macy kept running her hands over Parker's hair. She knew there was more she should be doing, but visions of Brent bleeding out flooded her memory, paralyzing her. *Parker can't die.* Parker's blood started to redden her Macy's jeans and her blue T-shirt. Parker's blood coated her hands, red and hot and sticky, and Macy was getting it in Parker's hair as she caressed it. She was rocking back and forth as she trembled. *Parker can't die. She can't.* If Parker died, she would kill herself. She couldn't imagine life without Parker somewhere in it.

Flashing lights soon filled the window through the gaps in the window dressing. Macy exhaled in relief. Parker couldn't die on her.

A team of cops and paramedics swarmed in.

"Quinn, what are you doing here?" One of the officers asked. He was a beat cop whose name Macy couldn't remember. "And why are you interfering with a crime scene?"

"Parker's a friend of mine. I came to check on her. She's in the middle of a messy relationship issue. And I saw her, and emotions took over. After Caldwell . . . I can't lose anyone else." Her blood-soaked hands wiped the tears from her cheeks, leaving smears of Parker's red blood war paint across her cheeks.

"Yeah, I forgot you were there for that." The beat cop gave her a sad look. "Your friend will be just fine, I'm sure. Did you happen to clear the scene?"

Shaking her head, Macy whispered, "No. I . . . I . . ." She couldn't finish the statement.

"It's okay, Quinn, I understand."

The paramedics moved Parker off her lap and began their assessment. Macy was lightheaded as she stared at Parker's blood-smeared, ashen face. She remained on the floor. She was dizzy and weak, her lap now cold where Parker had been lying before they removed her.

"Do you have your weapon on you?" Officer What's His Name asked.

"No. I had to surrender it when I went to desk duty." Her voice remained barely above a whisper as she kept her eyes on Parker.

"Do you know if she keeps weapons on the property?" He asked. She understood better than anyone that he was merely doing his job, but goddamn, this was the last thing she wanted to do right now.

"I know she keeps a twenty-two in her bedroom, and a nine in her glove box." Macy squeezed her eyes shut.

"How do you know that?"

"She and I went to the range together before. She keeps them because her client list is a bit sketchy. And she's received death threats."

"Do you know who the death threats are from?"

"Families of victims of the clients she's defended. A few of the women she'd hooked up with in the past were crazy, too."

"And you let yourself into her home and just found her like that?"

She couldn't focus with the sound of the paramedics working on Parker, and the detectives, whom she thought of as peers, were swarming over the house. `"No, yeah. I marked Parker's car in the drive, and the front door of the house cracked open. It's not like Parker. And the house was all dark. I turned on the lights and found her like this."

"Were there any other cars present?"

"Just Parker's Jag and mine."

Helpless, Macy could only watch as the paramedics loaded Parker onto a gurney and took her out as she rose off the floor to her feet.

"Were there any signs you could see of forced entry?"

"No. Just the door being left ajar." Macy kept her eye on Parker as the paramedics wheeled her out, fighting the urge to run after them and jump in the back of the rig with them.

"You said she's received death threats. Was this recently? Do you know if she has any enemies or someone who would want to see her dead?"

"Parker's dealt with death threats for as long as I've known her. Like I mentioned, some victims' families are not happy with her defending the suspects. But I don't think any of them would actually do it. It's just smoke most of the time. But she did just kick her wife out."

"Do you have her wife's name? Information?"

"Calypso Harrington. She drives an AMG, I think? Black? She's about five-three, maybe buck thirty-five? Tattoos on her neck, arms, and chest. Actually—" spinning to point at the large photo of Calypso's body on the wall—"that's her." She pointed. The unmistakable acid in her voice when referring to Calypso came out.

Another officer came down the stairs. "There's no twenty-two or any other weapon in the bedroom."

The light caused strange geometric patterns to reflect in the large pool of Parker's blood.

"If you have any further questions, you know where to find me. I'm going to go be with her in the hospital. Someone needs to let her family know, too."

Macy didn't have Parker's family's numbers. She remembered A.D. had them. She finally got off the floor and made her way outside. It would be the middle of the night in New York.

Her hand dragged through her hair, leaving behind streaks of Parker's blood as she dialed A.D.'s number.

When A.D. answered, her voice was thick with sleep. "Macy, what's going on?"

"I'm sorry. I wouldn't call if this weren't urgent. Parker's been shot. They are taking her to the hospital, and I think her family should know." Macy was walking to her car. She gave A.D. a rundown of what she had gone through minutes ago. "Do you know how to reach her family?" She was still blood soaked, but that didn't matter to her. She wanted to be by Parker's side and make sure she was okay.

"Yeah. I will call them. Keep me updated, okay?" A.D. sounded a hell of a lot more alert by the end of it.

"Of course. Thank you."

Parker was still in surgery to remove the bullets when Macy got to the hospital. Macy hated hospitals, ever since she was a little girl and her mother died. Hospitals were despair. Tragedy.

She was supposed to have had a therapy appointment hours ago. She called her therapist on the doctor's dedicated emergency line. "I couldn't come today," Macy said quietly.

"Why is that?" Dr. Bennet asked.

"My friend Parker was shot, and she almost died. I found her."

"Is this the same Parker you've mentioned in our meetings?"

"Yeah. That would be her."

"I'm sure that was very triggering." Dr. Bennet said cautiously. Macy wondered if the pun was intended. "If you would like to come in tomorrow morning, that would probably be beneficial. I can get you in early before my first appointment. Do you want to come in at eight?"

Macy ran her hand through her hair. She clearly understood that if she didn't go, it would look bad and possibly interfere with her getting off desk duty. "Yeah. I'll be there."

"Good. I have you down then. Meanwhile, I know this is a compounding trauma now. If you feel yourself getting overwhelmed, do your 5-4-3-2-1 sensory grounding."

"Got it. See you in the morning." Macy hung up the call.

By the time Parker came out of surgery, her parents still weren't there. She had spent the entire time pacing the waiting area, coated in dried blood. It was already after ten p.m. Parker had been sedated and was in a deep sleep. Leaning on the bed rail, she stroked Parker's hand. Parker didn't move. It was stillness with only the beeping of machines and the murmur of nurses talking outside the room. Doctors, nurses, techs coming and going. Adjusting a machine, putting something in an IV. A doctor asked if she was next of kin. Macy only shook her head no. He left. Minutes ticked by.

As Macy sat at Parker's bedside, Mr. and Mrs. Harrington showed up.

Mr. Harrington shook Macy's hand. "What happened?"

Macy gave the rundown for the third time.

Mrs. Harrington crossed her arms over her chest. It was the same way Parker did. "Do you think Calypso was capable of this?" she asked.

Macy sighed and bowed her head. "Did Parker tell you what I found out?"

Mr. Harrington nodded. "She did. Yesterday afternoon. Unbelievable. You did try to warn us. At the engagement party, you approached me and warned me."

"Is it really that unbelievable?" Mrs. Harrington snapped. "What did we really know about her history?"

Self-satisfaction at being acknowledged by Mr. Harrington for her acuity in warning him all those years ago flooded through her. Macy nodded. "Exactly. I think she is capable. The fact that no one can find or reach her, honestly, solidifies it. And they've been looking."

Taking a seat in the chair previously occupied by Macy and setting her Birkin bag on the other empty chair next to it, because God forbid the bag get germs from sitting on the floor, Mrs. Harrington left Mr. Harrington and Macy to stand.

26 FROM FLAME AND ASH

PARKER

*P*ain radiating through her left shoulder and her lower back, barely above her right hip, woke Parker up. The incessant beeping of the machines did nothing to ease her confusion as she tried to assess her situation.

Her mother squealed. "Parker, baby. You're awake!" Her eyes had deep, dark rings beneath them, and her normally perfect makeup was smudged. Setting her Starbucks cup on the tray next to Parker's bed, she stood up to take Parker's hand.

"Mom." Parker tried to shift and let out a pathetic yelp; everything hurt when she tried to move. No matter what your relationship is with your mom, sometimes you simply need her. Parker considered her mom to have been a good mom, albeit not necessarily always the most involved. Her mom tended to believe that children shouldn't be coddled or babied, for then they grow up to be useless mooches. That's not to say that she was *never* there. She stepped in and soothed Parker when she had her first heartbreak. She was there when Parker was frustrated because she didn't score as high as she would have liked in her AP classes. She was there for all of Parker's successes, including her first trial.

A nurse and a doctor came in with her father behind them.

"I thought I was going to die. I didn't die." Parker whispered with her throat dry. Her eyes were big. Her mom poured her a glass of water and handed it to her. She took a sip with a shaking hand.

"The bullet entered your left shoulder; if it were a hair to the right, you would have been dead. We also removed a bullet lodged in your lower back, hardly above your right buttock. You're lucky that the shooter was a bad shot." The doctor barely made eye contact with her as he explained her wounds. "If the bullet had been even a hair higher and a little left, we would be telling a very different story."

Mrs. Harrington dabbed at her eyes.

After a battery of tests to ensure Parker could move and breathe normally, the doctors broke the news to Parker that she would be staying for a minimum of three more days for observation. Parker tried to argue with them, because that's what Parker did. But no matter her argument, the doctors held firm in their opinion. She needed to stay.

As a nurse came in with a tray of bland food that Parker showed no interest in, a detective came in with Macy in tow.

"We can order you something better from DoorDash, sweetie." Her mother moved the tray away from Parker after noting Parker's dismay at the tray in front of her.

"Parker, this is my friend, Detective Aiden Jackson. He's taking your case. I promise you are in good hands." In a bold and assuming move, Macy took the liberty to sit on the foot of Parker's bed and fuss over Parker's blanket.

"Hi. I'm sorry, it hurts to move, or I would shake your hand." Sucking in a breath with a hiss, Parker fidgeting slightly.

"No worries, Ms. Harrington. Did you see your shooter?"

"No. I went to the house—I've been staying at a hotel downtown—to pick up some more clothes. When I pulled in, Calypso's car was in the drive, and the door to the house was cracked open. I went in, called her name, and then there was this searing pain in my shoulder, and then my back. And I hit the ground and woke up here."

"Calypso's car was there?" Macy asked, her eyebrow raised.

"Yeah," Parker confirmed as a nurse came into the already crowded room.

"How's your pain level, Ms. Harrington?" The nurse asked. "On a scale from one to ten."

"Eleven?" Parker responded.

She nodded and typed something into her computer.

"The only car in the drive when we arrived was yours and Macy's." Jackson wrote something on his pad. "Would Calypso have any motive to hurt you?"

"Hold on. I have something." In a frantic move that jostled Parker's bed, which forced Parker to hold back a whine of pain, Macy reached into the bag at her side and handed it to Jackson.

"What is this?" Looking at the file that was shoved into his hands, he furrowed his eyebrows as he shifted from the file in his hand to Macy.

"I dug this up on Calypso. She's wanted in New Orleans." Macy offered.

Dug this up? Parker was confused. She was pretty sure that's not what happened. Cocking her head to the side,

Macy fidgeted on the edge of Parker's bed picking up on Parker's unease. It made sense, Parker guessed, since Macy broke protocol to give this information to Parker directly.

Macy quickly recovered. "Detective Toussaint at NOPD is my point person there."

Trying to clear her painkiller-addled mind, Parker shook her head and answered Jackson's question. "I was going to void the marriage—Macy can tell you the backstory on that. It's in that file she handed you." The nurse uncapped a needle and injected it into her IV line. Before she knew it, Parker was swept into a wave of pain-free bliss almost immediately. "But if I void the marriage, the prenup is null and void. Per the prenup, if I'm the one who asks for the divorce, I would have to pay her out. And I planned to remove her from the trust."

"She stands to be a very wealthy woman if Parker dies." Her father finished. "She has several million reasons for Parker to be dead."

"What day is it?" Parker squinted at the daylight coming in through the window.

"Thursday. You've been out since last night." Her mother was the one who answered.

"The motion—" Parker's eyes popped open.

"Lloyd handled it. Everything is going to be okay; he's turning out to be very capable. So you can probably take the training wheels off now," Mr. Harrington reassured her.

Parker nodded and closed her eyes. But everyone in the room knew that was bullshit. Parker had always been a control freak, and there was no way she would release the reins.

When she opened her eyes again, the room was significantly darker, and Macy still sat on the edge of her bed.

"You don't need to stay," Parker mumbled.

Macy poured her some water and handed her the cup.

"It's not like I have anything better to do. I left for a little while before you woke up. I went to an appointment, and then I pulled some strings to make sure the best of the best would be handling your case since I'm not allowed to do it. But he's the next best thing."

Parker nodded. "Thanks. You're a good friend. Where are my parents?"

"They ordered you dinner. The driver can't come upstairs, so they ran down to meet him in the lobby."

"Awesome. I'm starving. What did they order?"

"Gnocchi and a salad from some Italian place you love."

Parker's stomach rumbled. "Can you turn some of the lights on?"

Obediently, Macy removed herself from the foot of Parker's bed and flipped a few switches before returning to her perch at the foot of the bed. "Parker, can I ask you something?"

"Depends on what you're asking." Parker tried to smile. But as she moved a shockwave of pain surged from her hip and shoulder. "God dammit." She hissed.

"Do you think Calypso shot you?"

"I don't know what I believe. I never believed she would be wanted for murder. But she wasn't comfortable with guns. She hated that I kept one in the house. At least that's what she led me to believe. But you know as well as anyone else does—money makes people do extreme things."

Macy's reply came on a sigh. "It certainly does."

"And on the surface," Parker continued, "she led me to believe that she wasn't into materialistic things. In the beginning, she asked me to stop buying her gifts. It made her uncomfortable—as she said it—like I was trying to buy her love."

"Five years of living a certain lifestyle will do that. She got comfortable. And then you pulled the rug out from under her." Macy was fidgeting with the corner of Parker's blanket.

"I can't believe this is my life right now."

Before Macy replied, Mr. and Mrs. Harrington returned with Parker's gnocchi.

On a lapse of memory regarding her current physical state, Parker attempted to pull herself up and yelped in pain. She couldn't believe she was in this position and was so grateful for food that had flavor. The nurse came in after Mrs. Harrington poked her head out and beckoned for her.

While Macy set up Parker's tray, the nurse helped Parker to sit up.

Propped up by pillows and with the head of the bed raised, Parker grabbed her fork. "Dad, can you please call Lloyd and have him bring me the files? I don't know where my fucking phone is."

"Parker! Language." Mrs. Harrington snipped.

Parker acknowledged her mom, albeit with obvious exasperation. "Sorry, Mother. I don't know where my phone is." She rolled her eyes as she said it. Her mother had always been prim and proper.

"It's at your house." Macy piped in. Parker forgot she was even there. Parker didn't even know why she *was* still there.

"No," Mr. Harrington cut in. "You need to recover. And the last thing we need is you working while you are on painkillers."

"I won't be taking them after tonight," Parker said defiantly.

"No, Parker. You need to recover."

"Dammit, Dad." Parker set her fork down.

"*Par-ker.*" Her mother shot a pointed glare at Parker as if she were still a small child, splitting her name into two distinct syllables.

"I'm not a child anymore. I'm going to need to work. I am

not going to sit and do nothing but think about Calypso for the next week. I can't. For fuck's sake. And no, Mother. I'm *not* apologizing for my language."

Mrs. Harrington huffed.

"How about a compromise?" Mr. Harrington offered. "We take it a day at a time. See how you are feeling when you get home in a couple of days."

"A couple of days? Are you serious?"

"Per the doctor, yes. You won't be discharged for at least another day or two. And you've been kept on a steady dose of painkillers. I don't foresee that changing while you're here. The last thing we need is for you to be handling files while doped up."

It was Parker's turn to huff as her mother had. Nature versus nurture. But as bratty as her huff was, it was her ability to negotiate and to know when to back away. Circle back at a later time.

27 BLURRY LINES

AUGUST 11

MACY

Four days after Parker had been shot, Macy sat at her desk in the station. She'd researched and gathered all of Calypso's information, only to have to turn it over to Jackson and his partner. She was salty she had to hand it over. She accessed the files and worked through the breadcrumbs, handing them over. After all, she may be close to the case, but she knew she would be the only one who would be able to figure it out. No one else could do it as well as she could.

As Jackson took her information, he showed a level of annoyance, but whatever. He would see, eventually, that she was doing him a favor. She would have loved to cuff Calypso herself. Meanwhile, she sat at her desk and tapped her lip with her pen. She wondered if she could work it out to at least be there when it happened.

He questioned the file from New Orleans, finding it hard to reach anyone at NOPD who would return his calls. On top of that, there were two Detective Toussaints at NOPD, and Macy couldn't remember what his first name was. Toussaint, Macy explained, is a super common name there, and she also tried to explain to him that they were drowning most days, and they didn't prioritize cases that were so old when they had fresh cases daily. He also questioned the time-stamps on the digital file. Macy had to explain to him that it had something to do with the digital transfer. He nodded and turned his back to her as he continued to read through other pieces of evidence that Macy wasn't privy to.

She was irritated that he didn't seem to take her seriously. She was a damn good cop. She knew how to build a case and make it stick. She had a higher conviction rate then he did for fuck's sake.

Later that afternoon, she got word that Jackson had found Calypso's car at the John Wayne Airport. But there was no record of her on any flight manifests, and no one matching her very distinctive look had been spotted going through the airport. The car was ditched there to throw off the investigators, apparently.

Jackson and his partner planned to visit Xochitl and Xander's house to question them that afternoon.

Parker was going to be released from the hospital soon. Her mom would be staying with her for a few days to ensure she was okay and comfortable. Mr. Harrington had forbidden Lloyd from bringing files to Parker's hospital room. Parker had asked that they at least be brought to the house. She asked her father to have Lloyd bring them, but she suspected her dad wouldn't call Lloyd, so she asked Macy to do it. Macy still hadn't. Lloyd was never considered Macy's biggest fan, and the sentiment was mutual.

To put off calling Lloyd, Macy arranged for a detail to

keep watch over Parker's home in case Calypso decided to show back up. God, she hoped Calypso would show her face at Parker's house. She probably wouldn't. But Macy still had hope. She offered to take shifts on the detail, but they denied her. Desk duty. *Stay on the desk, do what you are tasked to do. Let the real detectives handle Calypso.*

Macy reached out to Parker's parents and asked if they needed help cleaning up the blood. Mr. Harrington already hired cleaners to come and clean. Because of course he did. Macy wanted to be needed. Especially by Parker.

Macy decided to finally call Lloyd on her way to Parker's. She wished she hadn't. She told him Parker wanted the files brought to her house. He, of course, being the Harringtons' biggest sycophant, jumped to it. And of course, he was already on it and on his way.

Cleaners were leaving as she pulled into Parker's drive at the same time as Lloyd. *Yay. Fun.* Parker would be coming home with her parents any minute now. She was going to be stuck with that kiss ass for god knows how long.

Lloyd studied her as they leaned against their respective cars. "So . . . are you going to try to wiggle your way into Parker's bed now that Calypso is gone?" he asked her.

"Excuse me?" Macy glared at him.

"Everyone can tell you have been pining for her for years. And now you're her hero, you found her on the brink of death and called 911."

"No. Parker is a good friend, and that's all she is. That's all she will ever be." Macy's tone was defensive.

"Sure, Macy. Sure."

"Why do you care so much?"

"Parker's like a big sister to me. We spend a lot of time together. I know she's got to be absolutely broken about

Calypso. I just want to make sure you aren't going to try to take advantage of the situation."

The absolute desire to punch him in his smug face was hard to overcome. Her fists clenched, she tried to do the breathing exercises that the therapist gave her as Mr. Harrington's full-sized Range Rover was pulling into the drive.

Lloyd, the suck-up that he was, went running down the walkway, opened the back door, and assisted Parker out of the vehicle. Parker's left arm was stabilized in a sling, and she was limping. The second bullet had lodged itself in her hip bone. She wore sweats, and her hair was not in its signature pompadour, but Macy didn't care; she still found Parker to be unsettlingly good-looking. While she sat with Parker at the hospital, the nurses all flirted with Parker. Even if they were not aware of it. They would blush if her hand brushed against theirs or bat their eyelashes and laugh or giggle at the slightest self-deprecatory comment about being at their mercy Parker made when she asked for anything. Even the straight ones who had husbands. It had her wondering whether Lloyd was right, and, as he said, everyone had caught on that she's been smitten with Parker for years—was *she* that obvious?

Mr. Harrington got out of the driver's side and put his hand on his daughter's back as Mrs. Harrington went into the back and grabbed Parker's bag. As the ass kisser—Lloyd —assisted Parker on the other side of Mr. Harrington.

Macy followed behind them into the front door. When Mr. Harrington had the blood cleaned, he also asked that Calypso's portrait be removed from the wall. It was starkly empty in that spot now. For a brief second, Parker's eye went straight for the spot.

Hopefully, it was at the dump.

Once everyone was seated, Mrs. Harrington opened the

paper bag and pulled out Parker's medication. "Does anyone want anything to drink?" She asked as she put the pills in Parker's hand.

"Tea. I have some loose-leaf tea in the cabinet below the coffee maker." Parker's eyebrows were knit together in obvious pain as she leaned back against the couch and exhaled.

"Let me help you." Flying up out of her seat, Macy followed Mrs. Harrington.

"Water, please," Lloyd requested.

"Coffee." Mr. Harrington piped in as he made himself cozy in an armchair flanking the couch. Macy noted the similarities between Parker and her father. Parker appeared to be the female carbon copy of him, from the way she wore her hair in court to her bespoke suits to her all-day coffee addiction.

Lloyd gave her a subtle eye roll as she followed Mrs. Harrington into the kitchen. She fought the urge to flip him off. Or punch him. He was beyond annoying. Punching him would be preferable. Self-restraint was really a difficult skill to maintain.

"Tell me plainly, Macy. Do you think Calypso did this?" Mrs. Harrington asked as she made her way around Parker's kitchen.

Placing a mug from the cabinet and sticking it under the Keurig, before she pulled out the loose-leaf tea and the steeper, she tossed a glance at Mrs. Harrington over her shoulder before resuming her task. "It doesn't look good for Calypso." She packed the tea into the infuser, draped it into the mug, and selected the heated water option before turning to look at Mrs. Harrington as the water steamed and dripped into the cup. "I will tell everyone what I know as soon as we all sit back down."

Mrs. Harrington was definitely used to being a hostess.

She made her way around the kitchen, pulled out a tray from a cupboard in the island, put the glasses she filled with ice on it, along with bottles of alkaline Smart Water, took the mug of steeping tea, and set it on there as Macy put another mug in the machine and popped a Keurig pod in it. "How does Mr. Harrington like his coffee?"

"Black. Just like Parker." Mrs. Harrington smiled. She smoothed her hair before crossing her arms, as she leaned her hip against the counter. "I was so happy when I found out I was having a daughter. I imagined tea parties, dolls, dollhouses, pearls, dresses, and makeovers . . . She was never that daughter for me. She was always a daddy's girl. She would sit on the floor in his office and read books and listen to him as he talked to clients or sit in the war room when he prepared for trial. Once she turned, oh, I think ten? She was helping him organize evidence, and by high school, she was helping him prepare documents. She was aware from the time she could speak that she wanted to be a lawyer, exactly like her dad. She's his best friend. His shadow. His legacy. I had never seen him so scared in my life when A.D. called us." Her eyes, green and shaped identically to Parker's, wide with thick lashes, misted over. "We both thought we were going to lose her."

"Let me carry that tray, it's heavy." Placing the coffee mug on it as Mrs. Harrington made her way back into the living room, dabbing her eyes, Macy hefted the tray behind her.

Once the drinks were dispersed and Macy sat herself on the settee across from the couch where Parker sat, Lloyd sat to the right of Parker, nestled in the overstuffed cushions of the couch (because of course he was), Mr. Harrington in the armchair to Parker's left, and Mrs. Harrington in the chair to her right, Macy began. "Let me cut right to the chase with what we know . . ." She ran through everything, all of the information she had been privy to, not that it was a whole lot. The timeline, the car at the airport, the BOLO. And there was a theory that she was not working alone. They had questioned Xander, and were waiting for Xochitl to come back from a conference in Seattle. Calypso's bank account showed a huge withdrawal the day Parker kicked her out. She had been banking all of the money she got from the tattoo studio, and her occasional personal clients. Parker subsidized her life, so she allowed Calypso to accrue a hefty amount of savings. She cleaned out a little bit over $35,000.

"So that's it?" Mrs. Harrington asked.

"I think your best course of action would be maybe to do a press conference. Give the case more publicity. Get a wider audience for Calypso's picture. It would probably be more impactful if the public heard from Parker herself."

"No." Parker said with a quiet hoarse voice, shaking her head after downing her pills with her tea. "Absolutely not."

"Excuse me?" Her father's head nearly spun off as he turned to look at his daughter. "That bitch nearly killed you. You could have died if your friend here hadn't come by. And you say no? You want her to just get away with it?"

"I'm really not certain that she's the one who shot me," Parker whispered. "I didn't see her. I'm not going to do that without knowing for sure. It just . . . it doesn't fit with Calypso's personality."

"Parker," Lloyd began, his voice quiet as he put his hand on her thigh. "You said her car was here when you got here. But Macy said it wasn't here when she showed up. Everything points to her. Your gun is missing. The bullets were from a twenty-two, which is what you kept, and is now missing. Who else would know you keep a weapon and where it's stashed? "

"I understand that. But I still don't want to do a presser. I don't want anyone here to do it either. I know Calypso. She will come to me. And then I will decide how it goes forward from there."

"You are just going to let an attempted murderer go free while you hang on a bet?" Macy couldn't hide her incredulity.

Parker shot daggers in her eyes at her. "I'm very aware that the two of you don't like each other for whatever reason. And neither one of you will tell me why. I can speculate. I can guess. I've drawn my conclusions, and neither of you seems to want to tell me what it is. But if you or anyone else goes to the press with Calypso's information, I'm cutting off ties. No matter what our relationship was before this."

"Parker—" Mr. Harrington cautioned.

"You do *not* know everything, Dad. *I know* Calypso. And going to the press won't do anything to solve this."

"Parker," Lloyd intervened as if he were approaching a feral rabid dog in the street. "No offense, but you obviously don't know Calypso as well as you thought. You didn't know anything about her past. You didn't know she was wanted or under an alias. You may not know her as well as you thought you did."

Macy remained quiet and let all of this unfold around her. She was going to stay silent and allow the fallout to land on everyone around her.

Parker turned her glare on Lloyd. "I swear on all that is holy. Nobody goes to the press about this. I'm the one here who knows her best. She *was* my *wife*." She stood, sucking in a breath as pain shot across her face. Macy stopped herself from getting up and helping her—she knew Parker wouldn't have any of it. "Leave me to handle Calypso. Now, if you will please excuse me. I need to go lie down."

28 SHOW NO SHAME

MACY

With a pit in her stomach and acid on her tongue, Macy forced herself to remain calm. What the hell was wrong with Parker? Did she not understand she almost fucking died three days ago? "Parker—"

Parker turned her head and focused on Macy with a deathly glare. "You need to trust me. I know my wife."

"She isn't even your wife, technically." Macy challenged. She couldn't help it. She regretted it almost immediately.

"Look, I don't have the energy for this. I just want to go to bed. But none of you will go on the news and talk about this, or put Calypso's face on national television."

Lloyd stood to help Parker up the staircase. God, he couldn't be any more annoying. He had zero shame.

Mr. Harrington had an unreadable poker face. She waited until Lloyd and Parker were all the way upstairs, and she directed her question at Mr. Harrington. "Are you going to honor that?" She kept her voice quiet so Parker wouldn't hear.

"Parker is a smart woman. She knows how to handle her own affairs. If that's what she wishes, it would behoove all of us to respect it." Mr. Harrington gave a hard look at Macy. Biting her lip, Macy bowed her head down and darted her eyes away.

Upon returning from upstairs, Lloyd sat back in his cozy spot on the couch. "She's tucked in and out for the rest of the day. I can stay here, since I can probably better help her up and down."

A wave of disappointment crashed over Macy. She wanted to be the one to stay and help. "Do you want to take shifts? In case she needs something at night? I'm used to pulling overnights."

Lloyd gawked at her as if she had lost her mind. "I guess. She has two guest rooms."

Yeah. Guest rooms. What else did she think? She was going to snuggle with Parker? Sit in the chair in the corner of the bedroom and watch her sleep?

"We should get going and let her rest." Brushing imaginary lint from her pants, Mrs. Harrington stood.

Mr. Harrington took his cue from his wife and stood also. "Call us if you need anything." He clapped Lloyd on the back as he walked toward the door. t.

"Definitely. I think Macy and I have it under control." Lloyd nodded in their direction as they made their way to the door.

"Lloyd, you are for sure staying here and making sure she's okay?" Mrs. Harrington asked. "If you have better things to do, I can stay."

"I promise you, I have nothing better to do. She will be in good hands tonight. I won't leave her."

"Thank you. You are such a godsend." Mrs. Harrington smiled as she made her way out the door. Bile rose in Macy's throat.

After the door closed behind them, Macy sat back down. *Such a godsend. Whatever. More like ass-kissing sycophant.* Macy was certain Lloyd had a statue of Parker and of Mr. Harrington on some altar in his house that he lit candles in front of and prayed to.

After a couple of hours of sitting in silence in Parker's living room, scrolling her phone, responding to some emails, and paying some bills, she peered over at Lloyd.

Lloyd made himself cozy in the armchair previously occupied by Mr. Harrington, intently typing away on his laptop. He set his laptop aside and grabbed his phone, focusing with the same intensity with which he'd been working on his MacBook (that had a sticker with the Harrington and Harrington logo on it, because, again, of course). "What are you so focused on?" Macy asked him.

"Ordering dinner. Parker loves Indian food—so I'm DoorDashing." He got up and made his way into the kitchen, and Macy followed.

"I will pitch in. Can you add some chicken tikka masala?"

"Mm-hmm. How spicy?"

"Medium. How do you know what she even wants?" Macy put two twenties on the counter, and Lloyd picked them up without looking at her.

"I've worked with her for so long, side by side, hours on end. I know all of her favorites from every single restaurant."

"You're such an ass kisser." Macy lobbed at him as he finalized the order and set his phone down. And it felt so good to let it out.

"Look, Macy, I get that you're in love with her. I understand it. But you know she's not going to climb into bed with you because Calypso is gone. You staying here isn't going to change that. She didn't have to bring me in at her firm. But she saw something in me. And going to her firm was a huge pay raise for me. It's allowed me to help my family, who struggle. It's allowed me some room to breathe while I pay back my mountain of student loan debt. I owe Parker Harrington my life. So if I come across as a 'kiss ass' or whatever, it's for good reason. I'm extremely grateful for the Harringtons."

"Yeah. I may have deeper feelings for Parker beyond our friendship. But she's special. She's different." Macy sat on one of the stools lined up at the island and leaned onto her elbows.

"Parker is remarkable. I get that. But why waste so much time and effort on someone who will never love you back?"

A gut punch that nearly knocked her out. Macy shrugged. "I don't know. It's not like I have any control over it. I've dated other women. I got married. But nothing has ever slaked that thirst. And who's to say that one day, down the road, she won't learn to love me back?"

Lloyd shook his head. "Hope is a very dangerous drug. You don't think you have any control over that?"

"I don't. I thought if I had someone else, it would dissipate, and I would learn to love the person I was with. But no one compares to her."

"So you are going to spend the rest of your life waiting in hopes that she suddenly decides to love you back?"

"Maybe. I don't know. Meanwhile, I will just be here. I will be her friend. And I will hope from the sidelines that maybe one day she will. And if she doesn't, I guess just being her friend will have to be enough."

A throat cleared in the doorway. Both of them jumped and turned.

"Parker! What are you doing out of bed?" Macy cooed. Her cheeks flamed red hot. Parker was onto how she felt about her. Parker called her out on it while they were drinking at the bar. But it's a whole other thing to be overheard talking so candidly about it.

"I don't need either one of you to stay. I really don't. I will be fine." Parker sat gingerly in the chair at the head of the table.

"Your mom told me someone needed to stay. If I didn't offer, she would be here. I promised her." Lloyd justified.

"I won't tell if you don't tell. I'm not crippled. I'm not bedridden. I can manage on my own."

"Let me think on that over dinner." Lloyd smiled. "I ordered from Mantra. It should be here in about twenty minutes."

Parker grinned at him. "I knew I did right in bringing you on."

Lloyd shot a knowing look at Macy. Whatever he intended to accomplish with that look worked. Annoyance and jealousy mingled together inside of her.

"Macy, you don't need to stay." Parker insisted.

"I pitched in for that order. I will go home after dinner." Macy stuffed her disappointment down.

29 EVENTUALLY

PARKER

After Macy left, Lloyd glanced over at Parker as he cleaned up the dishes. "How much of my conversation with Macy did you overhear?"

"All of it."

"So you're aware of how she feels about you?"

Gazing up at the ceiling, she breathed in slowly. "I used to think that was why Calypso didn't want me around her. I've been painfully aware since Macy and I met. But yeah. She's not made a secret of it. I really hoped that when she got with A.D., she would let it go. And I hate to say it, but I've used it against her in court on more than one occasion."

"Whatever it takes." Lloyd laughed.

Parker didn't laugh. "I do care about her. She is a great friend. But I just don't think she's someone I could be in a relationship with. I don't feel for her that way." Lloyd handed

Parker her next dose of pills. "I've honestly never been big on relationships anyway. Not that I don't wonder what it would have been like if I were able to go there with Macy. She would make a good wife. She's smart. She has a good career. That level of devotion she carries for me is rare. But then I met Calypso, and Calypso, well, she took me by surprise."

"Do you regret it? Your relationship with Calypso?"

"No. Not one bit. It was nice to feel human. It was nice to feel loved and to give love in return. I think that's what I'm going to miss the most. And yeah. Maybe Macy sees a crack or opening or whatever. But you're right. It's not gonna happen. I don't think I can see her that way. I've never really seen her that way. If I have any regrets, it was sleeping with Macy. Not because it was bad, because it wasn't." Lloyd pulled a face. "But I kinda fucked her up. And believe me. It would be so much easier if I saw her that way. Or felt that way for her."

"Wait. Back up. You *slept* with *Macy?*" The look of utter shock and disgust took over his face.

"Eight years ago. We ran into each other at Mo's and had way too much to drink. She brought me home, and yeah. But she's been okay with being secured in the friend zone all this time. And then she married A.D. I thought it was done."

"She sat by your bedside in the hospital like a rabid junk-yard dog. I think you may need to put some distance between the two of you. For a bit."

Parker waved her hand. "It's never been an issue. I don't see it becoming one now."

"Tell me the truth," Lloyd sat back down at the table across from Parker. "Regarding Calypso . . . why don't you want to put her in the press?"

Parker shrugged. "I don't know. I have a nagging suspicion that she will reach out to me. When she does, I will know where she is, and when I know where she is, I will know if she really did it. And if I think she did it, really think she was capable, I will send the authorities. Meanwhile, I really don't want my business out there in the public. It's not for them to consume. This is my life."

"Where do you think she is?"

"I have no clue. I wish I did. If she's not with Xander and Xochitl, I have no idea. She doesn't have anyone beyond them that she is that close to. At least none that I'm aware of. And I guess, what do I really know about her after all?"

"One more question," Lloyd folded his hands in front of him. "You don't think it's odd—not at all strange that it was Macy who got Calypso's file from New Orleans?"

Parker shook her head. "I want to believe that my wife is who she said she is. That she wouldn't shoot me. That it's all some bizarre and manufactured conspiracy theory. But too much fits with this right now."

He only nodded, not saying another word.

* * *

AUGUST 18

House arrest was the closest equivalent to staying home for a week to recover. Parker rarely took time off and seldom had nothing to do. She took the time to change the gate code and the locks on the house on the chance that it was Calypso who shot her. She still had doubts about that, though.

She would have Lloyd bring her files, and then they would go through and discuss strategies together. He emerged as astute, and he caught on fast. In the beginning, he stayed quiet and soaked up Parker's knowledge. Slowly, he began to match Parker in ability and strategy. He brought the files to her more for her benefit than his own. They both recognized it. But it beat sitting in her house alone and brooding over her messy life.

Macy called her every day to check on her during her off time. She offered to go pick up food or run errands for Parker. It was sweet. Parker always thanked her and declined the offer.

Parker kept hearing Lloyd's voice in the back of her mind, suggesting that she put some distance between herself and Macy. When Macy volunteered to bring her food or help out, Parker told her she was fine. Everything was good. It wasn't. But having Macy come and complicate things further would do no one any good. Maybe she was being overcautious at this point. But right now was not the time to give in to crazy. Or messy. Or drama.

The hardest part of this recovery time wasn't the injuries. It was the absence of Calypso. Her perfume lingered in the room—a vanilla, orange, and lavender ghost hanging in the air. It permeated the carpet and fabrics of the house.

It was the empty bed beside her. Not having the warmth and softness she had grown accustomed to next to her.

It was the thought that Calypso had been living a lie and keeping it from her. The thought that Calypso would even do this to her. The utter betrayal. It didn't make sense. Not one bit. Parker was at complete odds with the entire situation. But she *saw* the file. She discerned the facts and the way everything had gone down from beginning to end. But she still replayed it obsessively again and again in her head, trying to find the different angles, trying to make it make sense.

The emotional side of her couldn't comprehend it. Her lawyer side—it made absolute sense. She planned on voiding the marriage to Calypso and Calypso would get nothing. As long as Parker hadn't changed the trust, Parker was worth a lot of money to Calypso if she died. The motive was absolutely there. There was no way around it. Money and sex. The top two motives for almost every single crime committed since the dawn of time.

But the emotional side argued that as well. Calypso wasn't necessarily materialistic.

But—she never turned down the gifts Parker gave her either. She wore the diamond necklace, the earrings, and the rings, drove the car, shopped on Parker's credit card, and quit her job shortly after the wedding. So maybe there was something to that motive. It doesn't take long to get used to the particular lifestyle Parker provided.

This loop running in the back of her mind would drive her crazy as she lay awake at night pondering this.

On Calypso's side of the bed, instead of her wife's warm body, Kitty would sit and stare at her. Kitty followed Calypso around the house as if Calypso were her chosen human. Kitty sat there and asking where Calypso was.

"I get it. We're all feeling the loss right now." Parker reached over to pet Kitty. She turned and jumped off the bed. "Wow. Remember who feeds you and puts a roof over your head," she grumbled as Kitty walked away with its tail straight up.

While she waited for Lloyd to come over and work on the case with her, she would put stupid, mindless reality shows on in an effort to quiet her thoughts. Nothing stopped her from turning the issue of Calypso over in her brain. It was constant and heavy. And she capably argued both sides, and it did her no good. She was no closer to feeling one way or the other. She had to wait it out and hope she was right and Calypso would come to her.

Standing in Calypso's closet, Parker thought about clearing out the remainder of what Calypso had left behind, but she couldn't bear it. After taking in the array of mostly black clothing neatly hung, she slammed the closet door.

As she walked past the empty wall in the living room, she wondered what her father had done with the portrait that hung over the couch. She called him, and he only said it was stored away for now. She made him swear that he hadn't thrown it away.

He told her she might want to see a therapist to help her through this ordeal.

That stung. But maybe he was right. She was on the verge of obsession with this situation. She couldn't believe she misread the whole relationship and Calypso's motives.

Lloyd would patiently sit and listen to her as she mulled it over again and again. Each time, he steered her back to the same theory. Calypso shot her, hoping to cash in on the trust before the marriage was voided.

"Have you voided it yet?" He asked her.

Parker flinched. "When the fuck did I have time for that?"

Lloyd shrugged. "The hours you are sitting here by yourself, I figured you might have worked on that."

"I'm not ready," Parker admitted. "Don't judge me."

"So, if she comes after you again, she gets everything? No judgment whatsoever." God, he could be a snarky little prick sometimes.

"If she comes for me again, she's stupid. She has to realize Macy's got everyone on the lookout for her. And Calypso's not stupid. So the likelihood of her even coming back for me is little to none."

"Point taken. But you think she's going to reach out to you?"

"She will. Eventually."

30 HIDING OUT

August 20
Calypso

STARING OUT THE WINDOW, but seeing nothing, really. Nothing registered, and nothing made sense. It was different here than in Southern California. She was surrounded by lush greenery and rain. Pine trees swayed in the wind, and the rain pelted the window. Not that she truly saw or could appreciate any of that. The chill, dampness, and constant gloominess of the weather did nothing to help her mood.

Friends are a great resource. But they were no replacement for Parker.

Calypso's heart couldn't take it. She couldn't take not having Parker in her life. And she couldn't believe that Parker would throw her out so easily. Things hadn't been great for a while, but she never would have guessed it would have ended so badly. Parker merely quit. Telling her she was nothing. Calypso thought they were on the road to work things out. Maybe she shouldn't have been so petty that night and stayed out with her friends, all because Parker ended up stuck at work. After Parker texted, Calypso turned the news on and took note of why. Parker's client was in a world of trouble after they found his girlfriend's body. She knew better. She was being immature and stupid. She acted out instead of being a grown-up and talking to Parker about it. She had planned to apologize and make it up to Parker when . . .

It was surprising to her how quickly she adapted to a domestic life. She enjoyed cooking for Parker. Being there for her. Having Parker come home to her. She even loved the Cat.

But here she was homeless. Licking her wounds at a friend's house, occupying a spare bedroom. That fucking bitch Macy Quinn threw a wrench in the whole ordeal. This had to have come from her. There's no one else who would have given this "information" to Parker.

Calypso should have known. She should have been able to figure out that Macy would not fade into the background and let her have her peace, have her life with Parker. Let her have her happily ever after. It was no secret that Macy was hopelessly in love with Parker. Did that crazy bitch actually think Parker would choose her if Calypso is out of the way?

She reflected on the last several months of issues with Parker. She thought about the fights. The accusations. The pettiness.

She regretted every second of it.

She thought about that night she woke up when Parker got home and . . . Her heart couldn't take thinking about it. She thought everything was going to be alright. Parker had promised to scale back after this trial was done. Parker had told Calypso to plan a trip somewhere. Any amount of time. Anywhere. She would leave her phone and laptop at home, allowing them to spend much-needed quality time together.

If someone truly loves you and trusts you, they don't throw you away without allowing you to give your side of the story. Parker wanted to be Parker. She didn't want to work on this marriage. She wanted to go back to life as it was before they got involved. To her former status quo as some sort of lothario. Win in court. Build a client list of notable figures. Rake in the money. Random hookups. A wife was simply an inconvenience in her life. But in those ever more rare occasions she did get to be with Parker, she got to be the beneficiary of that intensity and focus. And that feeling of being the center of Parker's world was intoxicating. A drug. And here Calypso lay, staring at the ceiling in absolute withdrawal.

She would never see Parker again.

She would never hold Parker again.

She would never know that kind of love again.

She left her car, her cell phone, and her wedding band behind.

She left Parker behind.

Calypso took a modest amount of cash from her savings, as she wasn't certain if this was a permanent situation or what she would need if it didn't get settled. She wanted to call Parker and talk to her. Talk sense into her. Hear Parker's voice.

The only person she had been in contact with after she left was Javier. It was an impulsive call. She asked him if she could still cash in on the favor he owed her. He laughed and told her anytime. She told him what she wanted, then immediately regretted it. She tried to walk it back. He told her he would think about it. An ask was an ask—she'd rung the bell. "Be careful what you wish for, chula. You might just get it." He hung up before she could say anything else.

A knock on the door to her room pulled her out of her

head. "Calypso?" Gilian called through the door of the guest room she was staying in while she un-fucked her life.

"Come in." Calypso was lying in the dark, staring at the blue patterns the rain-mottled windows cast. Essentially, how she spent every day since she arrived at Gilian's house. Calypso met Gilian in high school. They were unlikely friends paired together for a class project. After the project finished, they continued to talk and hang out. Gilian's parents had housed Calypso more than a few nights after her own parents threw her out. Gilian went on to walk the traditional path of going to college, joining a sorority, meeting a frat boy, and marrying said frat boy, who had gone on to become a doctor. Not that Gilian didn't have an impressive career working in human rights (inspired by Calypso's story). She became a grant writer for an international human rights coalition. And here Gilian was taking her in again after she had been thrown out again. It was no surprise that the first place she would go to would be Gilian's.

"Um . . . there's a story in the news from California. I think you need to see it."

Gilian handed Calypso her phone.

A picture of Parker graced the screen as Calypso scrolled through. It was one of her as she held a press conference after winning a case. She wore her cocky smile on her face, and her eyes were narrowed as she faced the sun as she spoke.

The headline read, 'Prominent Defense Attorney Found Shot in Her Home.'

Calypso scanned the rest of the article. It stated that they had no real suspects, as it could be a family member or loved one of a victim of a client she had defended at some point. But more than likely, the article said, it was Parker's wife,

Calypso. They wanted her to come in for questioning. But they can't find her, which makes it look even more suspicious. Her phone and her car had been found abandoned. At the airport. Keys inside. Parker's gun is missing.

Parker walked into the house, and whoever it was shot her once in the shoulder and once in the hip and left her for dead. According to sources, Parker was hesitant to consider Calypso as the suspect. And because it was dark and the perpetrator shot her from behind, she didn't see the shooter.

Calypso handed the phone back to Gilian. "Fuck." Was all she was able to say. She didn't have the energy to say anything further. She lay back down against the pillow and fought the tears that were threatening to flow.

"She doesn't think it's you." Gilian put her hand on Calypso's calf.

"It doesn't matter. Everyone else is convinced I did it. If I've learned anything from being married to Parker, the court of public opinion is almost as important as the courtroom itself."

Gilian sighed. "Maybe you need to reach out and talk to Parker." She was so hopeful. Clueless. But hopeful. She didn't know Parker, though. She only met her once at the wedding for all of thirty seconds.

"She made it clear that she doesn't want anything to do with me. And now I'm wanted for attempted murder. Just great."

"In the moment, sure, she said she wanted nothing to do with you. But, I would bet by now, she would love to hear from you. She would be willing to listen to what you have to say. She loved you. She married you. She almost died. That can change a person's perspective on things."

"She also took Macy's word over me mine. I may as well have been yesterday's trash the way she threw me out. She doesn't want me."

"Calypso, how would you even know? She has no way of contacting you. You left your phone—"

"Because she paid the bill."

"Your car—"

"That she bought."

"Whatever. Reach out to her."

"I'm not ready."

"She's not your mama and your daddy. She's your *wife*."

"Not for much longer. She said she was gonna void the marriage." Calypso rolled onto her side. She plainly saw she was being petulant; some of Parker's brattiness had worn off on her.

"I'm makin' my mama's gumbo recipe tonight. At least come out of the room long enough to eat."

Calypso couldn't resist Gilian's mother's gumbo. It was her absolute favorite meal in the world. If anything were going to coax her out of wallowing in the bedroom, that would be it.

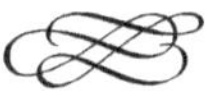

eptember 10
Macy

A month had passed since Parker was shot.

In that month, no matter what Macy tried to do to help Parker, Parker denied her. It was frustrating. Not because she still carried an unrequited flame for Parker, but because she genuinely cared for Parker and wanted to be there for her in any capacity Parker allowed her to be. She wanted to be included in Parker's life. Especially now that Calypso was gone and she *could* be back in Parker's life.

Meanwhile she spent her time at her desk. She would work eighteen-hour days so she could avoid the hollowness of her personal life. She was still quite literally the most dedicated detective in the department. Even if all of her work was relegated to a monitor. She was still one of the best.

It had been a long day already and it was only noon. The damn buzzing in the lights had her teeth on edge and the AC had to be broke. Sweat trickled down the back of her neck.

When Lloyd unexpectedly showed up and was escorted to her desk, her adrenaline kicked extra hard. Especially because he wasn't there for any other purpose than to speak to her.

"What brings you here? Slumming it?" Turning in her chair to better face Lloyd, she was skeptical of his presence.

"I'm just about to go grab lunch. Care to join?" He could be charming at times. And he had it on full bore right now.

Macy was deep in a file dealing with a geofencing case. The suspect's alibi and the location of his phone didn't match. She did a double take from the screen at Lloyd. "Me? You are asking *me* to have lunch with you? Is Parker not available for you to be lodged up her ass?" She started organizing the chaos of papers all around her desk, gathering the protein bar wrappers and old coffee cups and scooping them into the trash. She wasn't expecting "company." There was a spillover of her mess and chaos onto Brent's still empty desk. No one wanted to work that close to her. Which was fine. She preferred it that way.

"You're just jealous because you know that's where you would prefer to be." Okay. Back to our regularly scheduled program.

Macy turned back her to screen. "Why do you want to have lunch with me?"

"Because we both care about Parker. We are tied together because of our relationships with her. I want to maybe smooth things over with you so we can be friends. Don't worry. Juliana is meeting us there. You won't have to be alone with me." A playful grin spread on his lips.

"Why is Juliana coming? She's Parker's assistant."

"Because all three of us are concerned about Parker."

Macy turned off her monitor and stood, grabbing her phone and bag. "I guess. Fine. Let's do this."

She and Lloyd walked three blocks to a Mexican restaurant famed for its jalapeño margaritas, where Juliana was already waiting. Identical to her boss, she had a pen and yellow pad out and was busy working. Her pen wasn't a Montblanc like Parker's, but it was definitely nice. Expensive.

Lloyd pulled Macy's chair out and then sat at the table. Juliana finished the note she was writing and smiled genuinely at Macy, setting the pen down.

"So this all started when you exposed Calypso." Lloyd pointed out.

Macy's heart hammered hard. "Yeah. I got the file and I showed it to Parker."

"Where's the file now?" Juliana asked.

"Why?" Macy was having flashbacks to being on the stand.

"Just because I want to see it. Calypso and Parker were having issues, and this felt a little too convenient for Parker to create an excuse and kick Calypso out. Parker is like family to me. I just want to see what tipped the scales for her, and she won't talk about it."

"Maybe she doesn't want you in her business." Macy pretended to study the menu.

Juliana sighed. "Macy, I'm not trying to be difficult."

"I gave the file over to Jackson."

"But you had an electronic copy, right?" Lloyd asked.

Macy shrugged. She was really feeling attacked.

"You can send us the digital copy." Lloyd offered.

"They took away all of my access to anything that has to do with Parker or Calypso. I'm too close." Macy wondered if she could get away with having a margarita at lunch before going back. She wouldn't be drunk. She could probably do her job better drunk than half the department did sober.

She noticed Lloyd and Juliana exchange a look. She tried to ignore it but felt her cheeks flaming hot.

"So if I call Jackson, he will be able to send it?"

"No. It's an active investigation, and he wouldn't be

allowed to share it with you." Her answer came quicker than she wanted it to.

"Since when does your department follow the rules like that? I know firsthand you used to give information on active cases to Parker." Juliana crossed her arms over her chest. So much time with her boss, she was starting to imitate her mannerisms.

"That . . . that's different. I didn't give her actual evidence. I didn't give her hard copies or digital copies. She would get me drunk and coax the information out of me. And if that got out, I would be fired. I broke protocol for her because . . ." Her voice trailed off.

"Because you love her." Lloyd's voice was quiet. Understanding.

Macy felt the tears welling in her eyes. God dammit. She didn't want to show this kind of vulnerability to Lloyd and Juliana. With shaking hands she swiped at the tears.

"We all love her." Juliana placed her hand on Macy's arm with tenderness. The small gesture of it reminded Macy how lonely and starved of connection she had been. "Maybe not the same way you do. But we all love her."

"Why do you want the file?" Macy asked, forcing herself to get a grip.

"Just so we can try to understand why Calypso did what she did," Juliana explained.

"I'm sorry. I can't help you with that. All I can say is that Calypso was a fraud, liar, and killer. And now attempted to kill Parker, too."

"No love lost between the two of you," Lloyd called out.

Macy put her menu back on the table and walked out without saying another word. None of this felt right. Something was up with this whole situation. What did they know or think they knew?

* * *

MACY WENT BACK to the precinct and sat at her desk. Eyes were on her in every direction.

She fired up her screen and searched up Calypso's file. No one had been in it since she handed it over to Jackson. She could easily send it to Lloyd and Juliana but she didn't trust them, suspecting they were trying to trap her.

Jackson still hadn't received a call back from New Orleans. It had been weeks since he tried to contact them. He wasn't doing enough. He needed to be doing more. If they would let her work it, Calypso would already be in a cell, and a trial would be scheduled. She could easily track Calypso. She could make sure all of the evidence against her fit.

She clicked through Calypso's information. Known contacts. Gilian Viers was her best friend. Macy knew Calypso lived off and on with her family. She highlighted the contact and put a note in the file for Jackson to start there. Track her down and she would probably find Calypso. They were still close. Gilian and her husband were at the wedding.

God. Did she have to do everything? Did Jackson not know what's at stake here?

32 THE TEXT

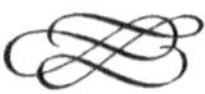

PARKER

*S*ix weeks after what Parker only referred to as "the incident," the trial she had been working on finally went into the hands of the jury. She delivered a searing closing argument. Having deftly brought the jury into the palm of her hands, she thought it was probably going to land in her favor. She studied them as she laid out the case for why her client should be found not guilty. She discerned exactly which ones were eating out of her hand, and those that she hoped she would win over. Normally, she enjoyed that rush. Not today. Today, she was empty. Depleted. She had been struggling to find her way back to herself since "the incident." But she was forever changed.

The judge gave the jury their instructions and called the court to recess until a verdict was rendered. Meanwhile, back in her office, Parker sat with the lights out and her feet on her desk. She was absolutely not herself. Her whole life had been thrown off center. She wasn't reading her mail. It sat unread, accumulating in a large pile on the kitchen island. It would have to be tended to eventually, but meanwhile, autopay was a saving grace. Meanwhile, she was in too much pain, physically and emotionally, to deal with anything more. It was enough that she was even working. She refused to take the painkillers the doctor prescribed for the last few weeks. The brain fog was not worth the relief from the pain.

The veggie burger she ordered for lunch was getting cold next to her custom Italian leather shoes on her desk.

Her suit jacket was hung up on a hanger on the back of the door, and her tie loosened. Life had been out of balance since she found out about Calypso. She hadn't been sleeping, and food held little interest for her. Not wanting to go home, she was hiding in her office—a dark and silent haven. It was dark and silent. Like her heart. She gagged at that thought. So dramatic. But it was true.

Leaning back in her chair, with her eyes closed, she didn't even bother to open them when Juliana knocked on her office door. "Parker?" Juliana popped her head in. "The jury is back."

She popped up with a groan. Her arm was still in a sling, and her hip still hurt with every step she took.

Lloyd was already out of his office. She tossed him her car key, so she could adjust her tie and put her jacket back on as they walked. Lloyd had caught her key deftly. "Really? I get to drive your Jag? That car is your baby."

"I trust you. Let's go." Truth was, she didn't want to drive. It required too much focus, and she didn't have much more to muster today.

"This isn't good. Them coming back so quick." Lloyd's forehead wrinkled with concern.

"Most of the time, no, it's not good. But I think this is

going to go in our favor. I could tell by their reaction during closing." Parker's voice came abnormally quiet. She didn't even recognize it. But in truth, nothing made sense to her. Any other day, running back to the court for a verdict would be a huge rush for her.

"Are you okay?" A look of concern in his eyes as he stopped in his tracks and turned to face Parker.

"No. But fake it till you make it, right?"

A slight nod, the concern not fading from his eyes and he kept moving forward.

* * *

LLOYD GOT them back to the courthouse without incident, despite his lead foot. Parker stared out the window the whole time. She was not used to feeling so out of step. She lived her life in total control. She couldn't remember a time when she wasn't.

As they sat in the courtroom and waited for the jury to come back in with the verdict, her phone vibrated on the table. Flipping the phone over, Parker picked it up and previewed the message. It was from an unknown number. It read: "Parker, this is Calypso. I need to talk to you."

Sitting bolt upright, Parker nudged Lloyd and gave him her phone. His eyes got big. Their client, who had been sitting at the table with them, drumming his fingers against it and vibrating his leg up and down rapidly, was impatient as he turned toward Parker and Lloyd. "Is everything okay? Is this about the verdict?"

"No. It's a personal matter." Placing her hand on his shoulder to calm him.

Lloyd slid the phone back to her. "What are you going to do?"

Before she could say anything more, the court was called to session.

Everyone rose for the judge and then sat back down as the jury was escorted back to their seats. Vision swimming and head spinning, her mouth went dry as she fought the feeling she was going to pass out. It was as if the world had tilted off its axis. She knew Calypso would reach out to her eventually. She called it weeks ago. But now that she actually had, Parker didn't know what she was supposed to do or say.

The judge sent the bailiff to take the verdict from the jury, but Parker was disengaged. All the sounds came muffled against the sound of her heartbeat in her ears.

The judge requested that her client stand for the verdict.

A verdict of not guilty was given. But Parker's head buzzed, and she couldn't breathe.

She was on autopilot. She hugged her client, shook hands with his family, and excused herself to the bathroom. It took everything in her power to keep everyone from thinking she was ripping apart at the seams.

As she pushed her way into the bathroom door, someone called her name. She whispered a quiet "fuck" under her breath as she turned around. Macy stood there, smiling. "Hey, Macy." Parker forced a smile. "I thought you were still riding the desk?"

"I had to drop some info off to Cameron. How are things?"

Parker nodded her head slightly. "Good. Hey, I got to use the facilities and head back to the office. Catch up later?"

"Yeah. But wait." Parker could see the hurt in her eyes. "Did I do something wrong? I feel like you've been avoiding me ever since you got back from the hospital."

"No. I just have a lot on my mind. I swear. I'll call you later." Parker hid in the bathroom. After checking to make sure she was alone, she locked the door, braced herself on the counter, and stared at her reflection. She didn't recognize herself. Her eyes seemed completely vacant.

Parker pulled her phone out of her pocket and opened the screen again. "Parker, this is Calypso. I need to talk to you." She read it again and again. Before responding, she filled her lungs with a deep inhalation. With shaking fingers, she replied, "Prove it."

The dots indicating a pending response appeared and then disappeared several times before a picture popped up on the screen. It was Calypso. A selfie date- and time-stamped for right now. Parker studied the picture. Calypso wore no makeup, and her eyes appeared tired and sad, like her own.

"What do you need to tell me? Sorry for shooting me and almost killing me? Sorry for lying to me about who you are?" Parker wanted to say *I miss you, come home*, but she understood that was the last thing she should type. She understood all too clearly that would be rock bottom and her father would lock her up in a mental ward.

"I don't want to talk about it on text or phone."

"Where?"

"I won't give that information on text."

"Why?"

"I don't want you giving the information over to Macy and her friends."

Parker sighed: "Call me tonight at nine."

Calypso sent a thumbs-up.

* * *

WHEN PARKER GOT HOME, she fed the cat, revisited the exchange with Calypso, and studied the picture Calypso had sent. Something didn't feel right. It didn't sit right, deep down. Karen had left her a crock pot of minestrone, which Parker unplugged and didn't bother to eat.

With her head still fuzzy and unclear, she went up to her bedroom and forced herself to persevere through her nightly routine. Brush teeth, wash face, put on PJs, and grab a book. The book sat open on her lap, and she tried and failed to read the words on the pages. The words were nothing but a blurry jumble on the page. Every so often, she would check her phone to make sure she didn't miss Calypso calling or texting.

At nine sharp, her phone rang with the same number Calypso had texted from earlier.

"Hey," her voice was flat as she rubbed her temples. She didn't have it in her to be anything other than neutral about this conversation.

"I need to start with this. Parker, you talked *at* me, not *to* me. You didn't bother to hear me out—"

"I *saw* the file with my own eyes. Are we really going to go there again?"

Calypso sighed on the other end. "I want to talk to you in person. Actually, I *need* to talk to you in person."

"So you can finish the job?"

"Parker, what are you even talking about?"

It was Parker's turn to sigh. "You *shot* me. *Twice.* In the back. I nearly died."

"I didn't—"

"Cut the bullshit, Calypso. You are the only one with motive and a history of killing her lovers."

"Fine. Okay. I'm not going to waste time trying to convince you of things you refuse to believe. Meet me in person so we can talk. Please, Parker?"

Parker paused. This could go two ways. It might be a trap, allowing Calypso to finish the job, or it might possibly be closure.

"Parker?"

"Where?"

"I'm in Washington state, in Gig Harbor, southwest of Seattle. I'm staying with a friend." Seattle. Didn't Macy say Xochitl went to Seattle for a conference? Makes sense. That's probably how Calypso got there. Xochitl would never admit that, though. Parker knew their level of loyalty to Calypso was fierce.

"When?"

"The sooner the better. I will be here for another week before I leave."

"Where will you be going after?"

"I can't tell you that. Not until we talk face-to-face."

"Is this the number to reach you at?"

"It's a number. Not mine. I will reach out to you in a few days and see if you're here."

"I will be there."

Calypso hung up.

Collapsing back against the pillows and staring at the ceiling, she was at war with herself. She was acutely aware that she shouldn't still be in love with Calypso. She should hate her. She should be turning all of this over to the cops. But she couldn't turn that part of her heart off. She couldn't flip a switch and not feel what she felt for Calypso. It wasn't that easy. If only it were.

PART III
THE RECKONING

33 I'VE GOT YOUR SIX

SEPTEMBER 24

MACY

Macy's phone rang at nine thirty with Parker's ringtone. She jumped on it (nothing like looking desperate). "Parker, hey."

"Hey. Hi. Sorry, it's so late."

Macy glanced at the clock. "No worries. None at all. It's not even late, really. Is everything okay?"

"Look. I need your help. But I need you as a friend. Not as a cop." Parker's voice sounded off. Macy couldn't put her finger on it, but something wasn't right.

"Yeah. Anything. What's up?"

"Calypso called me. She wants to meet up."

"What? Really? Where?" Macy perked up at this information.

"I don't want to tell you until I have your word that you're not going to feed it to your friends."

"I promise. You have my word."

"You're still riding the desk, right?"

"Yeah."

"Can you take time off? All-expenses-paid trip to the Pacific Northwest?"

"I suspected she left the state. I had a suspicion. I'm just shocked she didn't leave the country." Macy's voice was quiet.

"Macy, you can't tell a soul. I need to meet with her first. She's going to be in Gig Harbor, it's outside of Seattle. Once I'm able to talk to her, I will hand over the information, and then you can do whatever."

"I can call in sick for the next few days. But why me?"

"Because if shit goes down and she tries to finish the job, I know you can jump in and help."

Macy's heart did a flip-flop. Not only would she be going away with Parker, but Parker had confidence in her ability. And her self-confidence needed that boost right now. She needed to feel respected. And Parker respected her. Trusted her. Parker was choosing her to be by her side. It's all she ever wanted.

"I'm looking at flights right now. We can fly nonstop from Orange County to Seattle. The flight leaves at two in the afternoon. I'll pick you up at eleven. Can you be ready by then?"

"Yeah, that will work. How long do you think we'll be there?" Macy already began looking at a website for vacation rentals in and near Gig Harbor. It appeared to be a quiet, sleepy town, and it was off-season, so they were all cheap.

"Prepare for about a week?"

"I can get us a vacation rental."

"You don't need to do that. I can book us a couple of rooms at—"

"No. I want to. I don't believe in free rides." Calypso may

have been all about Parker's money, but Macy wanted to show she was independent and could handle things, too. Especially if the hypothesis about Calypso was that she was out for money. She would earn Parker's confidence even more by being able to provide, too.

"Okay. If you insist." Macy couldn't read Parker's tone.

"Thank you, Parker."

Parker laughed, but it was mirthless. "Why are you thanking me?"

"For having enough faith in me to ask me to come with you."

"Yeah. Of course."

Macy could only hope she would be there when Calypso met up with Parker.

* * *

SEPTEMBER 25

Parker arrived at Macy's driveway as planned at eleven sharp. After throwing her bag in the trunk Macy hopped in the passenger seat. Parker wore jeans and a black sweater. Her eyes shone extra green, albeit tired. As Macy clicked her seatbelt in place she inhaled the scent of Parker's cologne. Her mouth began to water.

"What do you think she wants to tell you?" Macy asked.

"I have no idea. I wish I knew. Can we talk about something else, though? I don't have it in me to discuss her."

"Of course."

Macy decided to talk about the latest with her efforts in trying to get off desk duty. Parker didn't add much to the conversation. She mostly nodded or asked a random question that made it appear as though she might be listening.

* * *

WHEN THEY BOARDED THE PLANE, Macy was not surprised that Parker booked them first class. She had, to this date, never sprung for first class herself. She was excited when she sat down, and a flight attendant immediately put a drink in her hand.

As they took off, Macy caught Parker looking at her but she couldn't decipher the look on Parker's face. Macy pulled her AirPods out and looked back at Parker, trying to figure out what the look in Parker's eyes meant.

"What?" Macy finally asked her.

"I just . . . It's nothing. No." Parker turned back the other way.

"Parker, we have two more hours on this flight. Just tell me. It's going to stress me out." Macy put her AirPods back in their case. "Do I need to remind you, I'm in a fragile state, too. I'm in mandated therapy for fuck's sake." She tried to smile and make light of the heaviness in the air.

Parker turned in her seat to face Macy and forced a smile at Macy's attempt at a joke before shaking her head and pausing to look up at the ceiling. "I just wonder sometimes. Because I'm so very aware of how you feel about me, it's not just because I overheard your conversation with Lloyd. I've always known. You've made it no secret."

Macy's face betrayed her, flushing deep red. "And you wonder what?" Her voice was a whisper, and her heart pounded hard. She worked to remind herself to breathe.

"I wonder what life would have been like if I had just chosen you." It all came out in a quiet breath, barely audible.

Macy faced Parker. "It's not too late." Tears prickled in her eyes, and she couldn't explain them. Hope bloomed inside of her.

Parker chewed at her lip. "I just . . . Macy, you have to

understand. This isn't easy for me. I can't just jump to you. I need to be able to put this behind me and see where I stand after."

The crushing weight of her continued disappointment settled back into Macy's chest. She leaned back against her seat and put her AirPods back in and let her eyelids slide shut. Part of her was angry that Parker, knowing how she felt, would say that. It was unfair.

Her hands were shaking. She pulled her hair up into a messy bun and took the AirPods back out, and again faced Parker.

Parker was looking out the window. "Parker—"

"Not right now, Macy."

"No. It's not that." Macy recovered quickly, even though it was what she wanted to talk about.

Parker turned her head away from the window and back toward Macy. "What?"

"What's your plan? With Calypso? We need to be clear on what we plan to do. Or at least I need to know."

Parker paused. "I need to talk to her. I need to give her a chance to be heard. And I need to understand why."

"Why what?"

"Why she lied. Why she shot me."

"Do you think she's actually going to tell you the truth?"

"Obviously, I have no way of knowing for sure. But I'm hoping she will. I'm going all the way out here to put an end to this."

Macy nodded and put her AirPods back in. The fact that Parker wanted so badly to get this closure—to have this conversation with Calypso—didn't bode well for her hopes that Parker stirred up and brought to life. *Fucking Calypso. She literally ruins everything.*

Parker went back to looking out the window. Macy wanted more than anything to take Parker's hand in hers.

She wanted to put her head on Parker's shoulder. She wanted Parker to see a future with her. To see that she could be everything Parker wanted and more.

The flight attendant came back with trays of food. Parker accepted her tray but didn't touch it. She continued to stare out the window. Macy held back from asking her what she was so focused on. She wanted Parker to talk to her. To confide in her.

She poked at her salad, ultimately putting the lid back on the tray and also forgoing the meal. Instead, she ordered another cocktail.

Two cocktails helped her relax and push aside thoughts of the conversation and hopes. Instead she closed her eyes and listened to the latest Fletcher album. God bless rum and coke. God bless AirPods and good music. And just like that, they were wheels on the ground in Seattle.

34 PLAYING WITH FIRE

PARKER

*R*egret. A feeling foreign to Parker. But Parker was experiencing all kinds of new feelings and emotions lately. And regret was huge right now. Parker regretted confessing to Macy that she often wondered how things could have been different if they had ended up in a relationship instead. It was true that she had considered it recently, albeit not with any depth. But in those unsettlingly quiet and lonely times when she was alone and in her feelings, it wasn't something she should have spilled to Macy.

She wasn't intentionally playing with Macy's emotions. Admittedly, she did exactly that in the courtroom. Which she knew full well made her kind of evil. She constantly leveraged Macy's feelings against her in court, knowing full well that Macy's coworkers would give her absolute hell. Knowing full well that she made Macy out to be an idiot.

When they landed, Macy also sprang for the rental car. Parker was impressed as Macy handed her the keys.

The town itself was surrounded by thick forest and beach land. Since it was a harbor, the waters were still and calm. The vacation rental was perfect. It had two bedrooms, a nice kitchen, and a view of the water from the living room. A covered porch with a swing outside the living room was calling to Parker. It would be a good place to sit and contemplate what a mess her life had become.

Macy paused at the doorway of the second bedroom. Parker pretended not to notice. Her emotions had her all over the place. She was not on her game at all. She was furious with Calypso. She was also at war with how much she still loved Calypso, and then add on to the top the complication that if she wanted a stable relationship with someone she could trust, Macy was right there. Macy would *always* be there. Maybe she had been blinded by Calypso.

Every time Parker checked her phone for a message from Calypso, which was frequently, there was nothing. Maybe Calypso wouldn't even follow through with the meetup. At the very least, she was getting a vacation in a peaceful location. And she had Macy. Macy, whom she seocnds ago told she would consider a relationship with.

The sun glinted off the waves, and the air was crisp and so much more fresh than Southern California. The leaves on several of the trees around the house were starting to change colors from green to gold and red. She pulled the air deep into her lungs, trying to anchor herself before she let it go. The possibility of being with Calypso ever again was dead. She lied. She took advantage of the situation. Parker also felt gratitude for the time with Calypso. It taught her that being in love and settling down wasn't the worst thing after all. She kinda enjoyed domestic life. Coming home to one person every night. Routines and traditions that naturally come to belong to only the two of you. The small intimacies and inside jokes. There's a value to that. That simple touch on the small of the back as you pass each other. The graze of fingers on the back of the neck. Those meant so much more than one would think. Especially Parker.

Macy came outside and sat by Parker's side on the porch swing.

There was no logic in it other than being deep in her feels, but Parker reached over and took Macy's hand in hers. Macy's hands were soft. She took in how Macy held her breath and closed her eyes at the gesture. No one would probably ever love Parker so deeply. Not even Calypso. And Macy was not a bad person. And it wasn't that Macy wasn't pretty, she absolutely was.

Macy never wavered in loyalty and devotion to Parker. Even accepted a role as a friend to maintain a spot in her life. And she respected Parker's boundaries that Calypso had hard-lined for her. That's love. True love. She loved Parker enough to set her free. Parker studied Macy's features as she sat there with her eyes closed.

Drowning in her own thoughts, Parker felt overwhelmed, lost, unmoored. Macy opened her blue eyes, and the look of apprehension pulled Parker back to the present.

Parker took her hand and ran it down Macy's cheek to her neck. Macy shivered slightly under her touch, and Parker pushed aside any trepidation and reserve that would hold her back and brought Macy closer in. She was less than a hair away from Macy's lips. She felt Macy's breath hot and insistent as she narrowed the distance between them. Macy's kiss was eight years of pent-up emotion. Hungry and deep, pulling Parker under in a wave of heat and need.

Parker backed away and pulled Macy to her feet, leading her to the bedroom she claimed only an hour ago.

She pulled Macy back into her. Macy's frame was firm

and toned from countless hours at the gym and refusing to be the stereotypical lazy cop. It wasn't the soft, lush pinup body of Calypso. Parker shut the comparison down. Thinking about Calypso now would do nothing for her.

Parker lifted Macy's shirt over her head and sat down on the bed in front of Macy, undoing her jeans and sliding them down Macy's slight hips. She pulled Macy to her, bringing her in closer. She inhaled the scent of juniper and sandalwood from Macy's soft skin. Her thumbs traced the lines of Macy's hipbones, and her lips grazed over Macy's belly. Macy straddled Parker's lap, locking her lips to Parker's. Parker pushed Macy's curtain of red hair away from her face. She expected to feel more. She wanted to feel more. She wanted the pain in her chest to go away—this time with Macy to be a Band-Aid to help her heal. Maybe, just maybe, it would get there if she let it.

Macy sat up and slipped her bra off. Parker rolled Macy onto her back, putting herself back in a position of command. If she were in charge of this, it would allow her to be in charge of her feelings. Her mind. Her heart. She slipped between Macy's thighs and teased her with her breath over her panties. Macy gasped. Parker dragged her tongue over the fabric and up to Macy's bare belly and into Macy's neck before bringing her lips back to Macy's. Macy clutched Parker tight to her.

Parker's hand slipped down and teased over the fabric. Macy writhed against Parker's touch, anxiously trying to get more pressure.

Parker gave in and slipped her fingers under the fabric. Slick and hot and pure need. Macy moved against Parker.

To Parker's delight, Macy came fast and hard. But Parker did not relent. She pulled Macy's panties off and buried herself between Macy's thighs. She would give Macy no reprieve. Not that Macy seemed to mind one bit as Parker recognized without a doubt that she owned every bit of Macy. Macy's whimpers and moans drove Parker harder. She allowed them to drown out any thought of the Calypso or the wounds she left behind—both physical and emotional.

Parker, for the first time in over a month, finally shut off all of her racing thoughts and surrendered herself. She pinned Macy's hips down with her hands so that Macy couldn't move and couldn't back away. Macy's thighs trembled over Parker's shoulders, and her back arched. Macy's breath was ragged as her fingers gripped Parker's hair. Parker didn't relent. She didn't give Macy a chance to come down. She kept pushing Macy over that edge again and again.

When Parker finally backed away and shed her own clothing and brought herself back onto a trembling and vulnerable Macy. Macy couldn't seem to hold her close enough. Her fingers pressed into Parker's back, and her legs around Parker's thighs, as if she let go for too long, Parker would disappear.

Tears streamed down her face as Parker kissed her. Parker wiped them away. "Are you okay?"

Macy opened her eyes. "I just . . . I don't want this if it's not real. If it's just something to distract you while you try to heal from your relationship with Calypso. I don't think I can handle that. And I'm scared that's exactly what this is."

Parker didn't have the capacity to discuss that. She didn't know exactly what *this* was or where it could even go. But deep down, she had every inclination that Macy was right. This was nothing but a distraction to put Calypso's betrayal behind her.

Macy released her grip on Parker's body, and her hands drifted through Parker's hair. "I'm sorry," Macy whispered. "I know that's a total mood killer."

"I can't promise or guarantee anything. I can't, Macy. I

can promise you I'm here right now. I'm willing to take it a day at a time. That's all I can do. Can that be enough for you?"

Macy nodded and pulled Parker back in. Her hands traced over Parker's body, slow and deliberate. Parker let Macy take her time exploring her body with her hands and lips. Parker let her eyes fall closed and dissolved herself into the right now, allowing Macy's touch—Macy's devotion—to carry her away.

35 THE IN BETWEEN

MACY

acy awoke before Parker. She paused, glancing at Parker sleeping, absorbing the realness. She waited eight fucking years for this. For every doubt she had, Parker made up for it last night. Even though Parker wouldn't give her a promise of forever, she was going to give her a day at a time. It's better than never. It's better than a booty call. It's better than being friend zoned.

Macy fell asleep last night with Parker spooning her. Her fingers trailing up and down her side. It was better than any dream or fantasy. Better than that first time when Parker was on the opposite side of the bed before bolting up and exiting the bed as if it were on fire.

Macy slipped out of the bed and tiptoed over to the other room where she had stored all of her bags yesterday. She slipped on a pair of sweats and padded into the kitchen.

They had stopped for groceries before making their way to the rental. She decided to make coffee and breakfast for both of them when Parker woke up. A slight smile curled on her lips—breakfast with Parker. Life couldn't be any better. A romantic getaway—even though that was not the intent of this trip, but still. Parker.

After making a cup of coffee, she grabbed a throw blanket from the couch and went out to the porch. She sat on the swing and watched the waves dancing in the early morning sunlight. A bald eagle swooped from the sky to pluck a fish from the water, and a ship's horn went off in the distance. She wrapped her hands around the hot mug, soaking in the warmth that enveloped her inside and out.

It was peace from within. It was an emotion she had given up on a long time ago. She was . . . *happy*. She hadn't been this content in over seven years, and it wasn't because she had great sex the night before. Sam and A.D. were both good in bed. But it was that irreplaceable chemistry absent from anyone else. The way Parker got under her skin and into her blood.

Before she lost herself in reliving last night with Parker, Parker made her own way out of the door, clad in flannel pajama pants and a UCLA (her undergrad school) hoodie, with a cup of coffee steaming in the chill air. Her expression was unreadable, but maybe that was only because she was groggy.

"Good morning." Macy lifted the blanket, as Parker set her mug down on the table next to the swing and got under the blanket, with her back against the armrest, her inside leg bent up at the knee, and the other leg hanging from the swing. Warm arms wrapped around Macy, scooping Macy closer, pulling the blanket up around them both.

Instinctively, Macy melted back into Parker. This couldn't be real. This was a dream. A fantasy.

Parker reached behind herself and grabbed her mug of coffee. "How are you?" She asked tentatively.

"What do you mean?" Macy asked quietly.

"Yesterday, a lot happened. A lot changed. How are you feeling about it?" Parker used her toes that were off the swing to rock it gently back and forth.

"I don't want to think about it. I'm afraid that if I do, I will wake up and none of it will have been real. How are you feeling?"

Parker sighed, and Macy held her breath. "I'm thinking a lot of things, honestly."

"Like what?" Macy still hadn't taken a breath.

"Like, I kind of hope that Calypso doesn't reach out. Like, am I going about things the wrong way, rushing into something with you? It's barely been two months since the whole Calypso thing. But I also know you. I don't have to question how you feel about me."

Using a sip of her coffee to give her time to formulate her words, knowing she would have to tread carefully, she took a beat. "I don't want Calypso to show up either. I'm afraid of her showing up and you taking one look at her, and I'm sitting here with a broken heart again. I don't think I can handle you rejecting me again."

The gentle sway of the swing stopped abruptly. "I never rejected you, Macy. I've always cared about you. I simply didn't want what you wanted. I wasn't at the same place you were."

Bolting up so she could turn and face Parker. "It felt like rejection. Especially when you went and did what you said you didn't want to—no, not didn't want to—*would never* do—but with Calypso." Macy paused. "Why her? *Why* did you choose her?"

Instead of facing her, Parker stared out over the water. "You've asked that before. And I don't know. There isn't a real reason or explanation. I was caught up. I mean . . . she was different. Unconventional in every sense of the word. She came over me like a tidal wave, and I got swept up in it. Looking back, I can see it now. It was all a mistake."

Her instinct was screaming that Parker was holding something back, but she wasn't going to push it. She studied Parker's profile. "I shouldn't have even asked that question."

Finally turning to Macy, Parker's eyes were dark and sad. "It's a fair question. I'm just not sure how to answer it fully. I don't think I will ever have a coherent answer on that topic."

Trying to bring some levity to the situation, Macy smiled. "The Great Parker Harrington doesn't know what to say. That's a first."

"This whole situation has me shaken—not you and me—everything around it. I nearly died, Macy. Can you even comprehend how fucking weird that is? I never considered my own mortality. My life. My choices until then. I've never second-guessed myself before. I was aware from eight years old I would grow up to be a lawyer. It was made clear that I would be taking on my grandfather and my father's legacy. I knew who I was and what I wanted since I was twelve years old. And now . . . I just don't know."

"What don't you know?"

Parker shrugged. "My priorities mostly. I revolve everything around my career. It's who I am. It's what I am. It's all I am. I've never had to deal with this messy, complicated emotional stuff. I don't know how to act or react with any of this. I'm book smart. I graduated *summa* in undergrad, and I was the valedictorian in law school. But I feel so fucking stupid and clueless right now. I'm only good at being a lawyer. That's pretty humbling." Parker wiped a tear.

"It's not all you are. You are a friend. A lover. A daughter. A mentor. You are a lot of things besides being Parker Harrington, Esquire."

Shifting her gaze back over the water, Parker remained quiet. Aside from the single tear she let slide, she composed herself.

"I tell you what. Let's just enjoy today for what it is. And take everything day by day, as you said last night. The past is the past. And we are here now." Macy put her hand up to Parker's cheek and turned her head so that she was facing Macy again.

"That's a good plan." Parker smiled, but it didn't reach her eyes. But Macy would take it. She would take whatever scraps of herself Parker was willing to give.

"There's a hiking trail not far from here. You want to check it out after breakfast?" Macy suggested. She wanted to keep it light. Parker was in a fragile state. She could respect that. And she feared that if she kept going down the road the conversation was going, she would scare Parker off.

Parker turned to look back over the water and nodded.

Keeping one foot in front of the other, Parker was quiet throughout the hike. She did reach for Macy's hand as they strolled through the quiet path.

"You're awfully quiet," Parker called her out as they were midway through the hike, on a thickly wooded trail. It was cold and it was damp, but Macy didn't mind.

"I'm quiet because you are." Macy shrugged. "I figured you aren't in the mood to talk much." Removing her hand from Parker's, she stuck her hands into the pocket of her hoodie.

"Just thinking about what we talked about this morning. I think I'm trying to make sense of everything. I've never been so out of control in my life."

"No one is expecting you to have all of the answers right now. Or ever, really."

"I get that it's no one else pressuring me. I just don't like it."

Macy squeezed Parker's hand. "I understand."

"I don't think you do, though." Parker stopped and faced Macy.

"Give me a little credit, Parker. Please."

"I am. I brought you here. I spent the night with you. I'm giving you credit."

Macy flinched. "Do you regret it?"

"No."

"It sounds like you do."

"Macy, we said a day at a time. If you are going to be insecure and question me about this, it's not going to work."

Macy's throat was tight. She nodded.

"You need to give me credit. I promised you I'm not in this to hurt you. Just understand I'm kind of a mess right now. A fragile mess."

"And I'm here for you. However you want that to look. But you need to let me in."

Pushing a low-hanging branch out of the way, Parker continued forward on the trail. They were near the end of the trail, which ended with a bench overlooking the shore.

Macy couldn't reconcile the thought that Parker was only settling for her—that she would never love her as much as she loved Calypso. It made her want Calypso out of the picture for good that much more. She ruined Parker. She hurt Parker. It was not okay. Macy glared in the direction of the water but saw none of it. Hatred for Calypso burned through her veins. Her cheeks flamed despite the cold.

36 A SINGLE ACT TO END IT ALL

OCTOBER 1

PARKER

*A*fter five very relaxing days with Macy, Parker was content and began to give up on the idea that Calypso would try to reach back out. And she was fine with it. They were a few short hours away from the Canadian border. Maybe Calypso skipped the country.

The more time she spent with Macy, the more she realized there was a possibility to be—well, happy may not have been the word—but she might find contentment with her. Maybe one day she could see herself falling in love with her. Perhaps she didn't need that closure from Calypso. Maybe it was all for the best if Calypso faded into the background of her life. Out of sight, out of mind, as they say.

This trip was not a waste of time. It was eye-opening at the least. She needed a real break from her life, and this was it. Macy cooked, baked, and fucked on demand. She was not Calypso. She was the antithesis of Calypso, who would challenge Parker. Macy completely submitted to Parker on every level. Parker had fun with it, and playing house for five days with her gave her a taste of what life with Macy could be. And it wasn't bad. Simply different. Parker was used to getting what she wanted as soon as she decided she had to have it. Plenty of her past conquests were submissive to her demands, but nowhere near Macy's level. If Parker asked, there was no questioning, there was no banter. She gave without question or hesitation. Parker kind of got off on it a bit.

Almost in a blur, their last day in Gig Harbor was there. The fog rolled in, and so did the rain. Everything became dark and oppressive around the town. Parker turned the fireplace on. The lights kept flickering until the power went out. Parker lit some of the oil lamps set up on various end tables. Very cozy. Fire lit, oil lamps casting shadows, rain coming down outside. Ideal for a romantic last day.

Macy sat on one side of the couch with a heavy blanket over her and a smutty lesbian romance book in her hand. Parker, on the other end, sat reading Temple Grandin's memoir. She put her phone on silent, but sitting face up next to her.

Macy must have been at a spicy scene. A devious smile played on her lips, and an eyebrow cocked as she caught her lip between her teeth.

"What are you reading over there?" Nudging Macy with her foot, Parker set her book down and teased Macy. Macy's cheeks flamed pink and Parker went with it. "You should read some of it out loud for me." Macy squealed playfully. "Are you going shy on me?"

Macy giggled. "It's so raunchy."

"That's fine. Let's hear it." Nudging Macy again with her toe. These were the little details where Parker saw it becoming something.

As Macy made a playful *ahem* sound as she got ready to read out loud, Parker's screen lit up with an alert. Parker glanced at her phone; it came from a number she didn't recognize with a local exchange: "It's Calypso. Can we meet this afternoon?"

Parker responded: "What time?"

"In an hour. Alone."

Parker sent the address.

Chewing her lip, Parker had to think fast. "Actually, I'm in a lot of pain. I forgot to bring anything for that. Do you think you can go to the store in town and grab me some Motrin, and some batteries for the flashlights and the lanterns?"

With narrowed eyes and her head cocked to the side Macy crossed her arms. It couldn't be more obvious Macy didn't buy it. She was, after all, a very esteemed detective.

"Please? You can read that scene in your book to me when you get back, and I will make it very worth your time."

Unmoving and still silent, Macy was playing chess with Parker. Parker understood and could totally play this game easily. Stay silent, and the other person will eventually say the truth, or bury themselves. She knew Macy to be a master at it. But she regularly outsmarted Macy. This was the first request that Macy didn't immediately jump to.

"Macy. Please. My shoulder is literally killing me." A gross exaggeration. It was stiff and achy because of the chill and rain. "It's radiating up to my neck. Or I would go myself."

Macy sighed. "Okay. Yeah. Let me just get dressed first." They had spent the entire day in pajamas, relaxing.

After Macy left the couch, leaving her throw blanket, and went into the bedroom, Parker put her head back against the back of the couch. Fuck. Sending Macy away may not be the smartest choice. What *if* Calypso came over to finish the job?

What would she even say to Calypso? What did Calypso even want? Probably a payout to stay gone. Which was fine. Parker would happily transfer a chunk of money to Calypso if that was what she wanted.

Pulling a cream-colored beanie over her red pigtail braids as she came out of the bedroom in jeans and a sweatshirt, Macy leaned in to kiss Parker, teasing, "You're lucky you're cute." She smiled. "Where are the keys?"

Parker and Calypso used to go back and forth with the *you're lucky you're cute* schtick. It sounded so wrong coming from Macy. Parker felt a chill down her spine looking at the smile on Macy's face. "On the counter in the kitchen." The rental included parking in the attached garage, with the door conveniently located right off the kitchen.

"Be back in a few."

"While you're out, would it be too much to ask if you would pick up food, too?"

Macy stopped in her tracks but didn't turn around. "Yeah. Sure. I will see what's open and call you." Her voice sounded quiet and monotone. Parker fathomed Macy had a good idea what was going on.

* * *

BARELY FIFTEEN MINUTES after Macy left, there was a knock on the door. Panicking, stunned, heart stopped, Parker sat frozen on the couch before pulling the curtain back slightly. Standing on the porch in an oversized black sweater and black leggings and boots, drenched from the rain, was Calypso. Parker's mouth went dry. She couldn't deny it. When Macy asked why Calypso over her . . . Calypso was . . . I mean, look at her. She was a status symbol. A trophy wife.

An extraordinary, unconventional, and rare one. But goddamn. She was also so much more than that. She was a whole package.

Parker exhaled and opened the door.

Calypso's honey-gold eyes were glistening with tears as she tilted her head up to look at Parker. Fat tears began to roll down her cheeks. Her burgundy–painted lower lip trembled.

The world suddenly tipped off its axis for Parker. Holding out her hand for Calypso, Parker was breathless as Calypso placed her hand in Parker's.

Holding her hand tight, Calypso walked in. There was no way to deny the connection—the electricity that coursed from Calypso to Parker.

"I've missed you," Calypso whispered. "I don't want to live without you."

She didn't want to let go of Calypso's hand. She didn't want to let go of Calypso. Her body was warm and soft when she pulled Calypso into her embrace and held her while she sobbed. Parker had never been in a position that made her feel so conflicted in her whole life. Calypso's perfume and the warmth and softness of her threw Parker out of sync with everything she had come to believe or think for the last almost two months. "I don't have any idea what I'm supposed to do right now," Parker murmured into Calypso's hair. "I'm not good at this. I'm . . . I don't know how to do this. Us. Not being good at something. Letting you down. Not being a good wife."

Calypso tipped her face up to Parker. "Will you listen to me? Can I tell you my side of this now?"

"Yes. I'm ready to listen. I have a lot of questions."

"You're alone?"

"For now. We have some time." Parker was about to release Calypso, but before she could think twice, she witnessed Macy bolt out of the kitchen. A flash of red hair, pale skin, and a flash of silver preceded a muffled wet sound, as cold metal grazed above Parker's hand. Parker's hand was suddenly wet, with hot blood, as Calypso went rigid. The sound repeated three more times.

37 IN THIS TOGETHER

MACY

Knowing what was going on, Macy didn't leave to go to town. She pulled down the street and watched as a Lyft driver delivered Calypso a few houses down.

That stupid fucking bitch was going to ruin this for her. She finally had what she wanted. She had Parker. And now Calypso was going to take her away from her again. Snatch her. And Parker was all she had left in this world. She couldn't lose Parker again. She couldn't lose another thing to Calypso. It wasn't fair.

Using the key to unlock the pedestrian door from the side of the garage, Macy let herself in. From where she was standing, she could see Parker leading Calypso in and hear Calypso's pathetic crying—begging Parker to let her say her side of the story. Fuck her side of the story. No one needed that. Especially not Parker. She slipped her tight leather gloves on.

When she heard Parker murmur that she was ready to listen to Calypso, Macy grabbed a knife from the block on the counter and charged into the living room, knife raised.

The most satisfying feeling in the world was the feeling of the knife as it penetrated through her tacky, ripped sweater —the rips in the back giving Macy better access as it forced through Calypso's flesh. It stuck slightly as she pulled it back. Using her hand to stabilize Calypso as she pulled it out and plunged it back in, relief poured through Macy.

Watching as Calypso went heavy into Parker, her eyes closed as Parker laid her down on the floor and stared at Macy. Freezing in Parker's glare, Macy held the bloody knife as Calypso's blood made a pattering sound as it dripped to the floor.

Staring at her own blood-soaked hands, Parker began to shake. "What in the holy fuck?" She whispered.

Fuck. This was not the reaction she was expecting from Parker. Her brain kicked into gear. Trying to play shocked might be the response. Forcing her eyes to grow huge, and dropping the knife, feigning shock, hoping that she was believable, "I thought she was attacking you. I don't know. I just saw her on you." Time to turn on the waterworks. Her eyes began overflowing with tears. "I'm sorry. I'm so sorry."

"She was *hugging* me. Hugging me. Not attacking me." Parker gaped at her own blood-coated hands and the body of Calypso lying on the hardwood floor. "We need to call the police."

This was not going to work. Those words pulled Macy straight out of her act. "This would ruin my career. You can't call them." Macy was frantic. "Parker. Don't. It was not intentional. It wasn't. And it would destroy me."

"What do you propose we do?" God, she was such a rookie.

"This is the off-season for the town. We can put her in the shower in the guest bath, clean up the blood, and go stay at the hotel airport." Her voice came calm and measured. Cold. Her tone was icy. She gave herself chills. Her plan was formulated off the cuff as it came out.

Parker nodded. "And when they find the body here, and you're the last person listed as renting it? We are on a flight manifest for Seattle? I mean, this would be a cakewalk case for any prosecutor, Macy."

"Seattle is a big tourist town. We could have been vacationing anywhere here. I will make it look like she broke in. Bust a window out. Also, I had a former CI book it under an alias. I figured it would be safer . . . we couldn't be accused of harboring . . ." Dropping to her knee, she grabbed Calypso under the arms, stood, and began to drag Calypso's heavy deadweight toward the hallway, leaving a slick and beautiful trail of blood in her wake.

"You really thought I would go away so easily. You really thought that you would have her forever." Macy's voice was a quiet and cold whisper as she dragged Calypso's body into the first bathroom right off the living room area.

Luckily, both bathrooms in this rental had walk-in showers—no tubs—so she wouldn't have to lift Calypso over the ledge. As she dropped Calypso's shoulders after dragging her into the tiled shower area, a wicked smile played on her lips as she knelt before Calypso on the hard, cold tile. The tile pressed into her knees through her jeans as she whispered into Calypso's ear, her voice ice cold. "I thought you would just go away. Maybe be arrested and maybe hauled back to New Orleans. But this is even better. This is a far more permanent solution to my issue. These last few days with Parker, I've been able to prove my love and devotion to her in the bedroom. The kitchen. Wherever she wanted me, however she wanted me. I've been able to be everything she ever wanted and then some. She didn't even miss you. She had no reason to. And she won't miss you, because I will continue to be her everything."

As she stood, she could hear Parker sobbing quietly in the living room. How could she be such a badass and so fragile at the same time? She would never understand this.

When Macy came back out, she went into the kitchen and grabbed a bucket from under the sink. Parker hadn't moved. She kept staring at the blood on her hands and streaked across the floor. In the dim light of the oil lamps, it resembled oil. Black, shiny, thick, and sticky. The metallic smell of copper pennies overtook the air.

She was going to have to take charge of this whole situation. Parker was going to have to help her. She couldn't do everything on her own. After filling the bucket with steaming hot water and a few different cleaners she found under the sink—it wouldn't be forensically perfect, but it would have to suffice—Macy grabbed some rags and came back out to the living room, where Parker stood, basically catatonic. She handed them to Parker. "Clean up the blood. I will go pack our things."

Parker shook her head. "I can't."

"Parker. Come *on*. We need to finish this. We need to leave. And the sooner the better." Macy shoved the rags into Parker's hands, setting the bucket at her feet.

Waiting for Parker to move before she went to handle any other business, Macy watched as tears poured out of Parker's eyes. Slowly, Parker got on her knees and began to mop up the blood with the soapy water. Tears wouldn't stop pouring. Rolling her eyes, Macy spun on her heel and went to the bedroom.

Haphazardly, she gathered all of their personal belongings except for a single change of clothes for each of them, wiped down all of the surfaces and threw that cloth into a garbage bag. All the while, Parker's quiet sobs came from the other room.

Going into the en suite she changed out of her bloody clothes, wiped down the bathroom, and threw the bloody clothes and rag into the garbage bag.

The lights flickered on, and the television came on, suddenly bright with the streaming menu.

Macy rolled their suitcases out as Parker sopped up the last bits of Calypso's blood off the floor. Parker threw the sponge back into the bucket and stood, leaning against the wall. Quiet tears streamed down her cheeks. God, she wished Parker would stop with the sniveling.

Macy turned on all the lights and inspected the floor and baseboards, ensuring that all the blood had been mopped up. It would have to do. She grabbed a hand towel, went out to the porch, wrapped her hand in the towel, and punched the window out so that the glass shattered on the inside. It made a loud tinkering noise as the shards hit the floor, sparkling and sharp. She took the bucket of water and dumped it out in the rhododendrons lining the walkway. It was all done with surgical precision. Deliberation. Actions ticked off a checklist. It wasn't the first time she staged a scene to fit her narrative. It wouldn't be the last time. And she wasn't the only one who did this. How did anyone think she learned to do things this way?

She came in and tossed drawers and furniture.

Macy shot a look over at Parker across the trashed space. "Let's go." She huffed out of breath as she pushed a stray lock of her hair out of her face.

Parker's skin was pale as her eyes stayed glued to the spot where Calypso's body had lain. Macy couldn't begin to fathom why Parker was crying over Calypso. It was such bullshit. It was beyond frustrating that Parker couldn't see what she might be throwing away. For Calypso at that.

"Parker!" Macy almost shouted. "We need to change and get a move on. I put your clothes on the bed." She handed Parker a plastic garbage bag. "Put your clothes in this. I put her in the second bath. Get ready in the en suite." Handing Parker another rag, "Don't forget to wipe everything you touch down."

Macy stood by the door, tapping her foot. Quiet sobbing came from the other room as Parker changed. When Parker made her way out with her clean clothes, freshened up, she thankfully had stopped her sniveling. Parker handed Macy the garbage bag with her bloodied clothes by shoving it at her. Some things need to be destroyed to fix the rest. Calypso needed to be destroyed. She was going to muddy the path of her and Parker's relationship. Out with the old.

Parker grabbed the keys and her luggage. Macy followed at her heels. They loaded everything into the trunk and Macy booked their room at one of the hotels near the airport.

As they drove through the forest roads, Macy asked Parker to stop along the roadside. The rain stopped, and they were on a small two-lane road with a scenic overlook. Macy took some of the clothes from the bag and dumped them over the edge. She got back in and instructed Parker to keep driving. She asked Parker to stop at three other locations along the two-lane road before they navigated back onto the freeway. She dropped clothes and the knife at various points. She had Parker exit the highway once the serene and tranquil forest roads gave way to suddenly bright and urban surroundings. She found a rundown liquor store with a dumpster and jumped out and deposited the empty bag in the dumpster.

When they got to the room, Parker sat at the desk while

Macy sat on the edge of the bed. Parker changed their flight to the earliest possible time, which would work well with their alibi. Their story was simple. They got into an argument and ended their trip early. Macy had made sure to rent a hotel room in her own name on the other side of Seattle before they left for the trip initially, and checked in online. She wanted to be prepared in case this happened. Frankly, she kind of hoped this might happen.

Macy was unsettled by Parker's cold and distant demeanor. Parker didn't speak one word on the drive to the hotel. She didn't speak when they checked in to the hotel. She stayed silent. Her jaw set tight. Macy studied Parker's profile, and she could see the muscles of her jaw tensing and pulsing as if she were clenching her teeth.

For the first time since they arrived in the Pacific Northwest, Parker didn't pull Macy close. She didn't kiss Macy goodnight. Didn't have sex. Parker went into the bathroom, where she stayed for an inordinately long time. If she had brought her phone in there with her, Macy might have been worried that she was contacting the authorities. But her phone sat on the bedside table. After some time, the water began to run.

While she waited for Parker to come out, she ordered room service and pulled up the local news. Nothing was reported. She was fairly confident no one would even report it for weeks at the earliest. And at that point, Calypso would be decayed beyond recognition, and they would probably write it off as an overdose or junkie. She was in the wind, and probably no one had a clue who she was or where she was.

An old movie played on the next channel, and she left it there as the room service was delivered. Red-eyed, pale, and freshly showered, Parker came out of the bathroom in her pajamas. Macy opened the lids to the plates. She had ordered them both the roasted vegetable penne Alfredo. "I ordered us some dinner."

"I'm not hungry." Parker got into the bed and rolled onto her side, facing away from Macy. Even though she was shaking, she used words. Progress. Macy thought Parker would be stronger than that. For the tough bitch persona Parker put on, she wasn't all that hardcore.

Setting her plate on the bedside table on her side of the bed, she turned to Parker. "Parker, listen to me. I can't go down for this. It would ruin me. We both know I'm a damn good cop and this would destroy that. And now you are also complicit in this. You more than anyone else can recognize that little fact. If I go down for this, you go down with me. We are in this together. I didn't have a choice. I didn't. She was going to—"

Parker flashed a hard gaze at her before turning back away from her. Parker didn't respond. The great Parker Harrington was again rendered speechless by Macy. But Macy gave zero fucks at this point. Calypso had to go, and if she had to go scorched earth and burn every bridge to make it happen, she would. Parker would understand eventually. She would come around and see that this was all for the best.

Hopefully, she would be back to normal by morning.

OCTOBER 2.

She wasn't normal in the morning either. When Macy got up, Parker sat in the wingback chair already dressed and showered. She silently stared out the window. She took a shot of espresso. She appeared normal. But she refused to look at Macy, and remained silent. There was nothing Macy could do to make her talk. *Parker only needs to process this, and then everything will be okay. It will.*

"Parker?" Macy came out of the bathroom after showering and getting dressed.

Parker turned her head and glared at Macy. Apparently, she planned to hold on to the silent treatment. And given the look of contempt in her eyes, she was still pissed off.

Macy went and kneeled in front of Parker. She was desperate. She couldn't lose Parker. They had barely begun. They scarcely established themselves together. Her heart ached as she glanced at Parker. The one great love of her life. "Parker, look at me." She begged.

Parker at least made eye contact with her. But that gaze stayed icy and hard. Macy's anxiety ramped to a fever pitch. *Please, don't walk away.*

Macy took Parker's hands in hers, and Parker yanked them away.

Macy gave a sigh. "Fine. I get it. You're mad. You're giving me the silent treatment. You have to understand, Parker. I did what I did because I love you. I've always loved you. I *will* always love you. That's not going to change. No matter what happens, or has happened, or whatever. You have to understand what I did, I did it for you. To protect you. I genuinely thought I was protecting you. Please. Talk to me. Tell me what you're thinking. Tell me you're okay. Tell me *we're* okay."

Parker turned the other way and moved herself as far from Macy as possible. Macy's throat constricted. It didn't seem plausible to go from five days of bliss to this. Calypso obviously still had some chokehold on Parker. Parker needed to understand everything she had ever done—she did because of her love for Parker. Nothing more, nothing less. The love that burned inside of her for Parker drove her to these depths. Parker was too blinded by Calypso to see that though. Maybe one day she would get it. She would. Parker would see. Parker already identified that no one would love her as deeply as Macy. Not even Calypso.

Macy hoped that no matter what else was happening, Calypso was rotting. Not just in the bathtub at the vacation rental, but in hell. Parker was hers. Parker would be only hers. She needed to be Parker's. And with Calypso out of the way, she had a clear path, once Parker opened her eyes.

PART IV
DIVULGENCE

38 WE ARE SO DONE

PARKER

The events of last night continuously played back in Parker's mind all night. She couldn't shake it. Not what happened, nor what her shock allowed her to be complicit in. A brief flicker of hope hit her when Parker thought she saw a flutter of Calypso's eyelids as she was dragged back. But that was impossible.

She wanted to throw up. *Macy is crazy. She's fucking crazy.* If Macy was crazy, it was because Parker made her that way. She felt crushing guilt. She was the downfall of Macy and Calypso. All of this was her fault. It was all on her. Consumed by fear, she complied. This was all her fault. She did this to Macy. She took Macy to this low. This was all her fault. She kicked Calypso out. She brought Macy here. She fucked Macy. She was still in love with Calypso. Macy knew it. Macy snapped. Guilt burned through her. All of this was on her shoulders.

Her heart was in a vice, and breathing was nearly impossible.

Her thoughts were jumbled and her brain was short circuiting. Attempting to make sense of what had happened and what was supposed to happen next was useless. How she even got here. It was all in fragments.

Vivid visions of the lights coming back on and the blood, the blood now glistening and red. The water in the bucket turning pink from Parker dipping the sponge in and wringing it out replayed in her mind all night. There was so much wrong right now. She couldn't think. She couldn't sort through any of this. Disbarment. Guilt. Too much weight being thrown around in her brain. Her ability to compartmentalize completely malfunctioned. She had done so much wrong and it all played out in a blur. She let her shock and sorrow and guilt overtake any rational thought. She allowed her emotions to dominate and in the process, she fucked up her entire life. The smell of the blood mingled with the scent of Calypso's perfume lingered, gripping a hold of her, short-circuiting her brain.

When she woke up—well, got out of bed, you couldn't call that sleep in the slightest—Parker didn't speak. Not through breakfast or on the plane. There was nothing left to say. Whatever Calypso needed to tell her, she would never hear it. She would never have that closure. Macy robbed her of that. The guilt she felt for Macy's behavior diminished as she saw the coldness in Macy. Macy would have done this regardless. Macy was capable of this long before Parker made the unfortunate decision of getting involved.

She barely tolerated Macy. Macy was calm. Collected. Smooth. Like she didn't just stab Calypso to death yesterday afternoon. Like she didn't have Parker mop up the blood. Like she didn't leave Calypso in the shower to rot. Parker couldn't comprehend how Macy could be so cold.

Every time Parker closed her eyes, she visualized Calypso looking at her in the rain with tearful eyes. Then she saw Calypso on the floor, her blood on her hands. And Macy, when she saw Macy, she was shaking. Parker thought it was because she was upset at first, and then she realized it. What she mistook for fear turned out to be pure adrenaline. She began to put two and two together. The vacation rental was registered to a phony name and ID. This had been Macy's plan all along.

There was a light in Macy's eyes that Parker only glimpsed when she was fucking her.

Macy got off on killing Calypso.

What the actual fuck.

What the *absolute* fuck.

And now Parker was complicit in this as well. There could be no turning back the clock. There could be no coming back from this. There would be charges of obstructing justice and accessory after the fact, for sure. Parker felt sick to her stomach. She may have fought dirty on occasion, but she never crossed the line into breaking the law. She pushed the limits, sure, but never dared to step over the edge. There could be no normal from here on out.

Macy stopped trying to talk to Parker after they boarded the plane. Parker couldn't look at her. Parker didn't *want* to look at her. Every time she heard Macy's voice or caught sight of her, she fought the violent need to retch. Macy made her viscerally sick. How low did she sink that she considered a relationship with that psycho? Parker felt dirty.

When they got into the car, Parker turned on the music and cranked up the volume.

Macy finally cracked. She turned the volume back down. "Parker? Talk to me." She pleaded.

"I have nothing to say to you, Macy. I'll drop you off, and then we are done. *Done.* I am not going to say anything because it fucks me over, too. I need to figure out how to deal with this now. But from this point on, don't call me. Don't talk to me. Don't contact anyone I know. Ever. Again."

"Parker . . . I swear I thought she was hurting you. She *shot* you. Or did you forget that?"

"She was crying. I hugged her. You *stabbed* her. You took advantage of my shock and made me complicit in her *murder.* Maybe that's who *you* are. It is *not* who I am."

Macy's lip trembled, and tears welled in her eyes. "So the last few days . . ."

Really? She's going to cry? She's going to be upset? The nerve. Pausing, teeth clenched, trying really hard not to backhand Macy, she gripped the steering wheel so hard it nearly snapped. She still wouldn't look at Macy. Couldn't stand the sight of her. "They were great. They were. I thought there was something there. But you lifted the veil, and I got to see the real you. The monster that you are. I'm done, Macy. *We* are done." Parker turned the music back up. She didn't want to hear whatever Macy felt the need to say from that point on. There was nothing she could say to change Parker's mind.

Macy turned and glared out the window. Not another word was said. Parker pulled into Macy's drive, got out, pulled Macy's luggage from the trunk, set it on the sidewalk, and got back into the car without saying a word.

As Macy got out of the car, she bent so she leaned close to Parker through the open window, eye-to-eye with Parker. "If we are truly done, you'd better keep quiet about this. Because if you talk, I can easily twist it around and say it was you who killed her. It's my word against yours. It's your DNA all over her. And you are the one with the reputation of fighting dirty."

Parker cocked an eyebrow and gave a bitter laugh. "In the courtroom. I dance on the line, but I don't dare cross it. My reputation is above board. And in my daily life, I don't do shit like this. I don't cross that line. I don't even go near that line. My reputation's solid."

"As is mine. So it's best if we both just forget it happened."

Not bothering to even respond, she simply drove off. Fuck Macy Quinn. Forget what happened? There is no way Parker would be able to forget what transpired over the last few days.

As Parker drove off back to her home, her hands shook, and the reality of all that had happened came crashing down around her. The bright Southern California sun beat through the windshield, hot and oppressive compared to the last week in the Pacific Northwest—Calypso's eyes, golden against the overcast grey. Warm honey. Parker's chest constricted, and she struggled to breathe.

With everything building within her, tears clouding her vision, she pulled off the side of the road and let out a keening wail. It ripped from her chest, and all of her pain, sadness, and frustration were coming out. And the choke-hold they had on her was heavier than it ever had been.

When she finally made it home, she closed the door and went up to her bedroom, where Kitty curled herself into a ball on the end of the bed. On Calypso's side. Because of course.

While she was gone, Karen came daily to feed it and clean its box. Kitty glared at Parker, and she swore Kitty could tell what Parker and Macy had done to her chosen human. Kitty's green and gold eyes narrowed at her as she stared her down.

"I didn't do it, Kitty. I swear. I wanted her to come home,

too." Until Parker spoke it aloud, she hadn't fully realized it. "I could have figured it all out. I could have helped her through whatever it was. I was selfish, and now we are both without her. And now, I'm losing my fucking mind. I'm talking to a cat like it's going to give me the answers."

A quiet meow came out of the Cat as it picked its head up. Parker sighed as she shook her head and moved to Calypso's closet; she was compelled to do it. She wanted to be close to something of Calypso's, thinking maybe she could conjure her back to life and back home. Her perfume was beginning to fade. It hit Parker even harder. She closed the door with the hope it would save what was left of her.

She walked out, and their wedding rings sat on the dresser where they had left them the day everything fell apart. A vice had been wrapped around her heart. Parker closed all of the plantation shutters in her room.

In the darkness, Parker collapsed on the bed, and Kitty curled up next to her, purring loudly. Maybe Kitty wasn't mad at her after all. She finally let it all go. All of the tears and anger she had kept under wraps for the last two days poured out of her. When all of this came crashing down, she and Calypso were in the process of finding a way back to each other. She had committed herself to do what it took to ensure they would make it through this rough patch. But now, there would never be any chance of going back. And the finality of it crushed Parker harder than she had ever anticipated.

Her phone rang and Macy's picture and name lit the screen. What didn't this bitch understand? Blocked. That simple. Parker had no desire to hear anything Macy felt the need to say. She thought she made herself pretty fucking clear when they parted ways. Parker went on all of her social media accounts and blocked her there, too. Macy didn't deserve access to her or any part of her life any longer.

Rolling over, she grabbed Calypso's pillow. A faint hint of her perfume lingered on the it. Parker threw it across the room. It was too much. Everything was too much.

39 PILING UP

PARKER

*P*arker didn't leave her bedroom for two days. She went downstairs to get food and feed Kitty, then returned straight to her bed. She saw the pile of mail on the kitchen island. She sorted the envelopes and saw at the bottom of the pile a large manila envelope. The black ink and flourished writing were a dead giveaway. It was from Calypso. Her stomach churned. She tossed it in the garbage. She didn't want to look at it. She couldn't. It didn't matter what she had to say anyway. She was dead. Her blood was on Parker's hands. Whatever she had to say would only make it worse.

Lloyd called her and left her several voicemails, none of which she bothered to listen to. She didn't have the capacity to socialize or discuss work, life, or anything else. Lloyd was aware that Parker had left on this trip to confront Calypso.

She'd suspected he would ask questions, and she wasn't prepared to answer them.

On Monday morning, Parker forced herself out of bed, showered, and put on her favorite black three-piece suit and Tiffany cufflinks (that Calypso bought her for their first anniversary). As she adjusted her tie before the mirror, she resembled Parker, but wasn't Parker. And her eyes, they didn't look right. She resolved to pull her life back into order and catch up on her mounting responsibilities. Perhaps if she attended to some of the business she had been neglecting, she would feel better. Unlikely. But maybe.

When she arrived at the office, Lloyd took one look at her and, with his remarkable ability to notice every detail and commit it to memory, sensed that something was wrong. You don't work that closely with someone for two years and not notice when they were off.

Following her into her office, he shut the door behind him and sat in the chair across from her black lacquered partner's desk. He laced his fingers over his belly and leaned forward slightly. "What's wrong?" His attention on her carried same intensity he treated witnesses on the stand.

Remaining quiet, she wouldn't meet his eyes. Panic mounted inside of her about what to say or whether she should ask him to leave her alone for now. She opened her mouth to say something, but nothing came out.

"Did you see Calypso?" Lloyd asked.

Parker squeezed her eyes shut. She could see Calypso's body on the floor and blood on her hands. Parker nodded. "Yeah. I saw her." Parker stared at her hands instead of Lloyd.

"How did it go?" His voice was tenuous as he sat, literally, on the edge of his seat.

"Not good. Not good at all." Parker didn't even recognize her own voice. It sounded meek and quiet, not at all the commanding and self-assured tone she usually spoke in.

"Parker, what do you mean 'not good'?"

She put her forehead in her hand, pushed her hand through her hair, and considered him. "I want to tell you, but I can't. But just hear this, understand this, stay the fuck away from Macy Quinn. She's not to be in this office, call this office, or have anything to do with me, or this firm or my home. She's a fucking psychopath."

A rabid dog with a bone, he wouldn't let it go. "Parker . . . did something happen on your trip?"

Parker laughed, but it sounded soulless and sarcastic. "Did something happen? Oh . . . that's one way to say it."

Lloyd cocked his head. "And you *can't* tell me, or you don't *want* to tell me?"

"I literally *cannot* tell you. In the off chance anything ends up coming back, I'm going to need you to defend me. I will leave it at that."

Lloyd exhaled. "Okay. Well, let's hope it doesn't come to that. I would prefer to know what might potentially be landing in my lap, though. But . . . I, um . . . I need to talk to you about something else."

She pinched the spot at the bridge of her nose between her eyes, squeezing them shut. "What? Is it essential that I know it now? Can it wait?"

"I don't think it can wait."

Placing her elbows on the desk and looking at Lloyd, she barely managed to answer. "Okay." It wasn't okay.

"I got a hold of the file Macy got on Calypso. It was sent to me digitally by a friend of a friend. I wanted to look at it because things just didn't gel with me with who Calypso is, and knowing what I know about Macy. I just felt like this is all too coincidental. Before I continue, can Juliana come in? She was part of this."

"Sure. Yeah. Whatever you need to get to the point."

Parker hit the button that paged Juliana. A matter of seconds later, she was seated next to Lloyd.

Juliana set a pen on Parker's desk.

"What's that?" Parker asked.

Juliana leaned over and unscrewed the pen. "Plug this into your computer."

Parker did as she was asked. The din of people talking, plates, and silverware came over her speakers. From there, a conversation between Juliana, Lloyd, and Macy about the file.

When the recording ended, Lloyd cleared his throat. "So, she obviously thinks I'm stupid. She lied, you got that. So red flags everywhere, right?" He faced Juliana for reinforcement. She nodded.

Parker raised an eyebrow. "Go on." There was pounding in her ears from her heartbeat.

"So, Juliana and I picked the file apart once we got a hold of it. The metadata doesn't match. It's counterfeit."

"Lloyd, what the fuck does that even mean?" Parker's patience was already razor thin.

He grinned. "I finally get to teach you something. You know both Juliana and me minored in computer science, right? It was a fallback for me if I couldn't make a go of being a lawyer. So, like I mentioned, it didn't feel right. So we got the file and inspected the metadata first."

"Honestly, I thought with Macy's training, she would have been smarter and fixed the metadata. But desperate people don't always think things through, do they?" Juliana added.

"Okay. Great. Good. Can you get to the point? Please explain to me what that means. Metadata. What is it?"

Still grinning, Lloyd launched into his explanation. "Think of a file like a letter. The words on the page are what you read, but the envelope it came in—the postmarks, the return address, the date—tells you where it actually came from and when. That 'envelope' is what we call metadata. When I checked this report, the envelope didn't match the story. The document says it was filed through the department's system five years ago, but the metadata shows it was actually created on August 1st, on Macy's personal laptop using Microsoft Word—not the police database. The author's field even lists her home user account, and there's no record of the file ever being stored on the department servers."

Juliana jumped back in. "Just to be absolutely sure, I called NOPD, and after some persistence, I talked to a detective there. Detective McMillian, and he knew Macy when she was there. He said she went batshit and put in her resignation and moved away. I asked him about the file, and he couldn't find anything on Calypso or Calliope or either name in any form."

"Basically, it's a forgery wearing a real uniform. All the digital fingerprints point straight back to Macy," Lloyd finished.

Her head spun. "Diabolical," she whispered. "Did you do anything with it?" Her voice was hoarse as she fought the tears.

"We wanted you to know first," Juliana said.

"I literally do not have the capacity to deal with this. Contact whoever you need to. She needs to be handled."

"Yeah. I can deal with it. It will be my absolute pleasure." A devious grin played upon Lloyd's lips. She knew he had little to no tolerance for Macy. "Now, do you think you can tell me what happened in Washington?"

Juliana got up and slipped from the office, closing the door behind her.

Parker paused and seriously considered it. Desperation with the need to talk about it, to unburden her soul, clawed at her from the inside. "Bring me up to speed on the McLoughlin file." Parker changed the subject. She planned on letting him take the lead on a new case. A television actor who got caught up in a situation involving drugs and hookers. Parker was glad she would be taking second chair on this case. She didn't have the wherewithal to give it proper attention.

Work proved to be the perfect solution, allowing her to set aside her own personal issues and focus on Lloyd and his case. As long as she kept herself in work mode, she didn't have to think about mopping up Calypso's blood. Or the smell of her blood. Or Macy fucking Quinn. Or the fact she had been completely played for a fool.

To keep from thinking about mopping up Calypso's blood, Parker pushed through a thirteen-hour day, working as she ate her lunch and dinner at her desk. Juliana popped in several times, and every time, her eyes carried a wary and concerned furrow on her brows. She gave Juliana the same instructions she had given Lloyd. Grant Macy Quinn no access to this office, Parker herself, or accept any of her calls. Juliana nodded.

Working would be the only way to avoid thinking about what she'd done. What Macy put her in the position to do. What she was complicit in. She tried to remember who the fuck she was and what she was good at and focus solely on that.

At one point in the day, she considered telling Lloyd and turning herself in, hoping to secure a plea deal for a lesser charge. Not being sure that she wanted to spend time in prison or be disbarred, she pushed it aside until she had time to research the laws in Washington. She didn't want to research it. The thought of her and Macy sharing a cell together also kept her from picking up the phone.

Meanwhile, she attended meetings with clients in a new high-profile murder trial to start prepping for, an NFL player who had beaten a man to death in a nightclub.

Amongst the million other things on her plate she also needed schedule a haircut because past experience with similar cases taught her that she would have to handle numerous press interviews for this case. The networks already began reaching out for comments as soon as they discovered she would be representing him. She would have to do damage control on his reputation. He specifically only wanted Parker on the lead when she tried to pawn it off to Lloyd.

As she texted her barber to schedule her haircut, Juliana came in and mentioned that Macy did, in fact, call requesting to talk to Parker. "Tell her that if she tries to contact this office again that she will be handed a restraining order." Parker didn't look up from her text. Lloyd would have her taken care of shortly anyway.

No one ever questioned her authority in the office. Ever since Mr. Harrington stepped back to enjoy his partial retirement (he would probably work until he died), Parker took charge, and did a damn good job of it.

It was well after dark before Parker left the office. Juliana was in the habit of waiting until Parker left most days. Parker appreciated it, and she had no issue covering Juliana's overtime. "Time to go home, Juliana," Parker called as she passed Juliana's desk.

"I should tell you, Macy Quinn tried to call two more times. I did tell her to stop calling, or we would be forced to file a restraining order. When she called the second time, I called Jimmy, my ex, who works at the Sheriff's department. So he hooked me up with filing the restraining order."

"That's a very nice ex." Parker rubbed her hand through her hair.

Juliana pulled her honey blonde hair out of its ponytail. She totally saw why Calypso would have been concerned. Juliana presented herself as gorgeous in the all-American girl next door, Taylor Swift type of way. Not Parker's type. Not that Parker ever had a type. But for someone with Calypso's, it would be a valid assumption that Parker would go for someone resembling Juliana. But Juliana worked for her, and she never mixed business and sex. And Juliana was also very straight. And she wasn't Calypso. No one would ever be Calypso. And now, because of her own stupidity, Calypso was lying dead in a vacation rental in the Pacific Northwest. Parker realized she was staring at Juliana.

"Is there something wrong?" Juliana asked.

Parker paused before giving a slight shake of the head. "No. Sorry. I'm just in my own head."

"Do you want to talk about it?" Juliana asked as she packed her Coach tote bag (Parker's Christmas gift to her last year) and grabbed her sweater.

"Before all of this bullshit with Calypso, did you know she accused me of having a thing with you?"

Juliana laughed. "O. M. Geeee. Does she not know you at all?"

"That's what I said. On top of that, someone else I know has a thing for you." Parker chided.

"Lloyd." Juliana laughed.

"So the cat's out of the bag?" Parker found this conversation to be a welcome distraction.

"I mean, he's not very subtle." Juliana laughed.

"Are you going to do anything about it?"

"I'm fairly certain when you hired me, you were adamant about no dating in the workplace."

"If it's something you two want, and can keep it professional, I might be able to turn a blind eye."

"I will keep that in mind." A sly smile crept onto Juliana's face. "He is kind of sort of hot."

Parker laughed at Juliana's candor. By this point, they had made it to the garage. On these late nights, Parker always made sure that Juliana got into her car safe before getting into her own. She watched Juliana unlock her car, throw her bag into the passenger seat, then get in herself.

It took Parker almost an hour to drive home when there was no traffic (which there almost never was if you used FasTrack, which, according to Parker, was worth every single dime). She had intentionally chosen her home to be located at a considerable distance from her office for several reasons. She needed the time to de-stress in the car on the way home. It served as a transition for her. She would turn her music up and work through shifting gears from work mode to home mode. This night, as she drove home, every single song that played reminded her of Calypso. Whether it was a single line, the vibe of a song, or a song that she knew Calypso would love. She and Calypso used to send each other songs throughout the day; it had been their thing, a way of communicating as they balanced busy lives. Now, there was none of that. There would be none of that ever again.

Turning the radio off and rolling down the window, Parker tried to clear her mind.

Relief washed over her as she pulled into her neighborhood. Until she saw a familiar car parked in her driveway. A large part of her was not surprised to see Macy's car in her driveway waiting for her. All of the peace she obtained from the drive disappeared, as rage boiled hot through her and she fought the overwhelming desire to throat punch Macy and then change her gate code.

"Get the fuck off my property," Parker growled at her when Macy got out of her car and attempted to follow Parker up the walkway. She thought about shouting all that she knew about the file. But she figured letting her get hit out of left field with an investigation would be more satisfying. Self-control, not being one of Parker's biggest strengths, was not easy to maintain at all times, but Parker patted herself on the back for not acting out violently or spilling what she knew.

"Parker, stop!" Macy grabbed Parker's arm.

"If you don't fucking let go of me and get the fuck out of here, I will call the cops. I mean it, Macy. Stay. The. Fuck. Away. From. Me."

Macy let go of Parker's arm. Tears rolled down her cheeks. "Parker, please . . ."

Parker pulled her phone out and the screen lit her face as she selected the keypad. "You have five seconds to turn around and head back to your car."

"You can't be serious?"

"Try me." She hit the 9, holding the phone so that Macy saw the screen.

Macy put her hands up and backed away. "Fine. I see." She went back to her car, where she sat for several seconds before turning the ignition on.

Parker wondered if that was the smartest possible decision given how unstable she realized Macy was. She had watched *Fatal Attraction* and *Single White Female* and dealt with enough criminal cases involving psycho women; she didn't have to guess that this would be a risk.

She didn't care. Right now, she wanted to be inside her house and far the fuck away from Macy.

She waited for Macy to back out of the drive before going back to her car and pulling into the garage.

Parker went into the house, where Kitty greeted her as she turned the light on. She paused before opening the pull-out trash drawer and retrieving Calypso's envelope from it.

40 THE TRUTH WILL SET YOU FREE

OCTOBER 5

PARKER

She took the envelope into her office and sat down, staring at it for what seemed an eternity. No return address was on the envelope, but the postmark was from Washington, the day before she was shot. Her heart beat hard in her ears.

Her hands began to shake. She put the envelope down on her desk, sucked in a breath, and sat back in her chair. The fine black ink and flourished writing were achingly familiar. She had at least a hundred scraps of paper with that writing saved in a drawer. Love notes. Poems. Sketches. Calypso. A sharp pain drove through her heart.

She warily eyed the envelope as Kitty made her way into the office and curled up in the chair across from her. It seemed as if Kitty sensed the presence hanging in the air. Calypso.

The ticking of the grandfather clock in the living room seemed suddenly loud. Kitty stared at her. Expectant. Parker understood that sounded crazy. Ridiculous, even.

As she finally mustered the courage, she tore open the envelope. Calypso's perfume emanated from the contents. Calypso's essence sat in the room with her. Kitty let out a small, quiet meow. She felt it, too. *That's insane.*

On top was a letter. Fine black ink and cardstock paper. Calypso. The name and the spirit of her overtook her mind and the room.

Parker's chest burned, and breathing became difficult. She exhaled and wiped the tears from her eyes before reading it.

Parker,

I left the keys to my car on the center console. My rings, as I'm sure you've already seen, are on the dresser in our bedroom. I figured if you didn't want me, I shouldn't take those with me. You can sell them. Keep them. Whatever. But I hope you keep them. And I hope you see this and read this. I have to tell you the truth about everything. It's time for you to know the whole truth. The entire history. I should have told you all of this a long time ago. You deserved that. <u>WE</u> deserved it. I regret that it is taking this moment for me to come clean with my truth.

I need you to read this, and read it very carefully. You were angry. I understand. You wouldn't let me talk, and I believe I have a right for you to know my side of the story. I was hoping to avoid all of this drama and put it behind me when I moved to California. But here it is. My truth. My side of the story.

I have high walls that I built. For good reason, too. I didn't do relationships prior to you for good reason. I was in love once before you. In New Orleans. Her name was Shae. After Shae, I couldn't bear the thought of being left again. I couldn't. But to be honest, I built these walls before her, even. They have been what kept me safe when I was on the street. They were what kept me safe through so much of my past.

I'm getting ahead of myself, though. So let me tell you everything. You know my parents kicked me out when I was sixteen. You know I lived for a few months with Gilian and her family. I didn't want to overstay my welcome, so I ended up getting a job at a snoball stand. The owner's daughter, Jodie, took a liking to me and we ended up in a relationship. When I got with Jodie, she was a lot older than me. I thought being with her would keep me safe. But then she was beating me. But getting beaten sometimes seemed better than being homeless. Until it became too much. And one night—that last night—as she was whaling on me, blow after blow after blow, I thought I was going to die that night. And to be honest, I don't even know what, if anything, fueled the fire that started it. I didn't realize until that moment that I didn't want to die. I wanted to make something of myself. Of my life. I reached across the counter, grabbed a knife, and stabbed her in the neck. She bled out and died. And you know what? I laughed. It was like I was out of my body, another person, not myself. I was watching myself from another part of the room. And I was laughing, covered in her blood. I didn't even realize there was so much blood in a body.

I don't know how long I sat there covered in her blood while she lay dead at my feet. I finally called the cops. By the time I called, the blood had begun to dry on my hands.

Macy was in the police academy at that time. She was on a ride-along. I was 19 years old. I was so young and naive. I didn't know the first thing about handling this situation. It was Macy who helped me get through the police interview. She would nod or shake her head just enough for me to see. She was helping me answer the questions. She helped me get a lawyer. She befriended me. That's when Macy Quinn entered my life. She helped me get the charges reduced. We hung out a few times, and she told me how she had recently gotten out of a long-term relationship, but they remained friends, and that she still wasn't over her. She thought her ex, who was Shae, could help me. And she did. Shae took me under her wing. She told me the other side of the story. The possessiveness. The jealousy. The clinginess of Macy. How she broke it off with Macy because she couldn't handle it. She, Macy, didn't take the hint. She called. She showed up at Shae's place. All the time. At all hours.

After apprenticing under Shae and working together so closely, we realized we were falling for each other. And it got serious fast. We moved in together. When Macy found out, she was jealous and angry. She accused me of violating her trust as a friend. She showed up at Shae's apartment, and when she saw me there, she shot Shae. Killed her in a jealous rage. I just remember seeing the flash from her gun, and my ears ringing. Shae fell dead onto the floor. I panicked and screamed. Macy grabbed me and pinned me to the wall. She told me that if anyone asks, Shae was attacked in a robbery gone bad.. I told her I didn't want to lie. She told me that if I didn't, she would come for me next. So I lied. And that's when I left. I moved to California to get away from Macy. Now there were two bodies linked to me. One that, yes, I was responsible for. But it didn't look good that yet another partner of mine was dead, and in our home. I had no choice but to leave. I needed to escape both New Orleans and Macy Quinn.

The reason I didn't want you to hang around with Macy Quinn is that I knew her before you and I ever met. I met her in New Orleans.

She followed me here. She said it was to keep an eye on me and make sure I remembered to keep my mouth shut. To remember that any given point, she could have me arrested and tried for Shae's murder. If I crossed her, she would turn me in for the crime she committed. She ultimately kept her distance. But in the back of my mind, she was always just around the corner. I would see her around town. I could feel her eyes on me from a distance. It was dumb luck that I fell for you, and she happened to be your friend.

However, you need to know that the "file" she showed you is false. It's a lie. It's all made up. I am not wanted, and my name has never been changed, except for taking your last name after we got married. I am who I have always been. The woman who loves you. The woman you married. The woman you fell in love with. I've never hidden anything from you, except for this. I wanted to keep it under wraps because I do fear Macy. And I figured if I didn't say anything, and we stayed away from each other, I would not have to worry about anything.

I knew from day one that she was obsessed with you, though. I had heard all of the stories and rumors. That's why I wanted you to stay away from her. That's why she married A.D.—to stay close to you. That's why I confronted her at our wedding.

She made this up knowing that you would believe it. She waited for the right time to drop it in your lap. She manipulated you. I'm sending proof of my story with this letter. I'm hoping you read this. I will reach out in a few days, hoping you've had a chance to read this, and maybe we can talk?

I miss you, Parker. I love you above and beyond everything in this world. You <u>are</u> my world. My heart. My everything. I am begging you—if you ever loved me—you will find it within your heart to read this and to look at all that I sent.

You said you would burn the world for me. Find it in your heart to burn that bridge with Macy. Trust me. Your wife.

Till death do us part.

I love you. I miss you. I need you.

Calypso.

Parker's hand trembled, and the salty, hot tears began to stream down her cheeks as she read the letter.

She set the letter down and studied the other contents of the envelope. Inside, she found a certified copy of Calypso's birth certificate. She was indeed who she said she was. Calypso Boudreaux. A copy of the police report from her stabbing her ex in self-defense. A newspaper article about the stabbing. A copy of the newspaper clipping from the story of the shooting. A picture of a younger Macy and a younger Calypso together on Bourbon Street with a tattooed woman Parker assumed must be Shae. Macy's arm slung around Calypso's shoulders and Calypso looking at Macy. Both of them laughing.

Parker's stomach lurched. Her thoughts scattered as she tried to put the pieces together. She put the contents of the envelope back inside and set it on her desk.

Macy Quinn was a monster. An unstable, psychopathic monster. Parker felt so stupid for being so easily manipulated. Of course Macy would have the ability to put together such a realistic counterfeit file. And everything Calypso wrote made sense with Macy's pattern of behavior after she killed Calypso. She was holding it above Parker's head the same way she did to Calypso.

Everything in Calypso's letter made sense. It all clicked. Everything fell into place. If only Parker had seen this before getting shot, or even before she left for Gig Harbor with Macy, things would have been so different. Calypso would still be alive. Calypso would be hers still. It made the pain of the loss and what she had done all the more painful. She betrayed Calypso and then ended up complicit in her death. It was a searing pain in her heart. She couldn't let Macy evade the consequences of her actions. Calypso deserved justice.

41 NO PLANS NO SOLUTIONS

PARKER

Sitting on all of this information was hard. Lloyd had contacted the precinct and reported all that he knew to the department. He said the timeline would probably be a few weeks before anything would actually happen in the way of an arrest. They would have to do their own investigation and not just take Lloyd's word for it.

Tuesday through Friday went amazingly well for Parker, keeping her mind busy. She ended up doing several press interviews for her client. Images of him on security video pounding on the victim went viral thanks to TMZ.

The optics were awful, but the defense strategy was solid. What the cameras didn't record was the words exchanged and the view of the events leading up to the very unintended death of the victim. The victim grabbed the defendant's fiancée's breasts from behind and made a lewd suggestion to her. That occurred an hour before the attack. From there, he kept pestering her. Grabbing her, touching her. The final straw happened when he held a knife to her back. That's when the defendant clocked him, sending him back. The knife fell from his hands, which explained why the knife did not appear on camera.

What happened to be going well for them was the number of witnesses who were present during all of the events of the night. Parker spun the narrative back in his favor. She pointed out that this case seemed to epitomize the villainization of a man of color. Portraying him as a predator when he was defending his girlfriend from a predatory assailant. She was confident that this case would be dropped fairly quickly.

Parker enjoyed working on this case as it kept her busy and distracted. It helped her regain a sense of who she always knew herself to be before this situation. Before Calypso. Before Macy. Also overseeing Lloyd's case—an embezzlement case involving a sitting senator. Lloyd made her proud. He did well on his own and didn't need her. He reported to her as a courtesy. She slowly began to let out the reins and let him do his own thing. He'd started to bring in his own clients at this point and handled it well. And he grew to be not only a junior attorney, but a friend as well.

Best of all, Macy Quinn, to her knowledge, had been leaving her the fuck alone. Her intuition told her that Juliana's ex deserved the credit for this small favor. But whatever it took to keep that psycho bitch out of her life.

Parker made her way downstairs. There was nothing for her to do today except focus on the ghost of Calypso.

She was unsure if she should confront Macy with the truth or not. She feared that if she did, Macy would kill her, too. Given her track record, it would be a pretty safe bet.

She thought about calling Lloyd and having him

come over, finally telling him the whole story, but she couldn't. Not yet. They were close, but she wasn't sure how close when it came to such an egregious violation of the law. And as she told him, she may need him to step up and defend her if . . . Let's not think about the ifs.

She called the one person she talked to about anything and everything. Her father. He would do whatever it took to protect her and to protect his legacy. That went without question.

When Mr. Harrington showed up, she ushered him into the office. He took one of the chairs across the desk from her, for once not taking *her* chair behind the desk.

"Daddy, I need to talk to you as my father. Not an attorney. Not my mentor. So put your dad hat on, and remove the attorney part of yourself," she said as she took a seat in her chair.

His eyes got big. "Parker, what is going on?"

"And you can't tell Mom anything about what I'm about to tell you, either."

"Parker, you're scaring me." The even tone of his voice made that hard to believe.

"Calypso didn't shoot me."

"Okay. How do you know this? I think you *want* to believe that, but the—"

Parker kept bulldozing on. "She's also not wanted by the police. And she's never changed her name. Macy made all of it up. Lloyd pulled the metadata from the file. It was all fraud."

"Parker. Slow down. How do you know all of this?"

She slid the envelope across the desk, and he took it from her and opened it, sorting through the contents, laying them out side by side. Starting with the letter, he picked it up and began to read it.

His eyebrows rose and his eyes became saucers as he read.

"How does this prove she didn't shoot you?" His attorney hat went back on. "Money is a powerful motivator. She may have felt entitled to your estate."

"Look at the postmark on the envelope. She sent that from Washington the day before I was shot."

"Why am I here as Dad and not a lawyer?"

"Hold on." Parker got up and moved to the shelf along the side of the wall, where she kept a bar shelf with a selection of single malt Scotch and glasses. She poured her dad a Scotch and one for herself. "You're going to need this." She handed him his glass and sat back in her chair. "Remember how I went to the Pacific Northwest with Macy? It was to meet with Calypso. Parker took a sip of the drink and let the heat wash down her throat and into her chest before summarizing the events of the trip to him.

The color drained from Mr. Harrington's face. "Why? Parker, *why* would you do something like that?" He tossed back the whole of his drink.

Taking another sip to stall and to numb herself, she attempted to explain the mental and emotional toll it had all taken on her, finishing with, "I was so scared, Dad. I was so afraid. I was in shock. I couldn't think straight. I just saw my wife bleeding out in front of me."

"Parker, it's really simple. We just need to make an offer to turn her over to the Washington State Police. You didn't kill her. You didn't hide her body. You were *scared.* How are you the brightest defense attorney in Southern California, and you can't see that?"

"Fear, Daddy. Fear. I was, and I still am scared. I was . . . I don't know. Traumatized. I just watched someone kill my *wife.* And then I helped her cover it up. And Macy is a fucking psychopath. An unstable, obsessive one."

He sat back in his chair and steepled his fingers under his chin; that's what he did when he strategized. Parker notably performed the same gesture. She had, of course, been emulating him since she was eight years old.

"Look up the town you stayed in, and the neighboring areas, and look for news headlines."

Her father remained the only person able to pull off bossing her around. If anyone else tried to order her to do something, she would have done the exact opposite solely to prove she was, in fact, the one in charge. She turned the monitor to show him as well.

"Look for the headlines. If Calypso had been found, it would be there."

Parker skimmed through all of the headlines from the day it happened until today. Nothing.

She glanced over at her father.

"Call it in. They need to find her. And then we go from there."

Parker put her hands flat on the desk and sat frozen, staring at her father.

"Parker, you can't keep going with this on your conscience. It will eat you alive." He leaned across the desk and put his large, warm, dry hands over hers. Parker studied them, noticing the blue veins and subtle brown age spots that had appeared on them. He gave her hands a gentle squeeze before she pulled back.

Parker held her breath and searched up the number for the Gig Harbor police station. She stared at it with her phone in her hand. Her father nodded in encouragement.

When they answered, Parker put it on speakerphone. But she froze. Her dad shot her a pointed look. "Hi. Um. I need to report a murder."

"When did it happen?" The dispatcher sounded bored.

"About a week and a half ago." The vivid picture of Macy dragging her down the hall played in her mind.

"Where is the body?"

"In a vacation rental. On Panorama Drive. It's the white house, with black shutters and a red door, a covered porch, and an attached garage. The body is in the second bathroom, not the en suite. It's in the shower stall. It's a woman. About 35 years old. Black hair, tattoos. Her name is Calypso. Calypso Harrington." Saying it out loud stabbed her in the chest.

"We were called to that address ten days ago. The cleaning crew went to clean and saw that there was a break-in. But there was no body found. Some blood in the shower, but that was it."

Parker hung up before the dispatcher could ask her any further questions. Her mind spun her back to Macy dragging Calypso's body to the bathroom. Calypso's eyelids fluttering. She thought she had willed it. That she was seeing things. But she didn't. It happened. Calypso is alive. "She's not there. She's not there. She's not dead. If she's not there, she's not dead." Parker whispered.

"What are you going to do?" Her father asked.

"I'm not sure. I don't know how to find her. And she probably thinks I tried to kill her and hide her body."

"Right now, I would just leave it all alone then. There's nothing you can do."

Parker leaned back in her chair and took another sip of the scotch. The color had drained from her face.

"Parker. Listen to me. I know you don't like loose ends. But there is nothing you can do right now. Calypso is in the wind, and there's a restraining order on Macy. You can only sit back and wait now."

"Where's Calypso's portrait? The one that hung in the living room?"

"That tacky thing?"

"It's not tacky. It's my wife. And I love that piece. And right now, it's all I have left of her."

"It's in the garage rafters. Before you say anything, it was covered in a sheet to protect it. But you're lucky I didn't throw that away. Your mother and I hated that thing. Even though we loved Calypso. That piece is god-awful."

After her father left, she called Lloyd and asked him to come over. Her arm was still giving her a lot of trouble. She wanted that portrait down from the storage rack and back on the wall, and she couldn't do it alone.

Once he realized why she called him over, he shot her a skeptical look. "Why do you want that down?"

"Don't question me. Just help me." Parker pleaded.

"She shot you, Parker. And ran off. Despite being framed by Macy. She still shot you."

"I'm not convinced she shot me. I never was."

"Parker, you won't tell me what happened in Seattle. You won't tell me why you want this down. You aren't acting like yourself. To be frank, you are acting kinda crazy. What's going on?" His impatience and frustration came through clearly in his tone and on his face.

"Lloyd, I promise. Once everything is settled, I will tell you everything. Just trust me right now."

He sighed, climbed up on the ladder, and pulled the large canvas down from where it sat stored, above Parker's bins of Christmas decorations.

"Thank you," Parker said once he came down from the ladder with the canvas in his hand.

Pulling the sheet off it lit a small glimmer of hope that Calypso might still be out there and would come back. A hope that maybe there was a possibility to make this right.

Lloyd folded the ladder and tucked it back into its original place.

"Can you help me hang it?" Parker asked him.

"Only if you promise to tell me what is going on," Lloyd demanded.

"Maybe I just fire you." Parker teased.

"I knew you would go there." Lloyd carried the canvas into the house.

42 RETURN TO SENDER

OCTOBER 1

CALYPSO

laying dead was harder than she anticipated it ever would have been. Not that it was on her bingo card of things to do this year, or ever. Giving her weight over and not fighting was against every fiber of her self-preservation. Holding her breath while Macy boasted about fucking Parker was the hardest part. Hearing Parker crying was the second hardest part. She fought a war within herself to stay still and hold her breath.

The pain was excruciating. But she forced herself to endure and wait it out for them to leave. Once the door shut, she counted to three hundred to be sure Macy wasn't going to come back. The one thing Macy missed was Calypso's burner phone in the pocket of her leggings, hidden under her sweater.

Calling the police was out of the question. Instead, she

called Beau. He and Gilian came and got her. He tried to convince her to call the police. Hard pass. She made them promise to keep it between them. She didn't need a public incident, and to be handed over to the police in California. Beau and Gilian—bless their little hearts—did not understand how things worked on this side of the law. She would be hauled in and stuck in a jail cell for God knew how long. And though she suspected that Parker had seen her, that she was willing to listen, she wasn't sure how far into her head Macy had been able to get. She would be stuck with some shitty public defender, and that would not work.

Beau and Gilian were reluctant when they picked her up, but she convinced them to keep this whole situation under wraps. Beau sat her on the edge of the bathtub in their bathroom and sutured her up.

OCTOBER 10

Now that she was mostly healed, it was time for her to go home and settle all of this. She was done with the games. She was done with the miscommunication. She was done with Macy Quinn.

"Thank you for letting me stay," Calypso wrapped her arms around Gilian.

"Are you going to be okay?" Gilian asked, concern in her voice.

"I have to be. I need to go back and make this right. Beau, are you sure I can't pay you for fixing me up?"

"Just take care of those stitches. Keep them clean. They should dissolve shortly." He was so incredibly ready for her to leave. She had been camped out in their house for months. Long enough that their kids even started referring to her as Auntie Calypso.

"I'm really worried about you," Gilian hugged Calypso.

"Call me when you get there? And if you need to come back, we are here." Calypso was positive that Beau did not share that sentiment.

Calypso wiped a tear from her eye. "I will."

"You know you can come back if you need to." Gilian grabbed both of Calypso's hands. The look on Beau's face made it clear he couldn't be any less enthusiastic about the offer his wife made.

Dropping her off at the car rental place, Gilian used her credit card to rent a small coupe for Calypso to drive back to California. Calypso gave her cash for the amount and planned to Venmo the rest if necessary. She was compelled to make this right once and for all. Macy Quinn needed to be exposed, and Calypso needed to put her life back together with or without Parker. But she would be damned if Macy was going to force her out of the state and out of her life. It was bad enough that she let Macy get the better of her and bully her into leaving New Orleans.

She got behind the wheel, and Gilian and Beau drove off in the opposite direction. She wore a black turtleneck that covered all of her ink and rocked a fresh haircut—her long hair shorn into a cute short, layered bob—think Marilyn Monroe, but jet black instead of platinum. If someone were looking for her, they would have to know her. She purchased a fake ID that cost an arm and a leg, but it was good enough to get her by until she reclaimed her life.

* * *

OCTOBER 13

Three days in the car alone turned out to be the hardest part of the whole ordeal. As she drove, Calypso's mind wandered back to the familiar scent of Parker's cologne and skin the night Macy tried to kill her. She felt in her bones that Parker would listen. Parker was too willing to hold her and hold her tight at that. They fit together. That embrace told her all she needed to know. She and Parker belonged together. She was convinced. They had a consistent gravitational pull that would keep them coming back to one another.

When she would stop for the night at hotels along the way, she replayed the conversation where Macy threatened Parker. The sound of Parker crying. What happened was not on Parker. This and every other shitty event in her life linked back to Macy Quinn as the mastermind of it all.

It would be a gamble going back to California now. A big one at that. If she showed up at Parker's, Macy might be there. She might wind up in a jail cell after all. With any luck, Parker would be home and alone.

As she crossed the state line from Oregon to California, she called Xochitl. "Hello?" Xochitl's voice sounded wary, answering a call from an unknown out-of-state number.

"Xochitl, it's Calypso. I know it's late. I'm sorry."

She gasped on the other end of the line. "Calypso! Are you okay? We haven't heard from you since I dropped you off in Seattle. Shit has gotten crazy on the news cycle. People think you shot Parker. The cops came here questioning us. You're wanted for attempted murder."

"I know. I know. Hey, I'm coming back. No one knows. But I'm going to see Parker. I need to tell her a few things. She needs to be told a lot of the things that I've never been completely honest with her about. But if it doesn't go well, can I crash with you guys?"

"Of course. You know you don't even have to ask."

Calypso let out a breath. "Thank you. You and Xander are—"

"Family. We're a family. You are our family. You've been there for us, too. It's a two-way street."

"I hate to ask, but can one of you pick me up from the airport? I will be in town around eleven tomorrow morning. I need to return my rental car there."

Xochitl covered the phone, nudged Xander, and a football game was playing in the background. There was some muffled talking before Xochitl came back on the line. "Xander will be there to pick you up."

"Thank you. Kiss him for me. A big fat wet one on his beautiful bald tattooed head."

Xochitl laughed on the other end. "See you soon."

Having at least another five hours on the road, Calypso pulled off to drive through Starbucks after she hung up with Xochitl. As she pulled into the brightly lit drive-through, she prayed to whatever gods that would listen to her that she made the right decision. She'd spent the last of her cash on this trip home, leaving barely enough to buy breakfast for her and Xander as repayment for him driving her to her and Parker's home. Well, hopefully still her and Parker's.

She believed that Parker still loved her. That there was hope. This was the biggest gamble of her life. Bigger than moving to California. Bigger than opening her own business. Bigger than marrying Parker. Her freedom and her life were at stake.

PART V

EXODUS

43 HOMECOMING

October 14

Parker

Parker hadn't slept well for three straight nights. She lay awake staring at the ceiling, wondering where the fuck Calypso was. Wondering if Calypso thought she was in on it with Macy. Wondering why, if she were still alive, she hadn't reached out to call her in these two weeks. She probably did think she was in on it with Macy. Parker wondered how she let things escalate to this point, which led her into a downward spiral of what-ifs. What if she never befriended Macy . . . What if she didn't believe Macy . . . What if she and Calypso worked a little harder to keep their relationship strong . . . It only fanned the flames of her guilt and regret.

As she rolled over and faced Calypso's empty side of the bed, she pondered how it would even go down if they saw each other again. She had no idea what she would say to

Calypso if she got to be near her again. She wondered if she *would* see her again. She hoped she would see her again. She *ached* to see her again.

She woke up after ten, which was unlike her. There was no telling what time she finally fell asleep, but it was as if she hadn't slept at all—like when she would pull all-nighters in undergrad, bar hopping, bed hopping, and then going to class in the morning. Only now, she awoke with stiffness in her neck and a raging headache. After a hot shower and throwing on sweats and a T-shirt she made her way down-stairs to the kitchen. She'd made the decision to text Lloyd and Juliana last night to inform them that she would be working from home for the next few days. She couldn't bear the thought of sitting in the office and trying to focus. She had a big meeting this morning and there was no way she would be able to manage it. Either Lloyd would take point on it, or they would reschedule.

As Parker stood in the kitchen waiting for her coffee, her mind still fuzzy from lack of sleep, she still couldn't stop obsessing over Calypso's whereabouts. To top it off, the fucking Keurig did not brew fast enough for her. She was desperately trying to pull her shit together in an effort to get some work done. And without caffeine, nothing was going to happen. She opened her email on her phone, but the words appeared blurry, and nothing made sense. After reading the same sentence three times, she closed the app and threw the phone on the counter. Finally, the stupid coffee finished brewing. Parker picked up her phone and her mug of hot, strong black coffee and made her way to her home office.

As she sat in the Chesterfield leather chair (that Calypso picked out when she was renovating her home office—a vintage piece lovingly restored), she heard a knock on her door and assumed that it was a solicitor or a Jehovah's Witness. She considered not even answering it.

Begrudgingly, with an angsty groan, she got up, made her way to the door, and opened it. She gasped at the sight before her and paused, thinking she was hallucinating. That she wanted her to come back so deeply that she conjured her. Tears began to fall, and she pulled Calypso in to her. Pushing Calypso's hair back and looking into her eyes. "I'm sorry. I'm so sorry." Her entire being flushed with fire in the best possible way.

Calypso nuzzled into Parker. Her arms wrapped around Parker. She couldn't get close enough. She wanted to melt into her. Her fingers dug into Parker's back, gripping her. She didn't need to say anything. Her presence said everything. She was here. She was alive. This was real.

There was no opportunity for talk or explanations. Parker didn't care how Calypso got there, or how she got past the gate. She only cared that Calypso was there in front of her. The world became right again when Parker brought her lips down to Calypso's. The world stopped. Everything that had been off balance came back to center. She wasn't going to let her go. Not ever again. Calypso's tongue glided over hers, and Parker had never been more certain that Calypso would always be hers.

Ascending the stairs to their bedroom, she held onto Calypso's hand. Calypso kept her fingers entwined through Parker's as she followed behind. Parker kept looking back at her as if she feared Calypso would disappear.

When they crested the stairs and made it into the bedroom, she brought Calypso back in to her and kissed her again. There was frenzy, there was hunger, and there was urgency in that kiss. Calypso let out a soft whimper. "You're really here." She whispered as she backed away and took it all in. Took *Calypso* in again. Memorizing every little detail. Her hair had been cut short, and she was dressed plainly in nondescript clothes, covering her tattoos. But it was her. It was her wife. All of the words she wanted to say, all of the apologies she wanted to spill out, disappeared.

Stepping in, Calypso closed the gap that Parker had created by stepping back in. Gripping the collar of Parker's sweatshirt, she pulled her closer and crushed her lips back to Parker's.

Fingers wrapping under the fabric of Calypso's shirt, Parker pulled it over her head. Exploring. Touching her tentatively as she traced her fingers over the black patterns inked into Calypso's flesh, soft and warm under her fingertips. It was her. Her wife. A woman whom she betrayed and cast away. She turned Calypso around and her fingers traced the marks left behind from Macy's brutal attack on her. "I'm so sorry." Parker couldn't say it enough. There were no other words she could say. After allowing her fingers to brush over each of them, Parker skimmed her lips over each of the wounds, raised and pink against the pale skin of Calypso's back, working her way to the back of Calypso's neck as she trembled against Parker's touch.

Mesmerized. Disbelieving. Overwhelmed. Breathing in her skin. Her perfume. Spinning back around to face Parker, her hands went up to Parker's hair. Her lips found Parker's again. Parker was overcome. Calypso's kiss became her life. She didn't realize how dead she was without her.

Calypso's touch was tentative as her hands skimmed down Parker's neck and to her face, her thumb gliding over Parker's lower lip. There was a look of awe in Calypso's eyes as if she couldn't believe this was real either. Parker's hands drifted down Calypso's neck and around her back, undoing her bra. Her mouth trailing down, inhaling the scent of Calypso's orange blossom and vanilla perfume, and the taste of her skin, sweet and salty, Calypso made a small gasp as Parker's lips grazed over her nipples, grazing her teeth against the metal of the rings in them. In desperation to feel

Calypso's skin against her own, Parker pulled her shirt over her head. She needed Calypso's warmth and velvet softness. There was an overwhelming want to feel every inch against her to know she wasn't in some beautiful fever dream.

Calypso's fingertips danced over Parker's back and over her front side, cupping Parker's breasts in her hands, sliding her hands down, taking Parker in. A shiver danced across Parker's skin as Calypso's fingers continued to trail over her.

It was unreal. Stepping forward into Calypso's space, forcing Calypso to step back toward the bed, her hands pulled Calypso's long skirt down. Calypso stepped out of it and kicked her sandals off as Parker lay her back onto the bed, pulling her own sweats off, bringing her body down, pinning Calypso's beneath her, relishing the sweet, soft warmth of her skin.

Planting a trail of kisses down Calypso's neck and down to her belly button, kneeling between Calypso's thighs, taking in her luscious body beneath her. Drinking in every nuance of Calypso's expression, the swell of her breast, the curve of her hip, Parker was certain there was nothing more beautiful than Calypso, lying bare before her.

Feather light, Parker ran her hands up Calypso's thighs and stopped, letting her fingertips graze over Calypso's center, watching as she moved under her touch, before bringing herself down between Calypso's thighs. Tasting what she thought she would never have again. Feeling Calypso writhe against her. Hearing her whmper. Calypso's fingers in her hair, pulling her closer. She was breathtaking. Beautiful and vulnerable. The surreality of having Calypso again. She believed down to her core that she didn't deserve this. Unworthy of Calypso's love or forgiveness.

Parker didn't care how Calypso got here. She only cared that Calypso was here with her. She only cared that she *was*. She only cared that Calypso wanted her still.

The doorbell rang below. Parker knew it was probably Lloyd checking on her. But work could wait. The world could wait. All that mattered was right before her.

Parker didn't waste time drawing it out. Calypso arched under her, crying out. Parker had never seen or heard anything more beautiful in her life.

44 OPEN THE FLOODGATES

Calypso

The day passed quickly as Calypso allowed herself to be lost in Parker's touch. Holding her close, Parker whispered her apologies so many times. She didn't need to, though. Calypso knew.

When Calypso managed to roll Parker onto her back, she read Parker's every reaction and predicted exactly where to go and what to do, how to move, to make Parker beg. She missed this. She missed the closeness. She missed the warmth. The familiarity of Parker. The closeness of someone only she knew so well. Something—someone—that only belonged to her.

Calypso didn't want it to end. She'd grown to be so hopeless when she thought Parker would never be hers again. She wanted to relish every second, every touch, every movement, every whisper, every kiss.

The room grew dark as the hours passed. Parker held her close, letting her fingers run up and down the landscape of Calypso's body. Calypso touched the raised scars on Parker's back, sending a shiver through Parker.

"What happened?" Calypso asked, her voice quiet, her fingers tracing the scar on Parker's shoulder.

"I came home to grab some things, and I saw your car parked in the driveway, and the front door was left open. I walked in, and it was dark in the house. I called your name, and then that was it. I don't know if I heard the sound of the gunshot first or if I felt it. It was just loud, and pain, and then I was out. Everyone assumed it was you. Your car was gone by the time Macy found me."

"I would never hurt you," Calypso whispered. "I can't believe you thought I would do that to you." Calypso was one part offended and one part disheartened, thinking Parker would assume she would do such a thing.

"It all circumstantially led back to you. I couldn't believe it either. Honestly, I always believed deep down it wasn't you. Couldn't have been you. Macy, my father, and Lloyd all wanted me to put you out there in the press so you could be found. I refused. But I knew you would come to me," Parker said quietly, her breath warm against Calypso's neck as she spoke.

Calypso pulled back a bit, turned on the lamp on the bedside table, and studied Parker's face in dim light. Parker rolled onto her back. Calypso propped herself up on her elbow. "I sent you the package before then. You should have known."

"No. I had no idea." Her head gave a slight shake. "It hadn't arrived yet, or if it had, I hadn't seen it yet. And even then, I only got around to opening it this week, ironically. I have existed in this fog since you left. It wasn't right. Nothing was right. Nothing made sense without you. And when I thought Macy killed you, a piece of me died. I was just . . . I was barely able to make it through each day. I called my dad. I prayed that you would know that I didn't want what Macy did to you to happen. That I would never want you to be hurt. I had hopes that you would come back to me. And you did. But after what happened in Gig Harbor, I was so unsure if you ever would. I mean, I thought you were dead." Parker's voice cracked. "I wasn't sure if you thought I was in on it."

"I heard you crying. I was playing dead to keep Macy from finishing the job. I was just there. And I could hear you. I *knew*. I heard her barking orders at you. I heard you fighting it. I knew. The way you looked at me. The way you held me, before she stabbed me, the words you had said to me . . . I *knew*. I knew we were going to be okay."

"I am so sorry I took Macy's word for it. I never thought she could be that diabolical. Who does something like that? I've defended some pretty fucked-up people, and never have I ever dealt with something like this."

Calypso paused and glanced over at Parker's profile. "I loved you. Even though you believed her. I loved you. Even though you left me for dead. I couldn't blame you. I didn't blame you. I love you. I think I will always love you." She always loved Parker when she was vulnerable, and not in her suits and work mode. She loved the bed-rumpled hair and the softness in Parker's eyes.

"I was so angry. I was so hurt. I loved you so much, and then I was just seized by this level of betrayal. You lied to me for years. No matter which way we look at it. You didn't feel like you trusted me enough with your truth. You lied by omission. And I don't know why you never trusted me with the truth. So much would have been different if I had just known the whole story from the jump."

"And you slept with the woman who went out for my blood. Who tried to ruin me." Calypso realized it was tit-for-tat, and she sounded like a bitter bitch. But she couldn't help it. The thought of Parker and Macy together infuriated her. No. Not infuriated. Disgusted her. "Not just several years ago. She thought I was dead, but that crazy bitch talked to me while she was dragging me into the shower. She told me you were together. She bragged about it."

"I'm not trying to make excuses," Parker's voice cracked and Calypso fixed on a tear that slipped down Parker's face. It reflected gold in the lamplight that spilled across the room. "I was so fucked in the head after all of this went down. It was so . . . I don't even know. . . It just . . . Nothing at all was right. I know I keep saying it—repeatedly even. But it wasn't right. I was out of sorts. It was all so sordid and twisted. I almost died. I thought you tried to kill me. I thought you were on the lam. And she had always been so loyal—"

"No. Not loyal. Obsessed. That's how she operates. She fixates on people and manipulates everyone around them. She's a cancer."

Parker nodded silently in agreement. "I see that now," she murmured.

Calypso sighed. "What do we do now?"

Parker wiped the tear from her eye and rolled back onto her side so she could face Calypso. "What do you mean?"

"About this. About us. About Macy." Calypso didn't know what she wanted Parker to say, or what she should say. But she needed a plan. She wanted to know this was not it.

"'About this' meaning what?"

"This whole fucked-up mess that Macy Quinn created for us."

"As for us . . . let's start there." Parker touched Calypso's face, running her thumb along Calypso's bottom lip.

Calypso backed away from Parker's touch. "No. None of

that until we figure out what we are doing. I can't handle it. I need to know if I need to distance myself from you. I need to protect myself. I told you I would always love you. But if you and I are done, I can't do this." Calypso motioned between the two of them, her chest tightened and constricted. She was aware that she should establish boundaries and that she should never have gotten into bed with Parker before laying those out. But she found herself helpless the second Parker's lips touched hers.

"Calypso, I told you. In our wedding vows, I promised that I would burn the world for you. I let you down. I gave up and stopped fighting. And I know I made some mistakes along the way. I know I should have been prioritizing you over my work. However, I need you to admit some fault in this as well. You never let me in. You didn't trust me." Calypso recognized that Parker spoke the absolute truth. And she took accountability, which was all Calypso ever wanted.

"I was afraid you would take her side. And look. You did." Yeah, that came out petulant, but the truth hurts.

"Maybe if you had been honest with me from the beginning, I wouldn't have. You left me to fill in the holes you left wide open. This isn't all on me, or Macy. You have some accountability in this, too." Parker's voice wasn't harsh or accusatory. It was soft, if a little bit stripped of sentiment. But that was simply Parker, how she dealt with things.

But those words still hit Calypso hard. "Okay." She whispered.

"I'm your *wife*, Calypso. You married me. We made vows. In good times and bad. I love you enough to want to work through this. But you have to learn to be real with me. Take down those walls. If you had told me all that you wrote in the letter from the start—"

"I was so afraid I would lose you. You come from this posh, privileged world. You don't deal with people like me—"

"I deal with 'people like you,'" Parker used air quotes, "for a living. It's my job to believe 'people like you.'" She used the air quotes again. "You need to give me more credit."

"But not in your personal life. I looked at your life and your family and friends, and I didn't—I *don't* believe—a story like mine would fit into a story like yours. And the way you looked at me every day. I didn't want it to change."

"I know the truth now. The absolute truth. And I still love you. I actually love you more than I did nine days ago, because I finally got to look into a side of you that you never let me see before. And you *trusted* me with your truth." Parker wiped the still-flowing tears from Calypso's cheeks. "I know we come from different worlds. But I also believed— and still do—that if anyone didn't accept you, I would have zero issues cutting them out of my life. And that stands today. That stands as long as you're mine. Are you still mine?" Parker's eyebrow arched.

Calypso knew Parker suspected what the answer would be. She was, and always would be, Parker's.

Calypso turned the lamp off and laid herself down against the pillow, allowing Parker to pull her closer, nose-to-nose on the pillow. "Forever. I'm not going anywhere. Not ever again." These were the times that she'd missed the most in the weeks they spent apart. Darkness completely took over the room. Calypso moved and buried herself against Parker's chest. She let the quiet and steady beat of Parker's heart, and the darkness, calm her. The quiet didn't last long. There was too much they needed to handle. She rolled onto her back. "So, us?"

"I'm still in if you're still in." Parker also rolled to her back. Her hand reached down and grabbed Calypso's under the blanket, intertwining their fingers. Parker squeezed her hand, holding on for dear life.

There was a sense of rawness and honesty that washed over her in a wave of peace. "I'm still in."

Parker released a breath next to her.

"So now what? What do we do about this situation and Macy Quinn?" Calypso brought the conversation back to the start.

"I don't want to think about that psycho bitch." Parker groaned and nuzzled into Calypso's neck.

"While we are laying everything out and talking through this . . . we can't just bury this and pretend it doesn't exist, that it never happened."

"Macy? I don't know what we can do. I can't turn her in because I was complicit. It would ruin me. There is an open investigation into the fraudulent file. It will take a few weeks, and then she will be in hot water and out of our hair."

Not at all what Calypso wanted to hear. The rawness and intimacy fled, replaced by incredulity and anger. Calypso sat back up and turned the lamp back on. "So she just gets to frame me for shooting you, and then try to kill me, and she suffers no consequence?"

"Calypso, it's not that easy."

"Okay. Fine. Karma will just work it out." Her voice was full of the bitterness sitting within her. She rolled onto her side, turning her back to Parker. *Parker can't possibly be allowing this to happen. Macy gets to hold two murders over them —one for Calypso and an attempted one for Parker.*

Parker placed her hand on Calypso's hip and her lips against Calypso's shoulder. "That's not what I'm saying at all. I'm just saying it's not going to be easy, and it's not going to be quick. We have a lot to sort through."

"She *cannot* go unpunished for all of this chaos that she's created."

"And she won't."

Calypso wished she could believe that.

"I can tell you don't believe me."

"I have a hard time trusting in anything regarding Macy Quinn."

45 EVERYTHING EVENTUALLY COMES TO LIGHT

OCTOBER 17

PARKER

*P*arker took three days off work, much to Lloyd and Juliana's surprise and Calypso's joy.

It wasn't only to stay and luxuriate in the bed. She wanted to work through all of the outstanding issues to the best of their abilities. They knew it wouldn't all be fixed, but a solid foundation was laid for healing.

It was long conversations about expectations while sitting outside overlooking the view, while they had morning coffee, continued with asking questions and answering with utter and blunt honesty while Calypso prepared meals. It was curling up in the living room with a movie on, not paying attention to the movie, but continuing to talk and explore their needs and their willingness to meet them. It was watching the sunset while they rehashed old memories and laughed.

There were boundaries and agreements made. Parker would make more of an effort to participate in Calypso's chosen activities, showing up for her friends' shows and openings, and learning more about art. Calypso would have more patience in dealing with Parker's cases. Parker would work on showing more appreciation, and Calypso would work on standing up when she felt Parker was being too demanding. Calypso would be more honest and would hold no more secrets. Parker would absolutely scale back and prioritize spending time together.

Emotionally and physically still exhausted, Parker dragged herself out of bed. She'd slept maybe three hours the night before. When she slipped out of bed, Calypso's eyes fluttered open. "What are you doing?" Calypso's voice was gravelly with sleep.

"I've gotta go to work." Parker ran her hand back through her hair. Any thought of working from home went out the window. Her father and Lloyd would be able to help get to the bottom of this bullshit with Macy, and they were at the office.

"Last night you said—"

"And I meant it. But I have to go in today. I have a meeting with a client at nine-thirty, and then I have a few more things to handle afterward. I promise, I will be home by no later than two or three." One of the many tasks on her list for that day was to set things up, allowing her to step back a little more. And she readily acknowledged she had a capable staff. It all came back to her own control-freak nature.

Calypso cocked her head to the side and raised an eyebrow playfully.

Parker knew the difference between angry Calypso and fun Calypso. "Don't look at me like that. Like you don't believe me." Parker smiled as she made her way to the en suite to shower, as she texted Juliana to make sure she had coffee ordered and ready.

Calypso dragged herself from the bed and followed her into the bathroom, where she perched on the side of the tub while Parker opened the shower door, started the spray, and stepped in. As she closed the door, Calypso stopped her and slid in with her.

"Are you *trying* to make me late?" Parker asked as she pushed her wet hair back off her forehead and grabbed the shampoo.

Calypso took the shampoo from Parker, poured it into her own hand, and worked it into Parker's hair. Calypso washing her hair was one of those things Parker missed so much when things went from bad to separation to thinking she was dead. "No. But I'm also not ready to be away from you right now." It was honest, and it was vulnerable, and Parker couldn't be mad as Calypso worked the lather into her scalp.

"We need to talk about something else." Parker rinsed the shampoo from her hair and moved out of the soothing cascade from the rainfall shower head, allowing Calypso to get underneath it.

"What's that?" Calypso asked as Parker tried to not to get distracted by the water flowing down Calypso's body, hating that she was going to have to leave. The last few days just were not enough.

"You're wanted. Everyone thinks you're gone. You need to stay home. Don't leave. Don't go anywhere. Not until this is resolved."

Calypso's eyes sprang open. "I didn't think about that. I can turn myself in, and you're the best defense attorney in the state." She placed her hands on Parker's shoulders.

"I wish it were that easy. Right now, it's your word against

Macy's and Macy's word against mine. This would only complicate matters. I cannot ethically represent you, nor can Lloyd or anyone else at the firm. I also don't trust anyone else to handle your case effectively. It's complicated."

"As everything that revolves around Macy is," Calypso mumbled.

"Does anyone know you are here?" Calypso removed her hands from Parker's shoulders. The absence was immediately registered, and Parker wished she'd put them back.

"Gilian and Beau—the people I stayed with in Washington—and Xander and Xochitl." Calypso worked the shampoo through her own hair.

"I know you can trust Xander and Xochitl. But what about the other two?"

"I've been friends with Gilian since freshman year of high school. I can trust them. Beau won't try to rock the boat with Gilian."

"Okay. Please, just don't go anywhere. And don't contact anyone else."

Calypso opened her mouth to say something, but nothing came out.

"Promise me, Calypso." Parker put her finger under Calypso's chin and tilted it up so she had to look in Parker's eyes.

Calypso sighed. "Fine. Okay. I promise." Parker sensed the irritation in her voice. This was entirely unfair for her. But until it was certain that Macy would be the one going down for this, on her own, she didn't want to risk losing Calypso again.

On her way out the door after forcing herself to finish getting ready, she kissed Calypso and kept her nose-to-nose. "I promise you, this will be over. We will get this handled."

Calypso nodded, straightened Parker's tie, and kissed her goodbye.

On the way to the office, she called Lloyd. "Where are you?" His voice was urgent. He was not used to Parker pushing it for time. "Everyone is waiting, and Juliana said your coffee is getting cold."

"I'll be there in twenty. I need you to go see if Dad is in."

"He is. I already saw him. Parker, what's going on?"

"I will explain after we meet with Blake," her NFL-playing murder suspect client. "I need you to make sure Dad's schedule is clear and so is yours. I'm going to need you both."

"What can possibly be going on that you, of all people, need help with?"

"Some things are too big for one person, and this is one." She hung up and turned the music up.

When she got to the office, Blake and his girlfriend were already there, waiting in the lobby. Parker came swooping in, Juliana running alongside her to hand her the coffee. "Blake, Tai, follow me." They got out of their seats and followed Parker into the meeting room, where Lloyd sat waiting for them.

Parker put her Hermes attaché case on the large mahogany table, pulled out all of her notes, and sat down, taking a drink of her now tepid coffee. Juliana would have to fetch her a fresh one.

Despite being exactly on time (which in Parker's world meant late), she made it through the meeting, and Blake understood her plan for his defense and walked away feeling good about it all. Tai asked good questions, and her story remained unwavering. Blake gave Parker a big bear hug on his way out as Juliana escorted him and Tai out.

Lloyd waited until everyone made it down the hall and out of earshot. "What kind of fuckery is happening, Parker? I know you've been going through it lately, but this is not at all what I'm used to seeing from you. I'd be lying if I said I wasn't worried."

"Just come with me. I'll explain once we are in Dad's office.

Parker and Lloyd walked down the hall to her father's office.

Without bothering to knock, she walked into his office with Lloyd in tow—something Lloyd wouldn't even do to Parker if he found her office door shut. Walking into her father's office unannounced was something Parker rarely did. But she found something comforting about Mr. Harrington's office from having spent so much of her life in that space. His dark-stained shelves were filled with leather-bound books. Her desk was a replica of his. However, his view was far superior to hers. Her office windows offered a cityscape view; his offered a view of the San Gabriels. The dark plush carpet under her feet had not changed since she was a kid, sitting at his feet, a sponge absorbing everything he said and did.

Mr. Harrington straightened his stack of papers, set them down, and cast his eyes on his daughter. "Parker, is everything okay?" To see her father concerned was a bit jarring. He took a hands-off approach to raising her, letting her make mistakes and learn from them. Coddling wasn't his thing.

"No." She sat down in the leather chair across from her father, and Lloyd took the other seat with his eyebrows raised. "Dad, bear with me. I need to catch Lloyd up on this first."

"Catch me up on what?" He ran his hands over his neatly edged haircut, smoothing it. His dark brown eyes narrowed in concern. "Parker—"

"Shut up and listen." Parker cut him off cold and then told him everything up to her opening the package from Calypso and reading it. Lloyd's jaw fell to the floor. Every time he went to ask a question, she held up her hand to silence him.

Mr. Harrington, all the while, sat back behind his desk

with his feet propped up and his hands steepled under his chin as he listened to the whole tale for a second time. He was analyzing and strategizing as he listened. "Okay, he's caught up. Now what?"

"There was no body found at the vacation rental. If there is no body, what can you conclude?"

"Calypso isn't dead," Lloyd whispered.

"She's home," Parker concluded.

Her father removed his feet from the desk and leaned over it. "What do you mean, 'home'?"

"She's at our house. Right now. She showed up a few days ago. That's why I've been staying home."

Mr. Harrington's eyebrows shot up, and Lloyd's jaw remained on the floor. It hadn't moved the entire time she told him the story.

"So what next?" Lloyd asked.

"That's what I need help with."

"If you turned yourself in," Mr. Harrington began, "you could still face charges. You would be disbarred. Besides, we don't know what kind of pull Macy will have with law enforcement up there, or how she will further manipulate this situation."

"I have no choice. If I get Macy to confess, and I record it, I will need to bring Calypso and one or both of you with me to turn it in. I won't do it alone. I can't do it alone."

"Your mother can never know about all of this. You'll put her in an early grave," Mr. Harrington grumbled.

Lloyd shook his head. "Parker, it's a huge gamble. Your cooperation will not guarantee a deal. Especially since you fled."

"That's why you two are going to help me. I need you to reach out and see what the environment in Washington is like for this and find me someone who is licensed there." Parker stood.

"What if this doesn't work?" Mr. Harrington asked.

"I haven't thought about that yet. We can deal with that after. Meanwhile, I have work to tend to." She made her way to the door. Lloyd scrambled up and followed behind her.

"Parker, this is insane."

"Juliana?" Parker called out, ignoring Lloyd as he caught up to her and fell in step.

Juliana magically appeared, walking in step with them as she made her way back to her office. "Yes, Parker?"

"Do I have anything on my schedule this afternoon?"

"You have a new client coming in to meet with you for a consultation at one. After that, nothing."

"Excellent. What do we know about the new client?"

"Parker—stop." Lloyd took her by the elbow.

Juliana paused. "Should I come back?"

Parker turned and faced her. "No. Just wait." She turned back to Lloyd. Parker lowered her voice to barely above a whisper."Unless you have a better idea, I'm out of options. My wife's freedom is at stake. My reputation is on the line. Do you have a better idea?"

Lloyd sighed and pinched the bridge of his nose. "No. And I do have your back. Whatever you decide to do. I will be there for you. I just don't like any of this."

"Neither do I." Parker turned back to Juliana. "Okay. Tell me about the new client."

46 THE BOTTOM OF THE BOTTLE

MACY

Macy sat on her couch, writing a letter to Brent as a part of her therapy. All of the things she never got to say to him. How he meant so much more to her than only a partner, he was kin—a sibling to be exact. She had the ability to trust him easily, and that was both important and rare. She sat surrounded by pages torn up and crumpled around her from having written and re-written the letter. It all sounded so hokey to her. This one, which she currently penned, would have to do.

She only left her condo to go to therapy, and that's it. She didn't even go sit in front of Parker's house. She couldn't. The department ultimately fired her because she was too much of a liability. She missed too many days and then showed up drunk for her desk duty with her history of violence and instability, it all finally fell apart. She no longer cared. They gave her a nice severance package: three months' pay and six months' insurance. So now, she stayed locked behind her doors. She went to therapy. And she drank. And she missed Parker. She didn't even know what day or what time it was. Her curtains and blinds remained shut tight. The only way she figured out it was time to go to therapy was because of the alarms she had set on her phone.

She couldn't believe that Parker was still angry with her. She didn't do anything wrong. She merely took out the trash. Cleared the path. Yes, she faked the file—not that Parker knew that—maybe she figured it out? Who knows. But she did it to *save* Parker. Desperate times. Desperate measures. It was super easy to create it. She was able to make a template and put a picture of Calypso through an age reversal program. Bam. It was a thing of beauty. It was done well enough to fool Parker of all people.

And it all worked for a minute. For a second. She had Parker to herself. Parker saw her. Parker saw how disastrous her choice of Calypso was.

She poured more vodka into a glass and added a touch of cranberry juice. That splash of cranberry kept her from thinking of herself as a total lush.

Her text alert went off, and she almost ignored it. It was probably a spam text asking for political donations or some shit. She tapped the screen and did a double-take. Parker's name scrolled across the screen. She made a habit of texting Parker daily, multiple times a day, for the first two weeks after they returned from Washington. Parker didn't respond to a single one. And every single one turned green—not blue —the iPhone tell of "you've been blocked." Macy created fake accounts to view Parker's social media. But Parker must have anticipated that—because all of her accounts were now set to private.

"Hey. Can we talk?" the simple message she'd been waiting for read.

Macy took a drink and stared at it. She picked up her phone after several minutes of staring at it on the cushion next to her as if it were going to detonate.

Her heart began hammering hard. She tapped a reply: "Please. I miss you." She waited a few minutes before hitting send.

Two angsty minutes later, Parker replied: "Meet me at Mantra?"

A dark and quiet Indian restaurant that Parker loved. Parker frequently picked it up on her way home from work. It was between her office and her home. Macy even memorized Parker's order, even though she had given Lloyd so much shit about knowing it by heart. Saag paneer, plain naan, mango lassi. She always got the same thing. It aligned with Parker's personality and very organized life. Macy questioned what it was about Parker that had her so stupidly in love with her.

This out of the blue text had her suddenly paranoid: "Do you want to give me a heads-up as to why you suddenly want to meet up?"

A long pause caused Macy to question the bitchy tone of her message. She watched as the dots appeared and disappeared. It was a lot of waiting and watching those dots before the reply came. "I miss you."

Macy's heart continued its hammering, throbbing in her head, a loud, hard tattoo. She wanted to believe it. She wanted *so badly* to believe it. She set the phone down, went into the bathroom, and examined herself staring back at her. She couldn't remember the last time she showered. Or slept more than a few hours. Her red hair, greasy at the roots, and frizzed at the ends. Her lips dry and cracked, and large black circles rimmed her bloodshot eyes. She looked like shit. She felt like shit.

She responded: "What time?"

The response came quickly this time. "Tonight. 7:30?"

Macy checked the time on her screen. It was a little after noon. She would have time to sober up and clean up: "I'll be there."

After assessing the bags under her eyes as she ran a hand through her greasy hair, she started the steaming water and turned on the shower. Parker wanted to see her. Maybe Parker finally realized that Macy did her a huge favor. Maybe Parker was ready to see what she and Macy could be. Together, they could be unstoppable. They could be forever. As Parker said, no one was ever going to love her as deeply as Macy. No one would go to the lengths Macy went to. Her heart soared, rising from the ashes that had been left when Parker went scorched Earth on her.

. . . Only for it to falter and drop as she considered that maybe Parker was getting ready to set her up. Maybe Parker would have cops waiting for her. She froze and pondered that option. But she knew Parker. Parker wouldn't have cops waiting for her. It was a huge risk for her. And Macy knew firsthand that Parker loved herself more than anyone else.

Macy stood under the scalding hot spray. She wanted to believe Parker still carried some semblance of love for her. At this point, she would even be happy with friendship again. She just missed Parker.

After getting out of the shower, she took the sweats she had been wearing for the last several days—maybe a week, she didn't know—and threw them in the washing machine, then sorted through her wardrobe. She settled on a pair of form-fitting jeans and a tight T-shirt. Her six-pack abs had softened from weeks of skipping the gym. She hadn't had a decent meal since her time in Washington with Parker. She had instead opted for a strict liquid diet of vodka since their return.

She had to get a grip. A serious grip.

After blowing her hair out and putting it up in a claw clip, she struggled with her makeup. It was taking her longer than she remembered. Her hands trembled. She put her eyeliner down and went to grab a snack. Maybe she needed to eat. No. She needed Parker.

The only edible item in her condo was a granola bar in the cupboard. She leaned against the counter as she wolfed it down. It helped, but only mildly. Her hands still trembled. She needed a drink. And Parker.

Even after Macy finished her makeup, she didn't recognize herself in the mirror's reflection. Even though she was dressed as she often did and her makeup was perfect, the woman peering back at her in the mirror was a complete stranger. A complete unknown.

She went to reach for the bottle of vodka, but decided against it. Instead she opted to blow the dust off and go for a drive instead. Staying sober needed to be her plan until she met with Parker.

The sun shone brighter and hotter than she remembered it ever being. She'd spent her last few weeks hiding indoors with her AC blasting. She put on her sunglasses and rolled down the windows. This helped more than the granola bar. The heat warmed through her skin and into her bones.

47 IDLE HANDS

OCTOBER 17

CALYPSO

Calypso sat in the house, bored out of her mind. She couldn't even set foot outside. Not until this shit with Macy was handled. Parker didn't even want her housekeeper coming over. She told Karen to take a paid week-long vacation. It was just Calypso and the Cat.

That manipulative redheaded bitch set her up to be the villain who tried to kill Parker. And everyone believed it. Everyone believed *her.*

It was so far off from the truth that it made Calypso's head spin. Anyone who so much as met her was very aware that Parker owned her whole heart. Her world revolved around Parker.

She wanted to have faith in Parker's plan. But she predicted there was no way that Macy would fall for it. Macy, a master manipulator, too smart, too underestimated by too many, able see the game five steps before anyone even realized she was playing along.

The biggest mistake ever made by anyone in Macy Quinn's path: underestimating her. That's what made her so dangerous.

Calypso finally did something she had been afraid to do since she left and started hearing the rumors that she was wanted. She went down into Parker's home office and tapped the mouse to wake the screen. She typed in her name in the search bar. She had only skimmed the one article that Gilian had shown her, but from that day, Calypso had avoided the news, the internet, and social media. She didn't want to know. But now, it was time to face it.

The first article from the LA Times featured her picture at the beginning. An older picture from her Instagram account. She and Xander were at a music festival doing cheap flash pieces for free admission. Her hair was wild, her makeup heavy; she was sticking her tongue out, her hands making the metal horns, wearing a shredded tank top with a black vinyl bra showing underneath. Below that, further down in the article, was a more recent picture of a refined Calypso. Lighter makeup. Tiffany jewelry. Though her clothes appeared far more conservative, they were still all black. To look at the pictures side-by-side struck her as a bit jarring. Did she change herself for Parker, or had she merely grown out of her past? Did Parker erase her identity and mold her into the shape she wanted? No. She was still there. She didn't *have to* wear the clothes or go to the events. She did it because she wanted to. She did it for love. She definitely assimilated into her new surroundings. The only remnants of who she had been before Parker were her tattoos and affinity for wearing all black. But that's because she chose to evolve.

She read the article. Specific lines stood out to her. ". . .

tattoo artist who fled New Orleans after a hurricane, was also apparently fleeing her own past. . . . homeless for nearly two years . . . stabbed her ex-girlfriend to death allegedly in self-defense . . . Now wanted on suspicion of another one of her former lovers' death, and the alleged attempted murder of her current wife, prominent defense attorney Parker Harrington. . . . once married, she stopped working . . . Harrington was found shot in the shoulder and hip from behind with her own gun . . . Harrington refused to comment . . . now on the run . . ." There was a picture of Parker standing at a podium at a press conference for a case. She wore a black suit with a teal tie and crisp white shirt. Her left hand was adjusting the knot in her tie as she looked out at the reporters huddling in front of her. It was an amazing picture. Parker in her natural element. It was no secret that Parker was preparing to run for a judgeship next year. Parker was ambitious. From the day she was born, she was refined and poised and crisp. She looked every bit the part of a future justice in that picture. And next to the picture of her and Xander at the festival, her image in this picture said she didn't belong with someone like Parker. *This* is why she never came clean about her past to Parker.

This article painted her as a gold-digging opportunist with a penchant for murdering her lovers. A black widow. Yes. She did kill Jodie. And she regretted it. Kind of. She wanted to live, so it was a necessity. That part, she didn't regret. She regretted that to live, she had to take a life. But once she made it to a position where she was able to live on her own, make her own meals, and not be at the mercy of handouts and strangers, she didn't even eat meat. Cruelty was not in her nature.

She couldn't bear to read the remaining articles. They would all be the same. Portraying her to be a monster. She was the one with the sketchy past. The nefarious and wicked villain. That was part of what she loved most about Parker—from the very beginning she saw past Calypso's outer veneer. She saw Calypso for her heart and her mind. She should have been able to recognize that. Parker was not one to settle for less than what she wanted or deserved. Parker *chose* her.

She swiped her tears away. Fuck Macy Quinn for ruining everything. Not once. But twice now. It was past her time to rot in hell. Or prison. Whichever would be more expedient.

Calypso picked up her phone and texted Xochitl: "Hey. Can we talk?"

Xochitl called her immediately. "Are you okay? Are you safe? Where are you?"

"I'm home with Parker. Well, not *with* her at the moment. She's at the office. But yeah. I'm safe."

Xochitl let out a shaky breath. "What's next? Is Parker going to clear you?"

"She can't. I'll explain all of the details another time. But it's complicated."

"Do you need anything? Are you good?"

"I just needed to hear the voice of someone who cares." Calypso's throat went tight.

"Of course. If you need anything at all, call me or Xander."

"Is he at the shop?"

"Yeah. He would love for you to check in. He's been worried since he dropped you off."

"I'm good. Parker and I are good. Well, will be once this is all settled."

"Give him a call when you can."

"Thank you for everything, Xochitl." Calypso ended the call.

She got up and walked to the window facing the street. The driveway was long and gated; the gate code had been changed, probably to keep her out. She easily guessed the code. It was so obvious that Parker probably assumed

Calypso *wouldn't* have guessed it. The day they met (not that Calypso didn't have to try a few others first). From inside the house, there was still a good view out over and past the gate since the house was elevated from the base of the long drive. However, those on the street would have a hard time seeing inside.

As she peeked out from behind the blinds, she locked in on a figure across the street, standing there, staring at the house. She grabbed her phone, opened the camera, and zoomed in. Macy stood there, staring at the house. It was quarter to two. Parker would be on her way home soon. But no one would know that. Anyone else would think Parker was chained to her desk at least until seven. Calypso's nerves went raw, and her heart beat hard and fast. She ran up the stairs, opened Parker's bedside table, and searched for the gun. It was gone. Of course it was. Whoever shot Parker (Macy) would have known that it was there and used it. The better to set Calypso up with.

She glanced out the window again. Macy still stood there. Psycho fucking bitch that she was.

Calypso stepped further back from the window. It was a good guess that Macy couldn't see her. But it still scared her. As far as Macy knew, Calypso had been dead for weeks.

Calypso sent the picture to Parker with no explanation.

Parker texted back: "on my way home. If she's still there in five minutes, call the cops."

48 THE WATCHER

PARKER

*P*arker was still ten minutes out when she saw the picture of Macy standing in front of her house. Part of her wished Macy would stay there and be caught off guard by Parker coming home early. The other part of her feared it. She had very little patience for Macy's bullshit, and she couldn't be sure that she wouldn't land herself in prison for life if she ran into her in front of her house.

Also, Macy would know something was up if Parker came home that early.

Parker had changed the gate code and locks again after she came back from Washington, after figuring out what Macy truly was, after she thought she killed Calypso. She also stopped keeping a somewhat accessible spare key in a fake garden rock. No one but her housekeeper, her dad, and Lloyd were given the gate code now or knew where she kept the spare key. Well, and apparently Calypso guessed it, or she wouldn't have been at the door. But of course she would guess it. Parker only kept a few select number combinations close to her—the day she met Calypso being one of them. And only the two of them would even know that exact date.

When she pulled down the street, she didn't see Macy. She didn't see cops either. Macy must have left on her own accord. She released her tightly coiled tension with a slow exhalation.

She checked the gate for any signs of tampering before entering the code to drive through. She had put drought-proof landscaping in after she and Calypso returned from their honeymoon. If Macy scaled the gate, there would be nowhere for her to hide. That didn't mean Macy wasn't in the house, finishing the job she had started in Gig Harbor.

Parker pulled into the garage and hurried inside. She called for Calypso as she made her way into the office. Hearing Calypso's footsteps come down the stairs gave Parker a welcome relief for so many reasons.

When she sat down at the desk, she noticed the article about the shooting on the screen. Seeing that article made her physically ill. Seeing Macy quoted and lauded as the hero detective, when in fact she was probably the one who shot her, filled her with a whole new sense of rage. It made sense, anyway. With a solid reputation of being a fantastic shot, Macy would know where to aim to stage a botched assassination attempt, without hitting anything lethal. Parker sat down heavily in the chair and exited the article.

Calypso appeared in the doorway wearing black linen cargo pants and a tank top, with no makeup, her hair held back by a scarf, backlit by the sun streaming in through the large living room windows, giving her a dreamlike quality, adding to the surreality of the last two days. "Hey," she purred, a small smile on her face. Parker was breathless, still disbelieving. The last few weeks would have broken a lesser woman. Yet here they both were, stronger because of it.

"Come here." Parker pulled Calypso in once she came within reach, grateful even to have Calypso back in the house.

Calypso nuzzled Parker's neck. Parker took it all in, wrapped in the warmth of Calypso's body against hers, and inhaled Calypso's perfume. Not the trace remnants. Fresh and mixed with the scent of her skin. It was real. She was back. And Parker committed herself to making it all right. Macy Quinn would go down for what she did.

"I hate this," Calypso whispered. Parker had suspected this would be difficult for Calypso. She wasn't the caged-bird type.

"It's going to be over soon. I promise." Parker whispered, kissing the crook of Calypso's neck before tilting her head back up to kiss her lips.

"I hate her, Parker. I fucking hate her. I don't like hating anyone. But I fucking hate her."

"I know. I do, too." Parker scooted Calypso off her lap and opened an app on her desktop screen.

"What's that?" Calypso asked, standing behind Parker's chair, letting her fingers roam through Parker's hair at the nape of her neck. The subtlety of her fingers in the closely shorn hair nearly made Parker short circuit and forget what she was doing, leaning back into the touch.

"Security cameras. I updated the whole system after the shooting incident." Parker clicked back to the time when Calypso sent her the picture, and the screen displayed a clear shot of Macy standing in front of the gate. She went back a few minutes earlier. She observed Macy on the recording as she pulled up. Macy attempted the gate code. When she couldn't access the gate, she stood there, watching the house.

"What's wrong with her?" Calypso said with a quiet, barely audible voice

"She's crazy." Parker mumbled as she pushed the chair back and stood.

"So, what's the plan?" Calypso asked as Parker left the office.

Calypso followed her up the steps. "I'm meeting her tonight at seven-thirty." Parker undid her tie as she entered the bedroom.

"I don't know that I'm exactly on board with that." Calypso sat cross-legged on the end of the bed, and Kitty jumped into her lap and rubbed her face against Calypso. She fidgeted with her wedding band and engagement ring, back, to Parker's joy, in their rightful spot—her finger.

Parker hung her tie on the rack and removed her jacket and vest. "Lloyd will be close by, just in case."

"How is he supposed to help? What if she goes full postal and whips out a gun or stabs you across the table with a knife?"

Parker laughed. "She's crazy, but I don't think she's that crazy."

"She killed Shae. She shot you. Or at least it can be deduced that she did. She tried to kill me. God only knows how many other bodies she's buried along the way."

"Babe, no. She won't do anything like that. Not in public."

"Hm. Okay." Calypso crossed her arms.

"You have to have some faith in me."

"I'm trying. So you're going to meet with her, then what? What's your plan?"

"I'm going to tell her I love her and I miss her—"

"Don't you think that's just going to fuel her obsession more?"

"No. Listen. So I'm going to tell her what she wants to

hear, and I'm going to coax the events out of her. All the while, I'm going to be recording her."

"How? She will know if it's your phone."

"The PI at the firm gave this to Juliana to record Macy previously." Parker pulled a pen out of her inside jacket pocket as she placed it on a hanger. She always kept her Montblanc pen there. This was a silver pen. It passed closely enough as something she would use, though.

"A pen?"

"It's got a recording device inside it."

"How do you know she's going to fall for it and talk?"

"It's not guaranteed. But I'm going to try. I'm willing to try anything right now. And that's what seems to be the most direct route."

"And what's plan B?" Calypso asked.

"I don't have one yet. But I'm all ears if you have any other ideas."

Calypso narrowed her eyes and bit her lip.

"I didn't think so," Parker said. "But, do you have any idea what I'm supposed to be doing between now and seven thirty?"

Calypso gave a little laugh. "I'm sure I can think of a few things to keep you occupied."

49 SEEING RIGHT THROUGH

OCTOBER 17

MACY

Macy arrived at Mantra at five after seven. She sat in her car and surveyed the parking lot. Sitting in utter silence in her car she wondered if Parker would even show up, or if she would be stuck waiting there all night.

She needed Parker to see her actions were for good. Calypso was a taker. Calypso took everything. Calypso took all that mattered from her. Again. Calypso was a greedy, evil succubus. She wasn't even human. Macy saved not only Parker, but the world. And when the world won't save you, you have to act. She merely acted in the best interest, not only of herself, but of Parker and everyone else.

Parker's car pulled into the lot ten minutes later. She couldn't help the physical reactions that overcame her when she saw Parker or sensed that Parker was close. It was Pavlovian.

Her breath hitched, and she was shaky as she tried to breathe in and exhale. Her jeans constricted her. Her sweater itched. She spent the last several weeks in pajamas and a bathrobe. And if she did leave the house, she wore ratty old sweats. She slid the sweater off and decided to go with only her T-shirt instead.

Nauseated and unable to stop the trembling, she checked her reflection in the visor mirror. She looked like Macy, but she felt like someone else—a stranger, an alien, or a skinwalker. She needed a drink. She needed to know that Parker was not playing with her emotions.

She got out of her car as soon as she observed Parker entering the restaurant. Something was different about her. Jeans, boots, and a black mock-neck cashmere sweater. She didn't want to appear too eager and be in the restaurant first. Parker wouldn't approve. It would make Macy look desperate. So, she waited outside for a few more minutes.

As Macy pulled the heavy door open, she spotted Parker seated in a dark booth in the corner. It's never busy at Mantra on a weeknight; most of their business on weekdays was their buffet lunch and take-out orders. There was only one other table seated, and it was a group of three elderly Indian ladies.

Parker noticed Macy and smiled. Macy's heart beat hard. She couldn't read the smile. Was it friendly or predatory? One could never tell with Parker. In Macy's experience, attorneys excelled at theatrics. She often wondered if law students were mandated to take drama courses.

Parker's attaché case sat next to her in the booth and a legal pad on the table. Typical Parker. Working. Always working. Parker set the pen on the paper and moved them off to the side once Macy made her way to the table.

What wasn't typical for Parker was wearing street clothes instead of her suit. If she stopped here on the way home from work, she would be in one of her suits. Something was off. However, perhaps Parker didn't have any client meetings or court appearances today. Maybe, just maybe, Parker was trying something new. But Parker rarely stepped outside her comfort zone.

Macy's eyes narrowed as she took in Parker's appearance. Yeah. Definitely not normal. She carried a sleepy calm about her. She appeared peaceful. She looked . . . happy?

Parker stood and went to hug Macy. Macy fought a total and complete war with herself. Her body totally betrayed her brain and she melted and warmed into the hug. Her brain was screaming to her that this was a trap. She hoped her brain was wrong.

"God, I've missed you," Parker murmured, holding her tight.

She wanted to believe it. She didn't. "Me too." Her throat tightened. This was a total setup. Every instinct in her brain told her so. After the way Parker left things, there was no way she would do such a big one-eighty.

Parker released her and sat back down.

"So, what's the nature of this visit?" Macy tried to be hard, but her heart was breaking. It physically pained her to look at Parker across the table, so she hid behind her menu instead.

"What do you mean?"

God, she's good. She sounded sincere. Maybe, just maybe, she was . . . a glimmer of hope burned deep inside of her. "You don't talk to me for weeks. You tell me to never speak to you again. Now—all of a sudden—you miss me?" Her voice trembled despite her attempt to stay calm.

"Macy, those five days in Washington with you were some of the best days of my life. And then . . . I mean . . . I got scared." Parker chewed her lower lip and inspected her hands. Out of habit, Parker played with her ring finger where her wedding band used to sit. And the Oscar goes to Parker Harrington. But maybe it was true . . . those last few embers of hope searched to catch flame somewhere.

"Scared?" Macy asked dryly, still looking at her menu. She was doing all she could not to climb over the table and wrap herself around Parker.

"But anyway, how are you? How have you been?"

"You know, same old, same old."

"How's work?" Parker tried desperately hard to make small talk.

"You didn't hear?" Macy's forehead crinkled and her brow crept up as the waiter appeared and stood expectantly over them.

"May I get you something to drink?" He asked.

"Vodka and cranberry, please." Macy was trying to read the situation. She was good at manipulating situations, but Parker did it even better. Parker made a living from it. To keep from falling into a trap, Macy kept her head bowed at the table. Parker's phone sat face up on the table, its screen dark. Macy set her menu down in a way that made the phone move, causing the screen to flash on. Her eyes darted to the screen discreetly—and saw no indication the phone was recording.

"Hear what?" Parker asked. As if she didn't know. Continuing to assess the table, the pen resting on the yellow legal pad didn't look like the pen she had watched Parker use a million times before. A heavy and pricy pen from some hoity-toity brand. This one was silver, and although it was probably a nice enough pen, it was far from normal. None of this was normal. As a matter of fact, that silver pen looked like Juliana's pen. That glimmer and those embers of hope began dying out.

"I got fired. After our little trip. They let me go." Pushing her menu to the side, she was desperately working overtime to stay unemotional even though her entire world was imploding around her.

Parker reached for Macy's hand. "I'm so sorry."

"I lost you. I lost my job. I lost everything." Macy let Parker take her hand. But it still didn't feel right. Parker's touch broke down the wall.

"I haven't been the same either. I think what we went through up there—it changed me. Watching what you did for me—once I processed it, I knew—no one will ever love me like you do." Parker never used that sort of purple prose, even during those five perfect days. This over-the-top performance didn't match Parker's character. Anyone who didn't know Parker as well as she did would have believed it. But Macy had studied and committed to memory every one of Parker's mannerisms, tones, and looks. She memorized them long ago. She would bet she had them down even better than Calypso ever did.

Macy pulled her hand back. This was a trap. She should have known. "I don't know what you're talking about."

Parker cocked her head to the side. "You don't remember stabbing Calypso?" The mask began sliding off. *This* is what it was all about. Calypso. She should have known.

Definitely a trap. "I never did such a thing. It was *you* who stabbed her."

Parker sat back with her arms folded over her chest. "Don't try to gaslight me."

"Who's gaslighting who?" The waiter delivered Macy's drink. Macy downed half the drink at once. It was weak compared to what she made at home. The burn of the vodka as it went down was barely noticeable.

"I don't know what kind of game you're trying to play,

Macy, but I'm here trying to bring us back together, and you're accusing me of killing Calypso?"

God damn. Give it a rest. She absolutely thinks no one knows what's going on here. That pen is recording this conversation. "You did, though, didn't you? You said it would save you millions of dollars to kill her, versus divorce her. Money and sex. The two main reasons for murder. You killed her because you didn't want to write the check."

"Considering she wasn't who she said she was, according to the file you gave me, I didn't have to divorce her. The marriage would have been null and void." Parker's voice grew cold. Ice cold. Here's the real Parker.

"You know, I don't think this was such a good idea." Downing the rest of her drink in one toss, she threw a $20 bill on the table and got out of the booth. "I was a fool to think you cared. I know what it is you are trying to do. You are trying to pin Calypso on me. It's not me. It wasn't me. You won't be able to pin that on me. Her blood is on *your* hands. You're the one with the motive, opportunity, and it was your plan to go up there and meet with her." Macy turned to walk out but stopped and turned to face Parker again. "You broke my fucking heart. I loved you. I would have done anything for you. But you—you used me and tossed me aside. You told me not to call you. You blocked me from you. You call me out of nowhere and bring me here, trying to play me like I'm stupid. I would have done anything —*anything*—for you. But I will not take the blame for Calypso. *That* was your mess. You need to fix it without me." Macy turned around before Parker could respond, and stormed out of the restaurant. The three elderly Indian ladies had grown quiet as they witnessed the drama unfolding. Macy shot them a look as she walked past their table.

When she got back in her car, she stared at the door, wondering if Parker would come rushing out after her. She somewhat hoped Parker would. But nothing. A keening howl came from the depths of her chest. All of her pain and frustration and sorrow ripped from her chest as she slammed her palm against the steering wheel. The impact should have brought her something, but it didn't. Fuck Parker Harrington.

50 FAILURE IS NOT AN OPTION

PARKER

$\mathcal{M}$acy walked out, leaving Parker with her jaw on the floor. This did not go at all as she thought it would. In the past, Macy would give up anything for her. She would take advantage of it from time to time, which she knew damn well was dick-ish. But still, sometimes you have to do what you have to do.

When the waiter came back, she placed her order: a double order of saag paneer, plain naan, and a mango lassi to go. While she waited, she texted Calypso: "It was a bust."

She responded almost immediately: "I knew it would be." Yep. She called it. But it was worth a try.

"I had to give it a try."

"Are you bringing take-out home?"

"Of course."

Parker's heart warmed at how easily they fell back into

their patterns. But with more openness and honesty, less brushing over of the past, and no more secrets. To think she almost gave this up. She realized she had been a fool for being so easily duped by Macy.

She texted Lloyd to come inside. Unlike her, he *was* coming directly from work, but he shed his coat and tie in the car.

When he noticed the empty booth, she read his face; he put it together immediately. "It didn't work, did it?"

"No. I had big hopes." Parker fidgeted with the pen.

"What do you think kept her from falling for it?" Lloyd pushed Macy's menu to the side.

"I don't know. I could feel her energy was different from the moment she walked in. She's grown—I don't know—I guess the best word is hard. Bitter even, maybe.

"We can think of something else tomorrow. I have to go. Juliana is waiting for me to call," he said with a sly grin.

"*My* Juliana?" Parker raised her eyebrow.

"Hopefully, soon to be *my* Juliana." Lloyd exited the booth.

"You better not fuck it up and change the office dynamic. Or worse. Fuck it up, and she quits. She's the best assistant I've ever had," Parker said, halfway serious, halfway joking. Juliana clued her in that she had the hots for Lloyd. Who was she to keep them from being together? Maybe it would work out and everything would be fine. But if not, hopefully the fallout would stay out of the office.

He laughed and walked out as the waiter brought her bag of takeout.

* * *

CALYPSO OPENED the door for her as she came in from the garage with the carry-out. Grazing a light kiss over Calypso's lips, Parker set the bag down. "Did the recording work?" Calypso asked as she pulled plates down from the cupboard.

She hooked the pen up to the the speaker while Calypso served the food onto plates. Standing side by side at the kitchen island, they ate as the recording played.

Parker watched as Calypso's face reddened with anger as she took in the exchange. "A master manipulator knows when they are being manipulated." She dragged a piece of naan through her dish to soak up the remnants of the saag paneer. A lock of her cropped hair fell over her left eye. Parker reached over and brushed it aside. She couldn't keep Calypso hostage in the house. A plan needed to be made. Something needed to give.

Parker paused and gripped the island. "If it comes down to it, I think I'm going to have to make a plea deal. The more I think about this, the more I can't just let her get away with it. Seeing her on the cameras earlier . . . we won't ever be safe with her rolling around out there. And it's not fair to keep you caged up in here for the rest of your life."

Calypso's eyes glazed with tears as she whispered, "No."

"What do you mean, 'no'?" Parker couldn't help being exasperated. She was tired of everyone naysaying her ideas without having anything better to bring to the table.

"No one will understand . . . and ultimately it will be her word against yours . . . and if they don't believe you . . . because she's a cop—or used to be a cop—she will know exactly how to present her side to make it look like it was all you. And I won't see you go down over that. You didn't do anything. I heard it all."

"You did. You were a witness."

"She will find a way to twist it. No."

"Calypso, what are we going to do? Have you stay hidden in the house for the rest of your life? This has to end some-where. Somehow."

"I have no intention of staying locked in the house for the rest of my life. Give me some time. I will figure something out. This *will* end." Calypso put her dish in the sink and rinsed it.

Her head dropped. She wasn't used to not winning. If she worked on a case that was hopeless, she prided herself on getting them the best possible plea deal. She could count on both of her hands how many times she had lost in a trial.

Parker always got what she wanted her whole life. But she was not prepared to deal with this. And she hated that she was letting Calypso down. She ran her hand through her hair. "I'm so sorry, babe. I really am."

"You're not the crazy bitch who kills people for fun."

"No. But I was friends with her. I slept with her. I never saw it. I should have gotten the message when you asked that she not come around . . . but I was so stupid."

Calypso wrapped her arms around Parker. "Blinded, maybe. But stupid never." Calypso kissed the crook of Parker's neck. "We will end this. That bitch will burn."

51 PLAN A / PLAN B

Calypso

Three days later, Calypso woke up after Parker left for work. She'd spent most of the night wide awake, staring at the ceiling. Her mind reeling, she climbed out of bed in the middle of the night, went downstairs for a glass of water, and stood at the window in the darkened house. Macy stood there again, in front of the gate. Staring. Seeing that made Calypso's skin crawl, which in turn made it harder for her to fall asleep. She considered waking Parker, but thought better of it and let her sleep. She should have been scared that someone so unstable was standing in front of her home in the middle of the night, pining for her wife. But Calypso planned on getting the last laugh. Macy had no idea she was in the house, alive, and with Parker. She crawled back in bed and curled up beside Parker, and the plan hit her. She smiled in the darkness. *This* would work.

In the morning, after Parker left for work, she made her way down the stairs with Kitty at her heels. She knew what she wanted to do. And she believed it would work. If not, she had a plan B worked out in her head. She thought through each of the steps in her head as she drank her coffee.

As she showered, she worked up the courage to go through with this. It was a huge risk. And if Parker had any idea what she was planning, she would throw a fit.

She dried off, got dressed, and, for the first time since she had been home, applied her makeup. Mostly, the makeup was an effort to stall enacting plan A.

When she couldn't delay it any longer, she called Xander and asked him to meet her at her house.

The good big brother he had become to her, he showed up with zero hesitation. "What are we doing?" He asked as she pulled him inside. He absolutely fit the part she needed him for. Dark black cargo pants, boots, and a tight black T-shirt. With his tatted bald head and sleeved muscular arms, no one would fuck with him. And no one would fuck with her as long as he stood by her side.

"You're going to come with me and be my bodyguard. My backup. My witness." Calypso informed him.

He laughed. "What? I don't think I heard you correctly. Bodyguard? Witness? What absolute fuckery are you planning?"

"I'm serious. I don't want to ask Parker. If I even told Parker I planned to do this, she would be pissed."

"Then maybe you shouldn't be doing whatever it is we are about to do?" Xander crossed his arms over his broad chest.

"It's exactly why we need to be doing this." Calypso grabbed the keys to Parker's Defender. Parker took the classic Jag to work most of the time. Parker was extremely uptight about her cars. She knew every scratch (or lack thereof). Every mile. Every setting. Calypso didn't even like moving one of Parker's cars much less driving them. She missed her car. She should never have left it with the keys inside. Now it sat in some evidence yard somewhere waiting while she was wanted for a crime she didn't even commit.

"With her car collection, you would think she would hang a British flag in her garage," Xander commented as he took inventory of the Defender and the Aston Martin. He was well aware that her daily driver was a Jag—he had drooled over it enough times.

"I think she did her DNA, and it came back like 90 percent British Isles. I think her cars are some reflection of heritage pride or something." Calypso unlocked the large black SUV.

Xander climbed into the passenger seat as Calypso got into the driver's seat. "Are you going to tell me what it is we are going to do yet?" Xander asked as she adjusted the driver's seat and mirrors. She said a silent prayer that no damage would be done to the car as she backed out of the garage, and that she would return the vehicle exactly as it left the garage.

On the way to their destination, Calypso updated Xander on the situation at hand. It took the entire drive to explain it all, from her history in New Orleans to Macy following her to California, all the way to what happened in Washington.

Xander stared at her when they parked in front of a row of condos. "Calypso, I think you need to go back home. What if someone spots you? What if—"

"I will not be a prisoner in my own home. I won't. I'm going to put an end to this once and for all. I'm not the crazy bitch who killed Shae. I'm not the crazy bitch who shot Parker to frame me. *She's* the crazy bitch. And she thinks she killed me because she stabbed me. I'm not the one who should spend her days locked up. She is."

She got out of the truck and slammed the door. Xander

followed behind her. "So now what are we doing exactly? What are my duties as bodyguard, witness, or whatever?"

"You are just going to stand by and be ready to intervene or call the cops or be my witness if necessary." Xander grabbed her elbow and stopped her.

"What does that mean, Calypso? Witness if necessary?"

"If I have to kill this bitch in self-defense." Calypso knocked on the door.

They stood there as if they had been waiting forever. "Maybe we need to go back home," Xander murmured.

Calypso knocked again when the door opened mid knock.

The sight on the other side of the door was not what she expected. Macy was wasted. Her disheveled and greasy hair, and old eye makeup crusted below her blue eyes, took Calypso by surprise. She wore sweatpants, a tattered shirt, and no bra. When it obviously registered who stood outside her door, Macy went extra pale. "How?" she whispered.

"Let me in," Calypso demanded.

"But you're—"

"Let me the fuck inside right now, Macy Quinn."

"Are you real?" She asked. "Am I letting in some sort of haint?" She began whispering a prayer and making the sign of the cross in front of Calypso's face.

Xander reached over Calypso's head and pushed the door in. Calypso moved past Macy and into the foyer that led to Macy's living room.

Calypso put her hand over her nose as the smell of despair and filth washed over her. She took in the disaster around her. Macy obviously hadn't cleaned in weeks. Empty vodka bottles were lined up along the coffee table. Various cups and glasses with pink sticky remnants littered the end tables. Macy herself smelled of body odor and vodka.

Macy turned around and stared at Calypso standing in

her living room. "Who is *that*?" Macy directed her attention towards Xander. Her words slurred slightly as Macy picked up a half-full glass of what Calypso deduced, from the empty Ocean Spray and Grey Goose bottles that littered the room, was some sort of vodka and cranberry juice mixture.

"Don't worry about that," Xander said, crossing his arms over his broad chest.

"I should call the . . ." Macy mumbled, fumbling for her phone in her pocket.

"You will do no such thing." Calypso snapped, knocking the cell phone out of Macy's other hand.

"You can't hurt me. You're a haint—just an evil spirit. I know because I stood over your dead body. I watched you bleed out on the floor." She pointed at Calypso with her drink sloshing over the rim and onto the dirty and dusty carpet. "But if you're a haint—what is he? Are you real?" She pointed at Xander, and her sticky fingers poked his arm.

He stared at her with hard eyes, lowered his face into hers, and said, "Boo!"

She backed away from him, making the sign of the cross in his direction, too, before turning back to face Calypso. "You're a haint," she said again, with tear-filled eyes.

"I didn't die, Macy. I wasn't dead. You silly bitch, you should have checked for a pulse." Calypso's voice came out hard and cold. "I am only here to tell you that you need to tell everyone that you faked that police record. That you tried to kill me, and *you* are the one who shot Parker. You need to face it. Shae was never yours, and neither was Parker. It's time to let it all go. Get help."

"Why would I do that?" Macy seemed to sober up. "What will you do if I don't?" She grinned, her dry lips cracking, causing a drop of blood to bubble up. Her tongue darted out so she could lick it like she enjoyed it.

"What will I do if you don't?" Calypso repeated the question before answering, "You don't want to know."

"Let's just say the solution would be permanent." Xander improvised as he cracked his knuckles. Calypso wanted to high-five him.

"I won't do it. I can't. It would ruin me. Forever ruin me. I will never—"

Calypso's following words came out in a frustrated yell. "You selfish cunt! *You* did this! This is *your* mess and now I'm here suffering for it!" She composed herself and lowered her voice back down to finish, "Again. I will no longer be a victim of your games and manipulations, Macy. You will figure this shit out. You will come clean with all of your lies. Get help. And then go the fuck to prison for a few years. Where you belong. Let me be. Let Parker be."

Macy's mouth turned to an ugly sneer. "Or what, *Ca-lyp-so?*" She laughed as she drew out her name into distinct syllables.

"I will *not* tell you. But once it happens, you will know it's because of *me.* But trust. I have plans. Watch me. I'm taking my power back. You cannot—you *will not*—mess with my life any longer."

Macy continued to laugh. "Get out of my house." Macy opened the door. "And be careful. I still have friends on the force. It only takes a phone call."

Calypso's heart hammered in her ears, her rage boiling over. "Suit yourself, Macy. Let's see who flinches first." Xander cracked his knuckles again and winked at Macy on the way out. He often played up the fact that he came across as intimidating, when in fact he didn't possess a single violent bone in his body.

Macy turned her steely gaze on him. "You both can leave." She opened the door and leaned against it. As Calypso walked past her she leaned in and whispered in Calypso's ear with her hot garbage and vodka breath, "Watch your back, *Calypso*. You never know if there will be another knife in it, or maybe some flashing blues in your mirror."

Calypso's blood went cold, and she tamped down the acid and bile that rose in her throat from the smell of Macy's unwashed body, her breath, and the stink of the room. "We'll see, Macy. We'll see." She forced herself to sound calm and collected.

She and Xander made their way down the walk and hopped back in the Defender.

"That was the most sad and disturbing thing I've ever seen. I've heard people claim to have reached rock bottom. Or say someone else had gotten there. But I've never seen it firsthand. That's the epitome of rock bottom." Xander buckled in. "What's plan B?"

Calypso shrugged. "I thought I knew. But now I don't know. I don't think I can . . . but I think I have to."

"What is it? What's your Plan B?"

Calypso shook her head. "I can't discuss it."

"Are you going to tell Parker?"

"About today or my plans?"

"Both."

"I have to tell her about today. I know Macy will run to her and say something. But she can never know my plan B."

Xander knew better than to ask any more questions. He recognized this fight was about survival and protection. "She's going to be *pissed*. You know, if you need a place to stay . . ."

Calypso rolled her eyes.

When they got back to the house, Parker was already home. "Fuck." Calypso whispered when she saw Parker's car parked in the garage. "I thought I would have more time to soften it."

"I'm gonna head out. Parker's an intimidating woman. I

don't want to see what she looks like angry. Good luck." Xander hopped out of the truck and bounded down the driveway to his car.

"Bye," Calypso said quietly as he waved.

Bracing herself for what was about to come down around her, Calypso walked into the house. Parker was leaning against the island. She hadn't even bothered to take off her tie or jacket.

"I'm not trying to be *that* wife. It's not my style. But for *fuck's sake*, Calypso, right now I have to be *that* wife. Where *the fuck* were you?" Parker's voice was exasperated.

Calypso hated to argue with Parker. Not because Parker was cruel or abusive, because she wasn't. But Xander nailed it—she was intimidating. She argued for a living, and her mind worked fast; she had the ability to argue every side of anything. And right now, Parker was angry even though she didn't show it. But that's because Parker's superpower was that she showed herself calm and measured on the surface. Showing anger and lashing out can lead to a loss of control. Calypso took a breath and braced herself on the opposite side of the island. She had to tell the truth. It was the right thing to do.

"*Calypso,* you need to answer me. Where. Were. You?" The exasperation had turned to a hardened tone.

"Macy's." Her voice sounded thin and weak. It was as if she were back to that day when she was a small child getting scolded by her mom for stealing that pack of Sour Patch Kids from the corner store.

"What the *absolute fuck*? Why?" Parker worked hard to keep her shit together, but Calypso felt the rage boiling under Parker's surface.

"I needed her to see I'm not scared of her and I'm not dead. And to try to persuade her to come clean."

"And exactly what did this accomplish?"

"Nothing."

"And now, you know what? She is fucking crazy. She may come to finish the job. Or—"

"Send her cop friends after me," Calypso whispered.

"That, too. Calypso . . ." Parker sounded defeated, moving to her elbows and putting her head in her hands. "I'm in the middle of a big case. I can't be here twenty-four seven with you. I don't know how to move forward right now."

"I know I fucked up. I know. But I had to try, Parker." She came around the island and put her hand on Parker's back. "I'm in this, too. And Macy was my problem long before she was *our* problem. It's not up to you to protect me. It's not up to you to be the only one to fix this. I'm in this, too, remember?"

Parker sighed. "It's just that I feel responsible for this. You asked me to keep her out of our lives. I let her back in, and now we're here."

Calypso put her arms around Parker. "I will burn it all down if it means she's out of our lives forever." Calypso never felt so sure of anything as that.

52 SOBER FACTS

MACY

*A*fter waking up hung over, Macy cleaned her whole house and poured out all of the remaining vodka. It was beyond time she opened the windows to air out the space. She looked around at the nest of filth that surrounded her and decided to vacuum, dust, wipe down the sticky surfaces, and clean the carpets. Once the house around her was finally clean, she showered, threw her linens and sweats into the washer, and ordered salad ingredients from Instacart. As she ran through all of these chores, she replayed the entire encounter with Calypso incessantly.

She had no choice but to get a hold of herself. Part of her decision to clean and clear all the clutter and sober up was that she couldn't be sure she had actually had a conversation with Calypso in her home. She wanted to make sure she wasn't hallucinating the entire encounter. She was fairly certain she had killed Calypso. But she was here with some big dude. She recognized him from the engagement party and the wedding. He gave Calypso away at the wedding, if she recalled. Yes. That's it. That's why he was familiar.

With her home clean, her mind sober, and her belly fed, she deemed herself clear enough to think.

She thought about calling her friends at the precinct to go haul that indignant bitch in. The look in Calypso's eyes when she threatened to call them was unmistakable. The hint of fear. She witnessed the shift within Calypso.

But there was risk involved in that. Parker would be interviewed. It would be the two of them against her. She was already disgraced.

She had done so much over the last seven years. Fake accounts to threaten Calypso into leaving Parker. When that didn't work, she started sending packages to Parker. That didn't work.

She also created the counterfeit file. That worked, in large part because she'd planted the seeds of doubt with everything she had done leading up to it. But once they called New Orleans PD, they would find out that Macy had made a fake file to frame the wife of the love of her life in an effort to get rid of her. How embarrassing. The things we do, the lows we sink to for love. This wasn't the lowest Macy had ever sunk. The lowest was killing Shae in a jealous rage. The lowest was killing (or almost killing) Calypso. The lowest was shooting Parker to frame Calypso.

And you know what? Macy was kind of proud of that last one. She knew she wouldn't fatally wound Parker. She was a damn good shot. And it all played out so perfectly, considering it was a spur-of-the-moment decision. Originally, she figured she would surprise Parker and take her for dinner. She didn't anticipate beating Parker to the house or Calypso's car sitting there in the drive. With the keys in it. Who does that? Parker had once told her where she kept the house key and where she kept her gun. Macy had a slew of CIs who would do anything for her to stay out of prison. She could easily have a CI move the car and stash the gun. So she did it. She was proud of having put it all together in a few short minutes. And it worked. Until it didn't.

But now she was out of options. Out of a job. Out of friends. Everything was out of her control. She had nothing. She was nothing. It was painfully clear.

She would never be anyone's choice. Not her father's. Her mother chose drugs over her. Her grandparents didn't give two shits about her. Shae chose Calypso. Parker chose Calypso. She would never, ever be good enough to be loved.

Her only option was to get the fuck out of here. For good. And she couldn't plan her exit drunk. She couldn't afford to screw this up. She'd screwed up enough along the way. She'd fucked up too many lives, including her own. And there was no hope of ever reconciling with Parker at this point. It was never going to happen, and it was time to give up on that ever being a thing. That hurt deeper than the loneliness. And without the vodka to dull the pain, it seared through her, burning hot.

Her entire life became one big fuck-up. She used to have so much promise. At one time, she believed in the possibility of making something of herself. She used to be an excellent cop and detective. And with the right person, she could have been a great partner. Loyal to a fault. Maybe that's what went wrong . . . to the fault. Her fault. Everything became her fault. She didn't merely cut ties; she burned the bridges. Scorched earth. Everything had gone up in flames around her. Tremendous, spectacular flames.

She would kick her plan into gear the next day. She couldn't bear to do any more today. She forced herself to finish her salad. She made sure to clean her dishes, put them in the dishwasher, and clean the remnants out of the sink. She wiped the counters down and ran the dishwasher. Her home was spotless. Erasing the evidence that the last several weeks ever happened.

Everything was clear. So clear. She'd burned everything down and all she had left was ash. Parker was lost to her forever. No one was ever going to choose her. No one could ever see that she did it all for the right reasons. Love. But it failed. Like everything else in her life. She was left with nothing. No one. It was time to exit stage left.

She brushed her teeth, washed her face, and put her dirty clothes in the hamper. She popped an Ambien, climbed into her freshly cleaned bed, and went to sleep. Before she fell asleep, she considered taking the whole bottle of Ambien and never waking up ever again. She put the bottle back on her nightstand and went to bed. For now, she only wanted that deep, deep, dreamless sleep.

53 THIS IS FINAL

OCTOBER 22

PARKER

*P*arker called her dad and Lloyd, stating she would be working from home for the time being. She didn't want to explain to them what Calypso had done. She didn't want to give them any more cause to worry. Though Lloyd asked a lot of questions, because he always did.

The next day, Lloyd and Juliana brought her boxes of files and notes for the cases she was working on. Whatever meetings she couldn't do via Zoom, Lloyd would be taking point on. They arrived together in Lloyd's Tahoe.

She caught the two of them making sweet eyes at each other as they unloaded and brought in large banker's boxes full of her files. "Gross, you two," Parker teased, trying to lighten the mood.

Juliana smiled and shrugged, blushing a little.

"Just no PDA in the office, okay?" Parker pushed a stray hair out of her eyes.

"Of course not." Juliana and Lloyd answered simultaneously.

"I'll never get used to not seeing you in a suit," Juliana commented. "It's kind of strange." Parker was wearing jeans, barefoot, and had on a plain white T-shirt. Her hair wasn't styled back in her signature pomp.

Calypso came down and helped bring in the boxes. "I kind of like Casual Parker." She hefted a box out of the way and hugged Lloyd and Juliana, respectively.

"I just assumed she wore three-piece suits at all times. Like she even slept in them," Juliana laughed.

Parker rolled her eyes.

"You should see her closet. I've never seen so many suits. And they are all hung a certain way. I'm afraid to even touch them." Calypso moved to stand at Parker's side, leaning into her playfully.

"Cute, you two," Parker teased, crossing her arms, trying to look peeved.

"But honestly, it's really good to see you, Calypso." Lloyd offered.

"I'm just happy to be home," Calypso said as Parker put an arm over her shoulder and drew her in. Juliana smiled before glancing at Lloyd.

"What's the plan?" Lloyd asked. "I'm assuming this has something to do with Macy."

Of course, he was too smart to let it go. "Calypso, do you want to explain what happened?" Parker figured she was the one who did it; she should be the one to explain it.

Calypso's cheeks flushed. "Not really."

Parker sighed. "Calypso and Xander went to Macy's the day before yesterday to confront her."

"Calypso, you didn't." Lloyd shook his head. "How? Why?"

Calypso crossed her arms over her chest, defensive. "With Parker not being able to obtain a confession out of her, I was just desperate. I assumed if I showed up out of the blue, with Xander, she would kind of freak out and then maybe do the right thing and disappear."

"Did it work?" Juliana asked.

"No. She accused me of being a haint. She was trashed. She smelled like shit. And she was just angry and bitter."

"A what?" Juliana asked. "What's a haint?"

"It's a southern thing." Lloyd offered. "It's an evil spirit. A deceptive one."

Calypso grinned at him. "How did you know that? You're a California boy."

"I was born here. But my mom's mom came here from Gulfport, Mississippi. My gran, she still paints her porch roof blue to keep the haints out, even though she's lived here for decades. Old traditions die hard."

Parker tilted her head. "What else did she do?" she prompted Calypso.

"She threatened me. It was vague. She was either gonna finish the job or call the cops."

"Which is why you are staying close." Juliana nodded toward Parker.

Parker nodded. "I'm not going to let her ruin Calypso over her jealousy or insanity or whatever the fuck it is."

* * *

OCTOBER 30

Parker kind of enjoyed working from home. With Calypso around, it was much easier. Calypso ordered a bunch of canvas and paint. She set up in the downstairs guest room, next door to Parker's office, converting it into a makeshift studio. She would often come in, sit in Parker's office, and read when she wasn't painting, cleaning, or cooking. It was the quietness and the simple peace of having her close.

One of Parker's favorite things about working from home was when Calypso would make them lunch and bring it into her office. She would pause her work and eat at her desk with Calypso sitting across from her. And to think she almost gave all of this up. Lost it for good.

When Calypso worked on a painting in the room next to her office, Parker would listen to Calypso singing along quietly as her music played while she worked. Parker would peek in and see Calypso with her hair pulled back in a scarf, intent on the canvas.

When Parker asked what she was painting, Calypso told her a scene of St. Louis Cathedral in the fog as Parker came to stand behind her to better see the canvas.

"That's in New Orleans, right?"

"For as much trauma as I lived through there, I still get homesick." Calypso set her brush down as Parker examined what had been completed on the painting. The stark white triple steeples poking out over the fog, the slick cobblestones wet with rain in the foreground, muted greens and pinks, and reds for the landscaping peeking through the mist. Looking at the painting, Parker was transported onto the rain-slick cobblestones.

"This is beautiful," Parker murmured. "We should find somewhere to hang it when it's done."

"I want to take you there. I want to show you the city that made me." Calypso set the brush down. "When this is all done, I want to go with you. I want to show you the French Quarter, and the cemeteries, and eat beignets and do all of the stupid tourist stuff we don't do when we live there. Preservation Hall. The food. The music. The shit we take for granted when you live there. I haven't been back since I moved here. And I want to experience it with you."

"We will. We will plan it. I promise."

Parker found herself more in love with Calypso than ever. They sorted through the issues that drove them apart. The downside to that was that Parker was more afraid than she'd ever been. Macy was a loose string, a dangerous one at that. Every noise made her jumpy. Every car that drove by made her hold her breath.

She pulled the camera footage one night to find Macy standing outside the gate. She chose not to tell Calypso. But she found it harder to sleep at night.

After eight days of working at home, and not leaving the house, of Instacart and DoorDashing, Parker received a phone call from A.D.

"Hey stranger, what's up?" Parker hadn't had any contact from A.D. since she moved to New York.

"I'm at the airport. I'm on my way back to California." She didn't sound excited or happy.

"Why? Not that I don't want to see you."

"Macy . . ." A.D. paused and took a breath that hitched.

"No offense, I know you were married to her for a minute . . . but fuck that bitch."

OCTOBER 30

CALYPSO

Calypso cocked her head quizzically at Parker as her burner phone, stashed in the closet of her makeshift studio, made its text alert. Slipping out of Parker's office into the next room, she opened the closet and pulled the phone out. A single text from Javier awaited her: "I assume ur off house arrest?"

Calypso responded: "What do you mean?"

"Meet me in 1hr @ ur shop. Alone"

She worried her lip. How was she going to get Parker to agree to that?

"Can you meet me closer to my home?"

"R u kidding me? u think i can pass for anyone who belongs out in that neighborhood? Ur shop."

"Fine."

Calypso paused. She got up and went to the garage

without even checking with Parker. She could hear Parker was still on the phone. She didn't want to interrupt, after all. And isn't it better to ask forgiveness than permission, she supposed. She grabbed the keys to the Defender and took off. She called Xander on the way.

She wouldn't be alone. She would have Xander in the parking lot behind the shop.

When she arrived, Javier sat waiting in his car out front. "Damn girl, you're looking fine as fuck as always."

Calypso shot him a look of disgust and unlocked the shop. "Let's get down to business." She sat in her typical chair, and Javi perched himself on the chair he'd already spent countless hours in.

"Consider my debt paid. Although your ask was way bigger than mine ever was." He smiled. "That ginger bitch has been 86'd as you asked. Although it benefits you and me both, really. You had my back at the trial all those years ago. You said you were never gonna ask for repayment. But I suspected you would. Eventually." A leer on his lips.

"Macy Quinn is dead? You really killed her? How? How did you do it?"

"Me and my homies pulled up and picked the lock to get inside. We surprised her for sure. It was a bit of a struggle. We forced her into the bathtub with a gun to her head. Made her confess to everything she did—which is how my homie wrote the suicide letter. That's when we figured out she had the gun that she used to shoot Parker stashed, which made it even better for us. So we made her go and get it. Made her sit in the bathtub, and she cried, and she begged for a little bit. I put the gun in her hands, wrapped my hand around hers, and pop." He was so matter-of-fact, a chill made its way down her spine when he smacked his hands together with the word *pop*, smiling the whole time.

A tiny pang of sadness and guilt made its way through her

chest. But it was fleeting. So very fleeting. A small whisper that was gone as if it never existed in the first place.

"So, we done here now, yeah?" He asked as he stood. "All debts paid and canceled. Nothing more for either of us to ask for."

"Yeah. Sure. Done." She was slightly stunned.

Javi got up out of the chair. "Do I at least get a kiss for killing the ginger?"

"Fuck off. No." Calypso smiled. Life was back to normal.

* * *

As she was climbing back into the Defender to head back home, Parker called her. "Why are you making me be that wife again?"

Calypso sighed. "I can't stay locked away all my life. I can't."

"It doesn't matter anymore." Parker's voice was flat.

"What do you mean?"

"Get home and I will tell you everything."

When Calypso pulled in almost an hour later, she saw an unmarked police car in the drive. Her blood ran cold. She contemplated backing out and driving far, far away. There was no way Macy's death could be traced back to her. There was no way anyone would know this was her plan B.

She pushed her hair back and decided she would go in and face whatever was waiting for her.

When she came in, Parker was seated in her office with two detectives across from her. "What happened?" Calypso asked tentatively.

"Macy killed herself. Shot herself in the head." Parker's voice was quiet.

"Oh . . . Oh my . . . I don't know how to feel." Hoping her tone came across genuine and surprised, she moved to stand halfway behind Parker's chair. *That's a fucking lie.* Relief. Gratitude. Peace. Joy. Partially guilty. *Only* partially. There were a number of emotions she experienced, but she didn't want to look like a callous, cold psychopath. That was Macy's role. Not hers.

"I know. Part of me is sad. Part of me is relieved." Parker scrubbed her hand over her face and shook her head. "It's kind of tragic."

A weighty silence descended over the office. Calypso couldn't move. She couldn't fathom that this all might be over for her. Fucking finally over. Nearly two decades of dancing around and walking on eggshells. Nearly two decades of fearing what Macy might do to upend her life.

Calypso didn't want to get her hopes up, thinking this might not be over yet. Not yet. She only nodded silently.

"There was a note left." One of the Detectives pulled a paper out of his jacket. "This is a printout. It was left on the screen of her laptop." He handed the paper to Parker.

Parker pulled open the suicide note and read it aloud. "To Whoever Reads This—I'm sorry. I've made a lot of mistakes. I've wronged a lot of people. At this point, I feel like I have no other choice but to end it all before I hurt anyone else. I'm tired of hurting. My heart has hurt for far too long. I need peace. Parker, I'm sorry most of all for what I did to you. I was the one who shot you. I was the one who set up Calypso. You will find the gun used, Parker's gun, in my hands. Funny to think about how closely I was connected to both of you. I cared for both of you. Now I just cause you pain. I'm sorry— With love and Sorrow—Macy Quinn."

Calypso raised an eyebrow. Quite poetic for one of Javi's goons. But who was she to judge? The cops bought it. And so did Parker.

One of the cops made eye contact with Calypso. She forced herself not to smile. "Wow. She was really disturbed."

The same detective who handed Parker the note said, "We haven't run the serial number yet," he said to her. "Why would Macy shoot you to frame Calypso?"

Parker addressed him. "No . . . actually, now the wounds make sense. She hit my shoulder and my hip. Not fatal wounds. She was a perfect shot. She had the capability to aim exactly where she could strike without killing me. But to anyone else, it would have made sense that it would have been Calypso, who is not familiar or comfortable with a gun."

The detectives stood. "We all figured Quinn to be batshit. Honestly, she was always kind of out there. But she was good at her job, so we let a lot slide. We also used to give her shit because it was so obvious she was in love with you. We were on to how she threw cases to give you wins or would bring you information that would help you."

Calypso rolled her eyes.

"I expect that the charges against Calypso will be dropped."

"We will put it all together and take it to the DA. The case is closed."

Calypso exhaled and felt her shoulders relax.

Parker escorted them out. When she heard the door slam shut, Calypso came out.

Calypso wrapped her arms around Parker and kissed her. "This is really over."

"I think we need to go upstairs and celebrate." That flirty, rakish grin that Calypso loved so much played again on Parker's lips.

"I will be up in a minute. I need to put some things away."

Parker planted another kiss on Calypso's lips and made her way upstairs.

Calypso went into her makeshift studio, took the burner phone, and dropped it in a jar of paint thinner before sealing it back up. She would dispose of it at the SAFE center the next day.

Macy was no longer a thorn in her side. No longer a threat. Her past was solidly exactly that—her past—and her future was never more promising or bright.

EPILOGUE

ASHES TO ASHES

DECEMBER 2

CALYPSO

The events of the past few months were unbelievable. Sometimes Calypso had to remind herself that it all really happened.

After it was all said and done and Calypso was officially clear, Parker took the letter from the DA clearing Calypso of all charges and apologizing for the disruption in their lives, the counterfeit file that Macy created to frame Calypso, and dropped them in the fire pit on the patio. Parker put her arm around Calypso as the flames consumed it.

She knew Parker suspected that Macy's death wasn't a suicide. Parker had doubts. As she sat next to Calypso while the fire blazed hot and the history they wanted to let go of was reduced to ash and flame, she turned to her and asked, "Do you think Macy actually killed herself?"

Calypso tensed subtly. Parker understood her body and

her energy so well. No one else would have noticed the subtlety of the shift. She could tell in Parker's expression. "Why?"

"I just wonder. It happened at the most convenient time. It worked out too perfectly."

"Does it matter?"

Parker bit her lip. "Did you have anything to do with it?"

"Really?"

"Yes, really. Stop answering questions with questions. We promised. No more secrets. No more withholding. No more lies. I won't ask again. I won't bring it up again. But I need to know."

Calypso raised an eyebrow, pulled the throw blanket up a little higher, and shook her head." Do you think I'm capable?"

"When it comes down to self-preservation, aren't we all capable? Self-preservation was your reasoning before."

"Some are more capable than others, I guess."

"So . . . did you or did you not have something to do with it?"

"Am I on the stand?"

"No. You are talking to your *wife*, Calypso. However, if it helps you answer the question, yes. You are on the witness stand under oath. How would you answer the question? Did you or did you not have anything to do with Macy Quinn's death?"

"No, counselor, I played no part in the death of Macy Quinn. But know that if I did have anything to do with it, I did it for us. For our peace. For our safety. For our future. Because honestly, isn't life better without her in it?" After all they had been through, she knew this one secret would have to be kept. Not just for her, but for Parker. Macy tried to make Parker complicit in her crime—but Calypso was going to protect Parker at all costs. This one secret would stay buried.

Just as Parker knew her so well, she knew Parker, too. Parker didn't fully believe her. But it was only speculation. She had no choice but to believe what Calypso told her. It was over. She wasn't going to investigate it. A.D. took Macy's ashes and spread them with no fanfare at some beach. There was no funeral or memorial service. And Calypso was right. Life was better without Macy Quinn in it.

* * *

APRIL 21

PARKER

Six months after Macy's demise, Calypso decided it was time to take Parker to New Orleans, finally. Now that Macy was gone and there was no threat of Shae's murder being pinned on her, she wanted Parker to see her hometown. It was a big part of who she was and what made her.

As they walked hand in hand through the French Quarter, a woman dressed in purple robes with wild gray curls stopped them in front of one of the touristy voodoo shops. "You are a beautiful couple." She smiled. She was soft-spoken and had a sweet smile as the breeze blew some of her curls back, revealing her deep brown eyes and subtly lined skin.

Parker pulled Calypso closer to her. "Thank you."

"I can see your future, you know."

Parker gave an amused laugh. "Can you now?"

"I can see your past, too."

"Really?" Parker asked, her voice thick with sarcasm.

"You," she pointed at Parker with a perfectly manicured red nail, "Avoided love at all costs. You were afraid that love would mean you would have to sacrifice your time, your career, and your money."

Parker's jaw dropped, and she side-eyed Calypso.

"These people speak in generalities. This isn't real. It's a scam," Calypso whispered into Parker's ear.

"That's not generalities. That's dead on." Parker whispered back. She turned to the old woman and handed her a $100 bill. "Keep going."

She folded the bill and slipped it into a pocket in the robe. "Follow me into the shop." She led them over the threshold of the small, cramped space. At the front a young man with dreadlocks tied in a ponytail that reached his waist stood at the cash register. He smiled at them as they followed the woman through the shop. Tables crammed with candles, tarot decks, crystals, bundles of sage, and various other accouterments were scattered haphazardly across the sales floor.

Calypso fidgeted as they walked into a back room with a small, round table covered in a purple velvet cloth. Crystals and rune stones littered the table. The woman sat down behind the table, and Parker and Calypso took the small wooden chairs on the other side. Deftly scooping the bone-colored stones up, the woman put them into a black velvet bag that matched the tablecloth and arranged the crystals. Clearing her throat, Parker choked on the heavy incense burning in the corner of the room and addressed the woman. "You have my attention. Please. Continue."

Closing her eyes, the old woman tapped the red nail on her index finger against a crystal on the table before snapping her lids open dramatically and considering them contemplatively, "You two were meant to find each other. You balance each other out. You've been through a very rough time recently. There was interference. Another woman. Meddling. Sticking her fingers where they didn't belong."

Parker turned her head slowly toward Calypso, and a waxy pallor took over her face.

"There were secrets. Lots of secrets. But those secrets no longer matter. All but one have been revealed." She locked her eyes dead on at Calypso now. "That one secret is coated in the blood of the meddling woman. But it no longer matters." She smiled at Calypso and winked. Goosebumps cropped up along Parker's arm as she turned toward Calypso, her mouth slightly open. She wanted to say something, but words escaped her.

"Okay. Enough. Parker, let's go." Calypso pulled Parker's arm and dragged her up out of the chair and away from the room where the old woman laughed.

"Dear, you can drag her away. You can hide your secrets. But it will never matter. She's never going to let you go. She's never going to leave your side. You're bound." The old woman called out.

Parker's mind was reeling. It went back to that conversation six months ago about the potential that Calypso could have had anything to do with Macy's death. Calypso had lied to her. Why else would she be so insistent on leaving? She let Calypso drag her out of the voodoo shop and into a neighboring gallery. Pinup art by Vargas and Olivia hung on every wall. Parker took a breath. "I don't like those people," Calypso said as she exhaled. "I don't like how they scam people and take advantage."

Parker nodded quietly. "Do you have anything you need to tell me?" Parker asked, her voice a thin whisper.

"No." Calypso shook her head. "Other than, I love you. And that old woman got one thing right: we are made for each other." She wrapped her arms around Parker and planted a kiss on the tip of her nose.

That night as they sat on the patio of a restaurant, lit by gas lamps, surrounded by revelers in the street, Parker set her gaze upon her beautiful wife, and she made a decision. The old lady was right. The truth no longer mattered where Macy Quinn was considered. Only the story as it was written now and would continue to be told mattered. And she and Calypso wrote it in flame and ash and silence. She said she would burn the world for Calypso, but it was Calypso who torched it all to the ground to save their marriage, and she couldn't be mad about it.